# The A[

# War of the Undead Day One
# A Zombie Tale by Peter Meredith

M000042890

# Peter Meredith

## Prologue

Benny hesitated, his foot coming off the gas to hover over the brake, his instincts to help someone in need, fighting against his better judgment and a natural inclination to laziness. Then, seconds later it was too late. The girl on the side of the road was behind him and just a diminishing blur in his rain-streaked mirror. She had seemed very small.

"Ah crap," he whined, his foot still uncommitted. He was a thin man and would have been considered short if not for his neck, which resembled that of a turkey's: long, thin and ringed. Just then it was torqued around as he tried to squint into the night. He never stopped for hitchhikers; it was stupid and dangerous. Yet this one had been simply a girl.

"Yeah, but I'm already late." He had downed three too many beers and now it was after one in the morning. In his mind he knew Jane would be waiting up. She wouldn't greet him with a kiss, instead she'd nag: *Where have you been? How much have you had to drink?* She'd ask even though she knew exactly where he'd been and that he'd drank too much.

He was late; it was cold; his wife would kill him...these rationalizations against doing the right thing failed when he thought how small the girl on the side of the road was. She had to be freezing out there and was probably scared out of her wits. He was on an upslope and without gas pushing his aging Jeep Liberty, he was slowing rapidly. Behind him, down the hill, the girl was only a wavy, ghost-like figure in white.

"She's probably a runaway," he said to himself as further argument to just keep going. Runaways meant all sorts of trouble: drugs, thievery, maybe even prostitution. Why would he want to bring that sort of mess home to the wife?

The Liberty was now crawling along and his foot went to the gas, but a last thought went through his head: what if someone else picked her up? Someone not so nice as Benny Robinson. A pedophile maybe, or a rapist, or, God forbid a serial killer?

He sighed long and wearily before putting the Liberty in reverse. It hummed back toward the girl, who was standing in the same place, drenched to the bone. She didn't even look toward the car heading right for her.

"Fuck. She's on drugs for sure," he said. Benny was all set to regret his decision to come back for her until he saw how fantastically young she was. She didn't look any older than eight. "Fuuuuck," he said again, this time slowly, letting the word draw out until he had backed the Liberty to a stop right in front of her. He leaned over the E-brake and opened the passenger side door, expecting her to jump in. However, she didn't. She only stood there wearing nothing but a hospital gown that clung to her skinny body.

"Get in," he yelled to her over the downpour and the slapping rhythm of the windshield wipers. She didn't budge. "It'll be ok," he cried louder. "I won't hurt you."

She swayed for a few moments and then moved with awkward and jerky motions. It was bizarre--she was bizarre. For some reason, she stepped up onto the seat instead of sitting on it. It was like watching a manikin that had come to life.

"No, step down there. Not on the seat. Put your foot...down there," he said, trying to guide her without being too "touchy." He was afraid she would bolt and he didn't like the idea of having to run around the forest trying to catch her. When she had finally folded herself properly into the car, he asked, "You ok?"

"I'm...fine." The two words crawled out of a phlegmy throat in a low growl. The answer had been an automatic reply, given without any thought whatsoever. Benny guessed there wasn't much going on in that bedraggled blonde head. She sat staring straight ahead, her mouth partially open, her eyes dull and unfocused. He glanced back up the road, wondering where the hell she had come from. There wasn't a hospital anywhere around there as far as he knew. He was just west of Hartford, Connecticut on a lonely stretch of road. There wasn't much around them but trees and a whole lot of rain.

With his long turkey-neck twisted back, his eyes fell on the gym bag he had thrown onto the rear seat. He started to reach for it but stopped as the girl finally came to life. Her head quivered on her neck and she bared her teeth like an animal about to attack.

*Freaky*, Benny thought. It was as though she wanted nothing more than to tear out one of his ribs with her small feral teeth. If he had to guess, what with the hospital gown and all the weirdness, he supposed he was dealing with some sort of mental case. But where there was a loony bin around there he didn't know.

"It's ok," he said, bringing up the bag nice and slow so as not to freak her out anymore. "I'm getting you a jacket to keep you warm."

In answer she pulled her lips back even further and in the dark her mouth seemed strangely virile and hungry. Her hands started opening and closing and she bunched in her seat, again like an animal ready to spring.

"Ok, you don't want a jacket? That's fine. I'll just turn up the heat." With exaggerated movements, he turned the heat up to its highest setting. "Is that better?"

The question confused her. She started rocking, staring out the front window, making a gurgling sound deep in her throat.

Benny gave a little cough. "My name is Benny...or Ben if that's easier. What's your name?"

She didn't answer. Instead she balled her hands into fists and her eyes grew large as if she were about to explode. Though it was dark inside the Jeep Liberty, he couldn't help notice that there was something wrong with the girl's eyes. They were very dark; the pupils were deep pits and seemed to be the size of quarters. The whites of her eyes were like those of a frightened horse. They were two little crescents below those black pits.

"You don't look so good," Benny said, putting the car in gear. "I think I'll take you…" He stopped in mid-sentence as her chin, a little point of a thing in her heart shaped face, jerked in his direction. Her lips were curled into a snarl. "Just relax. It'll be ok," he said, holding out a hand to her. She struck at it fast as a spitting snake, drawing blood with her ragged nails. She went to strike again and that was when he saw that she had part of an IV sticking out of her arm. Thick black blood oozed from it.

He pulled his hand back. "You need to settle down," he said sharply. "Or I'll kick your ass out. You don't want that." When Benny had seen what sort of shape the girl was in, he had figured he would find the nearest hospital for her. Now he changed his mind. There was a State Trooper station not far down the road. In ten minutes, she was going to be their problem.

He went heavy on the gas, one eye on the road and one eye on the girl, who had begun to pant. The rain picked up, thrumming hard on the roof. When he jacked the wipers to full speed she panted faster as if trying to keep time. Despite all this, Ben wasn't afraid—she was probably no more than fifty pounds after all. What he felt most was some sort of instinctual disgust. He was repulsed by her on a gut level, and when a passing truck illuminated the interior of the Liberty, that revulsion went beyond the subconscious.

Benny gave a glance at the girl and did a double take. He had thought she was a dirty blonde, but now he saw her hair was so pale it was practically white. It was on her scalp where the dark color showed through. Her skin was black with what looked like dirt, and there was more of it in her ears and down the back of her neck.

But it couldn't have been dirt, not with all the rain. It resembled black lichen or maybe mold…

Tha-dump…Tha-dump…Tha-dump.

"Whoa," Benny said, under his breath. The Liberty had drifted to the shoulder of the road while he had been staring at the girl. He corrected his course and then glanced again at her and saw that now she was staring back. Or rather she was glaring at him in hatred.

"Don't…stare…bitch," she said. Her words had come growling up from deep in her throat.

"Sorry. I'm just worried about you…" He glanced again at her in midsentence and she screeched over his words.

"No! Don't…stare!"

"Fine," he said, swinging his eyes back to the road and subconsciously accelerating. As much as he wanted them to, his eyes wouldn't stay focused on the road. Benny likened it to driving with an angry cheetah in the seat next to him and, of course, he had to sneak another look.

"No!" the girl screamed and then launched herself at him.

Her right hand grabbed the steering wheel, her left raked across his bare arm as she pulled herself towards him, her greedy teeth searching hungrily for his neck. In that split second he saw her gums were black like a dog's and that her tongue was coated with that same filthy, awful mold.

She was strong for her size, but still light compared to him, so he was able to hold her back from his throat. Her teeth snapped and gnashed the air just inches from the soft skin of his neck. She was absolutely wild and with some justification his right hand found her neck and he squeezed without regard for her age or her sex. He squeezed hard, hoping she would respond to the pain.

She ignored the fact that he was crushing her windpipe; all she cared about was tearing a chunk out of his flesh. Like some sort of snake, she twisted and slithered in order to get at him.

With a long grunt, he forced her back and held her at arm's length. Her right hand had never left the wheel, which meant…

[7]

Tha-dump…Tha-dump…Tha-dump! The sound was urgent, loud, and brief. In the second before the crash, Benny was filled with the dreadful knowledge that he had strayed too far over the edge of the road and that with this little fiend attacking him he'd never be able to right the vehicle quickly enough. In slow motion he turned from the monstrous thing he had by the neck and saw that the Liberty was pointed straight toward a steep embankment. Benny had been doing seventy in rain-slicked conditions and now he slammed on the brakes. They locked up tight and with dirt under the front wheels and wet pavement under the back, the Liberty spun.

Benny knew to turn into a skid; however his world had become a merry-go-round of flashing white teeth, of rain running sideways and of black forests going in every direction. He hesitated a half-second too long and then it was too late. The Liberty went off the road and began to roll.

During the first rotation, every window blew out and the roof crumpled down four inches. The girl let go of his arm to go ping-ponging around the interior of the car sometime during the second rotation. In the middle of the third, something struck the crown of Benny's head and the world went soundlessly black.

When he awoke, the night was quiet save for the steady ticking of the cooling engine and the pitter-patter of the rain. It was coming in through the front where the windshield had been and was striking him square in the face. The angle was strange; it didn't make sense until he realized that the Liberty had settled on its rear quarter; it was nose up in a sharp gully.

Benny tried to move, to look around, but a terrific pain engulfing his right neck and shoulder stopped him. With a shaking left hand, he explored where the pain was greatest and felt something jagged coming up through the collar of his shirt. It was his clavicle and it was an absolute misery to touch. "Oh, God," he whispered, wondering how the hell he was going to get out of there when he could barely move.

He began feeling around the door with his left hand when something behind and below him at the bottom of the car, stirred. It was the girl! It hurt like a beast to turn his head so far around, but he was suddenly petrified of the little girl. In those last few seconds before the crash, it was as though she had changed. She had stopped being human and had become a—his mind wanted to reject the word "monster", but it fit far too well. He remembered he had squeezed her throat so hard that it would have crushed the larynx of a normal girl but she hadn't even blinked.

With a whiney moan in his own throat he turned and saw that the girl had been injured as well. Along with many gashes and wounds, her left arm was folded beneath her at a horrible angle. Her elbow had been broken in the crash and now it bent the wrong way--her flesh was split open from the unnatural position and there was something dull and white showing through that resembled the cartilage off the end of a chicken drumstick. The sight of it, even more than his own injury, made him want to puke. The feeling grew worse when she ignored her mangled limb altogether and climbed to her feet. For a second, she stood where the back window had been, her bare feet in mud.

Then she started to climb, baring her teeth and drooling as though hungry, her eyes were all black now.

"No!" Benny screamed. He tried to turn; he tried to get away, but his right side was practically paralyzed and he couldn't reach his seat belt with his left hand. In desperation, he looked around for a weapon, anything he could use to stop this horrible creature, but there was nothing. Then she was on him, her small teeth tearing into his neck, her body shaking like a terrier with a rat until she tore off a chunk of hot flesh.

With Benny howling in misery and uselessly calling for help she chewed the flesh of his neck, slurped the hot blood, swallowed and went back for more.

# Chapter 1

## The Staff

## R&K Research Center

**1**

"Allow me, Doctoral Liggs. It would be honor to log all data for you." Eng's words were choppy. His Ls and Rs turned on his tongue, giving them the stereotypical Chinese mispronunciation. He didn't seem to notice or care. He sat in his stainless steel chair grinning up at his boss, like an eager child—or a simpleton.

"Are you sure?" Jim Riggs asked. The question might as well have been rhetorical since Riggs knew the answer, just like he had known that Eng was going to offer to log the data in the first place, simply because he always offered. And Riggs always allowed him to—the man seemed to love every aspect of the research project, even the dull as hell shit-work. All of which was just fine with Riggs who already had his afternoon planned: another attempt at Dr. Milner's new research assistant whose white lab coat could barely contain all that she had to offer.

If that didn't bear fruit, then a round of golf sounded nice.

"It my pleasure," Eng said with a short bow of his head, letting his black hair fall in front of his face. Culturally, the Chinese generally only bow in very formal situations, however, since it never failed to please his superiors, Eng was a frequent bower. He bowed in the cafeteria, in the parking garage and to everyone's amusement, in the bathroom. "I enjoy data. It where we find cure, ok? Cancer is most horrible of disease. Our work of much great importance."

Riggs nodded solemnly, hiding a look that suggested Eng was a complete sucker. What he didn't bother to hide was his condescension; it was far too ingrained. He considered Eng to be a very poor scientist and had very little respect for him. The man had no imagination, no insight beyond the ordinary. He seemed unable to make the intuitive leaps that would allow for the "Big" breakthrough which every real scientist strove for. But he was hell at cataloging data and would fetch coffee as if he were being timed.

"Have at it," Riggs said, trying to catch his reflection. He was tall, so had to bend at the waist to look into the glass of one of the cabinets, checking his ghostly appearance. After turning his head this way and that, he patted Eng on the back, saying, "I know you'll do a great job," before walking out of his lab wearing a smile.

When the door shut, Eng made a face. "Hóng máo guǐzi," he whispered—literally meaning *red furred devil*, a common Mandarin slur used to denigrate Caucasians. Since Riggs was blonde and very pale from spending all his days under the harsh florescent lab lights, *white furred devil* would have been more accurate. With a snort of contempt, Eng bent to his task, but had barely begun when the door opened again.

It was Dr. Thuy Lee. Eng felt his heart do a little jump in his chest, but he made sure not to react beyond reaching up to ensure his hair was in place.

"Where's Riggs?" she demanded. She didn't smile. Eng didn't either though he wished he could. He also wished he could kiss her or touch the silk-like black hair that hung halfway down her back, or gather the courage to ask her out…again. The first time had been a disaster. Some months before, in a moment of weakness he had opened his heart to her and she had casually stomped her four-inch stilettos right down on it. Neither had forgotten the incident though both acted as if it had never happened.

"Dr. Riggs is most very busy with great research project," he said.

Dr. Lee's dark and slightly slanted eyes closed to slits. "Why do you insist on talking like that, Mr. Eng? You sound like an idiot." He bowed his head in acknowledgement, which only made her angrier. "And, enough with the bowing! All you're doing is reinforcing a stupid stereotype. There's some idiot in procuring who bows every time he sees me. You have him thinking that's what all Asians do."

"My aporogies, miss Doctoral Tree Rhee," he said, butchering her name the same as always and making her want to spit nails. It didn't matter that her own mother had a similar accent; she was old, she had an excuse.

Through gritted teeth, she said, "One more time, Eng. My first name is pronounced Twee. Say it slowly, Tweeee. There's no R in Thuy, but there is an L in Lee, right at the beginning. Thuy Lee. If you're going to make it in America you're going to have to master these simple things. Now tell me, where the hell is Riggs conducting his so-called 'great research project' if he's not doing it in his own lab?"

Eng shrugged as only a recent Chinese immigrant would: with an exaggerated motion and a dreadfully fake look of pure innocence.

"Uh-huh," Dr. Lee said, dryly. She pursed her full lips, thinking. When she did, it showed off her high cheekbones and in Eng's mind made her look even more like a model from a magazine. He stared out of the corner of his eyes until she clucked her tongue.

"I bet he's trying his luck with that dippy Anna again. How they get anything done over there is beyond me. It's like Milner's trying to create a harem for himself."

Dale Milner was as unquestionably brilliant as he was pervy, which was how he was able to fund his "harem." Thuy had three research assistants whom she had carefully screened for competence. Riggs only had two but, since he worked Eng like a 19th Century "coolie", he didn't need more.

Thuy glanced at the stack of work Riggs had left Eng to catalog—it was two feet tall and she guessed that he would be at it well after dark. For a second, pity entered her cold heart. "Thanks for your time and have a good afternoon, Mr. Eng," she said, giving him the smallest of smiles.

"Good bye, miss Doctoral Rhee," he replied as though he had a mouthful of marbles. Her tiny smile dropped away to nothing as she turned for the door. She didn't think he had seen, however Eng, who was far more observant than he let on, noted it. When the door shut, he murmured, "Good bye Doctor Lee," this time in perfect English. "Have a good day Dr. Lee. Kiss my ass, Dr. Lee."

Angrily he looked at the stack of reports, wishing he could drop them in the nearest incinerator. More than that he wished he could show Dr. Lee who he really was and what he was really capable of.

"No," he said, taking deep breaths and calming by degrees. "Not yet. Maybe not ever."

It took a few more seconds of deep breathing to shrug off the interruption and then he went back to work, logging the data on the latest round of *Track 3* tests. As Dr. Lee had figured, it took hours for him to complete it all. Once the cataloging was complete, transferring a copy of the data to the facilities mainframe took less than a minute. His next assignment took much longer. The data had to be encrypted, compressed and zipped before it was loaded onto a flash drive. Later that night, Eng would visit his favorite McDonalds where the flash drive would be left in the wrapper of his Big Mac sitting, innocently enough on his tray. Who picked it up from there he didn't know and he didn't want to know. All that mattered was that eventually it would end up in the hands of Lieutenant Eng's station chief. From there it would be forwarded on to China just as all the other data he had ever touched had been.

**2**

Dr. Lee left Eng feeling a need to wash her hands. He

was a greasy man with a greasy smile and there was something about his eyes that bothered her. It was something hidden. She assumed it was some sick sexual perversion, and in that she was only partially correct.

With her four-inch heels clacking along the white-tiled hallways, she made her way to the *Track 2* lab where Dr. Dale Milner held forth like some petty noble in a petty kingdom. Dr. Lee was thankful the man had already been informed of the impromptu meeting; he was insufferable in his lab and rarely left it.

The same could not be said of Dr. Riggs whom she found in the front room of Milner's lab, leaning against a stainless steel table, with his elbow on an expensive centrifuge and laughing it up with Anna Holloway. She was one of Milner's hotter assistants and Riggs could barely contain himself as he let his eyes slip and slide along the soft curves of her cleavage.

"Thuy!" Riggs exclaimed delightedly. Dr. Lee could only assume that Anna's perfume had gone to his head, as he was not the least bit subtle as he turned from one beauty to the other. His eyes ran up and down Thuy's trim form as though she were a stripper and not a PhD.

"Hello Dr. Lee," Anna said, swinging her head so that her long blonde hair unfurled from her right shoulder to come to a gentle rest on her left where it rippled like a golden river. She flipped her hair frequently acting as though she thought it rude to let her hair come between her and the person she was addressing. "Dr. Milner isn't here. He hasn't come back from lunch yet."

Thuy knew this already. "Yes. He's in a meeting concerning the fate of the Com-cell project. I'm here to collect Dr. Riggs for the same purpose."

Riggs, who had been having a grand time chatting up Anna without Milner around to spoil it, felt his smile falter. He knew all too well that it wasn't normal for a senior research fellow to be sent to "collect" a colleague.

"Is it a status meeting? Or is it funding? Was it Rothchild or Kip who called it? Son of a bitch!" he cursed, jumping up and rushing for the door with his lab coat flapping. "I hate when they spring these sorts of things on us."

Thuy had followed him out but she didn't answer his question, instead she cleared her throat and jerked her head back to the lab. "Don't you want to say a proper goodbye?"

"Aw shit!" he exclaimed, and then turned on the spot and ran back to the door. "Sorry about that, Anna. The senior partners are up to their old tricks, springing surprise meetings on us like we have nothing better to do."

"You don't seem to have anything better to do," Thuy remarked.

Riggs' smile went tight. "I'll see you later, Anna. Maybe down at Hot Jack's Pub after work?"

"Maybe," she allowed.

Thuy took Riggs by the elbow and pulled him from the door. Anna's coy smile and her "maybe" had dislodged his fear of the senior partners. Riggs smiled down at Dr. Lee as they hurried for the elevators. "You cut that goodbye a little short. Getting jealous, Thuy? If so, you don't have to be, there's enough of me to go around."

"Maybe not after this meeting," she cracked.

Again his smile faltered. "What do you know?"

"Same as you. They want a meeting of all the track investigators." Just like Dr. Lee, his actual title was Independent Research Investigator, but like most, he preferred the term Research Fellow instead. He complained that the word investigator made him sound like a private eye.

"It can't be funding. It's just too early," Riggs said, trying to convince himself. He started to get a squirmy feeling of anxiety in his gut, because what if it wasn't? What if their progress wasn't what the partners were expecting? What if they wanted more? Kip was like that. The man was never happy with results until the *pills were on the shelves*. It was Dr. Lee who should have been sweating bullets, however she was her usual cool, composed self.

"We'll find out in a minute," she said, as though they were just out for a stroll.

"It's got to be a status meeting," Riggs decided. "And that's fine with me. Did you hear about my latest round of possum tests? Forty percent!"

"The same as your last test," Thuy noted.

"Yes, that's called consistency," Riggs replied, "And Kip likes consistency." They came to the elevators and, because there were a few other people waiting, they dropped their conversation. Once on, Thuy hit the button for the top floor and neither spoke until the last person exited on the fifth floor.

"And what did you learn from your consistent tests?" Thuy asked. "If your answer is nothing, then the second test was a waste of time."

Riggs, who didn't feel the need to justify his work simply answered, "We're still compiling the data." *We* meant Eng was compiling the data. "What about you? I heard your first round was a complete flop and your second was only slightly better. I told you *Fusarium* mycotoxins were too weak. The most you'll do is give the tumors the sniffles."

"My first round proved just that," Dr. Lee said, easily. Too easily for Riggs to be comfortable with. It was as though she was keeper of some great secret.

"What about your second round?" he asked as the elevator doors hissed open. "What did you learn?"

Thuy didn't answer; instead she smiled at the two women who manned the tenth floor reception desk. The lady on the right, Laura England, was just shy of forty and beautiful in a mature sort of way. The term MILF was bandied about quite a bit in the "lab-lines" on the third floor where the newbie scientists with lesser pedigrees competed to get noticed. Mrs. England was Dr. Kipling's secretary. She didn't know it, but she only had another year or two left, unless Kip managed to get into her panties quicker, then it would be a considerably shorter time.

The woman on the left, Dr. Rothchild's personal secretary, Abigail Unger, might have been beautiful decades before, now she was the matriarch of R&K Pharmaceuticals and the epitome of a Rothchild worker: competent, loyal, and always plodding forward.

"You're late," Mrs. Unger intoned, her lips drawn down in a frown—what was practically a permanent feature on her face. "In Dr. Kipling's office, please."

Riggs groaned. He had been hoping that Rothchild would be running the meeting. With Kip he knew that whatever was coming, good or bad, was going to be a headache. "After you, Dr. Lee," Riggs said, opening the door to Stephen Kipling's palatial-sized office. Not only was it palatial in its dimensions, it was also palatial in accommodations. In the center of the room was an oval-shaped table that could sit thirty people, though currently it held just ten, congregated at the far end.

The two principals were there: kindly, old Rothchild, who needed only a red suit and an extra twenty pounds to make him resemble a mall Santa, and Kipling, who was dapper as always in a three-piece Armani. The other six Track investigators were there, looking ill at ease in their lab coats, sitting stiffly in the humungous high-backed leather chairs

The other two men at the table were as different from each other as night and day. The first was a slight man in a grey suit sporting a nervous smile and a mustache of sweat across his upper lip. It was Jim Hartman, who headed up the procurement division—he was notoriously stingy, which was why Kip kept him around despite receiving complaints from every scientist who had ever walked through the gleaming R&K doors.

The second man was unknown to Riggs or Thuy. He was tall, with muscles that stretched the fabric of his suit jacket at the biceps and shoulders. He was somewhere in his late thirties and had quick eyes—they were a soft brown in color, but were sharp. Clearly, he wasn't a scientist. First off, he sported a warm tan, which meant he didn't spend his days with his nose pressed against a microscope. Secondly, there was his build; it was somewhat of a rule that true scientists couldn't wield their slide rulers without getting winded and this guy looked like he could twist Riggs into a pretzel and not break a sweat.

Riggs immediately pegged him as "security" which didn't bode well at all. It either meant that something had leaked or that the paranoia factor of the bosses was ramping up. Neither was good. Inwardly he cursed while outwardly he ignored the security man completely and brought out his most genuine fake smile. "It's good to see you Kip and you Dr. Rothchild.

Kip returned the fake smile with equal sincerity. He gave a warmer one to Thuy, asking her, "Where was the good doctor?"

"As if we don't know," Dr. Milner interjected before Thuy could do more than open her mouth. Several of the other scientists smiled at this. Behind her, Riggs cleared his throat and gripped her shoulders tighter.

Thuy, who felt as though Dr. Riggs had been using her as a human shield since they had entered the room, replied to Milner, "In the cafeteria, about to sit down for a late lunch."

Riggs tried not to let his surprise show as he escorted Thuy to her chair and pulled it out for her, something he never did. Rothchild watched the display of manners with a gentle smile on his wrinkled face while Kip waited with ill-disguised impatience until Riggs took his own spot at the table. Then he displayed his trademark smile that was supposed to put everyone at ease. It didn't fool any of the regulars at the meeting. A smile from Stephen Kipling could mean anything, from a promotion to a diagnosis of a terminal ailment.

"The Chinese symbol for crisis, as some of you know, is the combination of the characters for danger and opportunity." Here Kip paused and nodded to Dr. Lee. She was half-Vietnamese and half-American GI, and despite her extensive education, she didn't know one Chinese symbol from another. Still she nodded back in an attempt to get Kip's focus off of her.

"Crisis!" he exclaimed with a fist held in front of his chest. "It's where we find ourselves today. In the midst of danger and opportunity. I am proud to announce that *we* have finally solved our Com-cell puzzle. The cure for cancer is ours! It's a great leap forward, but not one without risks." He continued speaking in his self-aggrandizing manner, interspersing the word *we* frequently although he had done very little to help the project in any way. It hardly mattered what he said since the lead researchers weren't listening. They glanced back and forth from one to another, each wondering who had managed the impossible and what the breakthrough would mean to their position on the project. Only Thuy did not look around. She was more interested in the gentleman in the black suit.

Normally, the men who provided security for R&K Pharmaceuticals were aggressively anti-intellectual, most likely due to feelings of inadequacy. This man was different. His eyes were disarmingly soft and brown, but they were also shrewd. He watched the scientists, judging their reactions, seeing the fear in some and the haughty, god-like ego of others. He was literally in a room full of geniuses, but unlike the man in the grey suit next to him, he was completely unfazed.

Thuy was impressed, right up until he turned that piercing gaze on her. Their eyes locked and her inner calm broke like glass. Her feelings were suddenly jumbled and somehow he even seemed to notice this. She hadn't budged or jerked or reacted in any way, still he smirked in an irritatingly knowing manner before turning his chin slightly to look at Riggs.

Riggs felt like he'd had the rug pulled out from under

him. So far his track of combining stem cells with alkaloid producing fungi had shown the most promise in both the static carcinoma trials as well as with his favorite test animals: opossums. Still there was no way he could claim that he had perfected his version of the Com-cell. It was one of the others.

He snuck a peek at Thuy, forcing himself to look past her exotic beauty--*It couldn't be her*, he thought. Her choice of the *Fusarium* mycotoxins was so weak that nobody had given her any chance. Riggs had never been worried about her. If anyone was going to find the cure, other than himself that is, it would be Milner. Riggs would never admit it aloud, but he knew that Milner was smarter than he was. A glance in his direction, however, revealed the egotistical bastard looked about ready to shit his pants.

Kip seemed to be enjoying the uptight, near-silent chaos he had sown. "And thanks to my partner who has spared no expense bribing every one of our top-rated sleaze ball politicians, we have fast track priority from the FDA," he concluded.

"Meaning what exactly?" Thuy asked.

Kip's smile grew. "Meaning, my dear Dr. Lee, that we begin human trials five weeks from today. Congratulations."

The other scientists gaped at her and only Riggs was able to force out the word: "Congratulations."

Far from being ecstatic, as Riggs would've been, Thuy was irate. "That's too soon," she said. "We need at least one more round of animal trials before..."

Kips cleared his throat, loudly. "We will take that up later, but first we have some minor changes to announce. As of this moment we are discontinuing the other track research projects."

Riggs wanted to puke. Two years worth of work down the drain. What was worse in his mind was the fact that at best he would be relegated to some minor role in the new project where he would receive a hearty handshake and an "attaboy" when the cure was perfected. At worst he would be cut out completely--then there was the very real possibility of being fired. With the economy as crappy as it had been for the last five years, research dollars were drying up and with them, senior research positions seemed to be evaporating into thin air.

Rothchild saw the looks of dismay around the table at hearing the good news. "I would like to thank you all for your hard work. You all deserve an attaboy for your perseverance and dedication; however from this point on we will be advancing with a slightly smaller staff. Doctors Lee, Milner and Riggs will be staying on. The rest of you..."

Dr. Lipcomb leapt to his feet. "I can't believe you picked her track! It's...It's preposterous. Her work is crap. Her first trial showed only a three percent success rate for God's sake! And her second was only a little better at fifteen."

The senior partner nodded to the facts. "Yes," Rothchild agreed. "A five hundred percent increase in effectiveness. Her third trial was..."

Again, Kip cleared his throat. "Not yet, Edmund. I'm sorry Dr. Lipcomb we have made our decision, which brings me to an introduction I should have begun with. This is our new chief of security, Mr. Ryan Deckard. He has some things to announce."

The man in the black suit stood, glanced once at a small note and said, "Doctors Lipcomb, Rhagamesh, Beatty, Malinksi and Walters, I will need all of your notes pertaining to your research by tomorrow at noon."

Andre Beatty snorted, "Do you have an e-mail address?" This was Beatty's idea of a joke. The data compiled by each scientist over the last few years was more than enough to fill the hard drives of ten home computers. Beatty knew that e-mailing that much information would be a process of weeks.

"You misunderstand," Deckard said. "I want your hand written notes. The computers themselves are being seized as we speak."

This created another outcry larger than the first. Riggs barely heard. He was busy sighing in relief; the axe had fallen on someone else's head. Kip was glaring. "You each signed a contract. You each understand proprietary and intellectual property laws. And you each will comply with them or you will be subject to more lawsuits than you can afford in twenty lifetimes!"

Rothchild made a face at Kip's heavy-handed tactics. "I'm sure threats aren't necessary. These are all ladies and gentlemen of honor."

"Then explain the leak!" Kip replied. The scientists had been whispering or grumbling under their breath but at the word "leak", they snapped their lips closed and again glanced around at each other.

Seeing as any discovery was the intellectual property of the company they worked for, the quickest way--really the only way to get filthy rich, as a scientist was to play corporate spy. Undoubtedly, the cure for cancer would be worth billions to the pharmaceutical company that could patent it first, so it followed that any company falling behind would be willing to pay out tens of millions to the unethical man looking for the big payday.

Rothchild could only shrug. "I can't explain the leak. However I have full confidence in these men."

"And I have full confidence in Mr. Deckard." Kip nodded to the security specialist. Deck had been eyeing the scientists closely during this exchange; none of whom dared to meet his gaze.

"I appreciate it," Deckard said, without emotion, dismissing the talk of trust. "Now if we can clear the room." Under his intense gaze, the fired scientists filed out in various states of unhappiness. When they had left the room, Deck turned to glare at Kip. "My advice was not to discuss the leak. Now you've made my job much more difficult."

Kip, who never liked it when someone pointed out a mistake of his, made a show of being unconcerned. "Maybe not. Perhaps we've flushed the culprit out into the open. Perhaps since he knows we're onto him, he'll try to rush things and make a mistake."

Dr. Milner had been sitting this entire time tapping his pen on the desk, his face twisted into a sneer. He cared nothing about leaks when it wasn't his own work. Clearly unhappy to have been beaten to the cure, he rounded on Thuy. "How'd you do it?"

Thuy only smiled like a cat sitting in a pile of golden canary feathers.

## Chapter 2

## The Patients

**1**

## Erik Von Braun,

## Sing Sing Prison, New York

Erik Von Braun worked alone. He had no lookouts or anyone to watch his back in case things got hairy. He didn't have friends or accomplices and he really didn't want any. He liked working alone because he never had to worry about anyone snitching or letting their tongue wag after a couple of snorts of this or that, and he never had to fear that some jackass would start bragging in a moment of manly stupidity.

This self-enforced loneliness was why he was so successful at killing motherfuckers in the joint. For Von Braun there was only the name of his next victim and his payment: a dozen cartons of cigarettes. He didn't ask for instructions and he didn't take requests in the manner in which his victim would die; he kept things simple, having only one rule: he would not kill a fellow white man, unless, of course, that man was a proven nigger-lover. Then, Von Braun, who looked like the poster-boy for the Aryan nation, would cut his fee in half. Nothing burned his nerves and drove him into a rage more than a goddamned, motherfucking, nigger-lover.

This was not one of those times. This was a straight up revenge killing: *You kill one of mine, I'll kill one of yours*. For the most part he didn't give a rat's ass about the petty wars and stupid turf fights that went on in every prison in America. All he cared about was the kill, and this kill was only minutes from happening.

With the heel of his leather glove he wiped the sweat

from his blue eyes and tried to relax in spite of the fact that his knees were folded up to his chin. The cabinet he'd forced himself into was black as night and hot as fuck. The air had long before turned stale and tasted used up. It was so friggin' suffocating that it felt like he had shut himself up in his own coffin.

That thought gave him a second of pause, and he had to fight the urge to crack the door and take a breath. Instead, he kicked the thought out of his mind and concentrated on the challenge ahead. Tonight was a two-part kill: first the projectionist, who had the misfortune of simply being in the way, and then his real target, Malcolm X-Caliber.

"What a dumbass nickname," Von Braun whispered, trying to picture Malcolm. This wasn't an easy thing for him to do because, to him, *they* all looked alike. He had to pick out certain aspects of his victim to set him apart from the other coons. Malcolm had a shiny, slick head like an 8 ball, tats on both sides of his neck, Xs of course, and he was stick-skinny, which wasn't usual in the joint--men either went soft and fat or bulked up. Other than those little differences, Malcolm was simply a nigger like all the rest, and just like all the rest, he was a nigger with dumb-ass habits.

The dumb shit saw every movie that the prison ran, even the crappy ones, and he insisted on sitting in the very back of the theater just below the projector opening.

"Dumb, dumb, dumb," Von Braun whispered. His leg began to shake under the effect of the adrenaline that had begun to seep into his bloodstream and before he knew it, the neo-Nazi had his left glove off and was chewing on his thumbnail. The one thing he couldn't stand about killing niggers was the waiting. He was never nervous or anxious, in fact he had the opposite problem; he was always jazzed for the kill, eager, ready to spill blood. It made him want to go, go, go! But he couldn't and the long wait was killing him.

He was dying for a smoke. His chest thrummed and his

hands shook in his need for nicotine, but he never allowed himself a smoke while on the hunt and not smoking was hard shit for a man who went through four packs of smokes a day. It was why he let his nails grow between jobs. He knew that chewing them back down to nubs was the only thing that would keep him from going bat-shit crazy. Before the sounds of the first preview he'd nibbled all the nails of his right hand down to ragged points.

For some reason Von Braun couldn't understand, the inmates loved the previews almost as much as they loved the feature presentation and he could count on it that those packed in the auditorium would be sitting slack-jawed and wholly captivated by the moving pictures on the screen.

He pulled his gloves back on and, as the preview began to escalate in volume, eased the door to his coffin open and slipped into the dark projection room. There was Monty the Movie-Guy standing near the whirring projector with one beefy forearm thrown up against the wall as he leaned down to watch the preview through the little window. He was chubby and balding and as black as a friggin' tar baby. Monty didn't need to die. He was as pleasant a man as Von Braun had ever met, however he had three things going against him: he was black, he was in the way of his next target, and he was motherfucking black as hell.

The only question was how he would die. Von Braun had a shiv in his pocket, but it didn't feel right. He was a very organic killer, and always had been. If he found himself in a butcher shop he would use a meat cleaver. If his victim was in a lumberyard he'd use an axe or a table saw. In a bakery, he'd drown the motherfucker in a vat of chocolate icing.

In the projection room there wasn't much to work with. There was a bar stool unattended next to the projector; killing Monty with that would be loud and messy. Bolted to a heavy table was a small bladed film splicer that was probably too small to chop the guy's dick off. Next to it was a stack of film in circular metal tins. Von Braun hefted one;

it probably weighed twenty-five pounds--perfect.

Outside the little room, the sound of movie guns went off as though a battle was raging. The tin probably weighed twenty pounds—it was perfect. He stalked up to Monty who was just as oblivious as he could be, grinning out at the screen, his friggin' watermelon-eating teeth white in his black face. With a swift, vicious move, Von Braun drove the tin down on the back of his head, right at the base and Monty dropped with a soft thump that no one heard.

Monty's eyes were open. The left one stared up at Von Braun without understanding, the right one had slid back in his skull and was looking into his own brain. Von Braun hit him again, and again, and again, stopping only when Monty's face was unrecognizable. It was indented wrongly and bloody as fuck, but the projectionist was still alive— breathing wet and loud like a bull before a matador.

"Tough ole' buck, ain't you?" Von Braun said to Monty, as he pulled out the shiv. He had made it from a piece of scrap metal. Including the taped handle, it was eight inches long and as sharp as a dagger. Slowly, almost gently, he slid the blade into the soft skin under Monty's chin. The black man's one good eye flew open. His hand came up and grabbed Von Braun's arm; it was a weak hand. It was soft on his arm, more like a caress than an effort to fight back.

The knife slid deeper, slicing through flesh and muscle with ease, probing for one of the fat arteries that ran on either side of the trachea. A second later it pulsed rhythmically against the blade like a stereo's bass. Ten seconds after that, the black lost his rhythm altogether.

"There you go, Monty. After a lifetime, you've finally achieved 'good nigger' status." Von Braun gloated over the corpse until the first preview wound down and the second began in what sounded like the middle of a car chase.

He went to the projection window and glanced down at Malcolm X-Caliber eight feet below him. The dumb-ass coon was watching the run of images with his fat lips parted.

"Perfect," Von Braun said. Coiled around his midsection beneath his shirt were ten feet of braided wire. There was a noose on one end, while attached to the other was a short length of wood, part of a shovel handle that he had sawed off just for the occasion.

Malcolm was in for a good old fashion lynching. If it wasn't for the burning hate in his belly, Von Braun would have been giddy at the very notion.

The preview was in full swing when he dropped the noose softly onto Malcolm's unsuspecting neck. The black man jerked and swatted at his shoulder; for just a second he had the wild thought that a bat had attacked him. Then the noose zipped tight as Von Braun snapped back on the braided wire, and before Malcolm could draw another breath he was lifted out of his seat.

Von Braun was over six feet in height and was very strong. Using the muscles of his legs he hauled back on the handle until Malcolm was almost to the level of the projection window, at which point he tied the braided wires around the leg of the splicing table that was anchored to the floor.

Malcolm's friends on either side were so engrossed in the preview that at first they thought he was only standing up, choosing a real dumb-ass time to go to the bathroom. It was only when he started thumping the wall with his heels and clawing at his neck, that they looked away from the screen to see him being run upward like a slab of beef. Had either of them leapt in to help right away, Malcolm might have been saved. Instead, they both jumped back in fright and by the time they recovered, the wire had cut deep into Malcolm's flesh and blood was draining down into his lungs. Eventually, when he was finally cut down, it was discovered that his head had been close to being shorn clear away.

Von Braun did not stay to gloat over this kill. He sped out of the projection room door, shedding his gloves and the bloody outer shirt he had worn, dropping them without care as he went. There was nothing that would link them to him in any way. He took a practiced evac route and it was only when he was safely a cellblock away making sure that he was seen by at least one of the guards that he fished out a cigarette and stuck it between his lips.

He was slow to light it. For some reason he felt more winded than he should have and his head was a little dizzy. With the urgent desire for nicotine on him, he didn't wait for the feeling to pass fully and when he lit his cig, he immediately coughed up blue smoke like he was gagging on it, something he hadn't done since the second grade. His face went red as the coughing fit went on and on. In the middle of it he tried to take another drag on the cigarette. The heat of the smoke shriveled his lungs so that he felt like he was breathing through a very long, thin straw.

Behind him an alarm started braying.

"Shit," he said in a high wheeze. He put his hand out to the wall as his head went light and the floor began to feel strangely unsteady for solid concrete. Against all commonsense he brought the cigarette up once more to his lips, but it never got there. The cellblock began to spin around him. The fag dropped and sparked on the white linoleum and a second later Von Braun landed right beside it, slapping the floor with the side of his face.

He barely felt it.

With the last dregs of his consciousness, he tried to tell himself he was having an asthma attack, but beneath that thought lurked the word: cancer. It flitted on the ebb of his consciousness right before he passed out.

**2**

**Madison Rothchild**

**Manhattan, New York**

Maddy Rothchild balled her fists and stuck them on her hips. When she was determined, whether it be to stay up late, or to have Spaghetti-Os for dinner instead of salmon, she always struck this pose. It was by design. It told her opponent that he or she was in for a fight and that it would be best for all involved to just let her stay up those extra thirty minutes or to open that can of Chef Boyardee and be quick about it.

"Don't give me that look, Maddy," Ms. Robins said. "You are going to school and that's final."

"Mommy needs me," the eight year old replied, raising a pale gold eyebrow. She was a skinny, blonde child in $300 designer jeans. "She was up all night with a cough."

Ms. Robins nodded solemnly. "I am perfectly aware of the situation and it is nothing I can't handle. I will see to her needs."

"She needs her family," Maddy said, lifting her chin, knowing she was stepping well over the line. Ms. Robins had been Gabriele Rothchild's housekeeper, caregiver, and friend for over twenty years, and had long considered herself part of the family.

Her brown eyes flashed, and her lips went as tight as the bun on top of her head, but Ms. Robins was able to hold in her anger, barely. "And what could you do for her that I can't?" When Maddy dropped her gaze to stare at the marble floor, the maid/nanny answered her own question: "You can be a well behaved daughter and do as I have asked. That is how you can help her the most."

"Maybe," Maddy allowed. "If this was a normal day, which it isn't. She has her surgery tomorrow, for all darn it!"

Maddy wasn't allowed to swear. Her mommy said it wasn't fitting for a young lady of her station, so she made up her own curse words, sometimes to odd affect.

"Which is why I have already spoken to your teacher, requesting that you have tomorrow off," Ms. Robins replied. "Not today. And besides, this surgery won't be like the last one. It won't be nearly as bad."

Maddy, who thought that all surgeries were very bad and very scary, pretended to agree. "I know. She's having a *sleeve resection* done. It's when they cut out a section of the bronchi that's all tumored up before re-attaching the good ends." She had looked it up on the internet. There had even been a cartoon-like video that made the surgery look very neat and clean—no blood, no mess, no pale, sweating mommy who could barely talk afterwards and who sometimes cried. That was the real truth behind these surgeries. Maddy knew first hand.

And there was another truth, one that no one talked about. One that was supposedly this big secret to protect little Maddy: Mommy wasn't going to live no matter what they did. Everyone whispered it when they thought she couldn't hear. This was why she was staying home, because what would happen if they were right? What would happen if mommy went to the hospital and never came back out?

"I'm staying home," she said, firmly.

"You are not," Ms. Robins said with equal firmness. She held up her smart phone, and showed a text to Maddy. "I've already called Ricky. He'll be by with the car in twenty minutes."

Maddy's hands had not budged from her skinny hips. "No. Tell Ricky, I don't need him and his stupid limo today."

Ms. Robins looked sad all of a sudden. She squared her shoulders and took a deep breath. "I didn't want it to come to this, but you leave me no choice. If you don't get ready to go right this instant, young lady, I'm going to yank down those pants and give you a paddling like you haven't had in ages."

The little girl was, quite unexpectedly, unsure of herself. "You can't paddle me. You're not allowed. I know it's against the law. I saw it on TV."

"Wrong. I can paddle you until your bottom is as red as a tomato if your mom gives me permission to, and guess what? She already did."

Maddy took a step back. "No she didn't. When?"

"When she got sick again," Ms. Robins said in low voice. There were little tears in her eyes that she blinked away. "She told me to raise you like she would have."

"But she never paddled me at all."

"Yes she has," Ms. Robins replied. "I have seen it with my own two eyes. I was there for the first. You were not even one. You kept playing with an electric outlet and you wouldn't listen when she scolded you and so..."

"She spanked me?"

"Yes, ma'am, and it wasn't the last time either, but you were a smart cookie just like your parents and your grandparents, and you learned early to listen to adults when they asked you to do things, like going to school."

"This is different," Maddy said, though now she was less convinced of the infallibility of her position. Ms. Robins was not a big woman but she could be sharp at times and right at that moment her eyes fairly sparked with determination. If she was going to be forced into spanking Maddy, it was clear she was going to make it count.

"You are going to school," Ms. Robins stated as fact. "I'd hate for you to go there with a blistered bottom and tears in your eyes." Maddy was about to interject but Ms. Robins held up her large, pale hand. "Your mom needs her rest, however I'm sure she'll be up by the time you come home. You can help me then, ok?"

Defeated by logic and the threat of pain, Maddy rushed to get ready before the limo arrived to pick her up. She just managed to tiptoe into her parent's bedroom with enough time to spare to give her mom a kiss on the forehead. Gabrielle Rothchild, in her seven hundred square foot bedroom, under her two thousand thread count Egyptian cotton sheets, didn't stir.

"Love you, Mommy," Maddy said, wishing more than anything that her mommy would open her eyes and say it back. And she wished her mommy could jump out of bed and be happy again and healthy. But mommy couldn't, not even after three surgeries, not even when the best doctors in the country had been flown in to save her from the cancer.

There were some things money couldn't buy.

### 3

### John Burke

### Izard County, Arkansas

Sitting in his kitchen on one of his mismatched chairs resting on cracked and faded greenish linoleum and sweating like a fuck-all pig, with only a crappy, old ceiling fan ticking overhead, John Burke tried again to add the numbers so that he could get them to come out the same. So far he'd fed the numbers into his ancient sixth-grade *Texas Instruments* calculator three times and somehow had come up with three different totals.

He was on the verge of chucking that ole' Texas piece of shit at the wall, but he held back knowing if he did, he'd be fucked into summing up the math on a piece of paper; something he was none too good at.

"Lab work: forty-eight hunnert. Let's see…bi-opsy, shit, seven thousand each, and there was, let's see, six of those. The first hospital stay…fuck-all, twenty-one thousand…" The figures blurred as the tears started again. He took a swig of his beer, his third of that early morning. What did he care when he started to drink? What did he care if Mrs. Lafayette saw the can when she came to collect Jaimee? He didn't care one stinking bit.

After a deep breath he went on, "One copper and teak casket: f-for-forty-one hunnert. Fuckin' side-by-side plots…"

Jaimee walked into the room clucking her tongue like a mother hen. "Daidy, you ain't supposed to be cussing none. Momma said so." She had assumed all the motherly duties a six-year-old could attend to, which wasn't much beyond picking up some and making her own cereal. She could also stick bologna and cheese on bread, only her daddy hadn't gone to the store except to get beer and cough medicine. Sometime he went swig for swig, with a can in one hand and a bottle of nasty red syrup in the other, but still he would hack up strange looking hunks of who knew what.

John shuddered, wracked by another coughing spell. He was sure he was going to throw-up afterward due to the violence of the act, but he didn't and when the fit passed he took a drink of beer with a shaking hand. "She ain't here no more so I guess it don't matter none."

"We promised her," Jaimee reminded him. "We both made blood oaths to take care of each other."

That had been a year and half ago, and Jaimee who was having trouble even recalling what her mother looked like, remembered that oath like it was yesterday. So did John. It was why he was adding those hated numbers despite the cough that had sprung up and wouldn't leave and the pain in his joints that felt as though his bones were rubbing together. There was something very wrong with him and he was afraid. The one doctor's visit he'd had only made matters worse. Amy's old Doc had poked and prodded and listened and whatnot, all with a grim set to his lips. It wasn't good. No sir.

Amy Lynn Burke's cancer had been a doozey, but she had been a fighter. She'd gone toe-to-toe with that fuck-all champ—eight rounds of chemo that left her bald and wasted like one them poor Jews in Germany. Then they took a lobe from her right lung and then a few months later, one from the left. There were also the lymph nodes the doctors popped out of her, like fuck-all grey, lumpy boogers. They tried radioactive pellets and when that failed they resorted to laser beams.

Amy Lynn was a fighter to the end and she could honestly say she had won a moral victory. Even when they lowered her into the dirt in that goddamned expensive teak casket that would never-ever see the light of day again, people were singing her praises. Look how brave she had fought. Look at the courage she displayed. She was a right paragon of motherhood and wifely virtue to the bitter end. She was a fuck-all saint, a woman to be adulated and emulated.

And look at John Burke, that turd of a husband she left behind.

Sure, Amy had died, but she didn't lose her battle with cancer, John did. Her medical bills and hospital stays and pills and treatments had bankrupted them—and then she got sick again. They lost their home, their cars, their everything. John worked two jobs to pay for the fuck-all rinky-dink little place that was just a step up from a mobile home, and he wasn't no white-collar turd who sat his ass at a desk all day. No, he was a mechanic by day and a stock boy by night. He worked like a man, just as he always had.

It hadn't been enough and slowly their possessions had been taken from them and eventually, like a friggin' third grader, he found himself riding a fuck-all ten-speed to work because there were always new bills. Jaimee went about in cast-offs and sometimes John went without eating for days on end, all so Amy could be "brave" in the face of cancer.

She was the martyr and he was the unshaven, bleary-eyed goon who went about all the livelong day with dirt under his nails and grease stains on his *Goodwill* rejects.

It was an honest to God relief when she finally died.

[35]

That's what he felt when he saw her monitor finally flat line.
There were no tears or sorrow or grief. John never mourned,
not that anyone could tell. He left the hospital by the front
doors, got on his ten-speed and rode home. Once in the quiet
of his living room, he drank beer and watched *The Young
and the Restless* with his feet propped up on the arm of the
couch, and all he could feel was this great sense of relief, of
liberation.

By the time Jaimee was dropped off by the sitter that day
he had drunk all the beer in the house and was watching
Oprah and not understanding the draw whatsoever. "Why do
women like this shit?" he'd asked her.

"Daidy!" she had cried. She had an accent as thick as his
and when she said 'Daddy' it almost rhymed with lady.
"Momma's gonna be real mad with you when I tell her you
been cussing again."

"About that," he said. "I got some bad news. Momma
died this morning."

Jaimee was just like her momma and took the news like a
trooper. Oh yes, everyone marveled at how brave this little
four-year-old was. Look how she fought back the tears and
look how pretty she was in her little sundress that John had
dyed black. With her pale blonde hair and her pert nose, she
was the spitting image of Amy Lynn. Everyone just gushed
and marveled at her. They remarked about her toughness and
her spirit. They said: *Look at her strong jaw as she places
them flowers on her momma's grave. And look at that low
father of hers out drinking away his paychecks.*

This wasn't strictly true, however gossip was always
better than fact. He had indeed begun drinking with the
regularity of a Swiss watch, but he always made sure Jaimee
was properly fed, that is when he remembered to stop by the
grocery store. And he paid a local woman to sit for her and
take her shopping for clothes. And he made sure she went to
school and had friends.

He loved Jaimee just as much as he had loved her

momma. Though no one could tell from his reaction to Amy Lynn's death. He had loved his wife so much it had felt like torture. Her pain had been his pain every fuck-all step of the way.

Now he had to decide if he would allow Jaimee to be tortured just as he had been. His cough had started with a November cold and four months later it was only getting worse. It had been the same for his wife in the beginning and with each passing day he grew more certain that he had what she had. The symptoms were the same: a cough that wouldn't leave, frequent sickness, pain in the shoulders and back.

The big difference was that he was afraid of going to the doctors, not in the sense that he was a chicken, but in the sense he would have to face up to the shitty truth: he had lung cancer.

"I won't cuss no more," John told his daughter. "Or I'll try not to as long as I can get this fuc…I mean this ole calculator working."

"Don't use that one, Daidy. The seven sticks. I seen it. You should use momma's coupon calculator. Remember that little one she always brung to the market?"

"Oh yeah," John said, picturing his wife. Once upon a time, Amy Lynn could hold her shop list in one hand, her calculator in the other, balance a baby under one arm and fetch cantaloupes with the other, all the while guiding a left-veering cart with nothing but her breasts.

As Jaimee got her breakfast and fixed up her lunch, John went to fetch the calculator from Amy Lynn's coupon drawer.

The drawer hadn't been opened in three years. John didn't want to think about the neat stacks of cut out slips that were ordered, first by date of expiration and then again by desirability of the offer. He didn't want to remember how much time Amy Lynn had put into making sure she got the very best deals for her family. Quick as he could, he grabbed the little calculator with its vinyl cover and shut the drawer again, as if afraid that some spirit of Amy's would come wafting out of the drawer to berate him.

The great saint Amy Lynn would not approve of what he was planning.

He went back to the table and ten minutes and one more beer later he had his sums jotted in his childlike penmanship on a single piece of lined paper.

"What's that, Daidy?" Jaimee asked, before picking up her bowl and slurping down the Captain Crunch flavored milk that sat at the bottom.

"Nuttin'," he answered, suddenly embarrassed. He threw a forearm across the two columns. "Just some figgers. Budget stuff, money and the like."

The column on the left was a list of his assets. There were two items jotted on that list: an eleven-year-old Toyota Corolla, the one thing he had splurged on since Amy's death, and a savings account with a total of $107,254 in it. In a moment of pure ESP or precognizance or just plain maternal instinct, Amy Lynn, after a week with her strange new cough, had upped her life insurance to a quarter of a million dollars. The hundred grand was all he had left after paying the remainder of her hospital bills and her funeral expenses and that goddamned teak coffin.

Despite being church-mouse poor, he hadn't barely touched none of it.

The column on the right was a long list of bills he could expect to have to pay once he was diagnosed with the fuck-all cancer that was eating up his lungs and turning them black. When this was subtracted from the hundred grand, what was left was a depressingly large negative number.

"Fuck-all," he whispered, feeling the need to cough. He didn't, he was so tired of coughing. He just breathed through the nasty phlegm making a gurgling sound deep within his chest.

"Daidy, Mrs. La-fayette is here," Jaimee said in an urgent

tone. Her blue eyes went to the beer cans. She wanted them out of sight when Mrs. Lafayette came to take her on to school, but John didn't bother to hide them. What was the use? He was already regarded as a good-for-nothing bum by the high-class rednecks of Izard County. What did he care what they thought?

He was dying and no amount of so-called "bravery" on his part would change anyone's minds about what a fuck-all good-for-nothin' he was. And even if he could change people's minds about him, he wasn't going to put Jaimee through the same hell he had gone through. And he certainly wasn't going to leave her destitute.

As soon as Mrs. Lafayette unleashed her last look of disgust his way and left, John got into his battered Corolla and went to *Mac's Easy-Pawn* and for the first time ever he wasn't going to drop something off.

He was shopping for a gun.

# 4

## Stephanie Glowitz

## Newark, New Jersey

Since she was so tall the flimsy hospital gown came to rest just above her knees and though she frequently wore tiny miniskirts that her mother considered scandalous, Stephanie Glowitz felt embarrassingly exposed sitting up on the exam table.

In nervous agitation she kept tugging at the hem and flattening the wrinkles so that the gown lay smoothly on her thighs.

"It's going to be ok," her mom assured. Winnie Glowitz was a rock. She patted Stephanie's leg with a palm as dry and soft as talc.

"Yeah, it is. I know it. I feel good. No, I feel great; better than I have in years. And I think I look better, too. You know the sexy checker at the supermarket? Yesterday, when I ran to get your hair color, he was all like *dammmn, girl*."

The combination of chemo and radiation therapy had been the most horrid experience of her life. She had felt like killing herself almost on a daily basis, but it did have one plus: she'd lost a ton of weight and was fitting into clothes she hadn't been able to squeeze her fat ass into since high school.

Winnie made a face like she had smelled something odd. "That checker is a gay, dear. Everyone knows that. But it doesn't take away from the fact that you are looking so much better. I just wish your hair would grow back faster. Why aren't you wearing the wig? That fuzzy cap is…childish. You're twenty-eight not five. It just doesn't suit you."

"I kinda want to feel like a child," Steph replied, touching the soft *acorn* cap. It was pink in color and angora-soft. "All this was like a real big deal. I don't know how to explain it other than to tell you it feels like I'm reborn, you know? Like now I get this do-over. Like I get my life back but with a fresh start. I feel young again."

"I guess I can understand that." Winnie stared up at her daughter feeling a warmth of pride in her bosom. "Really, you do look younger with that cap. If your dad was alive he'd swear you were his little Bubbles again."

Stephanie choked and put a finger to her lips. "Don't ever say the *B* word out loud. You know how long it took me to lose that nickname?" The truth was that it took until she was a freshman at Vanderbilt where she traded in the nickname Bubbles for the name *Stone City*, though people tended to call her *Stoney* for short.

The reminder of her nickname, the newer one, not the sweet one her dad used to call her, had her jonesing for a joint again and her foot started to shake. That was the only positive to being on chemo—she was able to smoke all the weed she wanted and no one would say shit about it. Not even her mother. Whenever Winnie would catch Steph "self-medicating", her lips would get tight and her smile would turn crooked but she never said shit.

"Oh man, this wait is killing me," Stephanie said, her thumb subconsciously coming to her mouth. She started to nibble at the edge of the nail. "I mean, how long does it take to look at a CAT scan and say: clear, next."

"It's going to be ok," Winnie said a second time. "There were a lot of people in the waiting room, remember? Dr. Wilson is a great oncologist. He probably has just a ton of people to get through before…"

A knock at the door stopped her. She looked up at Steph and their eyes met—they were both suddenly afraid. The knock hadn't been Dr. Wilson's usual peppy knuckle rap. This knock had been two low taps.

"C-Come in," Steph said, her voice cracking.

Dr. Samuel Wilson was tall and dapper. His usual smile radiated from his deep brown face with confidence and showed a real pleasure in living life. His smile just then held a strong suggestion of pity.

Stephanie started shaking her head from side-to-side. "No. Uh-uh. I f-feel good. I feel great, ok?"

"Is it that obvious on my face?" he asked coming forward, not to listen to her heart with his stethoscope, or to take her temperature, but to hold her hands. "I'm sorry, but the first cycle of chemo wasn't successful."

Winnie stood up. Her eyes roved all around the room and could not find a single thing to settle on. They bounced from floor to ceiling to Wilson's shiny shoes. "Then we do another. Isn't that what you said? If the first didn't take we do a second round."

Dr. Wilson nodded but there was a hesitancy in the movement. "Yes and no. Unfortunately…unfortunately your daughter's cancer is no longer in the limited stage. It's progressed to the extensive stage, meaning we have found tumors, very small ones in the pleura and in her left lung."

Stephanie's eyes were doing the opposite of her mom's, she was staring at a button on Dr. Wilson's suit. It was round, grey, and wholly ordinary, but in some fashion it seemed to be hypnotizing her. "Pluera," she said and didn't know why she did.

"It's the membrane that encases the lungs," he explained. "When we find cancer there, it's a sure sign of it progressing to the next stage. I suggest we do a more thorough screening to find out exactly where the cancer has spread."

"Ok," Stephanie said. Her jonesing to get high was gone. In its place was a feeling of doom. "How long?"

"I'm sorry, I don't understand. How long is the test or how long until we can schedule it?"

"How long do I have?" Out of nowhere tears rushed from her eyes. "To live."

"That's not easy to say," he said, with a grimace. "It depends mostly on your genes. Most people don't realize this, but genetic predisposition is the main factor not only in getting cancer but also in fighting it. Your father's colon cancer advanced far quicker than the average and you, you're not even a smoker and yet you have lung cancer."

"She smokes pot!" her mother exclaimed. It came out like a combination of an excuse and an accusation. "If she promised to stop right now and never did it again would that help?"

Stephanie began to shake her head; her eyes still focused on that nothing of a button. "Marijuana isn't a carcinogen, mom. It's natural."

"I wish that was true," Dr. Wilson said. "The latest studies suggest that both tobacco and cannabis smoke contain the same cancer-causing compounds and, depending on what part of the plant is smoked, marijuana can contain more of these harmful ingredients."

"So she should stop, right?" Winnie asked.

The doctor puffed up his cheeks and gently blew out a long breath. "The doctor in me really wants you to stop, however the realist thinks that it won't make much difference at this point."

"How long do I have?" Stephanie asked again, her voice barely a whisper.

"It depends on…"

"How long!" she cried.

"Patients diagnosed with extensive stage small cell lung cancer have a median survival rate of six to twelve months. Possibly, with more chemo and radiation therapy, we can extend that."

Winnie leapt up. "Then that's what we'll do! You're going to be my partner in this Dr. Wilson. I want the next cycle started up as soon as humanly possible. Today if we can. I'll call into work; it'll be no big deal. We can lick this, Stephanie."

"No we can't." She was going to die. There it was. A doctor told her and that made it fact.

"With the right attitude we can," Winnie insisted.

Stephanie finally looked away from the button, but her eyes were so unfocused that she didn't really see anything. She shook her head. "No. No more chemo for me. I'm done."

## 5

### Chuck Singleton

### Norman, Oklahoma

When he got the news, Chuck said two words: "Well, shit." He stood up while his doctor went on talking about surgeries and tests and all the rest. Chuck wasn't listening. He tugged off his gown and was putting on his pants one leg at a time like he always did, or almost like he always did.

Unaccountably, he had left his underwear sitting on the floor.

His doctor, a young'un with a poor attempt at a beard scrabbling on his cheeks pointed at the under drawers. When Chuck made no move to pick them up, he went on, "Those are your treatment options. I'd suggest the brachytherapy. Mr. Singleton are you listening? Brachytherapy is when we install a catheter inside the affected bronchial…"

Chuck ignored the doctor's mumbo-jumbo just like he ignored the underwear; deciding at that point to go commando for the first time in his life. He slipped his boots on and pulled his t-shirt over his lean torso.

"Mr. Singleton what are you…um, where are you going?"

"Gonna quit ma-job," he replied. That seemed about right. No sense hanging around the shop as he wasted away. 'Sides, he needed a vacation. Chuck Singleton, at thirty-seven had never had what one would call a real vacation. Sure, he'd taken time off to go see his folks and every year he took a week during the season to go after white tails, and he enjoyed a four-day weekend on occasion to pull bass out of Canton Lake.

But just then he wanted more. "Think I'll go see a mountain. I hear Colorado's full of them."

"Um, yeah," the kid doctor said, uncertainly. "But what about your treatment? When are we going to start you on that chemo?"

Chuck knew what chemo was. He'd read what he had needed to on the subject and he'd be damned if he was gonna shoot radiation into his body on the off chance that it would kill his cancer. "What's the Vegas line on me, Doc?"

"Vegas line? I—I don't know what you mean."

"What're ma-odds?" he growled, feeling annoyed at wasting time. Seconds were suddenly a might bit more precious to him than they had been five minutes before.

"Odds, yes. Ok, with the right therapy we can likely increase your quality of life significantly. As for prolonging your life, we have made rapid advances in…"

"Let me help you," Chuck said, interrupting. "What're ma-odds of dyin' of ole age?"

The doctor started to hem and haw, but when Chuck turned his green eyes on him and gave him a hard stare, he sagged and admitted, "One in a thousand. Maybe not even that good, but it doesn't mean you can't have a good life between now and...you know."

Chuck had read about the sickness and the depression and the pain and the wasting away. Thanks but no thanks. "That's alright, Doc. You can save your radioactive pellets for the next guy. I'm gonna go see the mountains of Colorado and I think Hollywood. And, iffin I live that long, New York City. I just gotta see what all the fuss is about. S'long."

The young quack just shook his head, until his eyes fell on Chuck's tighty whities. "What about your underwear?"

"You can have 'em Doc. Maybe someday you'll grow into 'em."

## Chapter 3

## Opportunities

**1**

### Edmund Rothchild

### Manhattan, New York

"You can do this, Edmund," Kip said, flashing his white teeth and clapping his partner on the shoulder. "In fact, you need to do this. We are on the verge of something huge! Our Com-cells are going to be bigger than...I don't know, the light bulb."

"The light bulb is illegal in case you forgot," Edmund shot back. He considered the banning of the light bulb the biggest bit of tomfoolery he had ever heard of, besides global-warming, that is. Edmund was seventy-five years old and for the last twenty of those years he couldn't seem to get enough global-warming. Here it was seventy degrees and he had a sweater on under his suit coat.

Kip made a face. "I'm not going to quibble. We both know you become argumentative when you're nervous. It'll be ok. They aren't sharks."

Rothchild laughed. "You call them sharks, quite literally after every press conference."

"But this will be different," Kip shot back. He took Edmund by the shoulders and started to gently push him to the first floor conference room where a bevy of reporters were standing around eating expensive pastries and drinking gourmet coffee. "You see today we are announcing a breakthrough in the fight against cancer. They're going to eat it up. They're going to be more like sweet little kittens, you'll see."

Edmund wasn't convinced. "There are breakthroughs all the time."

"Not like this there isn't. You're the one who sold me on

the idea, now sell it to them." When Edmund looked unconvinced, Kip went on, still guiding the older man, "I'll be right next to you in case things get awkward. Just be yourself. Let the teddy bear out." Once upon a time, many years before, Edmund's wife had accidentally called him by his bedroom nickname while at a party. Very few had the chutzpa of Stephen Kipling to bring it up.

"Pissing me off isn't helping my nerves," Edmund said, as they approached the podium. He began to feel his pulse pick up and his smile felt phony and frozen. There was nothing in the world Edmund hated more than public speaking. The journalists, seeing them enter the room, went to their seats; those from the more important news outlets pushed to the front and stared up at Rothchild, expectantly.

Kip nudged him and after a shaky breath Rothchild launched right in: "First, I'd like to thank you for coming, especially on such short notice," he said. It seemed like a fine opening but for some reason Kip was smiling at him in a very strange way. Edmund tried to ignore him. "Um, I uh, have an announcement of some importance concerning a research project that has shown great promise…" Now Kip was grinning at him like a maniac. It was completely throwing off Edmund's train of thought. "One second," he said to the journalists and then leaned into Kip and asked, "What the hell is wrong with you?"

"Try smiling a little," Kip said, around a gentle smile of his own. "You look like you want to kill someone."

Whenever Edmund was particularly anxious the stress tended to settle in his face and neck. His muscles were so taut that he had to will a smile onto his wrinkled face. It was only marginally better. He'd gone from looking like a murderer to some creepy old, pedophile asking children if they'd like some candy or a ride in his van. It was the best Edmund could do under the circumstances.

Kip jerked his head towards the journalists, suggesting that Edmund should go on with the briefing.

"Right. As I was saying," Edmund said. "Through the tireless work of our scientists, R & K Research Industries has made a stunning breakthrough in the treatment of cancer, uh, lung cancer specifically. The technique is guarded by patent laws but I can tell you that small cell lung cancer which, as some of you know is the most deadly of all carcinomas, will no longer be the death sentence it once was."

He thought his statement was just fine, not realizing that when he had said the words: *death sentence*, the words were low and raspy and that he sounded like the crypt keeper. He went on, "The FDA has given us fast-track approval which means we will begin our first clinical trials in one month. We are now looking for proper candidates."

"What sort of candidates?" one of the reporters barked out. "Can anyone get in or are you going to screen them like you did with your insulin study? Isn't that what you're being investigated over? Skewing results?"

Edmund looked at Kip in surprise. What happened to the reporters being sweet as kittens? Kip raised a finger and answered the question, "We are not able to comment on a case that is still under investigation, other than to say the accusations are false and we look forward to being vindicated."

"I can at least talk about the candidates for our trial, correct?" Edmund asked his partner who nodded quickly and then looked emphatically at the journalists, who seemed amused at the befuddled, old man. "Sorry about this, it's usually Dr. Kipling who does these sorts of things. About the candidates, we are looking for second stage, or what's called extensive stage patients afflicted with small cell lung cancer. The only screening that we anticipate is age related and of course viability."

"What do you mean by that?" the same reporter asked with more than a hint of suspicion in his voice. "You only want the ones that will live anyway?"

Edmund glared down at the man, wondering: *Who was this jackass?* "First off, young man, I have a doctorate in microbiology and thus it is only polite to address me as Doctor Rothchild. Secondly, your question is so steeped in ignorance you should be embarrassed at having opened your mouth."

The reporter, who had been snarled at by scarier men than this old codger, shrugged and said, "By that, *Doctor Rothchild*, I take it you are refusing to answer the question?"

"The question was asinine. Once someone reaches the extensive stage of small cell lung cancer that person is deemed incurable. They are going to die no matter what. Do you understand that simple concept?"

"Yes," the reporter replied, this time without the sarcasm.

Edmund, who had become emboldened, went on, "By viability I mean a chance at a normal life after the treatment is concluded. There are some end-stage patients who have such extensive lung damage that even if their cancer were to be cured, they'd likely die Anymore questions?"

A woman raised her hand and started speaking even before Edmund acknowledged her. "Can you give us an inkling of the specifics of the cure? Is this a targeted genomic breakthrough?"

"It's not," Edmund said, grinning. "It's better, at least when it concerns lung cancer. We haven't have had the same success with other forms of cancer, yet."

The reporter, who had been rude earlier, smirked. "Sounds like a bait and switch. There are some who say that big pharmaceutical companies like yours don't really want to cure diseases. They say disease maintenance and symptom management is where the real profits are made. They say that companies like R & K are not in the business of cures because that would put them out of business."

Edmund's mouth came open and he began to splutter. "Who? Who says this?"

"People who think you profit from misery."

[49]

The reporter was a slight man, thin through the chest and when Edmund stepped forward with fire in his rheumy eyes, the younger man flinched back. Kip grabbed his partner before he could do something that would make the evening news and not in a good way.

Edmund, shaking in fury, said to the reporter, "I think you need to leave right now. Your questions are not befitting this press conference."

The reporter stood up and seemed about to leave when Kip stopped him. "Wait, I want you to have these." From the inner pocket of his suit coat, Kip produced two pictures. Edmund was surprised to see they were pictures of his wife and daughter. "If you think money is our only goal, I want you to talk to these two people," Kip said, heavily. "This is Gabrielle Rothchild, Edmund's daughter. She's dying of lung cancer even as you waste our time with these stupid questions."

"Kip, no…" Edmund said in a weak voice.

Kip ignored him and strode forward to stand in front of the gathered reporters, his face livid. "And this is his wife. She died of pancreatitis, so I guess you'll have a tougher time asking her if she thinks her husband doesn't want to find a cure."

Embarrassed, the reporter mumbled something that sounded like an apology and hurried from the now silent room. All eyes were on Kip. He held up the two pictures.

"Sometimes we are too eager to find a cure. Sometimes we want to help our fellow man so much that we rush things. That's where that investigation into our insulin study stems from," Kip said, lying smoothly. "Trust me, I wish it was all about money. Money is easy. Watching our friends and families die while we struggle against useless rules and regulations, and battle against pig-headed bureaucrats, that's what's hard to do." He paused, letting the silence work for him. He had such a natural understanding of dramatics that just then he seemed more like a stage actor than a scientist.

Kip smiled suddenly, breaking the tension that had built up. "But we shouldn't be worrying about any of that. Not today. Not when we have a cure for cancer in our sights. This is not another of the vague promises of some far away tomorrow that we've all grown accustomed to. I'm talking about a cure using a combined cell process that unleashes the natural healing power within all of us. Think about it, no more radiation, no more chemo, no more losing our hair. And what's better, no more useless deaths." Another pause allowed that to sink in. He nodded to each reporter and said, "I'm sure you have some more questions."

There were, lots of them, and he answered them easily, fluidly, and no one questioned Kip's veracity. He had cemented in their minds the concept that he and R & K research Industries were the good guys here. This had been his ultimate aim. Things had been going steadily downhill for the company; shareholders were losing confidence, stock prices were plummeting, capital was drying up right when he needed it to finish the new facility.

So Kip had orchestrated this little song and dance, and he had played the reporters like a virtuoso. No one asked if Mrs. Rothchild had died of a different form of pancreatitis than the one they were being investigated over. And no one questioned who the rude the reporter was. They had no idea that the man was actually a local actor and had been handsomely paid to play the villain. Not even Rothchild knew. Edmund was far too innocent, far too naïve in his view of the world. He stood there shaking, casting sad glances at the pictures Kip had made sure to have on hand just for the press conference. They would go back in his office drawer at the end of the day. They were, after all, just a prop to Kip.

**2**

**Ryan Deckard**

Peter Meredith

## Walton Facility, 60 Miles North of New York City

Deck was supposed to be impressed by the buildings and the grounds, then again the facility was supposed to have been completed by then. It wasn't.

"This is what happens when people can't make up their minds," Hal Kingman said in his own defense. He was the lead architect in charge of the Walton Facility and Deck wasn't impressed by him either. The man had on a blue chambray shirt with the sleeves rolled up to his elbows. The way he wore it seemed almost to mock the construction workers who were busy as bees in every building. It was as though Hal was *just* about to do some actual work. "Ask me what I'm supposed to throw all my men into today? Go ahead."

Deckard just kept walking to the main building. He wasn't there to play guessing games; he was there to check the state of security in this supposed fortress-like facility. In his opinion it looked like a college campus, and a pretty one at that. The existing trees had been preserved during construction so they could throw their shade over the winding walkways and the stately red, brick buildings, while shoots of ivy, perennials, and shrubs of all sorts were being nurtured so that in a few years Deck figured the place would resemble the Garden of Eden.

Other than a glance, he ignored the trimmings and the opulence just like he ignored Hal.

Hal's smile failed him, as Deck didn't play along. He hurried to keep up with the taller man. "Well, I'll tell you: yesterday it was security. Today it's the hospital. Do you know they want to have the fifty-bed hospital up and running in four weeks and three days? Who knows what they'll want prioritized tomorrow?"

"The fence," Deck answered him, stopping suddenly and pointing at the black, wrought iron fencing that went around the property. The fence was fine for stopping a few teenagers from getting in and sprawling graffiti on the walls but it wouldn't slow a professional for more than a few seconds. "At a minimum it should be fifteen feet high. I want a team replacing it tomorrow."

Hal looked at the fence in surprise. There was nothing at all wrong with it as far as he could tell. It was supposed to be a security fence and, by golly, it sure seemed secure; he was certain he couldn't climb it. "What's wrong with the fence?"

"It's too short."

"What? Too short? What do you mean? It's...it's..." Hal spluttered for a few more seconds and then smiled and threw up his hands as if the fence was nothing. "You want a new fence? Fine, but it isn't going to happen tomorrow. It's not that easy you know."

"It is that easy," Deck stated, flatly. "Hire another crew. Tell them you want the exact same fence only five feet taller. That should take exactly one phone call and five minutes of time. Do it."

The architect snorted, derisively. "Do you happen to know the first thing about codes and city ordinances? Or how much paperwork's involved? It's not like I can just snap my fingers and have it all magically happen. These things take time."

"Do what you need to do," Deck replied. "If a bribe is what it takes, do it, because we both know what Dr. Kipling will say when I give my report on the current state of his most 'secure' facility. The height of the fence was in my original report, if you don't recall."

Hal went white, remembering.

"And, what about the windows and doors?" Deck asked. "Are they at least to my specifications?"

The architect was on firmer footing here. "Yes and the roof access has been minimized to one egress site. Also the phone lines are all secure; no electronic data can be transmitted in or out of the main building. We are also on your timeline for adapting the computers to your demands:

single-piece towers, no USB ports, no Ethernet, and all of them are linked via the company intranet. There'll be no surfing the web with these babies." He tried to give Deck a smile, but the security officer saw the nervousness behind the look.

"And the surveillance equipment?" Deck asked. "Is it all in place and ready to go?"

The smile cracked. "No, but, look, it's not my fault. Getting guys with the expertise you ask for isn't easy or cheap. I still have to come in under budget. Have you forgotten that? Besides, there are precisely two firms on the East coast that can do this job and both are booked until August."

"Then fly in a West coast crew," Deck said. "Oh, don't give me that *woe is me* look. You bid this job, knowing the time constraints." Deck turned on his heel and continued his march to the main hospital. Over his shoulder he called, "I'll tour the place myself. You start making those calls."

"*You start making those calls*," Hal mimicked, falsetto voce. He was furious at how Deckard had treated him, however it was a testament to Kip's legendary anger that Hal pulled out his cell phone and started dialing numbers on the spot.

The second Deck turned away he put the architect out of his mind and focused on the job at hand: analyzing the current state of security. He opened the front doors and stood just inside the dusty lobby, trying to visualize how the building would look once it was complete. It would be a cast-iron bitch.

Sure it would be beautiful. Dr. Kipling had in mind the most picturesque laboratory/hospital money could buy. He was hoping to rival the fanciest private hospitals in the world. No expense was being spared in creating this curative wonderland, but all that gilding was putting Deck on the spot.

It was going to be his job to guard a twenty billion dollar

cure. It was roughly one-sixth the value of all the gold in Fort Knox and a million times easier to stick in your shorts and walk out the front door with. And to make matters worse, the cure had likely been half-stolen already. Rumors had been circulating in the research world, rumors that Deckard was quick to catch up on.

Setting up HUMINT--human intelligence operatives--in competing pharmaceutical and biotech companies had been his first order of business when Kip had hired him six months before.

For the most part, the operatives were passive agents, little more than "friends" in these other companies. They had been wined and dined, and "gifted" with small wads of cash. There was also the promise of more to come, simply for keeping an ear out. What they were supposed to be listening for had been, and was still, frustratingly vague. Scientists, even the ones he was supposed to be helping, were as secretive as CIA agents.

All Deck had to go on was the type of cancer they were trying to cure and the words: *Com-cell* or *Combination Cell Therapy*. He figured he would be just spinning his wheels, however there was such a uniformity of thought in the field that the term *Com-cell* had stood out.

Understandably, Kip had freaked when he heard Deck's report that a French company was kicking around a new concept involving a combination of mutated cells. It meant someone at R & K had given away or sold vital information. The next thing Deck knew he was on a plane to Canada to have a chat with one of his "operatives." Jean Basteau, a sweaty, little man, who tried to impress Deck with his spy chops by keeping his back to the door and jumping at every sound, had come by the information third hand. That had been two weeks before and Deck was still trying to chase down leads, but that too was turning out to be a bitch.

He simply didn't know enough about the Com-cells to ask the right sorts of questions; in effect he was basically clueless about what he was guarding. He found the one authority on Com-cells on the fourth floor of the Walton facility. When the elevator doors opened, Dr. Lee was standing halfway down the central hall, staring at what were going to be "her" labs for the duration of the clinical trials. She was visualizing just as Deck had been doing, though in her case she needed quite the imagination. The fourth floor was in such a chaotic state that it could either have been halfway to being completed or halfway to being utterly destroyed.

Without turning she said, "They're working in the back on the left, in the BSL-4 labs."

The irritation in her voice was too obvious to miss. "And you don't think they should be?" he asked.

Thuy turned and when she saw Deck, her eyes widened just the slightest. "No. Most of our work will be done in the BSL-3 labs and that is more of a precaution than because of any real danger." Biosafety levels or BSLs, range in containment practices and are designated a level based on the toxicity or the communicability of the pathogen under study. Deck, who had read up on the CDC safety standards, had already made it a promise to himself to steer clear of the category four labs if at all possible. He had no desire to see what the bubonic plague looked like first hand.

"So why don't you tell them to switch their attention to the other lab?" he asked.

"No, it's going to be alright," she said. "Mr. Kingman said he'll have it all completed in time." By the slight shrug and the tilting of her head, Deck knew she wasn't convinced of the architect's sincerity. After his earlier talk with Hal Kingman, Deck certainly wasn't convinced.

"Give me a minute, will you?" he asked and yanked out his cell phone. As he reamed out the architect, he walked past Dr. Lee and did a quick tour of the half-completed labs. Most of the rooms were without walls and one was without a floor. Deck found himself staring down at an electrician having lunch in the third floor cafeteria. It made little sense, but the cafeteria was as whole and complete as anyone could ask for while the far more important labs looked to have been ignored until only recently. In his ear Kingman was making all sorts of promises, but Deck didn't want to hear it and tore the man a new one.

"Mr. Kingman will refocus on the category three labs this afternoon," Deck said as he came back to Dr. Lee. "You just have to know how to speak his language."

"That's a language? I certainly don't curse as fluently as you, Mr. Deckard, but if things continue the way they are, I might just have to start." She was as clearly exasperated at the facility's level of unpreparedness as he was and when they locked eyes they shrugged at the same time and then smiled.

After a few seconds her smile faltered. "Is there anything I can help you with, Mr. Deckard?"

He swore inwardly at his foolishness—he'd been staring at her. It was hard not to when she smiled. Dr. Thuy Lee was absolutely, exotically beautiful. Her features were a study in perfection. After the first time they had met in Kip's office, he'd pulled her file: Thuy Heather Lee: age thirty-seven; Vietnamese/American war baby. Born in Saigon in the closing days of the Vietnam War and smuggled out of the country in a cardboard box by her desperate mother. She possessed a Bachelor's degree in chemistry from Yale University and a Doctorate in Molecular Microbiology and Immunology from Johns Hopkins. Among her many credits she had published thirteen papers, none of which held Deck's attention beyond their lengthy titles.

She was brilliant, but it was a toss-up whether her unique beauty was greater than her intelligence. Both left Deck a little tongue-tied.

"I, uh…yes. There is something more that I…I mean *you* can help me with." He coughed, making a pretext to break eye contact so that he could order his thoughts. "It's the

Com-cell. I need to know more about it if I'm going to have any hope of tracking the leak." Now it was her turn to look away. He let out a little barking laugh. "You don't trust the man who is supposed to be protecting you and your secrets?"

"I don't know you well enough to trust you," she answered, truthfully. "It's a question of motivation. Some people around here consider you little more than a mercenary and from what I understand about mercenaries, it's money that drives them. If that's the case I'm being wise not to divulge anything beyond what you need to know."

"Would it matter to you to know I did not seek this position out? Mr. Rothchild came looking for me because I have a reputation. This is not the first time I could have sold out my employers for a ton of money."

Edmund Rothchild had promised Thuy that Deckard was as honest as they came, however the Com-cell was worth a lot more than a ton of money. "Supposedly everyone has their price," she remarked.

"Except you of course," Deck shot back.

Her large doe-eyes narrowed slightly before she answered, "I don't think you can understand what motivates me."

This made him laugh. "Of course I can understand. In spite of how smart you are, you're still human. We all have the same underlying desires: success, security, popularity...love. Your main motivation is obvious: it's fame. You will be the woman who cured cancer. That is way bigger than money as a motivating force. It may even be bigger than love."

She flashed a quick smile. It was there one moment and then gone the next and though it was brief, it hinted that there was a deeper warmth to her that she tried hard to keep hidden. "Ok, sure, I won't deny it. Yes, it will be something to put my name on a cure for cancer. But that's not the only reason I began this research."

"Of course not," Deckard said. "Your mother, born Hue

Le, changed her name in '75 to Heather Lee when she emigrated to the U.S. She died of breast cancer in 2003. She had just turned fifty."

Instead of a return of that quick smile, her eyes grew more guarded. "You seem to know a lot already."

"It's my job. I know you scientists think of me as little more than a mall-cop in a nice suit, but I'm being tasked with guarding, not only a billion dollar secret, but billion dollar minds as well." There was the smile again! Like a shooting star, he caught just a glimpse and had to fight his lips not to reply in kind.

"Billion dollar mind is a bit much," Thuy said. "I'm worth maybe nine hundred million, tops."

Without realizing it he stepped closer to her. He was a tall man, thick through the shoulders and chest, normally very intimidating; she didn't step back. "I'll stick with my initial assessment," he said. "One billion, even."

For a moment she forgot herself in the smell of his cologne and his chiseled looks but the moment passed. "Ok, enough flattery," she said, laughing, feeling embarrassed and not understanding why. She leaned back, crossing her arms. "I won't give up my trade secrets so easily."

"I'm not after secrets, especially ones I probably wouldn't understand. I just need more of, I don't know, something. Something I can get my hands on or wrap my brain around. Kip wants me to find out how far the French have gotten and I'm running into brick walls. Can you at least tell me if there are exotic components that go into making this Com-cell? Plutonium? Iridium? Anything like that? Are there unusual flowers in it that are found only in the jungle or roots from the taro pant found only in Bora-Bora? These are the sorts of things I can trace."

"I don't know if I can help you. There's really nothing about the Com-cell that's out of the ordinary. You'll find almost everything that goes into it in every properly outfitted lab in the world. Except for maybe the stem-cells, that is."

His demeanor changed in a flash. "Stem-cells? Do you mean from babies?"

"No, not fetal cells. We use adult cells harvested from donors. Kip didn't care where we got them, but Dr. Rothchild was adamant: no fetal stem cells."

He relaxed a little. "Stem cells...I'll look into it. Anything else?"

Thuy opened her mouth to say something and once again their eyes locked: his were warm brown, while hers were so dark in color that they looked like wet coal. That darkness made them seem particularly wide and deep and slightly mystifying in a way that held him, as if he were on the verge of being hypnotized. It felt like a pull that went deeper than...

Dr. Lee blinked and glanced at the floor. When she looked up again that particular coolness of hers had blanketed her once more. "I'll let you know if I think of anything that will help you, Mr. Deckard. I won't detain you any longer."

Just like that, he'd been dismissed.

## 3

**Phillip Riggs PhD**

**Walton Facility**

In the cafeteria, the only part of the Walton Facility that was entirely complete, the three research teams were gathered around their tables waiting for the meeting to begin. Much as in a school cafeteria, the teams sat as cliques; no one daring to break the code and sit apart from their colleagues.

Riggs really wished they would. His six-person team had been handpicked by him, not for their wit or engaging minds, but to accommodate his dominant personality trait: laziness. His team of worker ants was not known for brilliance of mind, it was made up of worker ants; nose-to-the-grindstone drones who excelled when tedious chores were heaped on them. If brilliance was called for, that was where he would step in.

At least that's what Dr. Riggs PhD used to think. Then he was scooped by *her*. And he still didn't know how. Everything was being held very close to the vest. Too close in his opinion. In order to confound the spy who had leaked the information, Thuy had compartmentalized each activity: Stem cell harvesting and preparation was being overseen by Milner. Riggs' team was then transferring the mycotoxin-bearing organelles into the stem cells. Lastly, Thuy had assigned her team the work of growing the receptor cells and then "gelling" the receptors to the stem cells.

The end result was a miracle little molecule...supposedly. The results of her tests were also a tightly controlled secret.

He doodled *15%* on his note pad, wondering: *How could she have been the green light for a third round of tests with a fifteen percent success rate?* His own Com-cells, using far more powerful mycotoxins had a forty percent success rate in the animal trials with the unfortunate side effect of causing a rabid-like mania in nearly half of the subjects. A rabid opossum wasn't a pretty sight.

He was aching to be given the chance to figure out what had gone wrong, instead he was playing lab assistant to Dr. Lee. Riggs shook his head, watching her glance at her notes and then at her watch. She could've begun speaking already but she was always exact even when exactness wasn't needed. She'd called the meeting for three and Riggs knew it wouldn't start until three precisely. Thuy bent to pick something out of her briefcase that sat at the foot of the podium. Her tight skirt grew even tighter.

"Yowza," Riggs said, under his breath.

"What is yowza?" Eng asked. "Is this engrish?"

Riggs tried to keep the annoyance off his face. In the last few days, Eng had kept closer to him than his own shadow. Eng was scientifically curious to a fault. A very annoying fault. "It's nothing to do with the project. Why don't you read your handout?"

Eng had already read it once, but to satisfy Riggs he read it again. He was halfway through when Thuy's watch beeped at her. As usual she didn't bother with pleasantries or a warm up joke. She went right in with her opening statement concerning the funding status of the project and didn't pause until she noticed Riggs sitting with his hand in the air.

"Dr. Riggs, do you have a question on the current state of our funding?"

They'd worked together for the last six years so the skepticism in her voice was well warranted. "You know I don't," he answered. He only cared about funding when a project was his and his alone. "I want to know how you did it."

She glanced to Deckard, the security man, who was standing behind her. As far as Riggs knew the security man hadn't done much around the facility besides adding an aura of suspicion. He remained motionless save the raising of a single eyebrow, suggesting the decision was hers alone.

"Come on, Thuy," Riggs said. "The trial starts in thirteen days. You have us flying blind here and it sort of feels like we're about to fly into the side of a mountain."

"Yeah," Milner agreed; a rare occurrence.

Thuy knew she'd have to give up her secrets eventually, however the very idea that one of the people in front of her was a corporate spy galled her. It made her feel violated.

And yet the others deserved to know what it was they were working so hard on. "Fine," Thuy said and then sighed down at her notes. When she glanced up again she was a little shocked to find she had the room's full attention—they had all been drowsing through the funding report, but now every one of them was listening eagerly. "Ok, I like your enthusiasm. For those non-scientists, to understand the Com-cell, you must understand its parts. I'll start with what we call the receptor cell. We are using the 27Q proteasome because of the high affinity and specificity..."

Deckard cleared his throat, lightly and leaned in. "Maybe a little less with the specifics, Dr. Lee. There is still the leak to worry about and any little thing puts your competition that much closer."

"Of course. You're absolutely correct," Thuy acknowledged with a nod. She turned back to her teams. "All of you understand the concept behind the receptor cell: just like every other naturally occurring molecule, carcinomas have catalytic sites...docking stations if you will, where they receive nutrients and where they expel waste. Some of these sites are very specific to that particular form of cancer. This specificity allows the Com-cell to travel throughout the entire body and yet only latch onto the tumor."

"Mine didn't," Riggs stated in a loud voice. "And I was using the same proteasome as you. For some reason they built up along the meninges of my opossums with unfortunate side effects."

Thuy was unruffled by the outburst. "It is my theory that your mycotoxins were too powerful. Yes, they destroyed carcinomas, but I believe they also modified the Com-cells causing them to be able to dock at other sites." She paused to let Riggs respond, however he was picturing the Com-cell he had created and fearing she was right.

When he didn't meet her eyes, she went on, "The next step in creating the Com-cell is the merging of an adult stem cell with a fungal organelle; one that will release mycotoxins. In my first attempts with *Fusarium* the mycotoxins were too weak and too diffuse to make much of a difference against tumors larger than a gram in weight. I decided that instead of trying a more potent mycotoxin as my colleagues were, I changed tactics. Still using the weakest of the mycotoxins, I introduced the Com-cells via inhalation. This was a positive in a number of ways. First, the Com-cell was able to attack the cancer in the lungs right away without having to run up against the immune system. Secondly, the Com-cells were extremely concentrated allowing for the destruction of any sized tumors, and finally, the stem cells, having released their deadly payload were in a perfect position to replicate."

"Son of a bitch," Riggs said, in appreciation. "You kill the cancer and heal the lung at the same time."

"Yes. It's simple stochastic differentiation: the stem cell develops into two differentiated daughter cells. In layman's terms, the Com-cells, once their payload of mycotoxins is delivered, become simply lung tissue."

"The inhalation was your third test?" Milner asked. "What were the results?"

"Thirty out of thirty were healed completely," she replied and even she couldn't help the smile that crept across her face.

## 4

### Lieutenant Eng

Lieutenant Eng needed all of his training to maintain a calm exterior as he came to realize he had just been given the keys to the kingdom. He knew everything now, maybe more than any of them except for Dr. Lee. He certainly knew more than Riggs, who had barely glanced over the results of his two tests.

Eng had studied them until he had memorized every line. Cancer was easily China's biggest killer, accounting for over 1.6 million deaths a year—and that was just the official count. The real number was at least twice that high and with the pollution becoming thicker than fog in many cities, death from cancer would only continue to climb.

If he played his cards just right, it would be Lieutenant Eng of the People's Liberation Army who would get credit for finding the cure. To make that happen, he would just have to figure out a way to sabotage the efforts of Dr. Lee and by extension the French.

The first order of business was to force from his mind the visions of the parades that would be thrown in his honor and the justly deserved promotions he'd receive and all the hot patriotic ladies that would fawn all over him. These would come to him in due time. For now he had to make sure his cover of harmless, geeky "Chinaman" wasn't blown.

He sat there as Dr. Lee went back to her meeting's agenda. After the funding report, she introduced the members of the staff: Dr. Milner—a fat, pompous, ass. He stood and named his research team: three pretty ladies and three men from India with incomprehensibly long and complicated sounding names. Then Dr. Riggs stood and muttered the names of his crew; he looked stunned.

When Eng's single syllable name was mentioned, he smiled through squinty eyes and bowed his head in every direction. He was playing it up to the hilt, and no one noticed. Not even the security man. Deckard barely gave Eng a glance. He was too busy eyeing the new people to the lab: two oncologists, a radiologist, a mycologist, and the physician who would be present during the trial.

Eng didn't see Deckard so much as twitch until the mycologist was introduced. Then Deck leaned in toward Dr. Lee and Eng could read his lips: *What's a mycologist?* He took out a notebook and jotted down Thuy's explanation.

The last person to be introduced shocked everyone by what he had to say. "This is Mr. Blair," Dr. Lee said. "He's the trial recruiter."

Blair didn't hesitate giving his bad news: "I only have twelve subjects signed up. Sorry."

Only Deckard didn't seem to get worked up over the low number. Everyone else was floored. "That's not enough," Dr. Lee said. "From a pool of tens of thousands, you have twelve?"

The recruiter gestured to a stack of loose paper set out on the table in front of him. "Yes, only twelve, but the pool isn't as big as you think. A lot of cancer patients don't want to do any traveling on such short notice. Hell, most people on the West coast wouldn't even think of making the trip. Of those that are near I have to subtract the people who are too far gone, you know, physically and all those who have given up entirely. Then there are the people on the other end of the spectrum who think they still have a chance with chemo and radiation, or prayer. These people want to try what *quote, unquote* works."

"What about the ones who've tried chemo already?" Dr. Lee said.

"A lot of them don't want to waste their remaining time as guinea pigs and there are more who are just plain clueless about these sorts of trials. People worry that they'll get a placebo or a sugar pill or that the cure might make their cancer worse! I'm sorry, but it's these out of the blue, last minute trials that are the hardest to place people in. Maybe if you had billed it as something else, like chemo without the vomiting, I could have filled you up."

"So what do we do?" Thuy stared around at the room. She looked as though someone had sucker-punched her.

No one had a good answer. Eng had a self-serving one: "Maybe we postpone trial one year. Give time to get new patients."

"And let how many people die in the mean time?" Thuy demanded. "No, give me something else."

"We bribe them," Riggs answered. "Free flight, free cottage accommodations for loved ones. A big stack of *Benjamins*. Whatever it takes."

Thuy was ready to jump on any plausible idea. "Would that work?" She had asked Blair but it was one of the oncologists who answered.

"Yes," Dr. Samuel Wilson stated. "Many of my patients are hurting financially. If the bribe is big enough, I'm sure they'll come on board even if they have no hope of being cured."

Thuy smiled uneasily. "Let's not use the word bribe. I

think *incentive* is a better alternative."

## 5

### Chuck Singleton

In the middle of March, he stood fourteen thousand feet above sea level at the top of Pike's Peak looking out at the world. It was majestic, beautiful and surprisingly, fantastically cold and he coughed nonstop until he fled. A few days later, he rolled his jeans up and waded into the Pacific off Pismo Beach—it was also cold and he shivered the gunk from the insides of his lung and he spat up ugly matter. On the twentieth, he was in South Florida, riding his first rollercoaster and not really enjoying it. On the twenty-second, he was near out of money and the pain in his chest was a constant reminder that it didn't really matter.

It hurt to take a deep breath; it felt as though there were sharp edged diamonds between his ribs that gouged at his innards every time he sucked in air. Coughing made him wince and he couldn't remember the last time he was hungry.

"Guess I'm just 'bout done," he said. "Now it's just a question 'bout how I'm gonna go." The people around him on the observation deck pretended they didn't hear the lean and leathery man talking to himself. He was in New York City. Even at the top of the Empire State Building, there were crazies.

From thirteen hundred feet up, he watched the sun go down over New Jersey. It was one of the damned prettiest sights he'd ever seen. That evening he spent watching the people of New York live their lives. It was a bit overwhelming for a man from Norman, Oklahoma and his head spun at the sheer number of humans going this way and that.

The city brought out the best and the worst in people. They laughed over nothing and screeched in anger over less. They were suspicious of strangers but the love they showed their friends came off them in waves. New Yorkers were so different from him that he felt like an alien being and yet, at the same time, he could see there were many people just like him: people alone and in pain, on the outside of life looking in.

The next day he woke up in a Jersey City motel room with his lungs full of crap, and pain that radiated from his chest and up into his shoulder. "Well, shit," he whispered and then spat out a knob of ugly phlegm. He dry swallowed six Advil and when that didn't do anything he took six more. It barely helped.

"And that's why," he said, thinking about his upcoming suicide. Chuck had plenty of life left in him, but nothing to look forward to. He could expect every morning from here on in to be just as bad if not worse.

"A gun'll be messy. I don't wanna leave a mess for some poor shlub. That would be straight-up rude. And I don't like heights…" It was one thing to enjoy the view from the top of one of them skyscrapers, it was another thing altogether to intentionally take a step off of one into nothing. Using a car to gas himself to death seemed as fine a way to go as any, but seeing as he didn't have a car or a garage, that choice was out.

Chuck settled on pills as his one-way ticket to heaven or hell or whatever it was waiting for him. "And not some crappy Advils." He wanted to go out in style, maybe even with a smile on his face.

At ten that morning he stood in the High Point Oncology Wellness Center, reflecting on the dichotomy between the bright and shiny offices and the grey and listless patients waiting to be told what they already knew: that their remission had been canceled, their funeral date had been moved up, and that their chemo-fueled agony had been a waste of time.

"I don't have an appointment ma'am," he said to the brassy woman behind the desk. He tried not to stare, but east coast women were so strikingly over-worked in the looks department that he couldn't help wonder where the makeup ended and the girl beneath it all began. "I just need some pills. Ma-doc is Jeffery Montgomery outta Norman, Oklahoma. He'll vouch for me."

"We don't work that way," the receptionist said with a fake smile. Chuck figured that she never wore a real one. Her lips sported two different shades of gloss or liner or what all. They also seemed unnaturally puffy as if she was smiling up at him from around a mouthful of ass fat or silicone.

A few minutes later, Chuck found himself lying his way through a stack of paperwork. Phone number: first ten digits that sprang to mind. Address: 1428 Elm St, the original house in the movie *A Nightmare on Elm Street*. Mother's maiden name: Chiapet. Secondary Diagnosis: EPS— Enormous Penis Syndrome.

It was absolutely juvenile but he didn't care, he needed the laugh. All around him in the waiting room were people waiting to die and whenever he glanced at them he wondered if they would end up in the ground or if they would find themselves in something resembling a brass spittoon on someone's mantle.

When he was done bullshitting his way through the paperwork, Chuck stretched out his long legs, shut down his green eyes and tried to nap, but found that he couldn't because there was a cougher in the room. She would cough which would give him the urge to shoot one right back. What was worse she had that same loose-phlegm hack that he did. They traded cough for cough until he opened his eyes and saw the source: a very pretty girl—or rather she would've been pretty if she weren't in the process of dying.

She was tall and pale. Her skin was like white marble; it made the blue of her eyes stand out. On her head was a little acorn cap of soft wool that was girlishly pink. A very short tuft of pale blond hair stuck out beneath. They locked eyes

and each fought off the urge to cough. It became a contest—
again, so juvenile that Chuck marveled at himself.

The girl went pink in the cheeks, started blinking rapidly
and then coughed. Chuck grinned and coughed into the back
of his hand. "Squamous or small cell?" he asked.

"Small cell," she admitted. He nodded to suggest that he
had the same diagnosis. She glanced at the mass of brown
hair on his head. "Still have your hair, does that mean you
got lucky and they caught it early?"

"Nope. I'm into late innings and I figgered why go
through all that crap? Ma-name's Chuck, nice to meet you."
He stuck out his hand. They shook and he was slow to give
up the grip. Her hand was as satiny soft as his was rough and
leathery.

She didn't seem to mind. "I'm Stephanie. And you didn't
miss anything. Chemo is as bad as they make it out to be. It's
why I've drawn the line."

Their handshaking had reached an awkward point and
reluctantly he pulled his hand back. "You throwin' in the
towel?"

"I like the way you talk," she remarked instead of
answering the question. "Are you from Texas?"

Chuck's eyes blazed in mock fury. "Texas? Do I look
like a big hunk of bull crap to you? Next I reckon you'll be
asking me iffin ma-family is from France."

"Is it?" She laughed and then coughed. He did the same.

"Naw. I'm from Oklahoma. I'm out here seein' what all
there is to see before I get settled in for ma-long dirt nap."

"I should have done that," Steph said, "instead of that
awful chemo. Of course my mom wouldn't have let me
either way. Here I am a grown woman and she treats me
like…well she treats me like her baby daughter. I know I'm
lucky to have her around except she doesn't know the
meaning of the word quit. Right now she's in there with
Doctor Wilson conspiring to send me away to a top secret
facility where they have some sort of experiments planned."

"Experiments?" Chuck snorted. "Sounds like they got some newbie doctors who need practice with an anal probe. No thanks. They'll just have to wait until I've reached cadaver status."

"It's worse than that," Stephanie said. She lowered her voice to a whisper and added: "They want to inject a fungus into you. Is that crazy or what?" When he started to laugh, she put her hand on his arm and said, "I'm not kidding...oh shit, my mom."

Winnie Glowitz, looking small next to the tall doctor, stood in the waiting room doorway staring at Chuck with a great deal of suspicion. Dr. Wilson had a different look. "Could you wait out here for a few minutes, Mrs. Glowitz? I need to talk to this gentleman briefly. Charles Singleton?"

"You're in trouble with the principal," Steph whispered to him as he got up. Chuck flashed her a smile and followed after the doctor.

"I could've waited a few more minutes," Chuck said as they entered an exam room. "Twern't no need to call on me so quick like."

"You thought that was quick?" Dr. Wilson asked. "You were in that room for over an hour."

Chuck shrugged. "Some hours are better than others, I guess."

"With the right company, I would say you're correct. Now, my nurse tells me you're here for pills. Sorry, but we don't work that way. We follow protocols that are designed to..."

"I don't means to be rude, Doc, but I don't need protocols or chemo or any of that hogwash. I have some pain I need to deal with so, iffin you'll just write me a script, I'll be on ma-way."

"On your way, where?" Chuck shrugged in answer and Dr. Wilson saw right through it. "That's what I thought. I've been in the cancer business for over twenty years and I know when a man is done. You guys get that devil-may-care look in your eyes, and I'm alright with that. Who am I to say when life is no longer worth living? But, what about that young woman out in the waiting room?"

"Stephanie? What about her?"

"She's not ready yet," Dr. Wilson answered. "I see it. She may talk a good game but she's not ready to die just yet. She wants to try to live and I want you to help her."

Chuck gave a little laugh that turned into one of his longer coughing fits. Red in the face and gasping, he asked, "Help her, how? That fungus business? Are you serious? Look, I don't even know her."

"Yet, you two have a connection," Dr. Wilson said, entwining his long, dark fingers together. "It was obvious to me and it was most certainly obvious to her mom. You both are end-stage cancer patients. You're both staring death right in the mouth. And you're both young and pretty. You'll never meet a girl in a bar with connections that deep."

This brought out a laugh from Chuck. "I'm not that young." His smile dipped at the corners. He was all sorts of ready to die, but he knew the same couldn't be said for Stephanie. There was too much hope left in her. "So…is it this fungus business? Iffin so it sounds crazy."

"I'll make you a deal, Mr. Singleton. Let me explain the clinical trial to you and, if you still want to walk away from this chance, I'll get you your pills and you can go."

Twenty minutes later Wilson finished and Chuck left with his pills. He paused in the waiting room doorway. "Stephanie? You wanna come take a step around the block with me? I have a question for you."

**6**

**John Burke**

**Izard County, Arkansas**

The pistol, a snub-nosed .38 with a worn handle, sat under his socks in the top dresser drawer. John Burke had checked in on it once an hour for the last two days as if it were a cat ready to drop a litter under the stairs. He sighed with each visit. He sighed and he coughed.

But the gun would have to wait for just a little while longer. "Pretty soon, Amy."

Would she understand? Would Jesus? This was a big concern with John. Suicide was one of those things that didn't sit in a grey area. There wasn't going to be no asterisk next to his name when he was standing at the pearly gates waiting to be let in. *I got me some fuck-all extenuating circumstances there, Mr. Saint Pete.* That wasn't going to fly.

John shut the drawer. The time wasn't right. He was still waiting on answers from people who, it seemed, were hell bent on ignoring him. That he wasn't hearing from friends who'd stop returning his calls months before, wasn't surprising, but to be treated like a dog by family, well that just stung.

Downstairs, the kitchen door creaked open.

"Jaimee?" he called, suddenly nervous. Although Jaimee was a tiny thing, she was never this quiet, unless…

"Yessum, Daidy. It's me."

"Somethin' wrong?" he asked hurrying down to the kitchen. There most certainly was something wrong. Jaimee was white and there were tears on her face.

"Aunt Kathy came to see me at school," the little girl said. "They took me outta class."

It felt like a stone had done sunk deep down in his belly, but he tried to play it cool. "Oh yeah?"

"Aunt Kathy told me to tell you that I cain't come and live with her and that you have to stop callin' at all hours. Why am I supposed to go live with her? Is it your cough? Are you gonna be like mommy?"

The weight in his gut doubled. "Maybe," he said, chickening out. The manly thing would've been to sit her down and have a chat. Just then he felt no better than a dog.

"When do you go to the hospital?" she asked. Since she could crawl, her life had been one hospital visit after another. The weight in his gut grew. It was such a load that he sat himself at the kitchen table; it's one bad leg wobbling some as it had for years.

"I'm not going to the hospital," he told her. The room went very quiet

"Then how will you get better?"

He stumbled over the truth and tripped on lies, and all that came out of his mouth was a series of nonsense sounds. "I...I...uh...hey, is that the mail?" She had a little stack of envelopes in her hand; fuck-all bills and crap he figured, however the first one was addressed to Amy Lynn Burke. Normally, he would've chucked it without bothering to look inside, but just then he needed an excuse to not say what needed to be said.

"Who's it from?" Jaimee asked. She had latched onto the letter as well. It was like a life preserver from reality.

"Oh, just some pharmacy. Prolly it's a bill or a..." His mouth stopped as his eyes latched onto the sum $10,000. It sat midway down the paragraph. Was that how much Amy Lynn owed? No...he had to start over again, reading from the top to understand that it was how much they were offering.

"Who are these people?" John asked, looking at the front of the envelope. "R & K Pharmaceutical Research. Huh?"

**Chapter 4**

**One Day Prior to Trial Inception**

**1**

When it came to the labs, Dr. Lee could not have been happier. They were, at least from a scientist's perspective, beautiful. They were very bright, impeccably clean, and fantastically spacious—it was every scientist's nightmare to have to stumble over each other in order to get work done. She had the opposite problem, if problem was even the word for it. Each of her three teams buzzed and scuttled about in their own BSL-3 labs, preparing for the first trial, which was less than twenty-four hours away.

She watched through the glass windows, thoroughly satisfied as the final touches were being put to the Com-cells. She was so happy she had even been able to give Ryan Deckard a smile when he came scowling into the hospital just after nine that morning. Though to be sure, she kept it on the cool side. Whenever she gave him a warmer smile he returned it in the same manner and there would be a spark or something odd between them. Since she had no intention of getting involved with a co-worker, especially one who didn't even possess a master's degree, she kept her interactions on the lean edge of professional.

Deck wasn't happy. Not because of the cool attitude Dr. Lee was giving him, she was that way with everyone. No, he wasn't happy about the leak. His informant Jean Basteau had been open about where he'd come by his information: a professor of microbiology at Cornell named Ethan Rousseau who did frequent consultant work for Rhonofis, a French competitor of R&K's. The fat bastard had let it slip after three too many vodka tonics.

As expected, Ethan was not as forthcoming as Jean had been. In fact, Ethan was a dick in Deckard's opinion. So far, substantial bribes and threats of lawsuits had done nothing to change his mind about talking, and no amount of digging seemed to unearth anything concerning who the leaker was or how far Rhonofis was on their own version of the Comcell. Deck had run up against a stone wall.

But that wasn't his greatest problem. Most of his surveillance system was not yet operational and no amount of screaming at Hal Kingman would make it so by the following day when the trial would commence. For some reason Kingman had prioritized the perimeter cameras. Deck could see every inch of the grounds which was all well and good except the biggest threat to the cure was what was going on *inside* the facility.

Not only did he have a double agent to worry about, but there was also a sudden influx of people in the Walton Facility. He had the numbers memorized: forty-two patients, sixty-one family members, eight nurses, six doctors of various specialties, twenty-three members of the cleaning staff, fourteen cafeteria workers, thirty-one management and administrative positions. Counting the eighteen scientists, Deck's twelve-man security crew, and the construction workers, who still had so much to do, there were now two hundred and fifty-seven people crawling like ants all over the grounds.

To make matters worse, three of the patients were convicted criminals. In order to fill out the study to a respectable number, the recruiter had even scraped the nearby prisons. The prisoners had been secreted in by way of the loading dock and were now housed in the southwest corner room of the second floor. That particular room had been picked not because it was in any way more secure than the others, but simply because it had the worst view: the side of the parking garage behind the main building.

Deck checked on the prisoners personally. He entered without knocking and stood just inside the door. The room was crowded. A third bed had been crammed in with the original two and with it had come three portable monitors and an IV stand. There was barely room to walk between the beds.

The three prisoners perked up when he first entered. "Thought you'd be the hot nurse again," Von Braun said, speaking genially. After seeing the view: a grey concrete wall, he had chosen the bed closest to the door, reasoning he was not only closer to freedom but also closer to the *honeys* he hoped would be waiting on him hand and foot.

Deckard ignored the man. He went to the window, not to check out the view, but rather to inspect the glass and the rubber seal along its edges. With both palms he pressed hard against the window, leaving two ghostly prints behind.

Von Braun laughed at him. "You think we want to escape? You ain't too bright. Not only is this place practically a vacation, if we run away we don't get the fucking cure, moron."

Turning from the window, Deck stared at the hulking, blonde prisoner, assessing him, seeing the cold, cold eyes and noting the lack of emotion behind them.

"Check the glass once an hour," Deck said to the security guard who had followed him in. Strictly for the week long trial, Deck had hired three extra guards to oversee the prisoners. Each had been chosen for their large size and the easy way violence came naturally to them; the position didn't call for more than that.

"We're chained to the fucking beds," Von Braun said, lifting his arm halfway up and letting his shackles rattle.

"And check the chains as well," Deck ordered. "And I want to know if there's a single screw loose on any of these beds."

"What a dumb fuck," Von Braun muttered. He'd been sitting on the edge of the bed, now he laid back and nuzzled his head into the soft pillow. "Do what you need to do, just leave the remote and tell that hot young nurse I'm ready for my sponge bath anytime."

The other two prisoners were on the downhill side of middle age--one was grey in the face from his disease and lethargic from the meds. He was so far gone that although he was only fifty-eight, Deck had him pegged in his mid-seventies. The other prisoner had a great deal of body hair, but only a few wisps on his round head. He was chubby and sweated easily even in the thin hospital gown he wore. At the mention of sponge baths he sat up straighter. "They do that?" he asked. "I could get a bath from one of them?"

Deck's lip curled as an image formed in his mind. "Male orderlies only," he added to the security guard.

"That's bullshit!" the hairy prisoner cried. "I'm not a pervert. I got locked up for fraud, not for rape. And I got rights! You can count on a lawsuit if you plan on treating me..."

Dr. Lee stepped into the room; her beauty stopping the conversation cold. She did not advance beyond the doorway as every eye turned her way. "Did someone mention a lawsuit already? We haven't even begun the trial."

"Don't worry about it," Deckard told her. "Just some whining from the prisoners. That sort of talk never amounts to anything."

The hairy prisoner had already forgotten his threat. His mind and his eyes were completely focused on Thuy. "Whoa," he said as though in awe.

"Yeah," Von Braun agreed with his fellow inmate. "I don't normally go in for the squints but I'll make an exception for you, Doc. How about you draw the curtain around this bed and give me a full checkup. I have some swelling you might be able to help with."

Though Deck bristled, Thuy took the remark in stride--it wasn't the first time a man had made a jackass of himself in her presence. "You are nothing but a lab rat to me, Mr. Von Braun. When you've served my purpose you'll go back to your cage where you belong. Until then, be a good little rat and shut the hell up."

"You are a saucy little bitch," the prisoner replied, smiling, enjoying the attention. It had been eight years since he had even a conversation with a woman, and just then he had a fully engorged hard on.

"Yes," Thuy said, drawing out the word, somehow suggesting that Von Braun was inadequate by the simple syllable. "In case you are unaware of it, Mr. Von Braun, your fate is in my hands. If I want you off the study then you are out of here, and I don't need a judge or a lawyer or a court order, either. I simply put a line through your name and you'll be back in your cell by dinner."

"That would be a death sentence," Von Braun replied. "Are you so devoid of emotion that you'd be able to do that? Kill me with the stroke of your pen?"

Thuy didn't hesitate. "Yes. So, would you like to behave or go back to your cell?"

The pair locked eyes in a battle of wills only to be interrupted by the hairy prisoner in the next bed. "I'll be good. Herman, too. Don't lump us in with him."

She turned her cold glare on him; he blanched and touched the neck of his hospital gown with one of his hairy-knuckled hands in a gesture that was strangely dainty.

"I'll be good as well," Von Braun said. "You can trust me." He winked at her. As she started to shake her head, her phone began to ring.

"What?" she asked, brushing past Deckard and heading for the door. "What emergency do you have for me now?" she demanded into the phone just as the door swung shut.

"Did you see that body?" Von Braun asked the other prisoners. "Holy shit that was nice."

Deck gritted his teeth and turned to the guard. "Watch them. Anything happens, it'll be your ass on the line."

## 2

### Lieutenant Eng

The construction workers were going at it non-stop, hammering and drilling everything in sight. The nurses were like worker bees going from room to room, drawing blood, hooking up patients to monitors, and filling out charge notes. The scientists were sweating over the outcome of the trial before it even began and each was checking and rechecking the Com-cells or rereading their notes, or running computer simulations for the umpteenth time.

Strangely, the Chinese agent might have been the most relaxed person in the partially built hospital. With the hard part of his mission behind him he sat at his desk, playing solitaire on his computer and bowing his head like an idiot each time Dr. Lee rushed past. She was being run ragged, responding to every pseudo emergency that came up; there seemed to be no end to them and she was no longer the cool, professional scientist who had so confidently entered the hospital at dawn six hours before.

Secretly, Eng laughed at her and couldn't wait to see what she would look like the next day when her precious cure turned deadly; at least he assumed it would be deadly. When Riggs' possums had been given the *Alkaloid* Com-cells they had gone *diān*, crazy, biting through the wire of their cages to get at their brothers and sisters in the control group. Those that got through turned cannibal, gorging themselves until their bellies were swollen and the tips of their whiskers dripped blood.

It had been quite disgusting and yet Eng wanted an even more horrible display and so, when he sabotaged the trial by switching out the weak *Fusarium* mycotoxin with Riggs' *Alkaloid* version, he tripled the dose. It had not been easy.

With Riggs' team in charge of transferring the mycotoxin-bearing organelles into the stem cells, Eng was perfectly positioned to switch out the weaker *Fusarium* for Riggs's far stronger *Ergot Alkaloids*. It should have been simple, especially since Riggs barely paid attention to thing one in his own lab and spent as much time as he could next door in Milner's lab chatting up Anna Holloway.

When he wasn't around, Dr. Lee was always right there, asking questions and demanding answers about everything from the incubator temperatures to the pipette sterilization procedures. She wished to oversee every single aspect of the cure and was amazingly, annoyingly meticulous and had nearly caught Eng on two separate occasions in the middle of sabotaging her project. The first time he had crawled into a cabinet to escape detection and the second he had only saved himself by playing up his bumbling Chinaman stereotype to explain away why he was walking around with a tray full of *Alkaloids*.

Eventually Eng had to spend the night in the lab, working in the dark and dodging the guards to complete his sabotage.

On the other side of the double-edged sword was Eng's station chief who was not happy with Eng's latest reports. To be the real hero in the war against cancer, Eng had to keep *everyone* from making the breakthrough and that included his own scientists back home. In China, it was almost a point of pride to steal someone else's work for your own, something Eng was certain had been occurring since he was first placed on Riggs' team. It's why his last few reports had detailed the "poor" performance of the *Fusarium mycotoxin,* while at the same time he had hinted strongly that *Alkaloids* were the way to go.

That people would probably die, didn't concern Eng in the least. People died all the time in China. Life there was hard and short and quickly forgotten when it was gone. The state saw to that. China was a land where families are destroyed on a whim, a place where love was secondary to need, and a nation where personal honor rarely reaches maturity. It's a country where backstabbing and climbing over the warm corpses of your recent colleagues is a proven method of advancement.

Next door, in Japan, billion dollar deals could be concluded on a handshake, but Eng knew that in China a thousand page contract was simply an excuse to find loopholes. This sort of thinking breeds a form of selfish individuality that would be toxic in any other country--in China it was a way of life.


# 3

## John Burke

"You'll need to find a sitter," the admissions nurse said with a lift of one shoulder. After personally overseeing forty-one patients, she was too tired to do more.

"I ain't got no money for no sitter," John lied. He had plenty of money, however there was no way he was going to trust some stranger to watch over his baby-girl. *What about when you kick off?* A voice inside him asked. *Where is Jaimee gonna go then? Who'll watch over her?*

He still had no idea. His was a family of deadbeats, while Amy Lynn's kin had disowned him. He was practically shitting himself over the idea that his daughter would end up in fuck-all foster care when the cancer finished doing its number on his lungs and sent him to ride out all eternity in a cheap pine box. There'd be no teak casket for him--they was for martyrs who could gin up a hundred-person funeral service. Pine was for fellas like John who could only attracted people who he still owed money to and were there for one last shot at getting paid.

"She can sleep in mah bed. I can do stretchin' out on the floor." He had slept on worse.

"Mr. Burke, that's not how this facility is being run. We won't have people sleeping on floors like vagabonds." The admin nurse was stout and thick, almost the size and shape of a refrigerator. Her hair was the color of iron and cut short; if it wasn't for her dress and the nametag that read *Melinda Evans*, John would've thought she was a butt-ugly man.

"Then maybe this facility ain't right for me." He stood to leave and he wasn't bluffing. He had zero faith in a cure that he understood to be no more than jock itch powder in a test tube. He was there on a count of the money and since he'd already been paid..."Y'all have a nice day."

"Wait. Hold on, Mr. Burke. You can't just leave," Mrs. Evans insisted.

"Why not? I done spent all the money you'ins sent me." Another lie. The ten-thousand, along with Amy Lynn's insurance money was sitting in a trust account that couldn't be touched by anyone, including him, until Jaimee turned eighteen. John reckoned that if, by some miracle, he got a cure in him, he'd just go on back to work. The world was always in need of a good mechanic.

"It's not the money, Mr. Burke. It's the fact we have an honest to God cure for cancer on our hands."

"Y'all gotta cure for cancer, but y'all cain't round up another fuck-all cot or nothing?" Just then he remembered his promise about cursing and he glanced out at the waiting room where Jaimee was parked on a row of cold hospital chairs, swinging her feet a foot above the floor. She seemed very small and her skinny legs looked thin to the point of appearing brittle.

Mrs. Evans followed his gaze. She took a deep breath and sighed in defeat. "I'll see what I can do, but I don't think they'll let you keep her in your room." She picked up the phone and dialed and explained and then dialed and explained again.

She got nowhere.

Her immediate supervisor could be heard to scoff into the phone before offering to lend John fifty bucks for a sitter; Ron Blair, the trial recruiter gave up the number of one of the kitchen staff who had a sister who did daycare for a reasonable fee; the head nurse, a woman with two master's degrees and a blood pressure that was spiking near one-eighty yelled, "Are you kidding me?" and then slammed the phone down.

"Everyone's under a lot of pressure," Mrs. Evans said.

"You tried." John stood and had to grab the back of his chair as his head went light and his chest constricted. It was only a momentary thing and he took as deep a breath as he could, making a wheezy noise like a shot up bagpipe sitting in a mud puddle. "Y'all have a good evenin'."

"Wait, I got one more person to call."

She seemed so distressed that he sat down again, stretching his legs out in front of him. Jaimee wasn't the only one who looked brittle-thin. John's faded jeans hung off him and his ol' work shirt was so baggy he looked like a boy who'd raided his daddy's closet.

*Jes 'bout done in*, he thought. *An' still no one to watch over Jaimee.*

The thought, the long day of driving, the disease chewing him up and spitting him out had exhausted him. He dropped his chin to his chest, just thinking he would close his eyes for a moment. Thirty minutes later he woke as Dr. Lee, brusque and short, harried to the point of being rude, came in. "This does not constitute an emergency," she said after Mrs. Evans explained the issue. To John she asked, "Where is the child's mother?"

John blinked in slow steady beats as his mind tried to come to grips with being kicked out of a dead sleep. Before he answered Dr. Lee, he glanced into the waiting room to see Jaimee playing with another little girl. The two seemed like a matched set: equal in size, both pale and blonde with coltishly slim legs jutting from their pretty dresses. They looked ready for church.

John, in his grease-stained Levis might have been a bare step up from a hobo, but he made sure to keep Jaimee properly clothed. He turned back to Dr. Lee and spoke in a flat tone, "She dead. The cancer what got her two years ago."

Thuy's mouth came open for half a second, expelling nothing but a stunned sound, "Uhhhh...That's...I'm sorry for your loss, but that doesn't change the fact that we can't have extraneous personnel living in the rooms with the patients. We can help you find someone to watch the child. I'm sure there are a few daycare facilities around here. We aren't all that far from the city after all."

"But he doesn't want to use a..." the admissions nurse started to say.

Dr. Lee interrupted, "Mrs. Evans, it's a sad truth but sometimes we don't always get what we want."

"That's 'bout what I thought," John said, getting up. This time he forced himself to ignore the dizziness in his head and the ache in his chest, which made each breath, each second of his life a chore. "Come on Jaimee. We gotta get movin' on."

She looked disappointed that her playtime was being cut short and at the same time pleasantly surprised. "Did you get fixed already, Daidy?"

Up close the "twin-ness" between Jaimee and her new friend failed. The little girl smiled up at John, showing a rich man's set of teeth: straight and white--Jaimee's were already yellowing, and she'd be needing braces to close up the gaps in her ranks. The little girl also had perfect hair. It wasn't just cut, it was styled, and framed her face making her look like an angel. Jaimee's blond hair was limp and cut at right angles to box in her face, the limit of John's hair cutting ability.

The little girl's perfect smile slid away when John said, "I don't think there ain't no cure, darlin'."

"Mr. Burke!" Dr. Lee hissed as she hurried to catch up to him. "I can assure you there is a cure. But we have rules...the CDC has rules regarding this sort of thing. There are certain toxins involved that may not be healthy for children to be around."

"What about her?" John pointed at Jaimee's friend.

Dr. Lee glanced once at Maddy Rothchild. "She's different. That's the granddaughter of Edmund Rothchild, the man who fronted the money for all of this."

John smirked. "So she rich and so the rules don't apply. Typical."

"No...no that's not it at all," Thuy replied. She was having trouble grasping how a man, who was clearly in the end stage of cancer could walk away from a cure. It was mind-boggling. "Yes, Mr. Rothchild has a separate facility for his daughter, but Maddy still won't be allowed in the same room. You see we have to take special precautions against any pathogen with a measurement larger than point zero, zero, one micron."

She thought that was perfectly clear however John's brows came together to form a line across his forehead. "No disrespect, Doc, but you may know spores, an' varusses, an' macra-scopes, an' all, but you sure as hell don't know people. Tellin' me the rich got it better ain't exactly no surprise."

He started again to the lobby doors, but stopped when Thuy cried out, "But there is a cure! You can't walk away from it."

There were quite a few people in the lobby: two guards at the front desk, trying not to appear as bored as they felt-- Chuck Singleton with his back to the far wall where he could keep one eye on the elevators and another on the clock over the guard desk—Dr. Wilson who had stopped in mid-stride to respond to a text sent by his wife, she was unnaturally afraid that he was cheating on her and had texted and called eight times that day--Ms. Robins, chatting with one of the radiologists and wondering if his hair was real or if it was a rug.

They all stopped and stared at Thuy who only then realized how loud she had been. Her voice had echoed along the pristine white walls and the dust free glass. She'd even been heard down the hall where the secretaries in the admin offices all raised their eyebrows.

John shook his head. "So you say. People been sellin' snake oil since Adam and Eve. Iffin there's different rules from one to another then I'm a-guessin' there's gonna be different results, too. An' we both knows who'll end up holdin' the short end of the stick." He jerked a thumb at his own chest.

She glared at the insinuation. "You are being obtuse. Clearly, purposely so. And you're being offensive. Perhaps it would be best if you did leave." Her voice carried to every corner of the lobby and now people didn't even pretend not to have heard.

Dr. Wilson hurried over. "Did I hear someone mention snake oil? I have a case of it out in my car." Over the twenty years he'd been an oncologist, Wilson had developed a soothing presence. It was hard to be upset when he unfurled his broad grin in your direction. Thuy calmed, slightly, still her words were clipped as she explained John's irrational fears.

"What Mr. Burke is feeling is normal," Wilson said. "Doctors don't seem to realize how many times we are just flat out wrong. I had one patient who'd received sixteen different diagnoses before she found out that she was dying of endocrine pancreatic cancer. Each of her previous doctors were one hundred percent certain of their diagnoses and each was a hundred percent wrong. This affects the patients view, especially those in a terminal situation. It drains the hope out of them."

"But this time..." Thuy started to say.

John scoffed, "But this time y'all got it right? Sure." His skepticism was so obvious that even the two little girls, who were now almost an afterthought to the adults, caught it and shared a look.

"Right or wrong, Mr. Burke, this is your only chance," Thuy said, practically begging now. Yes, she needed him to flesh out her trial, however it was also clear to her that he couldn't last out the month without help. He was so bad off, swaying in place with sweat running from beneath his ball cap that she was on the verge of offering to watch the child during the evening, when little Maddy Rothchild spoke.

"She can stay with me. We can do a sleepover. It'll be ok, Mr. Burke. We'll just be in the big cabin. It's right nearby to the hospital."

John had seen the newly built houses on his way in; they didn't seem like cabins to him. Each was twice as large as his house back home and the largest was like a mansion.

"Asking permission first would've been nice," Ms. Robins said, cocking an eyebrow at Maddy. She wasn't going to argue too much. She had not been looking forward to entertaining Maddy single handily for the entire week. "But since you've offered already, I don't see why we couldn't have a guest. As long as it's ok with Mr. Burke."

Before John could spit, Jaimee had him by the hand and was begging, "Can I please? I ain't had no sleepovers in forever."

John wavered both in his mind and in his body. He staggered a little before righting himself. "Well, I don't know...I guess it'll be ok. If it ain't all that much of an imposition. And if y'all got the room."

"We have six bedrooms," Maddy assured him, holding up six little fingers. "And two of them are empty. But I think we should build a fort in the entertainment room. What do you think, Jaimee? We have all sorts of extra blankets."

The girls fell to planning and John was stuck with the real possibility that he could actually be cured. It was slightly unnerving.

**4**

**Chuck Singleton**

Chuck watched the little scene in the lobby with a level of understanding that none of them docs could possibly comprehend.

They weren't living with death practically hanging on their arm or constantly looking over their shoulder like some over-eager spy. They were able to sneeze without wondering if this was the little cold that would trigger pneumonia and then death.

Chuck felt like he spent every day with a cartoon piano hanging over his head suspended by an unraveling length of rope. When you lived like that it made little things huge and giant things small. He could see what that sick fellow valued and it wasn't his own fish-belly white skin, neither. It was the little girl and who would take care of her in the here and now.

For Chuck the big thing was seeing Stephanie Glowitz smile one more time. He was sure that when death punched his ticket he would miss icy beer on a summer's evening after work, and the feel of a woman's breast as he ran his hand up her shirt when she weren't wearin' no bra, and he knew he would miss all those Friday nights he got shit-faced with his friends down at Black-eye Pete's, but he knew what he'd miss most of all was Stephanie's smile.

He was tall and lean with a strong jaw and wide shoulders--there had been plenty of women before Stephanie, but there had never been that instantaneous connection before. Whenever he looked her way, he felt something he would've been embarrassed to admit to the *good 'ol boys* back home: he was in love.

This was why he had taken up residency in a little beach motel in Point Pleasant, New Jersey. Although Steph lived ten minutes away they'd only seen each other three times in

those fourteen days and two of those times were under the
unpleasant glare of Winnie Glowitz who was always
hovering around her daughter, setting a new standard in
over-protectiveness.

It was also why he had hung about in the lobby of the
hospital all day long. He'd been the first patient to check in
at a minute after nine that morning and since then he'd kept
a long vigil, watching as hundreds of people came in and out
of the little hospital. Of all those people, thirty-seven truly
caught his eye. He could spot others of his kind easily. It
wasn't just that they were frail and sickly, it was also
because they were the only ones who wore their fear so
openly.

Most people who came in through the gleaming lobby
doors marveled at the newness and the opulence of
everything like they were stepping into one of them fancy
New York hotels.

Not so the patients. Most of them cowered as if the
building was about to fall on them. They didn't pause to
gaze up at the marble walls adorned with renaissance prints;
they didn't look at the gilded sconces and fixtures or the
intricate tile that matched the soft squares of carpet. Instead,
in a hunched posture, they scurried through security, holding
their x-rays and body scans close to their chests as if afraid
someone would possibly want to steal them. They eventually
went in to see Mrs. Evans, whose make-up, hair, and overall
appearance slowly degraded throughout that long day.

From all outward appearances, Chuck had not changed a
lick. He had come in wearing the fanciest boots in his
arsenal, comfy, faded denim jeans and a white shirt that he'd
rolled to his elbows. He had foregone the cowboy hat that he
generally wore because Mrs. Glowitz always looked at it
with her lip curled and a tint of disgust in her eyes.

He waited and watched all for the chance to be smiled at
by the girl in the pink acorn cap. He had a long wait. She
came in just after one in the afternoon and she was different

than all the rest. Her eyes swept the lobby not in awe or barely concealed fear, but in hope. She hoped to see him, he knew it.

And she had smiled.

"Worth it," Chuck had said, under his breath.

When Winnie Glowitz wasn't looking, Steph pointed at the floor, meaning: *Wait here!* And he had for the next four hours, and again it was worth it.

During the middle of John Burke's confrontation with Dr. Lee, when the sun was threatening to clock out for the day, the elevator dinged pleasantly and from it strode Winnie Glowitz, alone. She looked neither left nor right, though somehow she was able to instinctively shun the unsightly Mr. Burke as she headed out the doors.

Chuck's heart began to pick up in speed as the minutes ticked slowly. Every time the elevator let out its merry "ding", Chuck stood up straighter and ran a hand through his brown hair. Four times the elevator chimed and four times he was disappointed, slumping back against the wall. After the fifth, Stephanie came rushing out into the lobby.

She had no idea what color the squares of carpet were or how many cherubs had been painted into the artwork, or anything else about the lobby, she only saw Charles Ryland Singleton. Unlike the other patients she had met that day, he wasn't pale and spindly. Yes, he was thin, thinner even than when she had first met him, but he didn't look brittle like the others...like how she felt. He looked tough like a strip of jerky or a knot of gristle. He was also tanned from living on the beach and he was so tall and handsome she caught herself staring.

"Sorry, I thought my mom would never...leave..." Her words seized up in her throat as he reached out and took her hand. With calm assurance he started heading for the lobby doors. "Where are we going?"

"I was hopin' to buy you dinner," he said in his rough accent. "I've been hopin' for going on three weeks now."

She'd been around her mother for so long that instant arguments popped in her head: *But that isn't allowed. But we'll get in trouble. But we're in the middle of farm town, New York.* She bit the questions back and allowed him to lead her outside.

The sun was setting, turning the tips of the western trees gold. Again it was the little things that seemed so important and they both stopped and stared. *How many more of these will I see?* Chuck asked himself. Next to him, Stephanie shivered in spite of the warm evening. "You want me to fetch a jacket for you?"

She was thin and her flesh had tented up around a thousand goose bumps, but she shook her head. The shiver hadn't been from the temperature. Her thoughts had run down the same line his had; if this new drug didn't work she'd be counting her remaining sunsets on her fingers and toes very soon.

"No, I'm..."

"What are you two doing out here?" Dr. Lee demanded, interrupting Stephanie. She was fast-marching from crisis to crisis as she had all day and naturally assumed the worst upon seeing two of her patients outside the walls of her hospital. "You aren't thinking about leaving, are you?"

"No ma'am," Chuck said. "Just thinking about gettin' us a bite to eat. Proper food that is. I'm just 'bout sick of hospital food."

Thuy arched an eyebrow at this. The cancer trial was her baby and she knew practically everything concerning it and that included her test subjects. She knew Chuck Singleton hadn't spent one night in a hospital since he'd been diagnosed. She also knew that he'd been instrumental in talking Stephanie Glowitz into coming on board. And it didn't take much of her natural genius to see that the pair wasn't just going for a "bite to eat."

"No alcohol," she said, with a stern glare. "And no drugs. And no eating after ten." She also wanted to add: And be back before midnight! But she already knew she sounded like a mother hen.

"Yes, ma'am," Chuck said, suppressing a grin. "I'll get her home safe and sound." He tugged Stephanie away, leaving Dr. Lee standing there looking exhausted. The pair headed for the Toyota Camry that Chuck had rented for the week. It wouldn't get much use beyond this first date but he didn't care, his horizons had shrunk to the immediate future. "You like ribs?" he asked as he opened her door. It was a purely perfunctory question for two reasons: One-who on God's green earth didn't like ribs? Two-there really was only one restaurant within ten miles of the remote hospital and it happened to be called Rib-King.

Stephanie enjoyed the ribs and the slaw, but, even more, she enjoyed Chuck's company, laughing at his jokes and how he talked, especially when he played it up for the waitress so that she kept saying, "Come again?"

She was tired by the end of the meal, but very happy. "I'm not quite ready to go back," she said when they climbed into the Toyota.

"Me neither."

The hospital held a certain finality to it that she wanted to hold off as long as possible. Going back meant there was only the trial to look forward to. Yes, she would be able to see Chuck during the course of the week, but what sort of shape would she be in? The chemo had left her sicker than a dog, her hair falling out, her skin checkered with nasty sores and blotches. What would a fungus do to her? Would her teeth go? Would it rot her gums or her lady parts?

Despite saying he didn't want to go back, Chuck started the engine and began driving. They did not go far, only to the edge of the little town where he pulled into the parking lot of a roadside motel.

"Chuck, I don't know if I'm ready." She wasn't a virgin or a prude by any stretch of the imagination, however she wanted something more from him than a romp on a well-used bed.

"I don't know if I'm ready neither," he said. His face had a pink glow from the neon sign canted on the motel roof. The light made him look healthy, but he, too, was feeling close on run-down. "I don't know what I'm supposed to be ready for cuz I ain't exactly sure what's going to happen in there, but I figger it'll be whatever we both want. Nothing more."

*Liar!* Her mother's voice echoed in her mind. Winnie Glowitz thought Chuck was a fake. She thought he was phony from top to bottom: the beat up cowboy hat, the down-home manners, the rugged good looks, all of it. She looked at him and all she saw was a slick operator who played up his country twang to charm her daughter when she was at her lowest.

Stephanie saw in him a man who had been ready to die, but had put it off for her sake. She trusted him.

"Ok," she whispered, worried about what he would expect, worried that she wouldn't be able to be what he wanted. She worried for nothing. He was sweet and gentle, and, though they both gradually came to want more that night, neither was physically able. They could barely kiss without breaking down and coughing.

They ended up entwined in each other's arms, sadly skinny like two lovers fresh out of a Nazi death camp.

"I'm scared about tomorrow," Stephanie admitted in a sleepy voice. Chuck thought about his own feelings for many minutes and by the time he said, "Me too," the girl in his arms was snoring lightly.


**5**


**Ryan Deckard**

Three rooms down from where Chuck and Stephanie lay snoozing, Deck sat in a dimly-lit room waiting for his contact. Light blared from a parking car and there came a soft knock. Deck eased his hand into his coat pocket where a CAI Canik 55 TP-9 9mm semi-automatic handgun with a 4 inch chrome barrel, sat hidden. It was for just in case. Things were never fully predictable, even when it was only a computer geek who was making a clandestine drop in the middle of the night.

"Come in," Deck said.

Casey Steinbach was alone and properly nervous--Deck was only an intimidating shadow in the darkened room. "Hi. I got it," he said, holding out a small metal square four inches on the side and an inch in height.

"Plug it in."

On the motel writing desk, next to the near useless stationery, was a computer setup, missing only a hard drive. Casey fumbled the stolen hard drive into position and clicked on the machine. "His user name is EDRousseau; caps on the first three letters. The password is Genius1!" Casey turned back to Deck and grinned. "Those scientist nerds are so full of themselves. Am I right?"

"Yeah," Deck said. "What about email?"

"The guy's got no sense of security. The username is erousseau at cornell.edu.org and the password is just like his computer password. I'd bet Genius1! is his password for everything. Not much of a genius if you ask me."

"I didn't ask," Deck said. In his left pocket was a stack of fifty dollar bills; there were two hundred of them, neatly banded together. He tossed the stack to Casey who fumbled the catch.

He came up from the floor grinning. "Hey, anytime you need a hand with computer related..."

"Get out," Deck said.

Still grinning Casey showed himself out. When the sounds of his car retreated back up the road, Deck went to the computer and started running down the files and personal documents--there were many thousands of them.

"Son of a bitch," he said, seeing the magnitude of the

work involved. With one hand he started breaking down the computer. With the other he started dialing numbers into his phone. "I'm going to be in late tomorrow," he said to his second-in-command, Ray Henderson. "I'll need you to make sure nothing goes wrong with the trial. I want you in with those prisoners when they get their treatment, you understand?"

"Yeah, it'll be a piece of cake," Ray said and then yawned into the phone. "I'll take Matt and Gottlieb with me. Those boys are bruisers; we won't have any trouble. What about you? You almost got the leak?"

"Hope so. A few hours will tell. If we do, we're going to have to jump on it with both feet."

"Overtime?" Ray asked.

Deck paused as he was unjacking the modem. He and Ray went way back; they'd developed their own code. What some had once referred to as "wet work", they called Overtime because of the extra pay involved. "I hope not." He had never been a party to assassination as a corporate security consultant and he didn't want to start now, no matter how many billions were involved.

**Chapter 5**

**Trial Inception Day**

**//6:14 AM//**

**1**

Nineteen-hour days had been the norm for so long that Thuy barely felt the difference between wake and sleep until she'd had downed at least two cups of coffee. It was just after six and she was already on her third as she headed into *her* hospital.

Mechanically, running on ingrained habits, she greeted the two lobby guards without even looking into their faces and in no way did she expect bad news to come from them.

"Uh, Dr. Lee?" one said, the discomfort clear in his voice.

Thuy rounded on him. "What's wrong?" There was always something wrong it seemed. In her opinion it had been a mistake to switch facilities so close to the trial deadline, especially when the new place was only half-built. *Dr. Lee, one of the elevators isn't running and we don't know why—Dr. Lee, the toilets are backed up on the second floor—Dr. Lee, all the centrifuges were calibrated inaccurately and have to be redone—Dr. Lee, the paint in the patient's rooms don't match. We asked for eggshell white and we received vanilla!*

She understood she had brought this on herself by the way she micro-managed everything. There was a deep need inside her to be a part of each detail. The cure was her baby after all.

The lobby guard could feel the weight of Thuy's responsibility in her cold stare. He blurted out, "We're missing two patients."

"Glowitz and Singleton?"

"Yes," he said in amazement.

Thuy was on the verge of using some of Deckard's colorful language but she bit back the string of expletives. "Call every hotel and motel in Kingston," she ordered. In her mind she pictured the map around the new hospital as she had seen it that first day when Kip had broken the news to everyone. He had wanted something secluded and picturesque and thus they were an hour away from anything remotely resembling a city. They were surrounded by farms and forests, with the first hint of the Catskills visible in the west across the Hudson.

Kingston, New York was the closest of the rinky-dink towns, but there were others. "If that doesn't work try Havilland and Millbrook. I don't care what you have to do, just get them here!"

This wasn't exactly in their job description, and yet both men started dialing without hesitation. They were well aware of the importance of the trial. Thuy didn't realize it, but, had the trial been as mundane as curing athlete's foot, her stress would've been ten times as bad. Apart from Eng, who had a very good idea how the trial would end up, everyone, from the guards to the janitors to the nurses to the lunch ladies, was working at a level that was almost unheard of. They felt they were part of something big, a part of something historical, and they were proud of it.

"Thanks," Thuy said to them, and then turned and began marching for the elevators, her heels clicking like a snare. She hoped that the two AWOL patients were going to be the only problems of the morning, however in keeping with her stress she asked the head nurse on the second floor: "What's going on?" By that she meant: what's wrong?

"We're missing two…"

"Glowitz and Singleton, I know," Thuy said, cutting her off. "I meant, what else?"

The nurse, a twenty-year veteran named Lacy Freeman, only shrugged. "Nothing really. We've had a few inventory issues, but my team busted their ass to set things right. We've cleared the floor of non-essentials and we're ready to go. We can start the prelim blood work any time."

"Begin with the prisoners," Thuy said. "They'll be getting the first treatment."

"Those three," Lacy said with a roll of her eyes. "I'd just as soon skip them entirely, especially that Nazi one. He gives everyone the creeps."

Thuy put a finger to her lips. She'd been warned by Kip that prisoners were exceptionally litigious and any loose talk could set off a lawsuit. "Just prep them and make sure you keep one of the security men with you at all times."

The prep work mostly consisted of a quick physical. Each patient was examined head to toe for any rashes or skin ailments that might be exacerbated when exposed to the *Fusarium* mycotoxin. They were then stuck with a large bore IV as a precaution against anaphylaxis or some other unforeseen medical emergency.

Although Fusarium was on the very lowest end of a class 2 biohazard rating, Dr. Lee wasn't taking any chances. The second floor was being limited to only essential personnel and the only people allowed in the rooms after the trial began were a handful of nurses who had been specifically trained to deal with the possibility of airborne disease. The treatment team would consist of three people: two would administer the Com-cells via an inhaler much like an asthmatic would use and a third who would operate the UV disinfectant light. Fungi are easily destroyed by ultraviolet light. All-in-all, Thuy was sure that the procedure would be quick, effective and safe.

She was supremely confident in her preparations. She wasn't even worried about the leak. It wasn't on her mind as she went back to the elevators. The leak had come too late for R & K's competition. Deckard had discovered that although a similar study by the French company was in the works, it was a month away from happening. It meant that Stephen Kipling's near reckless speed had paid off. The Com-cell was going to be a blinding success and everyone else was going to be spending all their time and energy playing catch-up.

The thought had her smiling as she went back up to her labs.

Dr. Riggs spotted her through the glass and hurried across the corridor that separated the two labs. Rubbing his hands together excitedly, he greeted her with: "It's go time."

She was surprised that he beat her into work, something that had never happened before. "You're in early... alarm clock malfunction?" she asked. "Or are you finally onboard?" Thuy couldn't say Riggs hadn't done his job over the last few weeks, however she had never classified him as enthusiastic.

"Yeah, of course," he said, as if he could sweep his past under the rug with a wave of his hand and a wide smile. "This is the cure for cancer we're talking about. And really I'm glad that it was you who got it right and not that jackass Milner. Don't get me wrong, my alkaloids would've worked in time...but, hey, you beat me to the punch."

"Is this your way of saying congratulations?"

"Yeah...I never..." he was suddenly too preoccupied to speak. Anna Holloway had come gliding out of the single operating elevator, all hair and bosom. Riggs watched her through the glass and if Thuy hadn't already been in her own lab she would've left him there drooling like an idiot.

When Anna was out of sight, he blinked, remembering he'd been in the middle of a conversation. "Yes, congratulations, Dr. Lee. That's what I meant."

She didn't bother to thank him. "Are you too preoccupied to oversee the blood panels? I'm especially interested in the lipids. If I have a fear over my Com-cells, it's that excess cells may become stored in body fat. It's something we'll want to be on top of right off the bat."

Riggs looked a little hurt at the suggestion. "I was hoping to be on the front end of things."

Lines wrinkled her forehead. "You want to be a part of delivery? That's what nurses are for....wait, are you expecting there to be some sort of immediate, dramatic response?"

He smirked, embarrassed. "So sue me if I like the idea of finally being able to help actually cure someone first hand."

Thuy understood the feeling. She'd been a doctor for fifteen years and today was the first time she felt like she had earned the title in the traditional sense. Even her friends, when introducing her would say of Thuy, *She has a Ph.D, but she's not a real doctor*.

"Sorry, Riggs, the administering team has been training together for two weeks. You'd just get in the way. Besides, I need your skills here.

**2**

The administering team, in their blue biohazard suits, proceeded solemnly through the labs and everyone stopped what they were doing to watch. Thuy had been pretending to read reports, too anxious to do anything of real value. Eng had been writing a letter to the INS describing how a certain Chinese scientist, himself, might have falsified data on his work visa. This would trigger an investigation which he would purposely fail and in six weeks he'd be back home in Beiping, where he would "magically" create a working Fusarium Com-cell and become a hero.

In Beiping, he would have his pick of women and all the money he could ever need. He'd be respected in a way he could never be respected in America. Lieutenant Eng:

military officer, scientist, spy, savior! The Chinese understood the value of each.

Riggs turned his head from the admin team and sighed, knowing he had missed his chance. He watched the team with their sturdy glass cart board the elevators and disappear behind the stainless steel doors. "So much for that," he whispered and then glanced at his spreadsheet again. Too late, he was seeing the problem with the alkaloids. The receptor cells in the Com-cells had been degraded by the alkaloids so that they no longer strictly went after tumors.

He cursed, seeing the obvious in the pathology reports that he'd only skimmed through after the first run of live animal tests. At the time he'd only been focused on tweaking the Com-cells and not on the effect they were having on the opossums, thinking that when they were perfected the secondary issue would taper off.

"What son of bitch?" Eng asked.

"I just figured out why our opossums all went mad," Riggs said. With a snarl he balled up the report and threw it across the room.

"What is what happen?" Eng went to pick up the wad of paper but Riggs stopped him.

"It doesn't matter. What does matter is that in about one hour we're going to have a fresh batch of panels to analyze. I want them churned out like clockwork so, if you want to get something to eat, or you have to use the bathroom, now's the time to do it."

3

John Burke watched the three-person team enter the prisoner's room with a feeling that was indescribable. Dread and hope seemed to battle within his guts, neither gaining the upper hand and both making him so anxious that he broke the cardinal rule the nurses had laid down. No matter what, he was to stay in bed. Only in an emergency was he supposed to get up. But what constituted an emergency? In John's mind having a heart attack while waiting for his turn was good enough.

Wearing only his hospital gown and a pair of white socks, he tiptoed across the hall and watched as the first prisoner, a very large, thickset blonde man started puffing on the short end of an inhaler. After a few minutes, the man pulled it away from his lips and said, "I don't feel any different. I'm starting to think this is just mist. Do you think you can fuck us over since we're prisoners?"

One of the admin team reached out a gloved hand to put the inhaler back in the man's mouth. "It's not magic," he said, the words coming out muffled because of the man's heavy face mask. "This is only the first of three treatments."

"If I find out that you're fucking me over…" Von Braun started to say, but was interrupted by one of the security men.

"If they're fucking you over, then you'll be dead, so you won't be doing shit. Now stick that tube in your mouth and shut the fuck up."

The guards were also suited in head-to-toe plastic, making John doubly glad that Jaimee was safe in the mansion that sat across a small park from the hospital. She and Maddy had become fast friends, amazingly fast. They had bonded like sisters separated at birth. Their one connection: cancer.

The night before, John had stood in the foyer of the great big, fuck-all mansion and yet he hadn't paid it any mind. His focus was on his daughter retelling the death of Amy Lynn. He was so caught up in it that he didn't notice that he was crying or that there was a gentle-looking old man standing at his elbow.

"We're going to stop it this time," he said, his words soft but gruff. "Sorry we weren't in time for your sweetheart."

John had stood there amazed at the man's sincerity and he couldn't think of one plum thing to say in reply. The old man, who turned out to be Edmund Rothchild and who had a net worth of nearly a billion dollars, insisted John stay for dinner. They talked of fishing and football, but not about cancer. The girls talked about school and whispered about boys.

It was the finest meal John had ever eaten and hell if he couldn't put a name on anything that had gone down his gullet. It was all very rich and wonderful, but near the end of the last course he started to tire and cough, and the dinner took on the feel of a condemned man's last meal. He excused himself, content that not only would Jaimee be well cared for but also extremely well fed.

Now, ten hours later, John watched the next prisoner get his treatment before slinking back to his room. There he waited a very long hour until the three-person team finally got to his room—they had been housed simply in order of their arrival, John had been last.

"Just breathe as deeply as you can, Mr. Burke," the attendant said, holding the tube between John's lips as he struggled against the overwhelming desire to cough. The Com-cell cure was completely without taste or smell. It was just like trying to breathe in a heavy fog. Midway through the treatment, a fourth person entered his room.

It was one of the nurses, though it was hard to tell which one as she was all got up in blue suit of her own. She pulled one of the men into the hall and he in turn pulled another of the three into the hall. When they returned, their smiles were as plastic as their suits.

"What's wrong?" John asked.

"Probably nothing to worry about," one of the blue-garbed men said. John immediately pulled the tube from his mouth and refused to put it back in.

"I'll be lettin' you know when I should worry," John told them. "Y'all jes tell me what's goin' on."

The three exchanged looks, not an easy thing to do when all they had were little card-sized windows to look through. Finally, the lady in charge said, "The prisoners are complaining about headaches. It's probably a mild reaction to the Com-cells. You have to remember this is an experimental procedure. There are bound to be side effects."

"What if it's more than that?" John asked. "Y'all said it was toxins and such."

"Fusarium toxicity presents as oral lesions and stomach ulcers," the lady explained. "Not headaches. It's also only extremely harmful when you're exposed over a long term and even then it's practically unheard of in someone whose immune system is still intact."

One of the other plastic garbed men thrust his entire torso forward and practically yelled. "Whatever it does it's going to be better than cancer. Also we have antifungal medications ready just in case. It's your best bet, my friend."

John didn't have friends; Amy Lynn had been the last person he could've called a friend. Still, the man was earnest and John was without options. He took the inhaler and sucked in the unnatural concoction.


**4**


The phone on the bedside rang, a shrill rooster that jarred Chuck from a coma-like sleep. It took a second ring for him to actually move his arm and open his mouth. "Yeah?" he asked.

"Is this Chuck Singleton?" The voice was tinny as a soup can.

"Depends on what y'all's selling." He was so slow in the head just then that he forgot that he'd paid for the room in cash and had signed the registry *John Smith* as a joke. No one should've known he was there.

"I'm not selling anything. This is Jack Cable, I work at R &K at the front desk and I…"

"Holy shit," Chuck said, realizing what time it was. Next to him, Stephanie was staring in horror at the clock while in his ear John was going on about how late they were for the Com-cell study. "Are we too late?" Chuck demanded, his mind solely focused on Stephanie. He would never forgive himself if he was the reason she missed her chance at life.

"I don't think so," Jack said, "but Dr. Lee is pissed. You better get in here as fast as you can."

"Tell them we're on our way, thanks." Chuck hung up the phone and then scratched sleep out of his eyes, still trying to come to grips with his sudden reentry into consciousness. "How the hell did I sleep so damn long?" He looked at Steph and smiled in spite of the desire to rush out of there. "It was you what done it."

"Me? It was you who…" A cough interrupted her and she went on long enough for Chuck to know they didn't have time for any more jawing. He waited patiently as she went pink and then red.

"Lay down," Chuck said, sitting her on the bed and then leaning her back. She went into the fetal position and it was five minutes before she could breathe properly. He brushed her hair back and said, "I need to get you to that cure before you spit up a lung. Is it safe to try?"

She didn't trust herself to talk, or even to move much; she nodded slowly. With quick hands, as if he was roping a calf, he put her sneakers on for her and then laced them up. He was even tempted to carry her, however his own cough had sprung up and he had to settle on letting her lean on him until they got to the car.

"Thank you," she said, and grabbed his hand just as he was getting ready to hurry to his side of the car. She pulled him close and jutted her chin as far up as it would go. He kissed her. There was no way he was going to trust his breath that early in the morning and so the kiss was all lip.

Still it was soft and warm and he knew that if he somehow lived to a hundred he would remember the feel of it to the day he died.

"Thank you again," she said when their lips parted.

He grinned. "Twern't nothing, ma'am," he said, laying the accent on thick. She smiled and climbed in. He was in his side a second later, feeling light in the head and fighting his cough. It would pass in good time, he knew. "Let's see what this rice-burner can do."

The Toyota was plenty fast, too fast, in fact. He was doing eighty when he saw the flashing red and blue lights in his mirror. "Can you act pregnant?" he asked Stephanie.

She puffed up her belly, held the pose for only a second and again began to cough. "About as well as you, I'm afraid. I'm practically worthless without my medicine."

He was as well and was a little ashamed to admit that in the last month he'd become hooked on hydrocodone. Without his pills his coughing would become so bad that he couldn't walk a block without going into a fit. Being near Stephanie helped, he was so focused on her that he barely felt anything when she was around.

They had lapsed into a silence when the State trooper finally got out of his cruiser. "Here he comes," Chuck said, fishing out his license and getting the rental paperwork. After the usual boilerplate questions concerning how fast he'd been going, Chuck explained that they were in the middle of an emergency. "We have to get to the hospital. We're late for an experimental procedure to cure cancer."

He had done his best to speak "Yankee" to show how serious he was and still the trooper smirked and said, "Right. Good one," before heading back to his car.

"You're one smooth talker," Stephanie said.

"I think ma-only chance is if you show some cleavage. Come on, let out the ladies."

She blushed and grabbed her shirt with both hands as if the buttons were going to undo themselves at his command.

"How would that help? He's got your license already. By the time he comes back it'll be with a ticket."

"I said it was *my* only chance. I'm starting to fade and I need to be revitalized."

On a whim, she flashed him and when his eyes went comically big she began another coughing fit that lasted until the state trooper got back. "You ok, ma'am? Because you're, uh…exposed." She hadn't been able to control herself long enough to button her shirt.


**5**


The labs were quiet. The eighteen scientists were working diligently on the fresh round of blood work. It was a somber atmosphere with everyone keeping their noses pinned to their microscopes or glued to computer printouts. Only Dr. Milner stood out in that he walked around with a smug *I told you so* look on his face.

The phone rang next to Thuy's elbow. She was afraid to take the call, especially in front of the entire lab. Every time the phone rang, everyone would look up and stare through the glass walls. Work was progressing slowly since the nurses on the second floor were calling every five minutes or so with new problems. The headaches were now universal among the patients and worse, they had progressed to migraines. Thuy had sent the staff physician down to begin medicating the patients, first with Tylenol, and then when the migraines had begun they had ratcheted up the drugs but so far they seemed always a step behind. The latest problem the medical staff was facing was a paranoid-fueled aggression that was bizarre in such a frail population.

"It's Rothchild," Riggs said, holding out the phone to Dr. Lee.

After a deep breath, Thuy spoke with as much confidence as she could muster: "Hello Dr. Rothchild, how is Gabriele?"

His daughter was still in the "Big House" being treated separately. Her personal doctor had come to pick up the first of her treatments just after seven. He'd been officious and dreadfully pompous, but, as he was the best physician money could buy, his attitude was pretty much expected.

"The good news is her O2 saturation rate has been steadily climbing. The bad news is that she's got a migraine, a pretty bad one," Edmund answered. He sounded tired and older than ever. "She's starting to become very agitated."

"Yes, it's what we're seeing with the other patients. We're prescribing *Relpax* for the migraine, with limited results. I've sent Dr. Lorry down to see what we should do about the aggression."

"Keep me posted," Edmund mumbled into the phone and then hung up.

"Same symptoms with his daughter?" Riggs asked. Thuy could only nod, feeling the sensation of impending doom hang over her head. If things got much worse she would be stuck using the amphotericin, an anti-fungal medication that would essentially destroy her trial.

Just then the phone rang again and she flinched. Riggs picked it up, listened for a second and said, "No, send them up here. Thanks." He set the phone down and said to Thuy. "The two love birds just showed up. I figured you wanted them up here."

"Sure, I guess." Thuy didn't know what to do with Chuck and Stephanie, and considered sending them back to whatever motel they had been shacking up in. Until they got a handle on what was happening she wouldn't be giving anyone any more treatments.

"It's early yet," Riggs told her, seeing the incipient despair in her eyes. "A migraine is a small price to pay for a cure for cancer. No, don't give me that look. The migraines are a setback, but look at the lung function, for goodness sakes! Except for that one patient, O2 sats are up across the board. That means the cure is working, and faster than anyone thought possible! Cheer up, Thuy. You can't let something small…"

The phone rang again and Thuy slumped. Riggs ran a hand through his sandy hair before answering. "Riggs," he said. "No, she's busy. What do you…Yeah? I'll—I'll tell her."

"What now?" Thuy asked.

"One of the nurses was attacked."

"By the prisoners?"

Riggs would have thought so, too. "No, it was one of the other patients, Mrs. Applewhite. Supposedly she just went crazy and bit Irene. They had to restrain her, which is nuts. She's like ninety pounds."

Thuy had memorized the particulars of every one of her patients—Sandra Applewhite; 54 years-old, married, mother of two; Five foot even; weighed in at ninety two pounds the day before. Four bouts of chemo had left her amazingly frail. "It's not nuts," Thuy said, hopping up. "So far the symptoms have been progressing based on when the patient received his or her treatment. It stands to reason that soon or later individual metabolisms and body structure will take over."

"Sounds reasonable," Riggs said, following after her. He stopped when he saw she was heading for the elevators. "Whoa, where are you going? Down there? Weren't you the one who said scientists belong in the lab?"

"I did." She hit the button and somewhere behind the walls the machinery whirred into life. "And weren't you the one who said he wanted to help people?"

"Right, but this? I-I wouldn't know where to start. We have forty-two patients…"

"Thirty-nine," Thuy corrected. "Mr. Burke is, for the moment, asymptomatic, and Glowitz and Singleton haven't been exposed."

"Ok, thirty-nine patients then, none of whom I'm at all qualified to help. You have a medical team, let them do their job. We should do ours."

She jabbed the button a second time. "Part of my job is finding out the facts. I have to see the patients first hand. Damn, this is taking forever." She turned and headed for the stairs but didn't get three paces before the elevator doors opened. Stephanie Glowitz and Chuck Singleton stepped out.

Steph started to apologize, "We are so sorry about being…"

Thuy spoke over her, "Riggs, explain to them what's going on. They'll need all the information we have to make an informed decision."

"Decision 'bout what?" Chuck asked.

She ignored him. "Set them up in one of the BSL-4 labs. We're not using them anyway." Thuy left them without any further explanation, dropping down two floors. The moans struck her as soon as the doors opened. The sound of pain—pain that she had caused—made her pause before stepping out onto the ward.

The head nurse stuck her head out of a patient's room. "Gloves and masks, Dr. Lee. We're still in the window for another two hours."

"Right," Thuy said. There was very little chance, statistically zero chance, that a healthy adult would have complications to Fusarium in the dry setting of the hospital, especially with all the precautions they had taken. Still, Thuy gloved and put on a surgical mask. She went to the nurse's station and found Dr. Lorry bent over a nurse, his gloved hands were wet with her blood.

"Is it bad?" Thuy asked.

Lorry was cleaning the bite wound, a ragged hole in the woman's shoulder. "Seen worse. It's going to need some stitches and it will leave a scar." He sat up, rolled his neck on his shoulders and looked at Thuy. "What did you give them? According to the literature, Fusarium toxicity shouldn't present in this manner."

"This is the first time anyone's been exposed to Fusarium in this way so it's no wonder that there are certain unforeseen side effects. I believe the symptoms are acute and will fade."

"And the amphotericin?" Lorry asked. "When is that on the table?"

"Not yet," Thuy said in a whisper. "We have to give them more time."

Before Lorry could say anything, a scream from down the hall cut their conversation short. It started out high and piercing and then dropped into a raging, curse filled rant. As Thuy stood rooted in place, first Dr. Wilson ran into the room and then the radiologist, Dr. Fenner. There was a crash and more screaming.

As if in a dream, Thuy walked to the patient's room and stared in at Sally Phelps who was swinging her IV pole like it was a halberd. The woman seemed no bigger than Thuy and the pole and the monitor must have weighed forty pounds, yet she swung it like it was a fly swatter. The first swing hit Dr. Fenner on the arm and knocked her to the ground. The second swing was like a strike from a sledgehammer. With full malice on her small features, Sally raised the pole and swept it downward looking to crush the radiologist.

Dr. Wilson yanked Fenner out of the way by her lab coat as the monitor exploded, sending plastic and surgical steel in every direction. "Help get her out of here!" Wilson bellowed at Thuy.

Dr. Fenner didn't need the help. She was already scrambling away, her mask turned halfway around her head, her mouth a grimace of fear and pain. Thuy stepped aside to let her get to safety.

"We need help down here!" Thuy yelled as Dr. Wilson started circling to Sally's right. Sally, who at one time had taught the third grade, didn't wait to attack. Her IV pole was bent and hung with the remains of the monitor; she swung it like a scythe, looking to decapitate Wilson. He dropped to the ground as the pole whistled overhead and crashed against the wall. Thuy reacted on instinct. She had a clear shot at Sally and darted in, tackling her.

They went down in a heap of flailing arms and legs. Thuy was younger, heavier, and far healthier. Sally was a demon possessed. Despite her sickly looking arms she was viciously strong and was able to pin Thuy to the ground. Thuy kicked and squirmed but there was little she could do against such strength. Sally opened her jaws wide and thrust for Thuy's throat, stopping just short of it as Dr. Wilson grabbed her by her hospital gown and pulled her back. Sally was tiny next to the large doctor and he was able to yank her off of Thuy, but not before Sally's nails dug three furrows along Thuy's arm.

"I need Diazepam, stat!" he ordered in a thundering voice. "Ten milligrams I.M." There was a rush of feet as Lacy Freeman and a second nurse sprinted into the room. Wilson held Sally down as Lacy jabbed a needle into her deltoid muscle.

"It's like she's on PCP," Wilson said, when Sally slumped back, her eyes slowly losing their focus.

"Or bath salts," Lacy said. "You know, that weird drug some of the kids are using that turns people into cannibals?"

Thuy struggled to her feet and stared down at the onetime schoolteacher. "I'll have my people check her blood for synthetic cathinone. It's the ingredient in bath salts that cause this sort of behavior. In the meantime I want every patient sedated."

Dr. Wilson, who was patting down his short afro stopped and looked at Thuy in disbelief. "Hold on now. We have two cases of bizarre behavior, but that doesn't mean we chemically restrain everyone."

"The two cases just happen to be the two smallest patients," Thuy said, pointing down at Sally, who had closed her eyes and looked to be unconscious. "Logic suggests that we will have eight more cases in the next half hour—all from the next smallest patients. And if you thought Sally was a handful, it'll only get worse. Wait until you try to subdue

Mr. Allen or the prisoners, especially Von Braun."

"I'm not really in the subduing business," Dr. Wilson said. "Maybe you're right. We can start on a lower dose, intravenously and move up if there are issues."

From the doorway Dr. Lorry said, "I want to know when we start the amphotericin. This trial is getting out of control."

"I'll call Kip," Thuy said.

"Why bother? You know what he'll say," Lorry shot back.

Everyone knew, however she felt she was out of options and called anyway.

"I forbid it!" Kip snarled into the phone. "The symptoms you describe don't fit Fusarium toxicity so treating for Fusarium toxicity is a waste of time and a waste of my god-damned money. Do you know how many millions I've sunk into this project?"

"There are lives in danger," Thuy said, ignoring his point completely.

"It seems so, but not from Fusarium. Find out what is causing the issues and treat for that. Hell, for all we know it is bath salts. We do have a leak, maybe they turned saboteur as well. If you need help with rowdy patients get Deckard to help."

"I would but I don't know where he is."


6


Deck stood up from his keyboard and stretched, kneading his knuckles into the small of his back and grimacing as the vertebrae popped and cracked.

"I'm getting old," he whispered to himself. Beside him the printer was spitting out paper, all the evidence he needed to secure a conviction, or at least a confession from the mole in R &K Pharmaceuticals. Seeing as all the evidence had been come by illegally, it was technically "fruit of the poisonous tree" but that was a legal matter. His first consideration was to the man who signed his paychecks.

He showered and shaved, dressing in black from head to toe, knowing it made him look particularly menacing. He liked having every edge possible when dealing with scum. He dropped the stolen hard drive onto the stack of printed e-mails and then went out into the gloomy day. The clouds were heavy and so low that it looked like he could reach them with a rake. Despite the threat of rain, children played hide-and-go-seek, running all around the thirteen guesthouses on the hospital property. One of these had been repurposed to accommodate Deck's security team.

A little blonde girl shot around the corner and nearly barreled into him. "You should be more careful, Maddy," he said.

"Ah'm not Maidy," the girl said in a molasses-thick accent.

"You sure aren't," Deck said. "Either way, you should…"

The girl screeched suddenly and went tearing off after a boy of about twelve. "…be more careful," Deck said after her. "Never mind." There were more cries and screams from the seven or eight children running around, and it was hard to tell if someone was being murdered. He assumed they weren't killing each other and walked the sixty yards to the hospital.

Right away he saw there was a problem. "Where's Jack?" he asked Earl Johnston, the lone security guard. Deck knew the guard rotation by heart: at all times there were supposed to be two guards on duty at the front desk, two more were stationed at the main gates, one was babysitting the prisoners and the last was supposed to be constantly walking the grounds.

"They needed him up on two. Some issue with the

patients."

"You mean with the prisoners?" Deck demanded.

"No, there was a fight between some of the patients. Some lady got bit. Nothing serious if you ask me." Earl had never been a part of a clinical trial and for him rowdy people were a daily occurrence. He wasn't concerned in the least. "He said he'd be back down in a few minutes. I'm thinking he's trying to chat up some of them pretty nurses."

Deck made a noise in his throat that was part growl— anything that drew a man away from his post was disconcerting. "Get the perimeter guard to cover Jack while he's away. And find Ray. I want to see him up on four."

He decided against checking on the patients; if there was more to the fight than just a couple of patients going at it, Ray would fill him in. Deck went to the fourth floor and even before he stepped out of the elevators he knew something was wrong there, as well. There was something in the muted atmosphere and how everyone in the glass-walled labs looked toward him when the doors opened. Tension ran on the air.

Dr. Lee spotted him and came fast-stepping in his direction. He didn't need any skill in reading people to know the tension was mostly stemming from her. "Where have you been?" she asked, scolding Deck like she was his mother. "Were you sleeping in?"

Since he'd been on the clock for the last thirty hours straight, this was particularly galling. Who the hell was she to question his whereabouts? "I was on a coffee break."

Surprised by the snarky answer, her dark eyes widened momentarily. She then set her jaw and hissed, "We need help and all you have to offer are flippant remarks? I was right about you; you're nothing more than a glorified mall cop... a self-glorified moll cop."

He glared and she matched it, completely unaware that the entire lab was watching them. Neither backed down and twenty seconds passed before the elevator dinged, pleasantly and Ray stepped out.

"Am I interrupting something?" he asked

Deck growled, "Give me a sit-rep."

"Sure…uh…" Before he could start, Deck stalked away, heading for the nearest BLS-3 lab. Ray caught up, walking quickly. "The prisoners are all accounted for; locked up tight. It's the other patients who we're having trouble with. There is something wrong with them, they're acting up, screaming and well, going crazy. There's talk between the medical staff that someone is attempting to sabotage the trial by putting PCP in the cure they were taking."

"It's not PCP or synthetic cathinone," Thuy told them. "We tested their blood. We don't know what's causing this."

"How about we ask the source," Deck said. "While I was on my coffee break I figured it out."

"You don't drink coffee," Ray remarked.

Deck chuckled. "Then it must have been when I was on a smoke break."

"You smoke now?" Ray asked. "You take that up when you stopped snorting coke?" He'd been with Deck long enough to know someone was getting their chain yanked. He just didn't know if it was their perp or if it was this cute lady doctor who was clearly getting worked up. Regardless who it was, Ray had eased his hand up and was resting it on the flat of his belly—his gun was five inches away in his shoulder holster.

"Will you two stop it and just tell me who did it!" Thuy demanded. She was suddenly furious and didn't notice that both men had assumed completely different attitudes. Ray was stiff, his muscles bunched and ready to spring into action. Deck was relaxed, his right hand holding the lapel of his suit. He worked better when he was relaxed; he was faster, fluid like a snake, and he never cocked up his aim by being overly tense.

Thuy also failed to notice Eng go rigid. He suddenly couldn't feel his feet, but he could feel his hand as it slowly stretched out to his top desk drawer where a pistol was hidden beneath a stack of papers.

"Stop what?" Deck asked Thuy, his eyes sweeping over the scientists. "This is what mall cops do. We hunt down bad guys when we're not sucking down an Orange Julius."

Eng had the drawer open and was fishing around beneath the paperwork as his heart began to whomp in his ears. He'd try for Deckard first and then go for Ray. If nothing else he would shoot Thuy simply out of spite.

"Just tell me who it is," Thuy demanded.

Deck's eyes swept to Lieutenant Eng who felt the steel in his hands. He gripped it like his hand was a vice and started to pull it out of the drawer when Deck jutted his chin to Eng's right.

"It's Anna," he said. The lady in question had gone white in the face and now she began to shake her head so that her pretty hair swung gently. Deck snorted out a half-laugh at her timid denial. "We should go talk somewhere private."

"I didn't do anything," she insisted, eyeing the stack of paper in Deck's left hand. "If someone has gotten into my emails, it's not my fault. Dr. Milner, tell them."

"I don't know what to tell them. If you're the one who did this…you're fucked."

Anna walked forward like she was in a dream. Ray met her and ran his rough hands over her soft body, searching for weapons. "She's clear." The two men immediately assumed a new demeanor: hard and quiet. They marched her away from the elevators to the relative isolation of the BLS-4 labs. Thuy followed along until they were at the pressurized door.

"We got this," Deck told her.

"Find out what she put in the Com-cells," Thuy said. "There are thirty-nine people whose lives are depending on what you find out."

"I didn't do anything," Anna whined.

Deck held up the stack of paper. "I have the emails between you and a certain professor at Cornell."

Anna opened her mouth but words failed her until she finally said, "You can't prove anything."

Brimming with hate, Thuy stared at her and had to fight against the overwhelming desire to punch the girl in the face. "Do what you have to do," Thuy said to Deckard. "I just don't want to know the details."

He tried to hide his look of amazement. Dr. Lee looked like the kind of person who couldn't even bring herself to jaywalk and here she was suggesting he should rough up a suspect. "I can sweat her and threaten her," Deck whispered to Thuy. "But that's about it."

Thuy tried not to let her dismay show. The patients were going downhill so fast it was frightening. "Do what you can," she practically begged.

Deckard grunted and shrugged—he wasn't about to commit to torturing anyone, especially not aloud. He and Ray frog-marched Anna to the back labs, while behind them Eng had to practically pry his fingers from around the gun.

**Chapter 6**

**//11:39 AM//**

1

Von Braun clawed his way out of the Diazepam stupor like he was digging out of a fresh grave. He came out bleary in mind, while everything around him was dim so that he thought he was wearing sunglasses. He tried to put his hands to his face but chains brought him up short.

"What the fuck?" he asked, squinting at the cuffs and barely seeing them twinkle. "Why am I chained up?" The only thing he really remembered was being angry, and that was because he was still angry, but at what, he didn't know. He was just simply furious. "What the fuck!" he raged.

"Shut up," the guard ordered. His name was Rory Vickers and he was very much tired of his assignment. The day before had been dull as hell just standing there as the prisoners griped or watched the TV or got hard-ons over every nurse that came in the room, but now he was annoyed as shit. Over the last four hours, the prisoners had become progressively more and more fucked up. They would rage and yank on their chains until their wrists bled. Worse, in his opinion, was that they would also scream their throats out.

Rory was ready to dash their skulls in. They were fucked up. There was a scientific term for it, he was sure, but he didn't know it and hadn't cared enough to ask.

When the docs finally got around to prescribing something to shut them up, Rory had literally thanked God. The second they were all asleep, he immediately switched the TV to ESPN and settled down on the edge of Herman's bed, hoping that the Diazepam would keep them sedated until his shifted ended, but that wasn't how his day was going.

Now Von Braun was awake and seething at him. "I don't have to shut up. You can't make me you dumb fuck. I have rights. I have a lawyer who'll sue your sorry ass. And all these doctors, too. And all the scientists who thought this…" Von Braun paused and squinted, mightily at Vickers. "Why are you wearing a mask? Are you fucking ugly, or is it something else?"

Rory wasn't sure why he was wearing the mask other than he didn't want to end up like these assholes. If he believed what the nurses said on the subject, the Fusarium had ceased being toxic two hours before and yet that hadn't stop them from remaining gowned, gloved and masked every time they entered a patient's room.

"You might be contagious or something," Rory explained. "Not going to take any chances.

"Contagious!" Von Braun cried in outrage. "Contagious! That means you fucks gave me a disease. That's why I can't see. You fucks are trying to blind me!"

This sparked a new memory in Von Braun's addled mind: People in blue suits coming for him…trying to poison him with some sort of gas. It seemed like a long time ago, or perhaps something from a dream, yet somehow it had been real. "You did this to me, you fuck! Let me go! Unchain me or I'll rip out your throat!"

This wasn't just an idle threat. Von Braun had a sudden need to get at this man's flesh because…because beneath it, he was certain there was clean blood. It would be red and warm and the taste…well, he wasn't sure what it would taste like but he knew it had to be better than how his mouth tasted now. His mouth tasted like dirt and shit.

"I need a drink," Von Braun said. All around the guard, the room was dim as if they weren't in a hospital, but in a dense forest where the sun's light couldn't reach and yet the man himself stood out distinctly and the swath of pale skin at his throat practically glowed. "Come closer, please."

Rory snorted in derision. "You sound like some sort of

kiddie rapist."

"Get over here!" Von Braun screamed.

"I don't think so, psycho. If you want a drink I'll page a nurse."

There was a call button next to the older prisoner who was thankfully still zonked out. Rory was still careful as he leaned over and hit the button. The old man stank.

Next to the button, there was speaker: "Yes?" a female voice asked.

"One of the prisoners is thirsty and I'm not going near him."

"He's got an IV, he doesn't need anything to drink."

Rory gave the psycho prisoner a shrug. "Your drink is sticking out of your arm, enjoy yourself."

Unbelievably, Von Braun bent over and yanked the IV out of his arm using only his teeth. He was thirsty alright, but instead of drinking from the little plastic tube, he drank the blood that came leaking from the little hole in his skin. "Fuck!" he cried, staring around, his mouth smeared with very dark blood. "This is dirty."

"What the hell?" Rory murmured, feeling just a touch of revulsion. With his lip curled he pressed the button again. "Hey, there. This jackass just pulled out his IV with his teeth. I actually think there's something wrong with him. His eyes are weird looking, too."

"Hold on. We'll send someone down there."

Von Braun was trying to touch his eyes with his fingers but was missing as if he couldn't see them very well. "What's wrong with my eyes? Huh? What did you do?"

"I didn't do anything," Rory said. "And I don't know what's wrong with them. They got some black stuff in 'em."

"What sort of..." Von Braun left off as two doctors came in, both of whom were masked and wearing surgical gloves. Rory recognized the smaller of the two by his bushy eyebrows. It was Dr. Lorry. He didn't bother to get very close and squinted at the prisoner from four feet away.

"I can't believe he's awake," Lorry remarked, making no move to get closer. "He's on a pretty good dose of Diazepam. Hold on…there is something in his eyes. What is that?"

The taller of the two stepped forward. "You can't see anything from there, doctor. Hi there. I'm Dr. Wilson."

"You're a fucking nigger is what you are," Von Braun seethed. "Get your black ass away from me." He couldn't believe they'd let one of *them* in a hospital with white people. The thought was sickening. "Get back to your jungle, Sambo."

"Sambo?" Dr. Wilson raised his hands as if surrendering. "After the morning I've had, I'm not even going to try. He's all yours, Dr. Lorry." Wilson left, shaking his head.

"Great," Lorry replied without any enthusiasm. He brought out a penlight and shone it into Von Braun's eyes. The prisoner cursed loudly and flinched back. "Photosensitivity," Lorry remarked to himself. "Also some dark matter which I don't recognize. Maybe dust. We'll want to do an ocular rinse to see if that clears it up. Alright Mr. Von Braun, open your mouth…holy…what is that?"

"It looks like mold," Rory said. Curious, he had leaned in over the bed and saw that the inside of Von Braun's mouth was lined with what looked at first like dirt or dried blood, however the way it coated the gums wasn't normal, it was like the insides of a dog's mouth.

Dr. Lorry worked the pen light back and forth and agreed, "It could be mold. We need a sample, Mr. Von Braun, so just keep your mouth open." Lorry produced a cotton swab and advanced on Von Braun, however the prisoner jerked his head left and right, trying to see the swab.

"What is that? Is that a needle? Get it away, you fucking cocksucker." To Von Braun the swab was thin and white against the backdrop of shadows. It didn't look right, especially in the hands of this little cock sucker. That thought stuck in his addled mind. "You're a fag, aren't you?

You're a nigger-loving fag."

"Does that ever get old to you?" Lorry asked with a sigh. "It was old for the rest of us fifty years ago."

Von Braun opened his mouth to reply and when he did Dr. Lorry ran the cotton swab across his gums. "What the fuck!" Von Braun screamed. Heedless of the manacles on his wrists he tried to reach Lorry, he tried to get at that throat, partially in anger and partially from a need to get clean blood. The doc had said there was mold in him and Von Braun was sure he was right. He felt dirty on the inside.

Lorry watched the prisoner struggle against his chains—it really was freaky. "Look, settle down, Nazi-boy before you hurt yourself. You're not going anywhere."

Von Braun's rage was so great he could barely think straight; all he wanted was to kill this fucking pipsqueak so that he could clean his mouth out. He had mold in his mouth! No wonder his tongue tasted like shit. Suddenly he stopped struggling as he hocked up an amazingly solid loogie and spat it at Lorry, striking him in the right eye with the black and green gob of snot.

"Son of a bitch!" Lorry yelled, wiping his eyes with his sleeve. He stormed out of the room, going immediately to the nurse's station where he cranked the hot water up on the sink. "That fucker just spat in my eye!" He yanked off his gloves and his mask, chucking them into the nearest biohazard container.

The nurses all took a step back. "You'll need to rinse that eye for a good fifteen minutes," Dr. Wilson advised.

"No shit," Lorry seethed. The doctor rinsed his eye with water and washed his face and even began a regimen of amphotericin as a precaution, not realizing it was already too late. The Com-cells insulated the deadly mycotoxins from the effects of the drug. In minutes the Com-cells were reproducing in his blood.

**2**

John Burke wasn't an idiot. He knew his diction wasn't more than a step up from a kindergartener's and that his accent was syrupy thick even compared to his fellow razorbacks, but that didn't mean he was void of common sense or that he couldn't read none. He had been told that the IV running into his arm was simply part of the treatment, yet right there on the plastic bag was the word Diazepam.

That was a narcotic. Amy Lynn had been practically hooked on the stuff in the last weeks of her life.

John didn't need a narcotic, he needed answers. All morning long he had lain in his hospital bed and listened as the other patients went through horrible changes. This started with the near-constant soft, pining tone of the nurses being called from one room to the other. Very quickly that sound was driving John crazy.

All he could think about was what was happening to the other patients, and when *it* would start happening to him? The tone soon gave way to the sound of people moaning in pain. This was horrible to listen to but what came next was worse.

*What did you do to me?*

*Don't come near me with that!*

*Stop! Stop, no...that hurts! Stop, you're killing me!*

People were caterwauling like they were being attacked in all sorts of dreadful ways. John drew the covers up to his chin and shivered like a child as his mind conjured up images of a thousand tortures he was sure the other patients were being subjected to.

During this there were fistfights. He'd lived what he would call a "hardy" life and knew a fight when he heard one. These battles occurred sporadically; one minute there would be only the crazy shouting and then in the next, there'd be crashes and thumps and the sound of running feet.

*Get his leg!*

*Tie him down.*
*Fuck! He bit me!*

During a lull in the commotion, John decided he'd had enough. If there was a cure, something he was beginning to doubt, he didn't think it was worth all of this. On tiptoes he went to the door and peeked out only to see a team of nurses and security men heading his way. Quick as he could, he jumped back in bed and pretended to watch the TV.

"Hello Mr. Burke," Lacy Freeman greeted him. Behind her biomask, her eyes crinkled at the edges, perhaps in a smile, perhaps in a grimace. "We need to add a medicine to your IV. It's for the trial."

*If it's jes medicine, then why do y'all need two other nurses and two goons to help?* John thought to himself. The men took positions on either side of his bed. They were burly, while John was feeling weak as a rat. He didn't resist.

"What is it?" he asked.

"Oh, just more medicine," Lacy assured. "It'll help you sleep."

John didn't want to sleep. It was the friggin' middle of the day. He watched the medicine drip into his arm and within a minute, the idea of a nap sounded very appealing. He started to close his eyes and that was when the men came at him.

They grabbed him by his flailing wrists and strapped him to the bed. The straps were padded and secured with Velcro. He strained against them but in vain. "What y'all gonna to do to me?"

"Nothing, Mr. Burke," Lacy said. "The restraints are for our protection as well as yours."

"What do y'all mean your protection? I won't hurt any of y'alls, I swear to Christ I won't."

"Just try to sleep. You'll feel better when you wake up."

There was no need to try to sleep, it was trying not to sleep that was the issue. The Diazepam made him groggy and his eyelids kept trying to drop over his eyes like a window shade that wouldn't stay up. At one point he blinked so slowly that by the time he forced his eyes back open, the room was empty.

"I cain't do this," he said, his voice sounding like some sort of cartoon creature speaking from beneath a lake or a pond or some such. He tried to focus on the IV. It had to come out. He tried twice to get at it before he realized that his hands were tied down. His feet weren't, however.

With a groan he tried to swing his knees up to his chest—they flopped back down. A second attempt was just as useless. He lay back, hearing the phlegm rattle in his chest with each wheezy breath. Before he knew it his eyes began to droop again.

"No," he whispered. He couldn't allow himself to rest. With barely focused eyes he looked at the IV sticking out of the crook of his arm. Was it really just Diazepam trickling into his veins, or was something more nefarious mixed in as well? Something that would turn him crazy or rabid like the others? "That ain't gonna be me. Fuck that."

He bent his left leg at the knee, put his right foot across it, and then heaved his lower body up, resting his weight on his shoulders and the back of his neck. In this position he could just reach the IV tubing as it came out of his arm with his toes. It took two tries to rip the catheter out of his skin.

He didn't feel any pain.

Even before his legs flopped back down, he had slipped into unconsciousness. It was an hour before he came too, blinking slowly up at the ceiling and wondering where he was. It was only when he tried sitting up that he remembered how he'd been bound and drugged. "Oh right," he mumbled.

For a few seconds he laid there collecting his wits, listening to the rest of the hospital, expecting to hear fresh screams cracking the air, however the second floor was eerily quiet. He knew it wasn't because everyone had suddenly gotten better. "They's jes drugged outta they minds."

Without the Diazepam clogging his thinking, John's fear grew into something close on paranoia. There was only one reason he knew of why a large group of people would be drugged like that and tied to their beds: they were being experimented on.

"Not me," he whispered. "I'm not gonna be anyone's fuck-all guinea-pig."

Again he laid his right foot across his left knee. This time he didn't even have to heave himself up to get at the velcro straps around his wrists--he simply had to torque his torso as far as he could to the left. His back cracked and he felt something pull in his abdomen, but he got his toes on the velcro. After six tries he was just able to grip the velcro, monkey-style, and pull it up.

One hand freed the other and in seconds he was out of bed and changing into his street clothes. When he was dressed he went to the door and cracked it, just in time to see a group of nurses enter a room two doors down. Opening the door further, he peeked out and saw one of the guards who had tied him down. He was leaning over a counter at the nurse's station chatting with someone John couldn't see.

John leaned back into his room and examined his choices. Stay and get poked, prodded, and in all likelihood, probed, or run away, and gamble on getting caught. Running was a bad bet. The guard was barely thirty feet away; surely he would see John out of the corner of his eye. And yet staying put was just plain dumb as hell.

He put his eye back to the crack of the door--the coast was clear. Without looking back, he left his room and fast-walked toward the exit at the near end of the hall. He just knew that at any moment the guard would spot him and there'd be a chase, which his weak lungs wouldn't be able to endure. He'd be dragged kicking and screaming back into his bed where they'd tie him down tighter than before in order to do their thing, whatever it was, on him.

The thought made him walk funny like he was on the

verge of crapping himself.

He made it to the stairwell door and went through without being seen. From there his movements weren't slowed by hesitation. He raced down the stairs only to be brought up short at the bottom. The exit had a bar across it with the warning: *Emergency exit only. Alarm will sound.*

John was back to being trapped.

# 3

Thuy rubbed her eyes and dropped the last printout onto the stack with all the rest. "There's nothing in their blood," she whispered. They had checked for practically every toxin and poison known to man: Anthrax, E-coli, Ebola, Marburg, rattlesnake venom, botulinum, cyanotoxins, hemotoxins...the list was very long. "I don't see how it's possible that nothing is showing up."

"Then it's the Fusarium," Riggs stated. "The Com-cells are the only thing that keeps coming up, the only thing they all have in common. Thuy, it's time to start treating with antifungals."

"No," she grunted, before running her hands into the silk of her hair and grabbing the roots like she wanted to yank them out. "Kip won't allow it."

"Rothchild might."

"I doubt it. Stopping the treatment is a guarantee his daughter will be dead in a month. It's true for all of them."

Riggs was undeterred. "You know if someone dies, we might be looking at prison time."

"Again, I doubt it. We have their permission *in writing* to treat them and we have followed every rule and procedure. They knew there'd be risks going in."

"Yeah well that all sounded ok back when we weren't killing them, now I'm starting to think it's not good enough.

We may not be 'real' doctors but we're still human. Suffering has to come into our calculations at some point. I think it's our duty to end the trial."

"No!" Thuy snapped. Fifteen scientists looked up from their work to watch the spectacle. Thuy didn't care. "First, they aren't suffering. They're sedated, remember? And second, they are doomed no matter what. If they die, maybe we can learn something from their deaths."

Riggs sneered, "That's cold. And if that's where we're at then I wash my hands of all of this." Next to him the phone began to ring. He shook his head at it. "You can get your own calls."

Thuy reached out a shaking hand and slowly brought the phone to her ear, dreading what she was going to hear next. "Yes?"

"It's Wilson down on two. I'm afraid there's an issue. Lorry is sick, very likely infected with whatever disease the patients have. He was spat on by one of the prisoners about an hour ago. He's been complaining of a headache but now it's gone over to a migraine. We've started him on antifungals but it's done nothing to slow the progression of the disease."

"Disease? This isn't a disease," Thuy said. "Fusarium is a mycotoxin; it's a byproduct of a fungi, not a fungus itself. It can't replicate on its own. He must have been exposed to the Com-cells in another manner."

"No. I've been with him all day and he hasn't broken protocol once. His blood work should show us something. If you'll send someone down here in full gear..."

Three lines etched across Thuy's brow. "Why can't you send it up? What's wrong?" The real question was: what else is wrong? Thuy almost didn't want to know.

"Oh, sorry, we have a lot going on down here. The CDC regulations state we have to quarantine in these situations."

Thuy lowered her voice and put her hand over the phone so no one but Riggs could hear her conversation. "Dr.

Wilson, please. We need to keep the CDC out of this. You're only guessing that Lorry was infected through the transfer of bodily fluids. Right now we don't have enough information to go to them with."

"The fact that we don't have information is exactly the reason I called the CDC five minutes ago." Wilson paused as Thuy began to sputter. When she went on too long without gaining any coherence he spoke over her, "Look, either the patients are contagious in some manner or the Com-cells are far more persistent than we've thought possible, either way we have to close this ward off. The entire hospital is on a seventy-two hour lock down. We also have to quarantine the Rothchild's home."

Thuy's grip on the phone grew so tight it began to shake. The CDC cared nothing about cancer or cures. They would trample all over the trial trying to contain a threat that really hadn't showed itself yet. Lorry could've been infected any number of ways and even if he had got it from the prisoner's spit, that didn't mean anyone else was in danger--as long as they took better precautions. "We're going to be hamstrung now, Wilson. You know that, right? You just made everything ten times harder. How are we supposed to send someone down to get the blood work when we're quarantined? You know each floor is supposed to be self-contained."

"I don't know. Maybe we can decontaminate the elevator and use it like a dumb waiter."

"No, that would break all sorts of CDC rules." They had so many rules it hurt her head to even think about them all. "The elevator has to be parked down on one. We're going to have to use the stairs. My team will use the south stairs, you can use the central. It'll keep us as separated as possible and still allow us to transfer samples. What else did the CDC demand?" she asked.

"That we are to begin treating the patients with antifungals and wide spectrum antibiotics. And of course the staff is to begin a prophylactic regimen as well. That's it. I'm sure it won't be that bad. We sit tight for a day or two, prove that we're maintaining a secure quarantine and they'll leave us alone. Speaking of which, where's Deckard? He has to be brought up to speed. If there are any leaks in the quarantine I'm sure the CDC will make our lives hell..."

As if on cue an alarm started braying from deep in the building. Thuy knew exactly what the sound was. Back when the idea of a CDC quarantine had been an academic matter, she had tested the door alarms as part of her inspection checklist.

"Someone just left the building!" she yelled into the phone. "Get a head count and call me back." She slammed the phone down and then swept her gaze across the glass walled labs: fifteen nervous scientists stared back. "No one leave!" she yelled, before running down the main hall to the BSL-4 labs. In one, Stephanie Glowitz sat holding Chuck Singleton's hand. In the other, Deck and his second in command stood like statues listening to the alarm. Between them, Anna was puffy-eyed and teary.

Thuy rammed open the door with her shoulder. "Deck, we're under quarantine. No one can leave, but...but someone just did. That alarm means one of the emergency exits just opened."

The word quarantine blindsided him and he was slower to respond that usual. "Quarantine? Why on earth..." as her brows came down, he stopped. "I'll call the perimeter guards. We'll secure the fence line."

Just as he began dialing his cell, another phone began ringing up front. There was a stunned silence reigning over the fourth floor and the sound of the phone jangled the nerves of everyone within earshot. It rang twice, just long enough for the scientists to hold their breaths.

"Thuy!" Riggs yelled from the front. "It was a patient named Burke who escaped."

She paused, half in the corridor and half out, her mind

bringing up an image of John Burke: southern white trash, a bare step up from a hillbilly caricature. She remembered his willingness to give up the cure to make sure his daughter would be properly looked after. She stuck her head back into the lab.

"Deck, have someone go up to the Rothchild's. Our escapee is John Burke. His daughter is staying up at the big house."

He began barking orders into his phone, after which came a tense thirty minutes as every guard, on duty and off, searched the grounds.

John Burke was nowhere to be found--the quarantine had failed already.

## 4

The last drip of his Diazepam had leaked into Von Braun's veins twenty minutes before, and now, in a haze of fading drugs and building rage, he climbed his way back into the highest form of consciousness he could manage.

He stared around the room. It was day and the lights of the room burned brightly, however Von Braun could barely make out the far wall. For him the world was filled with shadows. It took him seconds to focus on any one thing.

He saw the prisoner next to him sleeping under the effects of a full Diazepam drip. In the next bed over Herman was gnashing his teeth and growling. The portly, hairy little man had transformed into a beast: his eyes were black and his skin was mottled and blotched with something inky. Herman's IV was empty and had been for some time. Very dark blood had started backing into the line.

Von Braun saw and understood. Too much drugs in his system and he would sleep. Not enough drugs and he would be a monster. Just the right amount of drugs and he could think--sort of. His mind was filled with a deadly combination of hate and paranoia. He concluded that this wasn't a drug trial at all. They were doing things to him and the other prisoners--*experiments* his mind whispered. Yes, that was it! They were conducting tests like he was a lab rat.

With a snarl he yanked as hard as he could on his manacles, accomplishing nothing but causing the steel to bite harder into his wrists. "Son of a bitch! Let me out of here! You can't do this to me!" He ranted until a nurse came in with a fresh IV bag. Just the sight of it sent shivers down his back.

"Give it to him," Von Braun said, jerking his head toward Herman. "He needs it more than I do."

The nurse was different, or rather her garb had changed. When they had begun the first treatment the nurses were dressed like they were getting ready to operate with gowns and gloves and masks. This nurse wore a boxy hood with a plastic shield across the face and her gown was taped at the wrists above her gloves and at the ankles above her boots.

"What's wrong?" he asked. He had trouble understanding the outfit except that he knew it meant trouble or danger.

"Nothing," she said as she went to Herman's bed. "Just a precaution."

A precaution against what? His mind filled in the sinister answer: *Germs!* That was what the experiments were all about. They were being fed germs through the tubes; germs that would turn them into monsters.

When she was done hooking up the new bag, the nurse assured Von Braun: "I'll be right back with your medicine," before sweeping out of the room. He tried to fake a smile until the door shut and then he pulled as hard as he could on his cuffs once again. It was metal on metal and they didn't budge. The only way out was to get a hold of a key and the only way to get the key was for someone to get it for him.

A plan wormed its way through his haze-filled brain, however the nurse was gone for so long that his rage nearly put a halt to the plan before it began. Every minute that passed seemed to fuel his desire to kill and it was by the barest margins that he forced himself not to snarl at her as she came in. Instead he held himself so rigid that his manacles clinked against the rail.

She either couldn't hear the clinking or ignored it as she hooked up his IV. When she was finished he said, "The rail feels loose. Like I can break it."

In order to see through the little plastic window of her hood, the nurse had to make exaggerated motions. When she looked down at the rail, she bent her neck far over and thus did not see Von Braun's foot as he lashed out in a hard kick. His shinbone struck her on the back of the head, making a sound like two hunks of wood being knocked together. Her knees buckled and she fell into the side of the bed before slipping to the floor.

Von Braun grinned. The nurse's mask was in his left hand. His manacles were far sturdier than any hospital restraint, however they also allowed for a lot more freedom of movement. He had snagged the mask from her face as she slid down.

"Now, to make you become like me," he whispered before hocking up a nasty, black hunk of snot. He spat it on her face and then sat back, feeling the drug begin to mellow out his rage.

A few minutes later, the nurse slowly came awake, blinking her eyes, grimacing and touching the back of her head. It was some seconds before she remembered the plastic hood that should have been over her head. "Oh my God," she cried.

"Looking for this?" Von Braun asked. She stood, using the wall for support, but she didn't reach for the hood. "You a gambling kind of lady? I ask because while you were sleeping, I spat in your face."

Forgetting her training, she touched her gloved hand to the bare skin of her cheek. "Why? Why would you do that?"

"To make you be like me," he told her. Now it was his turn to blink slowly. The Diazepam was really kicking in, making the dim world seem nightmare black. Only the nurse's pale face was clear to him. "You will change and they will kill you and burn your body....Just like what they're going to do to me."

She shook her head. "No. They're working on a cure. I'll be fine."

"Then go tell them what happened and if you aren't sick now, you soon will...be. I have a...a plan." His lips were fat and heavy and his brain like mush. "Wake me when...you...you...you're...like me..." Von Braun's eyes closed, the demons in him finally caged by the drugs.

Lacy Freeman realized he had been right about one thing: if she told the others what had happened, they would stick her in the last bed available, the one next to Dr. Lorry who, only a few minutes before had to be restrained because his paranoia had made him dangerous. He was now on his own Diazepam drip and it wouldn't be long before she was hooked up to one of her own.

Every room came with its own bathroom. Lacy ran in and turned the hot water all the way over. She scrubbed her skin viciously as though she wanted to peel off the first three layers. As she washed herself, she began praying for a miracle.

## 5

The closest CDC office was located in New York City an hour's drive south of the hospital. A three-person team, headed by senior agent, Vince Oldham "sprang" into action. He made sure they checked their gear properly, he readied their paperwork to ensure they would be able to draw a *per diem* allowance, and he gassed up the van.

By a quarter to three they were out the door so to speak. The crew didn't get very far. The first stop on their trip was to Ray's Original Pizza where they took a half hour for a late lunch. After they paid with an agency credit card, they crawled through city traffic, heading north at an average rate of nine miles an hour.

Vince did not stress over their pace because he understood that the concept of emergency was relative. A single case of *possible* respiratory transmission of the Fusarium mycotoxin, though previously unheard of, wasn't likely to constitute much of an emergency.

He saw perfectly how the case would go down: his team would take some sample blood work, swab the place from floor to ceiling, levy some fines for code violations, make some recommendations that would carry the force of law, monitor a hysterical patient or two and then finish up by checking out what was playing on HBO at whatever motel was closest.

In the meantime he did his best to enjoy the ride and that meant he ended a squabble over the radio by the other two members of the team: Peggy O'Brian and Damon Green. Vince pulled rank: "We're listening to country;" he declared and then did what any good CDC leader would do, he leaned his chair all the way back and took a nap as Garth twanged in his ears.

The nap was briefly interrupted once.

Dr. Lee, the lead investigator at the Walton facility called reporting the breaking of the quarantine by a missing patient. Vince thanked her for the update and hung up. What he didn't do was turn on the siren and the lights, nor did he have Peggy hit the gas and start weaving through traffic. They were three people in one van, not a search team. He followed protocol and called the New York State Trooper station north of Poughkeepsie and alerted them to a possible infectious outbreak and a snafu in the quarantine.

He then went back to sleep. It was going to be a long ride

after all.

Only three police cruisers were dispatched to find John Burke--the troopers were, as usual, undermanned and stretched thin. Besides, this was just one man who was too sick to get very far and it wasn't as if he was a murderer.

## 6

There was no denying the headache, now. It had started as nothing but an occasional stab of pain, an annoyance that on any other day Lacy Freeman would've ignored. Now it was at another level altogether. It pounded in her temples, keeping perfect time with the thump of her heart. The pain made her grouchy...no, it made her angry. Lacy Freeman was pissed off, but, strangely, she wasn't angry at Von Braun. He was just one man chained to a bed.

No, she was mad as hell at R&K Pharmaceuticals and she was mad at the doctors and she was absolutely furious with the scientists on the fourth floor.

They had messed around with nature, they had tried to change the way things were supposed to be, and she had a dark suspicion they had done it all on purpose in order to trip her up, in order to infect her.

*I'm part of the experiment*, she thought to herself, not realizing that she was feeling the same paranoia all the other patients had experienced. *They're testing me...they're probably watching me.*

Lacy cast semi-secret glances up at the ceiling, trying to locate the cameras she was certain had been installed to spy on her. No one noticed. There were twenty people trapped with the infected patients on the second floor, eight nurses, the two oncologists: Dr. Wilson and Dr. Sinha, four cafeteria workers who had just brought up lunches when the quarantine trapped them, five construction workers, and the security guard, Rory Vickers. They sat around in various stages of exhaustion. Dealing with so many patients was draining but it was nothing compared to the stress of being quarantined with a virulent disease possibly floating in the air.

They had turned the nurse's station into a clean area by hanging plastic sheeting from the ceiling and then taping the bottom edges to the floor. It wasn't perfect, especially since they had to come in and out every thirty minutes or so to check on the patients, but it was working. No one had shown any symptoms...except for Lacy.

She was definitely sick, just like *they* had planned. Well, she decided she wasn't going to play by *their* rules. Von Braun had a plan. They didn't know about that plan she was sure. Oh, but she knew. She would just have to play it cool until she could find out what it was and escape.

A sudden spike of pain in her head caused her to grimace and that damned Linda Sheffield caught the look. "You ok?" she asked, leaning back and eyeing Lacy closely.

"I'm fine," Lacy said. It wasn't easy keeping the snarl out of her voice. "I'm just...anxious. Why haven't we heard anything? Shouldn't they have a cure by now? Or any clue what this is?"

"It's only been a few hours, Lacy," Dr. Wilson said. "We can't expect miracles."

"Why not?" Dr. Sinha asked in her lilting Indian accent. "Why must we expect only calamities?"

Lacy forgot herself. "Yes! She's right. There could be a cure. They probably have one already." She went to the phone and punched in the number to the fourth floor lab. It seemed to ring a long time before someone picked up.

"What's wrong now?"

It was a voice she recognized. "Dr. Lee? This is Lacy from the second floor. Is the cure ready yet?"

"Cure? There's no cure. We still don't know what we're supposed to be curing yet."

"How come?" Lacy demanded as if talking to a flunky as opposed to a doctor. "We've given you everything you've asked for: practically a gallon of blood, arterial gasses, fecal smears, urine, and now EKGs? What else do you want? What else could you possibly need to save us?" No one seemed to notice that she was practically hysterical.

"I know you're all scared, but we need time," Thuy said, wearily. "We're overloaded with samples and as of yet, the only thing that we've been able to figure out is that the Com-cells are collecting and reproducing in the meninges. It shouldn't be happening, but it is."

"So you don't know anything helpful?" Lacy asked, sounding like an imperious teenager. "You've been working on this project for like two years and you're pretending you don't know anything?"

Dr. Lee went suddenly cold. "I know enough to cease this conversation. Lacy, you need to get yourself checked out. You may have contracted the...the sickness or whatever it is. You don't sound like yourself."

"Of course," Lacy replied, now warmly. "I'll do that right away." She hung up to find everyone staring at her. It was as if they were trying to hurt her with their eyes.

"What did she say?" Wilson asked.

"Nothing really...except she wants me to check on the patients...to see if there's any changes in their, uh, level of consciousness."

"Sounds like busy-work," Wilson said.

"Yeah, but they're doctor's orders." Lacy went into the supply closet where they were keeping the gowns and hoods. Before she pulled them on she dug out a handful of Relpax from her pocket. It was about eight times the recommended dose for migraines; she swallowed them dry. They kept her migraine to a low frequency horror and relaxed the rage building up and up inside her.

Ten minutes later she was next to Von Braun's bed as he came awake. He smiled at her. "They're trying to kill us," she told him.

"We should kill them first," Von Braun said. "We should kill them and make us clean. Do you feel it? The dirt in you?"

"Yes." Lacy could feel the dirt crawling inside her, especially her mouth and in her ears and under her fingernails and beneath her breasts. It was driving her crazy. "I want to get clean, but there are too many of them and they're all in on it. They're all part of the experiment."

"Then make more of them like us," Von Braun told her. "Then we'll be the ones doing the experiments. We'll be the ones with the knives and the scopes and the needles and the chains."

This made perfect sense to Lacy. She pulled off her blue glove and reached out a shaking hand to touch Von Braun's mottled skin. His flesh was black and wet, alive with something evil and now it was on her hand. She hid it back in her glove.

"You should sleep *until*," she said, turning his Diazepam drip back to where it put him out.

In the nurse's station Lacy changed out of her gear and then went to the others holding her right hand out like it was a treasure to behold. Again, no one noticed. They were all listless and bored, except the two oncologists who were preparing yet another sample for the lab.

*More experiments*, Lacy thought to herself. The idea was acid in her mind and she went about touching the others with her special hand, leaving only Wilson and Sinha unaffected. Those two were different. They were with the scientists, the ones running everything, the ones who had done this to them

They would have to suffer.

Her stomach rumbled hungrily at the thought and she whispered, "Not yet."

## Chapter 7

**//3:15 PM//**

**1**

Two girls, both blonde and stick thin sat in the shade of the big house with their backs up against the brick. They weren't doing anything in particular because Maddy was concocting a plan.

Jaimee could only guess at the meaning of the word "concocting", it was one she'd never heard before. Her friends back in Izzard would have said they were "hatching" a plan, like it was something that came fully formed out of a neat little shell, only back home, plans were never so neat as that.

Like the time Jaimee had decided to become a beekeeper on account of the fact they were out of honey. That had not ended well, not for the bees, not for Jaimee, and certainly not for the postman who opened the mailbox to find thirty-eight very angry insects. He got all stung-up and Jaimee had her bottom reddened by her daddy, and ever since she wasn't keen on plans. And that was especially true of a concocted plan. It sounded like something a witch might do.

The pair had been there resting against the house for a good long time, long enough for Jaimee to have eaten up the two cookies and slurped down the iced tea that Ms. Robins had given her. Maddy hadn't touched her snack at all--she was too worried about her mother to eat.

"She's jes sleepin' is all," Jaimee said in an attempt to calm her new friend. "That's what y'all's nanny-sitter done said." Jaimee was also confused on what a nanny was. Ms. Robins sure looked like a sitter in her eyes.

"I think she was lying," Maddy replied. "Didn't you see her eyes? She was crying. Ms. Robins never cries and I think that means something's wrong. And besides, it's been hours and hours. They said the cure wouldn't take nearly this long."

Jaimee glanced across at the four-story hospital where her daddy was getting rid of his cancer by some sort of magic formala—a potion she reckoned. "Sometimes it takes a long time, don'tcha think? I mean theys take a long time to git sick so maybe theys git better slowly, too."

"Maybe," Maddy granted. She stood and looked down on Jaimee, who squinted up at her.

"Whatcha doing? Y'all got a plan all thunked up? Y'all gonna eat them cookies?"

"You can have them if you wish," Maddy said. "Hey, remember how my Grandfather confused you with me last night?"

It was something that Jaimee would not easily forget. She'd been on her lonesome trying to find a bathroom when this wrinkly, old man with great tufted ears like a screech owl and a nose bigger than a potato, had come up out of the dark and scared her near into wetting her panties. He had started talking strange, too.

*"Your mother is going to be alright. You'll see."*

*"My momma is daid,"* Jaimee had told him.

Rothchild bent down to look at her closer and with the big circles of his glasses doing a number on his eyes, his resemblance to an owl grew. *"Why, you're not Maddy."*

*"No suh. I'm Jaimee Lynn Burke. My Daidy is sick up in y'all's hospital."*

"I remember," Jaimee told Maddy as she pocketed the two cookies. "He was scarier than a striped haint."

"A what?"

"Y'all don't know what a haint is?" Jaimee asked, looking at Maddy in wonder. "Well, it's a ghost, don'tcha know. But a bad 'un."

"I didn't know," Maddy said, smiling as she frequently did at Jaimee's colloquialisms. "A haint does sound scary, but my grandfather isn't one. He's very nice. He just needs new prescriptions for his glasses, which is going to help us with my plan."

"Is that so?" Jaimee replied, wearing a false smile. She didn't want to go anywhere near the old man. Old people scared her, even nice ones. They was chugged full of awful smells and they were easily riled like a chained up yard-dog on a July afternoon.

"That is so. Hopefully he won't be able to tell us apart. The first thing we need to do is change clothes. I'll wear yours, you wear mine."

"Y'all want me to change out here where God and ever-one cun see?" Self-consciously, Jaimee pulled the hem of her shirt lower.

"Exactly," Maddy said, slipping off her shirt. "Except there's no one around. Come on, hurry."

Maddy was down to her panties and shoes in seconds. Reluctantly at first, but with growing enthusiasm, Jaimee switched out her Walmart sale duds for Maddy's Rodeo Drive name brands. Jaimee's clothes smelled of earth and little girl sweat. Maddy Rothchild's smelled of perfume and they were soft, and what's more Jaimee felt pretty for the first time since her mother died.

"Now we'll both pin our hair back," Maddy said.

Jaimee, who only knew the basics of ponytails, looked on nervously as Maddy's little hands pinned up her own hair. "That's kinda fancy. I don't reckon I could do that at all."

"It's easy." Maddy took charge and within two shakes had Jaimee's hair pulled into place in no time. "There we go. We're not quite twins, but we're close enough to fool my grandfather. Just as long as you don't talk, that is."

"I can talk like a Yankee iffin I wanna," Jaimee declared. She cleared her throat, stuck a pinky in the air and said as distinctly as possible: "How do you do? I am Madison Rothchild. I reckon I'm happy to be your acquaintance."

The two girls broke down in giggles. When Maddy recovered she said, "Other than saying 'reckon' that was pretty good. Can you say *Grandfather*, just like that?"

Jaimee repeated the word, Yankee style, and Maddy shrugged. "I think that's good enough. Now follow me and stay quiet."

Maddy led the way. They entered around back where the finished walkout basement opened onto a patio. It was dark and quiet, much like the rest of the house was when Maddy and Jaimee weren't tearing around it at full speed like they had been the night before.

The house was spacious, sporting seven bedrooms, eight bathrooms, two kitchens, a billiards room and a spa. The Rothchild's family physician, Dr. McGrady was staying for the week of the trials, he was billeted in one of the three top floor bedrooms with the other two belonging to Maddy and Ms. Robins. The master suite on the main floor had been converted into a hospital room for Maddy's mom, Gabriele. Edmund Rothchild stayed across the hall from her so he could always be near.

The two basement rooms were being used by the housekeeper and Edmund's secretary, Mrs. Unger, who was very stern and frightened Jaimee as much as the old man did.

"Go up to my room and make sure that you're seen by all the adults," Maddy whispered, explaining her plan. "When you get to the main floor, wave to them and then run upstairs. At the top, call my Grandfather, just like you practiced. He's always watching my mom's room like a hawk. Once he goes up to see you, I'll zip in, check on my mom, and then when I'm done I'll meet you in my room."

"What will I say to your grandpa?"

"Uh...tell him I'm playing hide and seek, and that I want him to find me. That'll keep him busy."

It was a sound enough plan and Jaimee was really and truly all for it--more than anyone, she knew what it was like knowing that your momma was dying and not being allowed in to see her. It was just about the most miserable, helpless feeling imaginable.

Jaimee went up the stairs from the lower floor, paused with her chin slightly turned away from the adults who were sitting around the island in the kitchen, talking solemnly. She gave a wave in their general direction and then started up to the top floor where she ran into Dr. McGrady.

"Hello Maddy," he said. "Wait, sorry. It's Jaimee, right? I thought you were Maddy. You both look very much alike."

"Yes," was all she could think to say. He stood there, smiling pleasantly until Jaimee was forced to walk away. She went to Maddy's room, hoping that the doctor would either go back in his room or head downstairs to be with the others. He did neither. He pulled out a cell phone and stood in the doorway to his room, talking about white blood counts which didn't make no sense to Jaimee. Everyone knew blood was red.

Either way the plan was all spoilt. Jaimee couldn't exactly call for "Grandfather" with Dr. McGrady ten feet away. She didn't know what to do and thus ended up doing nothing but waiting.

Down in the basement, Maddy sat in the shadows a good long time before becoming impatient. She couldn't understand what was taking Jaimee so long to say one simple word and eventually she made an attempt at gaining access to her mother's room with her grandfather still on guard.

She was caught and after a thorough dressing down was marched into a kitchen corner where she was made to stand with her nose pressed into the angle of the walls. "...And you're never too old for a spanking," Edmund admonished, when Maddy kept demanding to see her mother.

Jaimee witnessed this ill-treatment, as she saw it, from halfway down the carpeted stair. At the first hint of trouble she had come slinking down on cat's feet. *Why wouldn't they let her see her own mother?* she wondered. *Was it because she gone up and died or because she was on her way to being dead?*

There was only one way to find out. With all the attention on Maddy, Jaimee was able to pad-foot her way down the stairs and along the corridor without being spotted. She entered Gabriele Rothchild's room with her heart beating rapid fire in her chest, thinking she was going to be in a room with an almost dead person at best and a haint at the worst.

The room sure seemed a good place for a haint to grow attached to. The lights were dimmed and the shades pulled so that there was more shadow than light. The air-conditioning had been cranked up to a level that would keep a snowball round; quickly Jaimee's skin bunched into goose flesh and she began to shiver.

Just in front of her, a wall of plastic hung from the ceiling. It had been put in place to guard against any accidental release of Com-cells during the admin phase—it didn't look like it was coming down anytime soon.

There was a door in the plastic that opened by way of a zipper and Jaimee stepped through only to be confronted by a second plastic wall. Beyond this was Gabriele Rothchild. She was just a half-formed shape beneath a sheet and the little girl would've guessed she really had up and died had it not been for the fancy computer looking machinery around her bed that was still beeping and booping the way doctor stuff was supposed to.

Her daddy would've said: *That signifies*.

Gabriele was so still that Jaimee figured she was asleep, so she took extra care to keep quiet as she opened the second plastic door. She was greeted with the smell of bleach, which wrinkled her pert nose.

"P U," she said, under her breath. She couldn't understand the smell or the plastic walls or the full-body biohazard suits that had been hanging up between the plastic walls. None of it fit in with her paradigm of cancer and she simply chalked them up to things "rich" people did and thus was beyond her ken.

She went to the bed and gaped.

Maddy's mom didn't look like she was dying of cancer. Yes, her hair was short and patchy, just like Amy Lynn's had been. And she was skinny because it was the cancer what ate her up from the inside out. But that was where the similarities ended.

Something else was going on with Gabrielle Rothchild. She was leaking black slime from her eyes, and there was more building up in her nose and ears. It was even beginning to fill up the pores of her skin. Jaimee touched her cheek and then jerked her hand back.

Gabrielle's flesh had felt like the belly of a swamp frog— cold and clammy; it wasn't at all what any sane creature would call natural.

## 2

Deckard dropped down into the chair next to Dr. Lee's and sighed, staring up at the ceiling. "Anna's not talking."

Thuy had been comparing the blood panels for John Burke, trying to find any changes from the initial blood draw done that morning to the last one drawn two hours previously. As far as she could tell there wasn't any difference.

Platelets, hemoglobin, lipids, red blood cells, white blood cells, all within normal parameters and all basically unchanged. She had tested the blood six ways from Sunday, only to draw a blank every time.

In anger she balled up the sheets and threw them at the glass wall. Deck watched her, his face expressionless as always. "She called her lawyer and is talking about suing R &K for kidnapping."

"That's moronic," Thuy snapped.

"Before the quarantine we were basically holding her

against her will. It was mostly through intimidation rather than any overt physical or verbal threat, but I've heard of cases stick over less."

"Not with our lawyers it won't," Thuy assured him. "Especially with the possibility of multiple murder charges hanging over her head."

"Someone die?"

"Not yet, but if John Burke isn't caught soon he's likely to turn up in one of the little towns around here and rip someone's head off. Everyone else is pushing the maximum therapeutic limits of the sedatives we have them on. I'm afraid what Burke is like off of them completely."

"He's not exactly a heavyweight," Deck remarked.

"And neither was Sally Phelps, but it still took three of us to bring her down."

Deckard didn't bother to point out that the "three" of them included two rather small women and a middle-aged doctor. He wasn't all that worried about bringing down Burke if he happened to come back. He glanced at her bandaged arm. "You were scratched by her. Are you infected? Do you have a case of the crazies?"

She wasn't infected by anything as far as she could tell, however that didn't stop her from peeking beneath her bandage from time to time. The scratches were red but not inflamed—they looked like normal scratches. "I'm not and neither is Irene Watts who was bitten on the shoulder. If the fungus is contagious, there's clearly an incubation time before the spores mature."

He pulled back from her slightly. "It's a fungus doing this? I thought you called them toxins."

"It's all one in the same," Thuy said, turning from Deck to look at her computer. She really wasn't in the mood to give a high school refresher class in basic biology, but since he was trapped there because of her, she hit the highlights: "Mycotoxins come from mold of which there are over four-hundred thousand varieties. Mold comes from fungus of which there are over a hundred thousand types. What it is leaking out of their eyes, we just don't know yet. Maybe spores, maybe gametes, maybe some sort of byproduct."

"Gross," Deck said, mildly. Although he wasn't a fan of germs or viruses, or any of that sort of thing, he had a special dislike for fungi. It made him, a rock-hard, grown man feel a little squishy inside.

"Yes, I suppose it's gross. Now, if you'll excuse me, Mr. Deckard, I have quite a bit of..." A gunshot went off in the building. It was distant yet still distinct--there was no mistaking it for anything else.

At the sound, Thuy blinked and, somewhere in the fraction of a second in which she had her eyes closed, Deckard had pulled his gun. "Was that a gun?" she asked.

Deckard didn't answer. He was already charging out of her office. Ray stood about fifty feet down the hallway, his weapon drawn. Deck jutted his chin toward the stairwell and the two started toward it at a sprint. As they ran, Deck pulled out his two-way. "Shots fired, south stairwell! Proceed with caution."

"No!" Thuy yelled from behind them. "Don't proceed anywhere. You can't break quarantine."

Deck paused at the door. "With all due respect, Doctor Lee, but fuck that."

3

Wilson tried not to let the near overwhelming fear that shook his insides, and made it a struggle to breathe without panting, show as he put on his blue bio-suit hood back on properly.

"I'm sure we can handle this," he said to Lacy, smiling toothily, hoping the new sweat wasn't showing across his brow. "It's just a routine check of the ward. Why don't you go relax with the others?"

In another time that might have been considered a joke. The others were far from relaxed. Sometime in the last ninety minutes or so, the rest of the medical staff had become infected and their symptoms were progressing rapidly into the paranoia stage. They were being egged on by Lacy Freeman who, if her hate-filled eyes were any indication, was clearly on the brink of murder.

"What were you doing out there for so long?" Lacy demanded. "Were you upstairs with them? With the scientists? Is that what you were doing? Planning more experiments on us?"

He and Dr. Sinha had only just realized their danger a minute before. For the last hour, the two of them had been collecting cerebral spinal fluid from each of the patients, a very tedious chore in a full body biosuit.

Not realizing that the medical crew had been infected and had already gone passed paranoia and were now into *dangerous,* the two went back to the nurse's station to find the others clearly in the middle of something that he and Sinha weren't supposed to hear.

"If…if that's true, then of course they have to die," the security guard, Rory Vickers, was saying. "Just like the rest of them upstairs."

"Who has to die?" Dr. Sinha asked as she pulled off her hood.

Eighteen sets of eyes bored in at her with such intensity that she stepped back into Wilson. "Do you see…?" she started to say, but he stopped her words by squeezing her shoulders, hard. The signs of the contagion in the other medical personnel were obvious: migraines, the aggressive paranoia in their eyes, the squint that the patients had developed in order to see through their fading eyesight.

Lacy was the worst of the lot. Her eyes were already black and her mental state, alarming. She hadn't attacked anyone yet simply because she was self-medicating to a dangerous degree. As they stood there, she opened a bottle of Valium and tipped six pills into her mouth. She chewed them slowly, almost daring Wilson to say something about the criminal breach of narcotic regulations.

He only smiled and said, "We're going to go check on the patients." No one smiled back. They were agitated and on the verge of violence. "Come on, Dr. Sinha, let's get our...our gear back on. Everyone else should stay here."

Unfortunately, Lacy followed them demanding to know what they'd been doing "out there" for so long. Wilson explained about collecting the cerebral spinal fluid, however Lacy clearly didn't believe the truth when it was offered to her.

"Sex," Dr. Sinha spat out suddenly through a strained smile. Her hands shook as she zipped up her bio-suit. "We were having sex in the men's room. Please don't tell my husband. He's very jealous."

"He's jealous because you're a skank," Lacy hissed. "You're a little skank. A little bitch. A little fuck bitch." She started advancing on Dr. Sinha who was a tiny Indian woman and seemed as defenseless as a child.

Wilson yanked the hood over his head and stepped between them. For a few frightful seconds, he was blind as he straightened it on his head. "Yes, you're right, Lacy. We were...oh, there you are...we were wrong to have sex. And because we were wrong, we should atone. We...we're going to check on the patients and...and empty their urine bags. How does that sound?"

With desperate hands, Sinha dragged the hood over her head and zipped up. She and Wilson were now fully gowned and had backed to the edge of the plastic curtain. "You should not follow us," Sinha said. "The ward is contaminated. You don't want to end up like the patients."

As they were already infected, it wasn't much of a threat. Lacy kept advancing and right behind her were the others. The smaller women among them were practically growling while the two largest men see-sawed between bestial hate and stark confusion.

"What are you really going to do out there?" Lacy demanded. "More experiments? Is that it? We already know you and the other scientists have a cure and are just laughing at us."

"Nope, just changing urine bags," Wilson said. He put an arm behind him and gave Sinha a push out into the hall. He followed her, letting the curtain swing into Lacy. The plastic confused her and she seemed to have trouble reorienting on the suited pair as they backed down the hall.

The other eleven parted around her and continued to advance. "Do not come closer," Sinha begged. "We are simply changing urine bags. See?"

She started to duck into one of the patient's rooms but Wilson stopped her. "We can't let ourselves get trapped," he hissed, pulling her back. To the others he spoke loudly, saying: "We can handle this. The rest of you please go back to the nurse's station where you'll be safe."

"You mean where you'll leave us to die?" Lacy asked from the back of the group. "That's what he's going to...they're running!"

That "they" were running was a surprise to Wilson who'd been standing his ground. He guessed that Dr. Sinha was making a run for it, and before anyone else could react he turned and ran after her, his plastic suit making a ridiculous swishing noise as he sprinted at his full speed.

Behind him, the wild bunch chased after. The sound of their shoes thundered down the hall, coming closer and closer. He barely reached the stairway before them and had just enough time to throw his weight against the door. Dr. Sinha was right beside him. Through the square of clear plastic he could see her white teeth gritted as she strained against the weight of bodies piling up on the other side.

The two were slowly forced back. They struggled against the door until it made sense to run again. Without warning they released the door. It flew open and the nurses fell into the stairwell piling over each other. Wilson was about to leap over them to try to go down stairs but a gunshot rang out and something blinked off the railing right next to his hand.

He went numb from shock and took two steps back— they were shooting at him! How was that even possible? How had the day gone so wrong? How was he going to explain getting shot to his wife? He froze in place, his mind whirling as he saw something more impossible than being shot at: the patients were coming out of their rooms.

It was impossible because they had been sedated *and* restrained. And yet the black-eyed demons were shuffling down the hall, their hospital gowns open, their genitals flapping about, completely ignored. Most growled, some ground their teeth and others raked at their eyes with hooked fingers. All of them exuded hate. It seeped from their pores, pooling in the air around them.

There was no way Wilson could have known that the infected patients were looking to kill and maim and drink the blood of those who were still clean, however, somehow, in some crazy way, he did. On some elemental level he understood that the patients were no longer precisely human.

Just then a hand came down on Wilson's shoulder and gripped the plastic. Dr. Sinha was pulling on him. "Let's go!" She was close to panic.

Awkwardly, he turned, losing sight of everything but the inside of his hood. He had to hold one hand on the rail and one on the hood to keep the clear plastic part centered on his face in order to see anything. Behind him, the nurses who had fallen through the door were clambering to their feet, and Lacy, who had hold of Rory Vicker's pistol was aiming again, slowly, as if she were lining up a fieldpiece. Wilson was three steps up when the gun went off a second time.

Although the bullet missed, Wilson felt a zing of adrenaline shoot up his spine, while Dr. Sinha let out a shriek. Before Lacy could shoot again, they rushed up the stairs and stumbled into the third floor hall, tripping over each other in their fear.

Dr. Sinha was terrified and running blind. The hood of her biosuit kept pulling around so that all she saw was yellow plastic. She'd yank the hood back into place time and again, but eventually it slipped in front of her face and she tripped before she could get it seated properly again.

Wilson, who had been running sideways to see if they were going to be followed, stumbled right over her, catching her in the chest with his knee. He went flying as though he'd been tackled, while she lay flat on the ground, stunned.

The gunshots in the stairwell and the sound of running feet in the corridor had attracted attention. A number of people, including Dr. Hester, stepped out into the hallway. He was startled to see two people in bio-suits on the floor at his feet.

"What is it?" he asked. "What's going..." Just then four more gunshots went off, echoing up and down the south stairwell like thunder trapped in a mine. Everyone stared down the hall, waiting to see what was going to happen. Seconds later the stairwell door opened and five or six of the medical team charged out into the hall. They were gibbering and snarling like lunatics.

"Get back in your offices!" Wilson screamed through his plastic hood. "Barricade yourself in!" Not for a second did he realize he had just damned the thirty-two people quarantined on the third floor to a horrible death and an appalling afterlife.

He looked down at Dr. Sinha. "Get up!"

"Can't...breathe..." she gasped.

Wilson bent down and hauled her to her feet. They had to run. They had to get away or risk becoming infected, as well. That was what he told himself, at least. He didn't want to think about the hunger on their faces or how their mouths seemed to stretch wider and wider.

"Come on!" he screamed at Sinha. She couldn't stand;

she was still fighting to breathe and so he pulled her up and half-carried her to the central stairs. She was crimped inward at the waist and her slick, plastic biosuit made it difficult for him to keep hold of her.

Desperation drove him.

Next to the elevator in the center of the building there was another stairwell. He made it ahead of the infected medical personnel, took two steps down and then stopped-- there were people somewhere on the stairs below them, heading up. They were infected, emitting barely human growls that echoed up at the two doctors.

"Holy...shit," the fifty-six year old Wilson cursed between gasps. He had just run the equivalent of a seventy-yard sprint in full bio-gear, half of which had been spent carrying another person. The air in his hood was as hot and ill-used tasting as exhaust from a car and he couldn't seem to be able to catch his breath. The best he could manage was a strident wheeze.

Dr. Sinha was worse off. When he had crashed into her, his knee had cracked two of her ribs; she could only take futile little sips of air that never satisfied. She felt like she was suffocating and it took all her willpower not to rip off the hood of her suit.

With Wilson's help she trudged upward, making it only three steps before the door right below them opened.

"Come...on!" he urged Sinha, struggling to hold her upright. She made a great effort, sucking up the pain and ignoring the dizziness that was making her head swim. Four steps later the first of the infected people caught her by the ankle.

Before Wilson knew what was happening, Sinha slipped out of his grasp and was pulled down into the greedy arms of the people below. With one hand on the rail and the other holding his mask in place, he turned ponderously in time to see Dr. Sinha's murder.

Those infected had no construction of reality beyond the

need to vent their hate. They swarmed her, stomping her and punching her until her suit was little more than a bag holding blood and meat. They then tore into the plastic and, as Wilson watched in paralytic shock, they began eating her like a pack of jackals.

He turned and fled up the stairs, his face behind the plastic twisted with mental agony. Despite the horror he had witnessed, he was dreadfully slow. Terror and a middle-aged, sedentary life had robbed him of his strength, leaving him without either of the classic options: fight or flight. The best he could manage was a dull trudge and had he been followed closely by any of the infected people they certainly would've dragged him down, too.

Reeling like a drunk he stumbled onto the fourth floor. "We... need...help!" he yelled.

To the left of the elevators and the central stairs was the south "wing" where the BSL-3 labs were; to the right were the BSL-4 labs where only two people were in view: Chuck and Stephanie. They hadn't seemed to have heard Wilson's cry.

Wilson tugged off his hood, gulped down two huge breaths of air and cried, "Singleton! We...need to...barricade this door. Ms. Glowitz, help him with that table. Come on!"

The earlier gunshots and the urgency in Wilson's voice got them up and moving and while they struggled the table through the doors, Wilson gripped the stairway door handle with both hands. Seconds later his strength was tested. The metal handle was almost pulled out of his grip, but with his arms shaking and cords rising from his neck he held on, but barely.

"Open up!" a woman screamed. "Give me the fucking cure!"

Wilson was shocked to realize that this was one of the nurses, Jill Sams, all one-hundred and thirty pounds of her. She was practically ripping the door from his grip. "Jill, it's me, Dr. Wilson. There's no cure just yet. But..."

"Liar!" she raged. The door slid inward three inches before he was able to stop it. "We know you have it. We know you're just playing tricks on us. Now give it."

"I'm not lying, Jill," he said desperately. His gloved hands were slippery and it was only a matter of time before the door was pulled from his grasp. "Listen, all this was just as much a shock to us as it was to you. Remember this morning, how we had coffee together? We talked about your son?"

"Is that when you poisoned me, you motherfucker?" She grunted and heaved; the door slid further back. The strength in his arms was ebbing.

"Jill, please! I didn't poison you. There is no cure. You have to believe me." He glanced back at Chuck and the others but they were so absorbed in trying to move the table they didn't see his predicament.

Now the door was far enough back that Jill was able to jab her foot in the crack of the door. Her face appeared next--her jaw was smeared with Dr. Sinha's blood. "If you don't have the cure, you can at least make me clean." She was staring at his neck where he could feel his pulse pounding— it was an obscene, hungry look that seemed to feed into her mania, lending her strength.

Jill pulled harder and the door opened relentlessly, bringing Wilson into the stairwell with it. Suddenly, he let go, hoping she'd go flying, but she grabbed the arm of his suit and started pulling him into her embrace. Her mouth gaped and from it came a smell like death, like rotting flesh, like an old grave.

Compared to her, Wilson was kitten-weak and despite the size difference between them, Jill flung him down.

"Don't," Wilson begged.

She had him pinned and for just a second she gloated and leered over him, before slashing in with her hell mouth gaping open. He would've been ripped open from ear-to-ear except there came a smart "crack" sound and she sat up looking confused.

There was a man on the stairs. He had come slinking up quietly and in his hands was a length of a 2x4. He cocked it over his shoulder like it was a baseball bat and swung for the fences, striking her across the cheek. Jill fell off Wilson and stared up at the ceiling.

"Come on, hoss," the man said. His face was twisted in disgust as he nudged Jill down the stairs with the beam. "Get up, Doc. I done knocked a few of them out, but there's a more headin' up, lookin' to raise cain."

Lying on his back in his bio-suit, Wilson was like a turtle and was slow to get to his feet. "Mr. Burke?" he asked as he realized who the man was. "Where have you been? I thought you ran away."

John didn't like the way that came out, like he was yellow or something. "I never ran. I have a daughter to look after. I jes opened that door downstairs to make them think I was runnin'. I done reckoned I'd get caught in the daylight and so I jes found a spot to burrow down in. Then I saw these…whatever they is. They don't barely look like human beans."

"How come you're not like them? You're…you're normal. If you had the same treatment, you should've…Look," Wilson said, pointing down the stairs. It was another one of *them*.

Burke grunted at it and then cast a glance at Wilson's sweating face and his trembling hands and said, "I'll hold the door, y'all go scoot them along with that barricade."

Wilson hurried away, the plastic of his suit making a friendly swishing noise. John set his length of wood aside and confidently took hold of the door handle. Holding the door shut against one of them was not so easy as John had assumed it would be. The infected man, and John used the term loosely as these things didn't seem all that human to him, was incredibly strong.

Very soon John found himself weakening and, just as it

had with Wilson, the door began to slide inward once again.

Chuck Singleton arrived when John's arms were beginning to tremble. "Leggo," he ordered. John released his failing grip and a split second later Chuck slammed his shit-kicking cowboy boot into the door, sending the diseased man flying down the stairs. His head fetched up hard against the cement, making a grisly *crack!* sound that suggested his skull had caved in. Regardless, the infected man scrambled to his feet and made to climb back up.

"What the hell?" Chuck whispered.

"Don't let them touch you," Wilson yelled from the hallway.

"You don't have to worry 'bout that none," Chuck murmured. He had no intention of letting any of them freaks get close. He and Stephanie had hauled a conference table to the stairwell and now he heaved it down the stairs at the infected man. It struck him square and drove him back against the wall.

"Much obliged for the hep," Burke said, calmly, in his Arkansas twang.

"If y'all could hold the table in place, I'd be mighty pleased," Chuck drawled right back. The weight and the leverage of the table allowed John to pin the man in place as Wilson, Chuck and Stephanie brought more furniture. Chairs and tables were stacked high into the stairwell creating an effective barricade against the single infected man.

Unfortunately, there were many more of *them*. Half a dozen infected people came up and began tugging down the makeshift barricade, working tirelessly. Soon, Wilson began to panic.

"Stephanie, go check the north stairs. Run!"

She was back in thirty seconds, coughing and gasping. "There are more of them. They're...they're growling. What's wrong with them?"

"I don't know. But they're dangerous. Go find Dr. Lee. Tell her we have lost containment on the second and third floors...and tell her that all three stairwells have to be blocked up. And tell her that they're killing people now."

**4**

Deck and his second in command, Ray, entered the south stairwell half a minute after Lacy Freeman's second gunshot. They advanced with guns drawn, making their way to the flight of stairs just above the third floor. It was there they encountered nearly the entire medical staff, looking crazed out of their minds. Just behind them was Rory Vickers.

"Rory, where's the shooter?" Deck asked. His eyes roved over the fifteen or so people, looking for the gun, sensing the danger in the little crowd and not quite understanding it. The group was primarily made up of women; nurses and a few cafeteria workers. They were leering up at the two security men in a way that made Deck's stomach uneasy.

"Why are you with the scientists?" Rory demanded. His face was tortured by a combination of rage and confusion. It turned him ugly. "You should be with us. Come down and be with us."

Deck and Ray glanced at each other uneasily and took a step back. "What are you talking about?" Deck asked. "There is no *us* just at the moment. We're all in a quarantine situation. There's nothing up here that you can't find down there. So, please stop, all of you, before someone gets hurt."

The ones in front kept coming and both Ray and Deckard had to give up more ground, reaching the landing midway between the third and fourth floors. "I said stop!" Deck bellowed, not quite knowing what he was going to do if they ignored him.

"Then give us the cure," Rory demanded. "We know there's a cure."

"Yes, the cure! The cure!" The group began to shriek,

demanding a cure that Deckard was pretty certain didn't exist.

"There is no cure," he said. The crowd was only four steps below him. They weren't stopping. He raised his gun. "I said stop! Go back..."

Just then Lacy Freeman fired the pistol she had taken from Rory, earlier. In the enclosed space it cracked the air so loudly that it stung the ears. The bullet missed wide--Deck's double tap did not. He fired twice in the space of a fraction of a second, shooting through a six-inch window between Rory's shoulder and the left ear of one of the cafeteria workers. The first bullet holed Lacy above the heart, the second passed through the hollow of her throat and out the back of her neck carrying blood and bone in a spray that spattered the wall behind her.

She dropped, but before she hit the ground there was a fourth shot from right beside Deckard. Ray had fired his weapon, which made no sense to Deck. Their assailant was down and the others were unarmed. To shoot like that was so out of character for Ray that Deck immediately knew something wasn't right.

As if in slow motion, he turned to his friend of eleven years only to see him crumpling forward, falling down the stairs, his muscles, after the final convulsive jerk that had caused him to shoot his pistol, had gone flaccid. Too late, Deckard reached for him, but his hand slid off Ray's suit coat without gaining any purchase and the man fell down the stairs into the greedy hands of the crowd below.

That Ray was ex-military was obvious in a number of ways: his trim build, the way he carried himself and his weapon, the fact that he always backed into parking spots, and how he always wore his hair high and tight. Deck could see the hole in the back of his head through his razored hair.

Confused, Deck turned halfway around to see who had shot him, but there was no one behind them. There was, however, a gouge in the concrete of the stairwell wall where

Lacy's shot had missed. Ray had been hit by a ricocheting bullet.

"Fuck!" Deckard cried in a mixture of anger, sadness, and shock that once again death had reached out its long, bony finger to touch those around him while leaving him inexplicably alive. Hot misery wanted to come boiling up out of him, but there was no time for it.

A hand scrabbled at his dress shoes, marring the shine he had worked so diligently on. He took another step up the stairs, moving just out of reach, giving himself time to analyze the situation. He came to the very quick conclusion: that these people were crazy!

The ones in front had launched themselves at Ray's corpse and were tearing at his flesh. They were all over Ray, and as Deck stood there dumbfounded, he saw a small white hand with fingernails painted pink, reach out and dig into his friend's face, gouging the flesh as though he was made of cream cheese.

Deck raised his gun for half a second and then lowered it. They were clearly dangerous and crazy and yet they were still human. They were suffering from some sort of mold-induced mania, which, in the eyes of the law, was not sufficient justification for killing them outright.

Felling he had only one option left to him, he turned to run back up the stairs, but stopped and stared in horror--Lacy Freeman was pulling herself off the ground.

"Fuck," he said again, this time in a whisper. It was impossible that she was still alive and even more impossible that she could still move. The holes in her chest oozed a thick, black blood, the exit wounds in back looked like he could put his fist into them.

He stared without understanding until another one of the nurses, a slim little number he had chatted up twice the day before with the idea of asking her out, made it to the landing. There was murder in her eyes. Without hesitation she attacked. His reaction was not instinctual. Again the idea of being legally responsible for every death entered into his calculations—when all was said and done, who would believe that this young lady was a true danger to a man of his size? Instead of shooting her, he snapped a front kick into her sternum, sending her flying back into the rest, bowling them over.

Deck left them scrabbling over themselves and ran back upstairs. At the top he found a gaggle of scientists staring at him. There was fear gathered in the air around them and they cringed at his stern look.

"What did you do?" Milner asked

"Only what I had to. The med staff on the second floor have all been infected."

"And who is doing all the shooting?" Riggs asked, eyeing the gun in Deck's hand. "Are you killing them?"

"Just the ones that piss me off," Deck growled, annoyed at the stupid questions. "Unless you want to end up like them, we can't just stand around. Let's get this door barricaded, they're on their way up. They say they want a cure and I don't think they're going to leave without one."

## Chapter 8

**//4:07 PM//**

**1**

In the hour before the hospital broke down into bedlam, Nurse Lacy Freeman had downed half a bottle of valium to keep, what she thought of as the real monsters from taking over her mind. The face that shone out from the valium haze, the one Dr. Wilson had looked upon and thought capable of murder, was an innocent babe compared to what lurked beneath.

As much as she had wanted to let them free, she had held the real monsters back in order to do her duty. She had followed after Wilson and Sinha as they had gone around the ward doing their spinal taps. In their suits, they had been oblivious to her. Her mission, given to her by Von Braun had been to slow the Diazepam drips on all the patient's IVs and loosen their restraints.

She also told them about "the plan."

It was a simple plan, because it had to be. The patients could not understand higher reasoning beyond: *let's kill the ones who had done this to us and drink their blood*. Most of them ignored the IV bag that Lacy pinned to their shoulders in order to keep their minds functioning in some fashion. Others resented the bag or looked upon it as part of the problem. These people tore the catheters from their arms and hurled the bags away from them. In minutes, their minds descended into a state of hell that was beyond all control.

They no longer understood "the plan", they only understood the need to feed and the desire to rid the hated dirt from their throats. It felt like their intestines were backing up and they were choking on shit. Instinctively, they knew their bodies were toxic and instinctively they craved clean flesh and pure blood. They were drawn to it.

Three such evil monsters came after Paolo Garcia.

Along with forty other people he had been quarantined on the third floor where he'd spent the day playing cards in the hospital kitchen with his friends. The first gunshots in the stairwell had found him up two hundred dollars—he had a veritable pile of green in front of him. While a few people ran to see what was going on, Paolo quickly dealt another hand. He was hot and didn't want anything to disturb his run of good luck. It didn't hurt that the man right next to him, Hernando Dias, was a fish who wouldn't stop accidentally flashing his cards to Paolo.

"It's probably nothing," Paolo said of the gunshots. "Let's play."

Four others stayed in the game and by luck, ill luck as it turned out, Paulo dealt himself two aces. Two people folded in front of Hernando who raised, "Veinte dólares."

"This is America, moron," Paolo seethed. "Speak English. Say twenty. Tw-enty." Paolo wasn't just legal, he was an actual citizen, a rarity among the lower paid members of the staff. It had taken him eight years of endless paperwork, dull hearings, and hoops to jump through but he had persevered and now he possessed legal papers and a fairly overbearing attitude toward the *illegals*.

"Tenty," Hernando said.

"It's *twenty* but since you were close enough, I will see your..." Paolo was interrupted as more gunshots went off when Deck put two into Lucy Freeman. One of the other players got up and ran to the door that separated the kitchen from the cafeteria. While he stood there staring through the crack, Paolo re-raised, "Twenty more."

Hernando sucked his teeth as he thought over his options. Outside the cafeteria people were running and there was a scream. "Hurry up!" Paolo said. Hernando shrugged and dropped another twenty dollar bill into the pile. Quickly, Paolo dealt the flop, turning over three cards. Another ace sat staring up at him.

"Bet," Paolo said, impatiently, running a hand through his black hair. "Let's go."

They were the last two left in the kitchen. There was a lot of shouting, out in the halls as well as in the cafeteria, but no more gunshots.

"*Shek*," Hernando said.

"The word is *check*," Paolo snapped. "Ch-ch-check. Say…"

He stopped in midsentence. A woman in a hospital gown banged into the kitchen—black goo was running from her eyes. Hernando took one look at her and jumped up. He was running even before his feet were under him, causing him to stumble. The woman chased after.

Paolo watched in shock as the two disappeared heading for the back where the freezers ran in a line of shining metal. "I had aces," Paolo yelled, scooping up his money as fast as he could and stuffing the bills into his pocket. He had no clue what was happening but, with the screams and all the running, he felt he should be armed. The prep line was the closest source of weaponry; he grabbed two gleaming, sharp knives, each a foot in length.

He was challenged almost immediately. Three strangers, all in hospital gowns came barging in from the cafeteria. All three had the same black-dripping eyes and the same murderous rage on their faces, but otherwise appeared to be normal people. "Stay back!" Paolo yelled, holding up the knives.

Acting as though the knives didn't exist, they charged.

Despite the fact that he was armed and they weren't, Paolo ran. He made a break for the dining hall, slamming open the swinging doors with his shoulder and charging through; only to be brought up short by what he saw: there was a full-on battle raging right before his eyes. People were fighting back and forth across the entire room: *Black-eyes* versus the *Cafeteria workers*.

His people were losing badly and already bodies littered the floor, lying at ugly, twisted angles with pools of blood around them. Blood seemed to be everywhere: red puddles on the tile, handprints on chairs, spatters across tables, and footprints tracking from body to body.

Paolo stared a second too long. Behind him the doors banged open and he spun. The first one of the black-eyed things was on him in a blink. It had been a man: white, bald, middle-aged. Paolo didn't hesitate and slammed his foot-long knife into the man's chest. The blade was brand new and sharp as a razor. It parted the man's sheer hospital gown with ease, slid through his flesh like it was warm butter and went deep into his right lung.

The man didn't seem to notice the knife that had skewered him. He kept coming, grabbing Paolo by the arm and lunging at him with his mouth gaping wide. Paolo saw there was more of that black stuff in the man's mouth. His tongue was coated with it and more of it dangled from his teeth.

Paolo screamed. He never thought that he'd scream in a life and death situation, but out it came nonetheless. He screamed and twisted and stabbed blindly with the other knife, desperate to get away, however the man with the black eyes and the diseased mouth was far stronger than he looked and had him in an iron grip. The two, as close as lovers locked in an embrace of death, fell over, hitting a table on the way down.

They struck the floor hard, but Paolo didn't feel it. The pain of having teeth rip into his flesh was horrific and galvanizing. It overwhelmed everything else. The diseased man's teeth sunk into the side of his neck and tore out a huge hunk of meat and skin. Paolo's screams rattled the windows. He screamed again and again until the man chewed his way into Paolo's larynx. Then blood poured into his lungs and, for a time, Paolo was dead.

**2**

The first two gunshots were so unexpected that it was a few seconds before the lobby guards reacted.

"Was that a gun?" Jack Cable asked.

They were seated behind the desk, twenty feet from the front doors. Earl Johnston had his head cocked with an ear to the ceiling. "I think so."

They just sat there in somewhat stunned disbelief until Deckard came over the two-way: "Shots fired, south stairwell! Proceed with caution."

As Jack and Earl were unarmed, being cautious was their only choice. The hospital was so small and so out of the way that the original security plan consisted of allowing only the supervising agents, Deck and Ray, to carry weapons. With the prisoners being a part of the trial, Deck had hired on three more guards, all with the proper firearm permits. Rory had been one of these.

The other two armed guards, along with all the other off-duty guards, had made themselves scarce hours before, not wanting to be caught up in the quarantine if they didn't have to be. They were at a pool hall in Poughkeepsie thirty miles away—close enough to be called into work when the quarantine ended, if they were sober enough that is.

Jack stood and looked around the desk as if he would find a gun that he had previously overlooked. "Shots fired…this is crazy. What the fuck are we supposed to do against someone with a gun?" he demanded.

"We have our tasers," Earl said, touching the bulky weapon at his side. He'd never fired one in anger before, yet he was relatively confident. Someone with fifty-thousand volts running through them wasn't going to do much except piss himself, even someone with a gun.

Earl led the way to the stair exit and drew his weapon. Jack came right behind him, grimacing in fear. "This is fucked," Jack whined. "First the quarantine and now this. I need some fucking combat pay if this keeps up. You know what I mean? Fourteen dollars an hour isn't going to cut it."

Behind them someone hissed, "What's happening?" A few of the more curious and daring Admin workers had crept down the hall and were now peeking around the corner. Earl waved them away. "Get back to the break room! We have the situation under control."

There were almost forty people quarantined on the first floor where the Administration offices and the large entrance lobby were located. They had, for the most part, sat gaggled in the break room where they gossiped or complained, watched TV or read books. For reasons that were beyond them, Jack and Earl hadn't joined them. They had stayed at their post although it wasn't really necessary since all the exits were locked and the two gate guards were in charge of turning people away.

Now, Jack and Earl were crouched at the south stair door; their eyes went wide when three more gunshots went off, one after the other. Jack wiped his hands on his polyester pants. "If no one comes out, do we go in?" he asked, nodding at the stairwell door.

"I'll call the boss," Earl said, with a shrug of his broad shoulders. "Deck, this is Earl, over. Come in, Deck."

It took two tries before Deck came on. In the background Earl could hear bangs and crashes, metal on metal. It sounded like his boss was in a scrap yard. "You two ok?" Deck asked. His voice was uneven and his breath was drawing heavy.

"Yeah, we're doing fine. What's going on? Who was doing all that shooting?"

"Hold on!" Deck shouted. Under the sound of his heavy breathing, they could hear what sounded like growling. There was another crash and then swearing. "Get that end…No, turn it on its side. Damn it, hold that one back. Don't let him get too close to you."

Jack and Earl shared a look. "Deck!" Earl shouted into

the two-way. "Come in, Deck." For three minutes all they got was more of the same: crashes and curses and the strange growling.

Finally, Deckard came back on. "You two have any activity down there?"

"What sort of activity?" Earl asked.

Deck blew out. "You wouldn't believe it if I told you. Listen, what I need you two to do is to evacuate the first floor. Take everyone, and…and I don't know, take them to a police station or something. Just get them out of here and try to maintain the quarantine. Keep them away from other people. Just in case."

"Ask him just in case of what?" Jack suggested.

Deck was quiet for a moment. When he came back on he sounded equal parts mad and embarrassed. "Just in case they *turn*. You'll know what I mean if it happens. Now get moving."

Earl tossed his keys to Jake—they were brand new and flashed in the light. "Unlock the front doors, I'll get the others."

They were hurrying to the center of the building when the middle stairwell door opened and three people came out. "Get on back upstairs," Earl ordered. "Go on, you're under quarantine."

"What's with their eyes?" Jack asked. He was suddenly very nervous. The people weren't right; they were dirty and they walked strangely, as if they weren't sure how to coordinate all their moving parts. "They have stuff coming out of their…" He stopped in mid-sentence. The three people started to charge the two security guards.

Unlike Jack, Earl wasn't afraid. The three people were clearly patients and not only were they unarmed, they weren't overly large or striking in any way. Earl stepped forward and waited until the first of the dreadful looking people was practically on him before he fired his taser.

The twin spikes struck one of the cancer patients that he

and Jack had checked in earlier the day before. Earl even remembered the man's name: Mr. Mumford. He'd been a jolly little man despite that he was practically at death's door. Now he resembled some sort of ghoul, discolored, leaking black fluid and smelling nasty.

The taser burned two holes in his gown as it lit him up. Mr. Mumford stopped in place and stared vacantly ahead as if the electricity had done nothing more than short a system in his brain.

"What the fuck?" Earl breathed, stepping back.

Another of the patients charged around the manikin-like figure of Mr. Mumford. This one was bigger. It was a woman who hadn't gone through chemo and who had managed to retain her appetite until the last few days. She weighed over two hundred pounds and, when Jack's taser struck her she didn't stop coming at him. But she did slow down... horribly so. It was as if someone was running a film of her at quarter speed. It wasn't human.

"That's sick," Jack said. Her movements were so robotic that it was hypnotic. "That's just so sick." He stepped to the right just as she came within arm's reach, dodging her easily.

Then the third one was on them; it went for Earl lunging at him with both hands extended. Earl tried to throw the crazed man off him but was surprised to find he wasn't strong enough. The two went down in a heap and struggled in an unearthly quiet.

"Earl!" Jack cried, rushing up and kicking the patient in the side. Jack wasn't a small man and the kick should have broken ribs, only the patient didn't even seem to notice. With his taser spent, Jack had no other weapon and so he kicked the patient again and again and again until the man finally looked up from what he had been doing to Earl.

There was so much blood. It ran down the patient's chin as though he had been lapping it up out of a bucket like a dog. Earl was dead, his throat had been torn out in seconds.

"Oh shit, oh shit, oh shit," Jack said, backing away, his

eyes like lamps staring at the body of his friend. The woman he'd tasered came at him, still very slowly. Jack hauled off and punched her in the mouth. The blow rocked her head back and cut his knuckles, but was otherwise without effect. She grabbed at his coat, fouling the navy blue uniform with her diseased hands.

When the man who'd killed Earl got up, his mouth dripping red juices veined with black, Jack ran. He sped for the front door, fingering the keys as he ran. Behind him the south stair opened up, causing the crazed creatures to turn away and giving him the seconds needed to find the right key. Then he was outside and sprinting madly for the employee lot where he'd parked his Mustang.

As he climbed in, the first rain dotted his windshield. It went unnoticed as he gunned the car toward the gates, leaving steaming rubber in his wake. The gate guards stepped in front of the speeding Mustang; Jack frantically tried to wave them away but they wouldn't move and he was forced to slam on the brakes.

"Get out of the way, damn it! All hell has broken out in the hospital. The disease…" Jack paused as his mind brought up the image of the crazed man's mouth, there had been flesh in his teeth. "Earl is dead and Deck is trapped on the top floor. The quarantine has failed and now they're running amok."

"What kind of disease is it?" one of the guards asked.

"It's turning them into cannibals," Jack answered, speaking so quickly his words ran over themselves. "Earl had his throat ripped out. We tried tasing them but they just walked right through it."

"Where are you going?" the second gate-guard asked, first eyeing the Mustang and then the hospital.

"I don't know. Somewhere away," Jack said. "Whatever they have, it's contagious…they leak black stuff out of their eyes and it's making them crazy! I don't want that to happen to me. You guys should get out of here, too."

"I'm staying," one said.

The other barely gave it any thought. "And fight them with what? We don't have guns for fuck's sake. I'm not staying. They don't pay me enough to get some disease." He climbed into the Mustang and wouldn't look the other gate guard in the eye.

"But our posts," the first said.

"This isn't the fucking army!" Jack cried before taking a look back at the hospital. He could see a number of the patients walking around. Remembering the inhuman way they moved gave him the shivers. "Stay if you want. Be a hero for fourteen dollars an hour."

The guard changed his mind a second later. He opened the gates and then climbed in next to Jack. The three of them couldn't think of anything better to do but to drive the half-hour to Poughkeepsie to find their friends and tell them what had happened. Jack decided against mentioning that he'd been touched by one of *them*. He had a pretty good guess what would happen if he did. Instead, between shots of tequila, he told the other guards that he had run back to the desk to get his keys and when he turned around he saw Earl being swarmed.

"There was nothing I could do," Jack said, finishing in a whisper. By the third re-telling, the number of infected patients attacking Earl had jumped to ten. Jack wore a grimace as he spoke—his head had begun to ache. He prayed to God it was just the stress getting to him.

More alcohol helped, and when both the gate-guards began to complain of headaches also, Jack kept the denial going by ordering each of them a bottle.

**3**

On the fourth floor of the Walton facility, twenty three people were fighting a losing battle keeping the barricades in place. There was simply not enough furniture in the labs. Thuy had been particularly proud of the sleek, modern look that deemphasized clutter, however now there just wasn't enough heavy material to block-up the stairwells properly. They would throw a table down the stairs and a minute later the infected people would pull it further down the stairwell. Had there been just a single door to defend this might have gone on for many hours, resulting in a draw, instead there were three stairwells they had to barricade.

The scientists were so hard-pressed keeping their pathetic defenses from being breached that the telephone went ignored and three calls from the CDC went to voice mail.

On the third floor there were only six people left alive after the massacre. They were huddled in a side room of the radiology department where PET scans were performed. They were deathly afraid to make any noise. If they spoke, which was very rarely, it was in whispers. They cried in silence and mourned in silence and shook in fear in silence. The little group had no plan but to sit there as quietly as possible and not die.

Eventually, they decided to risk calling the police. "Help," Dr. Hester breathed into the phone after dialing 9-1-1.

"What is the nature of your emergency?" a bored voice asked.

Even the tinny, little voice coming from the phone seemed too loud and the others silently begged Dr. Hester to hang up. He said one more word, "Zombies," before hanging up. To him it was a very legitimate word. He could think of no better way to describe what the patients had turned into—they fit every criterion he could think of: they were unstoppable, mindless, cannibals who looked like they had been spawned in hell.

Unfortunately the word "Zombie" was not legitimate in the eyes of the police. The dispatcher turned to the girl sitting next to her and said, "Get this, Courtney. Some guy just called and when I ask him the nature of his emergency, he says zombies!"

"He didn't!" Courtney Shaw practically yelled.

"He did. It was all in a whisper, too, like zombies have super-hearing."

"I bet it was a kid pranking you. I'd flag the number or they'll keep calling. Remember the dude who kept calling to say an alien was probing him? Lieutenant Pemberton bitched up a storm when I finally sent a trooper to check it out."

Back at the hospital, on the second floor, Von Braun wiped at his eyes and tried again to make sense of the writing on the little IV bag. Everything was so small and blurry and the lettering only confused his swirling mind and made him, if it was possible, even angrier. Without warning, he punched a hole in the wall next to him and then tore down part of the plastic curtain around the nurse's station.

"It doesn't matter," Herman hissed. "We know where the cure is. We just have to get it."

"Yes it does matter, you stupid fuck," Von Braun said, grabbing the sides of his head and crushing his hands inward, trying to smother the fire of hate that was beginning to interfere with his ability to think on a second grade level. "If I can't think straight, how will I know what is the cure and what is a bottle of piss?"

"I don't care if you find it or not," Herman said. "I like being like this." He'd been in prison for tax evasion though that was only because the prosecutor couldn't get enough evidence to make the pedophile charges stick. He'd been certain that Herman was guilty, and he'd been right. Herman, a short, fat, hairy little perv, liked to feel powerful and the only time he ever had was when he was around little children.

Except he was feeling exceptionally powerful just at that moment. He felt he could do anything he wanted without any fear of the consequences, and just then he really wanted to hurt someone. He wandered away from Von Braun. He knew where people were. They were trapped upstairs.

Von Braun didn't notice him leave. His Diazepam drip had run out a few minutes before and his mind was regressing quickly. "It starts with a 'D' I know that," he said. He also knew the IV bags were small. It narrowed his choices to one. After a five-minute struggle as his hands and brain fought against each other, he finally got the new bag in place. The calming effects of the drug were immediate.

"Yes," he whispered, enjoying the peace in his mind. He still wanted to kill and he still knew that "they" had done something to him, something that called for revenge, and he still felt dirty on the inside, but at least he could think. "The cops will be coming. I need a gun."

He had a vague memory of a nurse with a gun; he went in search of it.

One floor down the "authorities" finally arrived. Vince Oldham and his two EIS officers parked the CDC van directly in front of the building. "Full gear?" Damon asked. He'd been an *Epidemic Intelligence Services* officer for only three months and the training videos were fresh enough in his mind that he still asked about going full on, every time out.

"I think so," Vince said. He liked to gear-up. Without the bio-suit, people only saw him as nothing more than an over-bearing, officious bureaucrat. The suit, whether it was needed or not, lent him an air of urgency and it did quite a number on the psyche of people. The biggest corporate bully was always a bit more circumspect when Vince came in suited up.

Too bad the CDC suits were canary yellow. He had pleaded with his superiors for them to be changed out to black—for recruiting purposes—he had argued, but had been shot down.

The three of them began gearing up: full bio-suit, rubber boots and gloves, goggles, and the P-100 filtered mask. Before he put the mask in place, Vince tried to call Dr. Lee one last time. It was a courtesy he extended to her simply because he'd looked her up after the initial call and thought she was smoking hot. Normally, he would march right in, hoping to catch the offending company desperately trying to clean up whatever mess they'd made.

"Went to voice mail again," he said

"What about trying the state troopers one more time?" Peggy asked. He'd called an hour earlier to check on the run-away situation only to sit on hold for fifteen minutes. Eventually some tired sounding dispatcher had come back on to tell him that they hadn't found anyone matching John Burke's description.

"I'll call the state police after our initial run through," Vince told her, noting that the rain was really starting to come down. Who knew what it would be like after another lengthy stint on hold? "Burke's probably holed up somewhere, safe as a bug in a rug."

Vince wasn't close in his assessment. John was four floors up, trying to cut a length of carpet in two using only a scalpel. He and Chuck Singleton were rolling up the flooring and using it to stuff the cracks that kept opening up in their barricade—they had run out of furniture and were getting desperate. The zombies were tireless in their attack.

"Let's do this," Vince said. He opened the van door, stepped out and shouldered his pack. They went to the front entrance and noted that the door was unlocked. "First violation," he remarked.

"Second violation," Peggy said as they stepped in. No one had put tape over the elevator or the stairwell entrance. The three of them were so absorbed with picking at the breaches in the hazmat code that none of them saw the body of Earl Johnston lying behind the waiting room chairs.

"What's that banging?" Damon asked. A great deal of thumping and crashes were coming from somewhere down the north hall. As there was no one around to escort them, they decided to follow the noise. They passed through a right-angled field of cubicles and found a small group of people hammering on a door with their fists.

Peggy and Damon turned with a rustle of plastic to share a look that each interpreted as: *What the fuck?*

Vince raised his hands and said: "Excuse me! What's going on here?"

The group turned as a unit. There were nine of them and Vince saw right away that seven of the nine were in bad shape. They were leaking what looked like old blood from every orifice; their eyes being especially affected.

"Is that hemorrhagic fever?" Damon asked, taking an involuntary step back.

"I really doubt it," Vince answered. "If it is then it's awfully advanced, and these people seem too energetic to be in such a late stage." The *victims,* as the three CDC agents saw them were staring, turning their heads this way and that as if they, too, were trying to make sense of what they were seeing.

"Thank God we wore the suits," Peggy said. "We...we should call in some back up. This is bigger than just Fusarium."

Vince had to agree. "We will, but first we have to see what we're dealing with. We have to get a handle on the scope of the situation." He stepped forward, hands out in a calming gesture. "Hi. We're from the CDC. We're here to get you people some help, but first, can any of you tell me where I can find Dr. Lee?"

One of them, the man that used to be Mr. Mumford, shambled forward. Vince saw the fresh, red blood that ran all down his chin and assumed it was part of the disease. "Hi," Vince said, this time nervously. Mumford reacted to the sound of his voice and stood on his toes trying to see into the tiny plastic window. They locked eyes. "Yes, I'm trying to find Dr. Lee. She's the head of…"

Mumford, realizing there was a human inside the strange yellow suit attacked Vince. His hands were like claws, raking at the plastic hood, turning it around on Vince's head. The CDC man was basically blind, staring into the side of his hood, while doing his best to keep it from being ripped off altogether. Peggy leapt to his aid and struggled with the growling Mr. Mumford.

Damon took another step back. The junior agent had the strong, near-overpowering urge to just point his feet at the door and hightail it out of there. His training had not prepared him for the idea that the victims of the diseases would actually attack those trying to help.

"Get him off me!" Vince screamed. "Get him off!"

Peggy began slapping Mumford on the top of the head with her clipboard. He seemed not to notice; he was fully focused on getting Vince's hood off, and when he did, things went from bad to worse.

Seeing Vince's red face was like a signal to the rest, they swarmed forward, tackling Vince and sending Peggy sprawling. In that split second, Damon made up his mind to help, however in the next second Mumford reared back with his mouth wide, exposing hellish looking black teeth; he then bit down on Vince's exposed neck. Horrifically, he began rooting around like a pig, chewing and swallowing until he found the source of Vince's clean blood.

It came geysering up in an arc of red. Vince had been screaming and fighting like mad, but now he went limp. Then it was Peggy's turn. There were two of the infected patients on her tearing at the yellow plastic, looking like children at Christmas, ripping into a present. She'd been struggling with all her strength and instead of screaming she was grunting with the effort, but when her suit tore she let out a terrified screech.

Damon did the only sensible thing: he booked it out of

there at top speed, racing for the van. The booties of his suit were as slick at the rest of his outfit and he fell twice, both times knocking the wind out of himself. In his panic, he barely noticed. He made it to the van just ahead of three of the infected patients. Jumping in, he began swatting down the locks one after another. When the last was down he let out a sigh of relief that was cut short—he didn't have the keys to start the van! And worse, the diseased people had ringed the vehicle.

They immediately started pounding on the glass with their fists, uncaring what sort of damage they were doing to themselves in the process. The driver's side window cracked first. Damon only had time to say, "Oh, God, no," before the glass shattered. He tried to escape by crawling to the passenger seat however something on his bio-suit got hung up on the emergency brake and held him tight.

They crawled in after him and began to eat.


**4**


In the 'big house," Jaimee sat on a gurney swinging her feet and wondering why the adults were fussing so. Yes, she had a headache, but that didn't mean she had the cancer. According to her dad, the cancer was got by living in the "bestos" house, and Jaimee had never lived there, not for one day.

So that only meant she had a cold. She hated being sick. She weren't never allowed out to play when she was sick.

A long, tired sigh escaped her and for the millionth time she wished she hadn't been caught sneaking in to see Maddy's mom. There was no way Jaimee could've known there were cameras watching all over the place as if there were gold and 'jules' stashed somewheres in it.

And boy, howdy, she had gotten a talking to! "That Dr.

McGrady is such a cranky-puss," she muttered.

"We can hear you," Ms. Robins said, her voice magnified by the hidden speakers.

"I know," grumbled Jaimee.

"Did you want us to hear you?" Dr. McGrady asked.

"I don't know. I don't really care iffin y'all hear me or not. How much longer do I gotta be here? My Daidy will be 'specting me when he gets better."

"Are you mad at me, Jaimee?" the doctor asked. "Do you blame me for keeping you here?"

"A little cuz I ain't sick. 'Ceptin for my head a little like I told y'all before."

"Can you describe the headache?"

Now, Jaimee was getting mad. She pounded her fist down on the gurney. "I already told y'all. It's thumpin' what good, now can I git?"

"Not yet, Jaimee. Can you take your temperature again for me?"

"I jes did it!"

"We need you to take your temperature every fifteen minutes in order to track the progress of your sickness. It's something your father would want you to do."

"But I ain't sick," she muttered, forgetting how sensitive the microphone was. The thermometer was on a cart across the room next to Gabriele's eternally sleeping body. Jaimee went to it, swiped the little instrument across her forehead, and read the numbers "It has a nine and an eight and there's a little bug of a number that says seven. Is that good?"

"Yes, that's good," McGrady said. "Now put the thermometer in its place. Good." He was in his room two floors above her, sitting at a desk staring at one of the three monitors.

Beside him, Ms. Robins asked, "Why do you insist on taking her temperature? Dr. Lee hasn't mentioned anything concerning a fever."

McGrady gave her sideways look before answering,

"You are correct. Fever is not a sign of the disease, however failing eyesight is. I'm trying to judge her acuity based on how well she can read the numbers." He sat back for a moment, tapping a pencil, looking lost in thought. "If she's changing, it's at a rate far slower than that of the others."

"Is that significant?"

"Everything is significant, my dear," he replied, pompously. He had a mountain-sized ego and rarely did anything to keep it in check. "Unfortunately, we frequently find out why too late." He chucked down the pencil and picked up the phone.

In the hospital eighty yards away, Dr. Lee answered, however she was so engrossed in the latest blood work that she had snatched from John Burke that she wasn't really paying attention to the phone. "How can that be?" she asked herself at what she was seeing on the readout.

McGrady looked at the phone, confused. "Uh, this is Dr. McGrady...How can what be?"

"There's no sign of the Com-cells in his blood."

Her floor was being attacked on three sides, her co-workers were desperately trying to hold the barricades in place against foes who never seemed to tire, and they were running out of anything to stop up the holes. In other words they were running out of time. Deckard was down to pulling out the toilets in the men's room. And yet she was still so engaged with the puzzle that the Com-cell represented, that she was practically oblivious to her danger.

"Dr. Lee, This is Dr. McGrady, were you talking to me?"

She blinked, remembering she had just picked up the phone. "Is the girl sick? It's been over ninety minutes."

"If she is, the disease is not following the same pattern as your other patients. Her only real symptom is a headache and a very slight personality change, though this last is hard to know for certain since I don't have much of a baseline. Everything else, pulse, BP, O2 sats are just fine."

Thuy frowned. "I do not construe 'just fine' as actual

data. Email me real numbers. I'll need to know..."

Milner stuck his head into the lab, interrupting her. "Lee! Is that the cops you're talking to? When are they going to get here?"

"No, it's McGrady from over at the Rothchild's. I don't know when the police will be here. I haven't called them. I've been busy."

"You've been busy!" he shouted. "Haven't you noticed there's a fucking crisis going on all around you?"

"I'll call you back," she said to McGrady and then hung up. "Show me." Of course she had noticed the people running around and the fact they always seemed to be carrying items, however there hadn't been any more gunshots and she had assumed Deckard was in the process of containing the problem.

She followed Milner out into the hall where the sight of her hospital being destroyed, piece-by-piece struck her, viscerally. The scientists, being led by Deckard, were tearing up everything they could lift and throwing it down into the three stairwells. There was so little left in sight that she figured the stairwells had to be filled with so much debris by now that nothing could get by, however the infected people were just as quickly yanking everything further down the stairs in their effort to get up. Succinctly: it was a hell of a mess.

"Nice of you to join us," Deck said. His suit coat was flung on the ground and the sleeves of his black button-up shirt were rolled to the elbows. He stood three steps down, wielding a push broom, knocking back a couple of nurses who had come too close to the top of the stairs. There were another dozen or so clawing their way toward him, basically swimming upstream against metal and glass. In their eyes was hate and murder. They were beyond any understanding of a cure. Now they were only interested in killing.

Just above Deck, at the top of the stairs, Wilson stood breathing heavily. He held a monitor in one hand and a computer tower in the other. Casually he flung them down the stairs adding to the confusion.

Seeing the infected people so intent on their destruction focused Dr. Lee's mind in a snap. "I'm sorry...I was busy working on a cure," she said, defensively to Deckard. "Can you give me a status update?"

"Sure, we're fucked." Despite this assertion he was calm. He was the only one.

"We have to start killing them before it's too late," Milner stated.

Thuy was wholly unaware of the massacre on the third floor or that even then the door on the first floor break room, where dozens of people were trapped, was only minutes from disintegrating under a voracious attack. She still thought of the infected subjects as people. "These are our patients, Milner! We did this to them. We should be trying to find ways of helping them, not hurting them."

She thought Milner was being hysterical and she looked to Deck to back her up, but he shook his head. "We either kill them now while we have the advantage or we wait and kill them when they're up here."

There had to be a better way. "What about wounding them? I bet you're a pretty good shot. Maybe go for a leg or something."

Milner laughed, high and loud. It was a hysterical cackle that was unnerving coming from such a straight arrow. Thuy tried to step back from him, but Milner grabbed her arm and pulled her away from the stairwell. "Let me show you what *you* created. Remember, this was your project."

He tugged her to the central stairs where they stood over a chest-high pile of what used to be fantastically expensive lab equipment. Below them were fifteen or sixteen of the infected, struggling to pull down the pile.

"Look! Look at that one." The one stood out from the others. Thuy couldn't help but gasp at the sight of it. It had once been a person, now it was some sort of creature's whose face was covered in black bile, which leaked from its eyes, nose and mouth. It was altogether hideous, but what made it worse than the others was that the creature had a twelve-inch carving knife planted in its chest. It didn't even seem to notice it. It went about the business of trying to kill them without so much as wincing.

Deck had come up behind them."You see now?"

Dr. Milner laughed again. "This will be on your head, Thuy, not mine. I was just doing what you told me to. I even have the proof that it was..."

Deckard grabbed him by the shoulder and hauled him around so that they were face to face. "Go get more of those computers and shut your trap while you do it, too." Milner flinched, snapped his jaw closed, and scurried away. Deck cracked a small smile and said, "You hit a man in the face once and he learns to fish for life."

"You hit him?"

"Just the one time; he needed it. Let's get out of the way."

Riggs had just come into the stairwell carrying a shelf and a pile of books. He was sweating and there were dark circles around his eyes. "The cops?" he asked.

"I'll call them right now," she told him, touching his arm. Riggs tossed his load down onto the pile. The infected swept it aside almost as soon as it landed.

"They couldn't possibly get here in time," Deck said. "There's almost nothing left to chuck down on top of the creatures. That's the bad news, the worse news is that I only have twelve rounds in my gun and there's got to be at least sixty of those things trying to get us. We're going to have to fight hand to hand. My question is, how contagious are they?"

She had to make assumptions in order to answer, unfortunately they were safe assumptions. "I'm afraid they're very contagious."

Deck made a face as though he smelled something bad.

"Fuck. Excuse my language but we are just about as fucked as can be. Your scientists are…let's just say they look very doubtful when it comes to fighting."

A number of the scientists were nearby looking sick with fear. Thuy had to agree with Deckard, they would make terrible fighters. The scientists were either skinny, shallow-chested nerds or saggy, plump, and pushing fifty. Only a few, Riggs and Eng for example, were in shape enough to put up some sort of fight.

Next to Deck, Riggs was nodding in full agreement. "Look at us, we're pathetic. We can't fight, but what about the elevator? We can take it in shifts and be gone before any of these things even know it."

"We can't," Deck told him. "The elevator is parked on the first floor and I can't get a hold of the front desk guards who have the keys. I'm afraid we're going to have fight, one way or the other. We should arm ourselves as best as possible."

"Wait! Please…I'll figure something out," Thuy said, looking around at the door and the painted concrete walls and the now emptied labs. She grunted, "In the meantime, don't kill them."

Deck shrugged. "You have about five minutes before that choice is no longer mine to make."

Thuy stalked away down the corridor and saw the destruction of her labs first hand. The rooms had been stripped of everything that could be torn down by hand and carried away. Even as she was standing there Eng walked by with her computer in his arms. "So solly," he said in his ridiculous accent.

All her work was in that metal box. "Hold on," she said grabbing him by the shirt. "Not that."

"But Doctoral Ree, we need must stop zombie from getting up."

She made a face at the word "zombie." It was hardly scientific. "What you're doing isn't working," she said. "Or it won't work for much longer. We need to hold the doors closed...somehow." She again stared at the door of the closest stair, her mind ticking easily. The doors opened into the stairwell, so barring them in some fashion wouldn't work. They would have to rely on simple physics to keep them closed. They would have to apply an equal or greater amount of pull on the handles as that which could be exerted from the other side.

Force against force. Pull against pull...unless...

"Put that back," she said to Eng, slowly, still not quite in the present. "And then get me some rope or wire. Lots of it."

"Yes, wire is easy. Machine have much wire. Wittle wires, though."

"Just get what you can." There wasn't enough tensile strength in a single strand of wire to work, but if they could find enough to braid together, it might hold.

She was just picturing what she would need when a voice said in her ear, "Are you just going to stand there while we get attacked?"

Thuy blinked in surprise to see it was Anna who had spoken. "You?" she demanded in shock and outrage. "What are you doing..."

"What am I doing walking around like a free person? Like I'm an actual citizen with rights? I'm trying to save our asses from whatever it is you did to those poor people."

"Me?" Thuy thundered in a voice that could be heard down both ends of the hall. "You're the two-face traitor who..."

"Not now, ladies," Deckard yelled as he swept past with his arms filled with binders to hurl down the stairs--they were getting desperate. "Save it for the hearing."

Thuy stepped back, her soft lips pressed hard against her gritted teeth. "Fine. I can be civil. I need rope or heavy wire. Can I trust you to handle finding some?"

"What about steel cable?" Anna replied, holding in her own anger by the barest margins. "All the lights in the BSL-

4 labs are hung by cable."

"Get all of it," Thuy demanded.

Shortly, she had all the cable she could need. They came in four-foot lengths, each with fish-eye hooks at the ends. Eng, Anna, and Thuy daisy-chained them together and then went to each door, shooed people away, and strung the cable from the handle of the stairwell doors and attached it to whatever was convenient across the hall. In two cases it was attached to a railing, in the third it was to the handle of another door.

No human, no matter how possessed of demonic strength was capable of pulling open the doors now. The scientists stood around sweating and staring at the simple contrivance and feeling somewhat stupid that they hadn't thought of it first.

"That was smart," Deckard remarked, casually, wearing that awful, handsome smile on his lips once again. It was the one Thuy always felt the strongest desire to respond to.

"Smart is what I do," she replied, laying on just enough chill to dampen that roguish smile.

Now that she'd said it, she had to prove it beyond figuring out how to lock a door. Thuy went back to her desk--the only one left on the fourth floor--hooked up her computer and sat, drumming her fingers, her eyes unfocussed as her mind grappled with the two anomalies generated by the trial: John and Jaimee Burke.

John was apparently immune to the Com-cells, his natural defenses destroying them completely, and Jaimee seemed resistant to the worst effects. The question was why them? What made them so special?

The obvious answer to this little puzzle lay in genetics. In other words, a random quirk of nature was keeping them from turning into mindless, cannibalistic, killing machines. It was obvious, yet with her lab in shambles there was no way for her to test the hypothesis. A part of her was ok with that. A positive genetic confirmation would mean the other infected people were simply screwed.

"We'll move forward working on the assumption that their immunity is based on environmental factors," she said to the empty lab. Everyone else was still in the hall, listening as the infected people made it past the heaps of refuse in the stairs and were now testing the doors. For the most part they hammered on the metal with their fists. The doors shook and shivered from the blows, making the scientists feel ill at ease.

Thuy ignored all of it--the stairwell doors were up to code. They were metal, as were their frames, and so banging or pushing would have even less effect than pulling. She stuck her head out into the hall.

Before she could say anything, Milner asked, "Are the cops coming?"

She shrugged. "Don't know, I never called them. Burke, I need to talk to you in my office, now."

Chuck sniggered at him, "Sounds like y'all just might get a paddlin', son."

## Chapter 9

**//4:51 PM//**

**1**

Other than Dr. Hester's whispered phone call about "zombies", no one had yet called the police. The attacks on the third and fourth floor had occurred with such rapidity and brutality that there had been no time for anyone to make a call, except for Dr. Lee that is and she hadn't understood the extent of the problem until it was practically too late.

On the first floor, after Earl had been killed and Jack sped off, but before the CDC personnel were eaten with their canary yellow wrappers still on them, the admin employees were under the assumption that everything was being taken care of. Yes, they had heard what sounded like gunshots, but nothing more had come of it.

They were sitting in the break room, following the quarantine protocol and were utterly bored by it. Eventually, Morgan Pierce, whose fingers and teeth were yellowed and whose skin was more akin to leather than to flesh, stood up, straightened her skirt and said, "I need a smoke."

The head of human resources, Preston Stuart, a man who couldn't let the littlest things go, said, "You know the rules. We took the same class together, Morgan. You can't leave the building."

"Fine, I'll smoke in the bathroom."

"You're not allowed to smoke in there!" Preston found cigarettes to be an abomination and crusaded against them at every turn. "You'll just need to wait."

Morgan had done enough waiting. So far all they'd done was wait. "Then I'm going to go take a dump," she stated.

"You can't smoke in the bathroom," Preston argued.

"Right, you said that. Anyone else wanna take a dump with me?" she asked, patting her purse. She had two takers, friends who could always be counted on to lend her a puff when she needed one.

She also had one tagalong.

"I can walk down the hall if I want to," Preston noted with a childish air. He stayed eight paces back, escorting them all the way to the bathroom, whereupon he leaned up against a wall next to the door. "I can lean here," he said at their look. "It's a free country."

"What you're doing is really close to stalking," Morgan noted. One of the main reasons she had taken the job with R&K was that she had been working as a data processor for eighteen years and was heartily tired of it. She was looking to sue somebody for something and the fact was R&K was loaded and could afford a sexual harassment suit. She'd even read up on the subject and knew that documentation and witnesses were the key to entrapping someone with harassment.

"I'm not stalking anyone I just like to lean here. It's not my problem that it just...happens to be..." His words faltered as a fresh indignation caught his eye. A person had just walked out of the central stairwell door. "Is that one of the patients?"

"I think so," Morgan answered. "He might be leaving, and that's against the rules. Why don't you go harass him?"

Preston stalked off, thinking to do just that. "Hey! You can't leave!" he yelled. "We're under lock down. That's..." Again his words ground to a halt. The person had turned his way and there was something not quite right about him. Black orbs seemed to have replaced his eyes and there was a viscous goo leaking all down his face. What was worse was how he had turned at the sound of Preston's voice; he had done so with naked aggression.

"You need to get back upstairs," Preston said, with less of an imperious tone.

He was ignored. The man neither turned left nor right, he headed for Preston with his mouth wide open, clearly looking to take a chunk out of him. Preston didn't wait to be bitten; he punched the crazy looking man square in the jaw. Preston might have been officious and a tad overbearing but he could fight. His raw personality made it almost mandatory.

And yet the blow, delivered with all the righteousness he could muster, didn't even faze the patient. And neither did the next punch, or the one after that. The man just kept coming on, stupidly with his mouth agape. Preston focused too much on the gaping, hungry mouth and didn't realize there was so much danger in the man's outstretched hands. The fingers were like talons and once they got a hold of Preston's sweater they would not let go.

The man pulled him into his embrace and it was everything Preston could do to stop those blackened teeth from tearing into him.

"Help! Shit, fuck! Morgan, help get this guy off of me." The patient was so strong that he easily wrestled Preston to the ground and was bending back his arms in order to get to his soft throat. Morgan and her two friends tried to help.

"Get off!" Morgan yelled, kicking the patient with the toes of her shoes. One of her friends joined her, stomping with wicked stilettos, while the third woman picked up a three-hole punch and started beating the man on the back of the head. Preston was going spastic, screaming and writhing, kicking his legs uselessly as his head was bent further and further back.

Preston knew what was coming—the crazy man had already bitten him on shoulder, the cheek, and his right ear, which was torn in two and dangling by a membrane of skin. He was in intense pain and there was blood flowing, urgent and hot, but he knew it would be nothing compared to what would happen if the deranged patient could get to his neck.

And yet there was nothing Preston could do to stop him. He was weakening and all he could do was scream in anger and fear...and then in pain. It was an awful, terror filled sound.

At the cry, Morgan stepped back uncertain what to do. Blood ran like water out of Preston's body. It darkened the tan carpet, leaching outward, quickly. It almost seemed to her that the blood would soon spread under her feet to cover the entire corridor in red. As she took a fearful step back, Preston's cry turned into a wet gurgle and his hands suddenly shot out, frozen in a rigid posture. They stood out like that for half a minute and then dropped with two little thumps.

"Oh, shit," the woman with the three-hole punch said.

The lunatic made a slurping noise as though he was sucking up milk from a bowl when the last Cheerio had been fished out. Then he took another, larger, bite out of Preston and shook his head like rat-terrier. Something...some part of Preston, flew up and slapped onto Morgan's wrist. She couldn't tell what it was. It slid off when she turned her arm over, leaving a wet stain behind.

"Oh, God," Morgan whined, shuddering and backing away. The other two women did the same, tiptoeing, not wanting to disturb the crazy patient, not wanting him to look up and see them, not wanting to suffer the same fate as Preston. At the edge of the cubicle maze, they turned and fled, running as if there were a dozen more lunatics after them.

There actually were. The sound of Preston's screams had attracted every one of the patients who had wandered down to the first floor and now they were converging on the three women. When Morgan saw them she kicked it into high and sprinted for the break room at top speed, yelling: "Open up! Let us in!" She had this insane fear that the break room was going to be locked when they got to it, unfortunately, for all of them, there wasn't a lock on the door.

Jodi Schmelling opened the door and stood blinking in confusion at what she saw. Morgan plowed right through her and the other two women trampled them both. "Lock it!" one of them screeched.

Instead, Dean Redman looked out over the admin area. At the sight of the black-eyed monsters rushing the door, he jerked as if an electric eel had chomped down on his testes. "Oh, shit!" he cried, slamming the door practically in the face of one of them. There was an immediate crash as a body smashed into it.

"Lock it! Lock it!" Morgan yelled. "They killed Preston."

"Who did?" Jodi asked. Dean was staring down at the doorknob in disbelief, his mind seemingly incapable of grasping the concept that not all doors had locks.

"Some guy," Morgan cried. "One of the patients from the trial. They did something to them and now they're like..." The door banged again and the wall shook.

"There's no lock," Dean said. He turned slightly and pointed at the knob. "It's got no lock."

"We can barricade it with the sofa," Jodi said. "Everyone move out of the way. Someone give me a hand." Jodi, who was normally quiet as a mouse, began commanding the others. They hopped to. Both couches were stacked one atop the other in front of the door, while the heavy chairs were pushed into supporting position on either side. They also armed themselves with whatever was available: one man held a coffee pot as though it was a hammer, another had a mug, a third had a broom.

Morgan took out her cell phone and she punched 9-1-1 with shaking hands. After a minute of near useless questions and hysterical answers she told the others in the room, "They said it would be fifteen minutes. We should be fine, right? Those things haven't even tried the doorknob yet."

Everyone looked at the knob. It hadn't turned. The patients were hammering on the door with unrelenting fury, but the knob hadn't even been tried yet. It was a fine door for what it was made to do: opening and closing, and perhaps offering a modicum of sound privacy. It did not possess a solid core and had not been constructed to act as a first line of defense.

After a minute, a crack opened up on the hallway side and soon the repeated blows turned the crack into a gaping hole. The beasts tore at it in maniacal rage and then they began to attack the near side panel. The door got a sudden reprieve when they heard someone talking from the other side.

"It's the CDC!" Jodi cried upon hearing Vince Oldham. There was a cheer from the trapped admin workers and then as the screams began on the other side of the door there were only tears. Soon the door was back to being hammered on and after five minutes the trapped employees could see the death that awaited them as the door began to fall apart.

When it finally came apart, they tried to hold the couches in place, but the top one toppled over. Jodi then ordered the men in to attack with their "weapons". The coffee pot lasted a single swing, the mugs shattered on first contact and the broom snapped in two--they had gained three minutes.

## 2

Six miles away, New York State Troopers Heines and Brown were racing their cruisers at breakneck speed. They had spent the last three hours motoring along the narrow back roads east of the Hudson, trying to track down a single man: John Burke. That sort of thing was the dullest of police work and both were glad for the break.

"Say again, dispatch?" Brown said into his mike. His wipers were slapping back and forth and, combined with the rain and the roar of his engine, he was having trouble hearing. "Is this a terrorist attack?"

"We're trying to make some sense of this, Charlie-6," the dispatcher said in her usual, bored as hell voice--nothing ever seemed to get her excited, not even the possibility of a terrorist attack. "We advise caution until the situation clears up."

"Dispatch, this is Charlie-Sierra-5, we roger that," Heines affirmed. "Possible gang or terrorist attack. We'll be judiciously cautious."

Brown snorted. Judiciously cautious meant Heines was going to do whatever he felt like doing and talk his way out of any trouble later. The man had a silver tongue that Brown envied. He glanced at his GPS and was shocked to realize he recognized the address. "Dispatch, is this the hospital that's under quarantine?" he asked into his mike.

"Just a sec, Charlie-6," the dispatcher said. She was away from the mike for a couple of minutes; when she came back on she still didn't seem all that concerned. "That is affirmative. A research fellow just put a call into us. You will be facing a biohazard of unknown origin. There are CDC agents on the grounds. Make contact with them to receive any follow up directives."

"Already a cluster fuck," Brown snarled to himself. Heines pulled up beside him, glanced over, and shook his head. "Yeah, I'm right there with you," Brown whispered. The idea of Ebola or small pox or any of those nasty diseases, was one of those threats police forces simply hated. You couldn't shoot a virus, you could only pray you weren't going to come in contact with some of that nasty shit.

The hospital came up too quickly for Brown's tastes. It looked shiny and new, an unlikely spot for terrorism, however the gate was unmanned and there was a dead body in the CDC van sitting out front.

"Holy shit," Heines said, staring in at the remains while rain water fell off the brim of his campaign hat, what all the troopers called *smokeys*. Beneath it, his lip was curled in disgust, making his caterpillar-like moustache poof up as though it was about to crawl off his face. "Call it in. I'm going to check the lobby."

Brown had been staring at the body feeling the starch drain out of his uniform. It was a moment before he could turn away from the sight of Damon's partially eaten corpse. "Dispatch, this is Charlie-6." Even in his own ears his voice sounded like someone had tweaked his testicles something good. "We are on site and request back-up and ambulance support. We have one CDC personnel deceased."

"Roger, Charlie-6. Do not touch the body. I say again do not touch the body. We are routing extra units in your direction."

"Out," Brown said. He glanced up at the hospital, feeling his insides do a little dance. He didn't want to go in. First, the germs and now the CDC man...something had torn great hunks of flesh out of him; it had looked as unnatural a death as Brown had seen in fourteen years as a state trooper.

He took off his *Smokey* and was wiping the sweat from his brow when he saw Heines waving at him urgently from just inside the lobby. "Shit," Brown whispered before ducking into his cruiser. In the glove compartment were latex gloves and surgical masks. He donned them as quick as he could, grabbed an extra set for Heines, and then ran for the front doors. One step in and he understood what Heines was so frantic about.

There were screams coming from deeper in the building. "Put these on." Brown shoved the mask and gloves into his partner's hands and then took off at a run. His body was charged with fear but he couldn't ignore a cry for help, being the *good-guy* was simply too ingrained in his psyche to run *from* danger. The trooper ran into the admin section, staying low, pausing where the cubicles formed little hallways.

At each turn, he poked his head out, glanced back and forth and then ran on, faster. The cries drew him on until he found the source: a room near the end of the building. Its door was in pieces, hanging from bent hinges and there were what looked like claw marks on it.

His first thought: *What the fuck, is there a bear in the building?*

Brown ran to the door, weapon drawn. What he saw

inside shocked him into inaction. It was a wild melee. Thirty or forty people were battling with hands and feet and in many cases with teeth! There seemed to be no rhyme or reason to the fight, only the result: death. Blood coated the floor, dripped down the walls and was spattered across the furniture that had been uprooted and now pointed at strange angles that made not a lick of sense.

Some of the people fighting were dressed in hospital gowns, some in surgical scrubs and others in business attire--most were women. Brown had never seen a brawl like this between such normally mundane individuals and it was a few seconds before he bellowed: "Everyone freeze!" Amid the grunts and growls and the blood-curdling screams he went unheard.

Heines came up beside him and his eyes went comically large over the top of his mask. "Mother of God, what the fuck is all this?" he asked.

"Who the hell knows," Brown replied. "I guess we should try to separate them, somehow. Let's just start grabbing them and pulling...shit! Look at her."

One of the brawlers, a woman with graying hair, had been kicked square in the chest by a spectacled man in a button up shirt. The blow turned the woman around and now the two troopers were looking the hideous woman square in the face. The entire orbs of her eyes were black as coal--*Like a demon*, Brown thought.

She was covered in a smear that resembled ink. It seemed to leak from every orifice except from her mouth. Her mouth was wide and gushing blood that was just as bright red as Santa's coat.

"Kill her!" someone screamed.

*But she's unarmed*, Brown was thinking. Regardless, his weapon came up. In response, the woman spat out a hunk of something onto the floor that had once been part of a person's face. "That--that's a nose," Heines said in disbelief.

Brown believed it, just like he believed that what was

held in the woman's right hand was a tangle of hair and at the end of it were the still bleeding remains of someone's scalp. "Stop right there," Brown ordered. She didn't. She oriented on Brown's voice and came at him with her mouth stretching wider still as though she would swallow him whole if she could.

"Do it," Heines said. "Plug her."

Brown put a hole in her chest, nine millimeters in diameter. Other than jarring her back a step, it seemed to have zero effect. He shot again; the second shot was as useless as the first. "Mother fucker," Brown hissed and pulled the trigger a third time. The last bullet passed through the fourth intercostal space and spun at a shallow angle before blasting out her vertebra. With her spinal cord cut she dropped like a ragdoll.

"Mother fucker," Brown said, again in a whisper.

"Yeah," Heines agreed. He pointed into the room with his service piece. "Look, there's more of them." With all the commotion and the blood and the screams, the faces of the fighters had blurred together, but the canon-like gunshots had paused the fighting and the people came into focus. There were ten others with the black eyes.

"Should we try to cuff them?" Brown asked. Killing that first lady had unsettled him mightily and although the others seemed as mindlessly violent, he didn't think he could just shoot them out of hand.

Heines shrugged. "I don't know if we can. But we can try."

The two officers charged into the fight and in seconds they realized that handcuffing was not an option. They wrestled one man down to the ground, however he was all gnashing teeth and rending claws. He was also fiendishly strong and somehow got atop of Heines and was within a whisker of tearing out his throat when Brown shot him. Just like the lady, it took three shots before the man slumped.

With a grunt, Heines threw him off. "Forget the cuffs!"

he yelled, getting to his feet. In a terrific rage, Heines strode into the battle and began shooting without regard for anything that resembled proper procedure. There seemed to be little choice. The "normal" people were losing the fight. Many were pouring blood from gaping wounds and a few were stretched out on the floor, unmoving.

Stunned, Brown just stood there watching Heines blasting away, until he saw one of *them* come up behind him. Then Brown reacted and put two into it, in quick succession. After that he joined what some would've considered a mass execution if only any of the crazy looking people had actually died. The bullets did their thing: tearing through muscle and bone, ripping apart organs and vessels, spraying blood everywhere, but the black-eyed creatures came on and on, regardless. They took their awful punishment in unholy silence. A few times a single shot would do the trick, but generally it took three or more to bring them down. Still, none of them actually died. When they dropped, they would continue to crawl at the troopers if they could or stretch out grasping hands, or just lie there growling, snapping their teeth.

When the grisly work was complete, or as complete as Brown and Heines could make it, the room was eerily quiet. There were a few tears and sniffles, and one poor woman who'd had all the fingers on her left hand bitten off was rocking back and forth, moaning, but other than that the room was shrouded in a stunned silence.

"An ambulance...we should...we should get an ambulance," Brown said with a stutter affecting his tongue. He felt hollow through and through and his fingers had lost all sensitivity; he couldn't feel the gun he held in a death grip.

"Hold on, will you?" Heines asked, putting out a shaky hand. He was gasping for breath and staring all around with wide eyes. "Just give me a moment to think."

"Your mask," Brown said, pointing with his pistol.

Heines touched his face and felt the blue mask that had slipped cock-eyed from his mouth. He put it back into place and then looked at his gloved hands: they were wet and black. "Is that stuff on me?" he asked.

"Yeah," Brown said.

"Shit. You got some on you, too. Right above your eye. No, don't touch it. We got to call this in and tell them that we…that we might be infected, too."

Brown began shaking his head as if denial were a strong component of a plan. "We don't know if we're infected. We don't even know what's going on." He looked around and his eyes fell on Morgan. "You, Miss, what's wrong with these people?"

"They have cancer," Morgan answered.

"Cancer that comes out of their eyes?" Brown asked, feeling a little madness begin to creep around the edge of his reality. To counter it he tried to rely on his training. "We should call an ambulance."

Yeah," Morgan agreed. "We gotta get out of here. There's more of them." The other admin workers all agreed to this. Some of them were bent over their injured co-workers trying to help in what small way they could, while others had backed to the corners of the room to be as far away as possible from the black-eyed creatures who were still struggling, however pathetically, to get at the living.

"But we're still under quarantine," Dean Redman said. This silenced the room again. Everyone stared around in fright, wondering if he was right.

"It'll be ok," Brown said. "We have guns, and we can get back up. You'll be safe."

"I'll call it in," Heines said. Without waiting for a response he began stepping gingerly towards the door. The floor was covered with the dead and the ghastly creatures that couldn't seem to die.

"Wait," Brown said, sharply. The madness inside him hadn't retreated a lick. It felt like it was growing inside his brain and was even then slipping under the lid of his realism.

Heines paused, expectantly, however Brown could only think of selfish things like running out of the room as fast as he could, or begging to be the one who got to call in the attack. He was deathly afraid that either he had already been infected or that he would be if he stayed one second longer. He was fearful of taking too deep a breath. And yet he was no coward. He bit back on the madness. "Have them bring lots of ambulances," he said.

"Right. Good idea. I'll make sure they bring four or…" Out of the blue, Heines cried out and pitched forward.

For a split second, Brown thought his partner was infected and actually took a step back, fear overriding his thinking. In truth, Heines had already been infected, they all were, however his issue was more acute. One of the crazy people they had gunned down had lurched forward, and grabbed hold of the cuff of Heines' starched uniform. Its mouth gaped and before Heines knew what was going on the infected person had bitten into his lower leg severing his Achilles tendon.

The pain was magnificent. It was fire and ice raging up the back of his leg and right up his spine. A scream that put all the other screams that day to shame, tore out of his lungs. Brown had never considered himself much of a quick draw, yet his service pistol cleared his holster in a quarter second. He fired at a downward angle into the monster's head and blew brains and a good deal of blood onto the carpet.

The creature, who had been Dakota Oswalt earlier in the day, was the first person to actually die in the Walton facility since Ray took an unlucky bullet to the back of his head. The others: Paolo and those massacred on the third floor, Vince and the CDC people, Preston and Earl, weren't as dead as they seemed. Even then some of them were beginning to twitch. The Com-cells had never stopped reproducing and the stem cells within them healed at a rate no scientist could have believed.

When the scream had run its course, Heines said through gritted teeth, "I'm fucked."

"No, you're not," Brown insisted. "Let me see." There was an outrageous chunk missing from the back of his ankle. "You'll be fine," Brown lied after swallowing loudly. "Let me just get these fuckers out of here and then I'll get you that ambulance."

"What about us?" Morgan asked.

"You're not even hurt," Brown snapped. He stood and surveyed the room. "Those of you who are hurt will get an ambulance. The rest of you, drag these things out of here." He showed them how by grabbing one by the ankle. Ineffectually, it tried to turn itself around to get at him. "Just keep out of reach of its mouth and you should be fine."

He hauled it out into the corridor and then as soon as he saw some of the survivors helping he left them to call his dispatcher. Brown jogged back to the front lobby and stopped just at the end of the admin section. There were more of the black-eyed people wandering around the lobby.

"This is the sickest," he said, before changing out the clip in his weapon. He knew that if any got within five feet of him he would shoot first and not stop to ask questions.

"Here we go," he whispered, psyching himself up. With a deep breath, he ran for the doors. Two of *them* saw him and shambled after. They were quicker than he expected and he thought it safest just to shoot them: two into the one on the left, three into the one on the right. Brown then turned and ran for the doors where another was simply standing there squinting and turning its head like a curious dog. He brought his gun up to drop this one too, but it spoke.

"Don't shoot," it said and then raised a hand.

Brown was so surprised he almost jerked off a round accidentally. He slid his finger off the trigger. "Ok, man. It's going to be cool. I'm going to call ambulances for everyone. I won't leave you behind."

The creature had a name, though he barely remembered it

even with the Diazepam dripping into his veins. The hate in his brain was like one long explosion that drowned almost everything else out. "Ambulance? For me?" Von Braun asked. "What about for them?"

He pointed behind Brown, who turned. At the last second, when he felt the barrel of a gun jab into his spine, Brown realized he had fallen for the simplest trick in the book. Von Braun pulled the trigger and there was an ear-splitting retort and then a strange combination of pain and numbness within Brown that flooded outward in waves from the point of impact.

Brown fell and Von Braun descended on him with his mouth wide like a modern day Dracula. The blood was good and fresh and it made Von Braun feel alive and, for a few minutes at least, clean.

## 3

Thuy had not meant for the questioning of John Burke to feel like an interrogation. She had also meant for it to take place in private, instead twenty of the twenty-three people trapped on the fourth floor were arrayed around the man in a semicircle. Thuy ordered everyone to leave, however Milner pointed out that she no longer had any authority and that if she wasn't fired the second Kip and Rothchild heard about the fiasco, he would quit.

"Why don't you go call them while we take care of business here," Deckard advised. His hard tone and his cold eyes left no room for misinterpretation: Milner would leave or Deck would throw him out. Having already been punched, Milner made a quick getaway.

"Her, too," Thuy said, pointing at Anna. Thuy knew she may not have authority over the others but there was no way she was going to let that traitor bitch stay. Anna left without making a scene, which was wise, since the other scientists were glaring at her harshly. "Riggs?" Thuy asked. "Do you mind keeping an eye on her? I don't want to even think about what sort of mischief she might get into if she were left alone."

"Is there something going on with her?" Stephanie Glowitz asked. She could barely keep herself propped up on Chuck's shoulder. It had been a long, disappointing day for her—first being late, then finding out that there wasn't a cure after all, and, lastly, the hard work of helping to fill up the stairwells with anything she could carry. She was coughing again and the ache in her chest felt like she had swallowed a nine-volt battery that had gotten lodged behind her sternum.

"Anna did all this," one of the scientists declared.

"We should throw her down the stairs," another demanded.

"Everyone quiet down," Thuy snapped. "We aren't going to throw anyone down the stairs. And if you wish to stay, you need to shut up. Now, so far, Mr. Burke you are the only one immune to the negative effects of the Com-cells and there has to be a reason why. I need to know everywhere you've been in the last two weeks, and everything you've eaten, everything you drank and everything you snorted or shot up or whatever."

"Everthin'?"

"Start with yesterday," Thuy said.

It lasted twenty-five minutes and not one of those minutes went by without someone asking a follow up question—*Did you have any sauce with that? What did you take your pills with? When did you go to bed?*

Thuy charted everything from what motels he had stayed in, to what cars he had driven. Just then it felt like a waste of time, but there was no knowing what the information would mean when more facts were in. In the middle of Burke's questioning there came the sound of more gunshots from lower in the building. It was Heines and Brown in the break room; the mumbly bangs went on for close to a minute.

Milner came running in. "They're shooting downstairs!"

"No shit," Chuck drawled.

John, who was happy not to have everyone staring at him for once said, "It's prolly the police finally done showed up."

"Maybe you should call the State troopers and see if they have any new information," Thuy suggested to Milner. "And find out what's going on with the CDC. Their agents should have been here ages ago." When he left, Thuy ignored the whispering that had sprung up and went back to grilling Burke.

Eventually, no one could think of anything else to ask John. In the quiet that followed, Stephanie said to Thuy: "You never really answered me, what was with that lady? What did she do?"

Thuy gestured to Deckard who replied, "What we know is that she's been slipping information concerning the Comcells to one of R&K's biggest competitors. We have email confirmation of this."

"That's what we know," Thuy said. "What we're very sure of but can't prove just yet, is that she also sabotaged the trial somehow. What's happening to those people isn't anything found in nature. It couldn't have just happened by itself."

"And you're just letting her go about free?" Stephanie asked. A small part of her was happy that she had dodged a bullet concerning the sabotaged trial, another part was furious that someone would do something like this. "She should be...someone should...I don't know what, but I'm mad as hell. This was my only chance." Tears sprang into her eyes and she put her hands out to Dr. Lee as if begging. "If you find out what went wrong, will there be another trial?"

"Maybe," Thuy answered, not meeting her eyes. "But if there is, I won't be heading it and it won't be in time for you two."

"Son of a bitch," Chuck said. He had a very slow fuse, but when it was lit it stayed lit. "Someone should do something."

Again Thuy and Deck traded looks and she again nodded to him to answer. "There's nothing more we can do until the authorities get here and take over the situation. Everything will come out eventually, I'm sure."

"Not in time for all those poor people in the stairs," Stephanie said. "And not in time for us."

"I'd do sumptin' but I has my baby girl to think on," Burke said. Thuy nearly choked. She hadn't yet told Burke about his daughter being infected.

"Then I'll do it," Chuck said. "All that shooting means the cops are here and everyone knows she'll hide herself behind the law just as soon as she can. If y'all want real answers out of her, now's the only time you'll get 'em."

"What are you going to do?" Thuy asked as Chuck stood up. With his boots on, he was the tallest man in the room and very intimidating when he squinted down at her.

"I think you know."

She couldn't comprehend what was on the verge of happening. Was Chuck Singleton suggesting torture?"You'll get in trouble," Thuy whispered.

"It not America way," Eng declared. "This not right." He didn't care about America and clearly right or wrong didn't mean all that much to him—he cared about himself. Anna hadn't sabotaged anything, and wouldn't be able to answer the simplest question. If she endured the torture, some would think she was telling the truth and their suspicions would go elsewhere. In Eng's eyes, it was better for the American police to investigate. They were notoriously slow and inept; every good Chinese citizen knew that.

"Thanks for the civics lesson," Chuck drawled. "You'll make a great American when you can speak the fuckin' language." He clapped Eng on the back and headed for the door.

"Deck?" Thuy asked, flicking her dark eyes at Chuck. She was still the boss as far as Deckard was concerned. He stood and cleared his throat.

Chuck paused at the door. "You ain't the law, boy. Don't pretend otherwise."

"I'm not pretending. I know I'm not the law. It's you who seems not to have a grasp on the fact. We don't know what happened here and you jumping in half-cocked isn't going to make anything better."

The Okie was flinty-eyed and though he gave up fifty pounds of muscle to Deckard he wasn't one to back down. "Just to let you know, I don't do anythin' halfcocked. If that woman's been up to no good I'm gonna to find out."

"You people may want to give us some space," Deck said to the scientists between him and Chuck. Deckard didn't really want to fight. There was no real honor in beating up a man on the verge of dying. Sadly, it looked like Chuck wasn't going to give him any choice.

As the scientists scrambled for safer seats, Chuck cracked his knuckles. "Law or no law, there's a thing called justice, boy. If she been stealin' for some big corporation it don't take much of a leap to think she been-a sabotagin' for it, too."

"That's what evidence is for," Deck said coming forward. "And let's say you are right. If you hurt her, you have to know her lawyer will turn that against the prosecution. She might end up going free."

"And I might end up savin' some lives."

They were eye to eye, neither giving an inch, when the phone rang. Dr. Wilson, who didn't know which side to come down on, picked it up, hoping it was the police with some news.

"R&K Industries," he said. "Dr. Wilson speaking." Wilson had a deep, soothing voice that he had cultivated over the years. Cancer patients seemed to find it calming. It was a distinctive voice.

"Oh, hey, it's the nigger. You still thinking you can be a doctor just like white folk? Don't you know they keep you around to amuse them? You're like a chimp that rides a tricycle."

"Von Braun?" If it wasn't for the racist crap, Wilson wouldn't have recognized the prisoner's voice—he sounded like he was speaking around a throat full of razor blades.

"Yes. Good job, chimpy. You earned your banana, now let me talk to the gook. She's got something I need."

The name Von Braun had caused the room to go still and quiet. Wilson held the phone out to Dr. Lee. "He wants to talk to you."

"I can't believe he can talk," Thuy said, excitedly, hoping that this meant the negative effects of the Com-cells were temporary. "Hello, Mr. Von Braun! It's so good to hear your voice. Where are you?"

At first there was nothing on the other end of the line except heavy breathing then Von Braun hissed, "Cunt! Whore! Bitch!" Shocked, she held the phone out and stared at it as he went on, "You have the cure and I want it."

"I'm afraid there is no cure yet. How are you doing this? Talking I mean. Are there others like you who can talk?"

"Stop your lying!" he screamed into the phone. "You have it. I know it. Now give it or I will kill all of you. Believe that, bitch. I want the goddamned cure and if you don't give it over in thirty minutes, I'll fucking kill all of you!" He slammed down the phone.

The good feeling drained out of her. She believed Von Braun. He would try to kill them and given the fact that he could talk it meant that he could also think, at least on some rudimentary level. It might be enough for him to get past the doors.

"Find Milner," she snapped at Deck. "See if he knows when the police are coming." As he hurried out of the room, she turned to the other scientists, the three patients and Wilson. "That was a man named Von Braun. He was a prisoner who was treated this morning along with all the rest. Somehow he can talk, which means he can still think. He says he going to kill us."

"He's probably taking barbiturates of some sort," Dr. Wilson said. "Nurse Freeman was able to function better than her...I almost said colleagues. That's funny. I should say, she was doing better than the others who were infected because she was popping mega-doses of valium."

"Oh," Thuy said, disappointed. "Well, that information should help us, I hope. But for now..." She faltered as Deck slipped back into the room. "What is it, Deck? Where are the police?"

"Milner's been on hold with the CDC this entire time. He doesn't know anything except that there should be CDC agents somewhere on the property, but they aren't answering their cell phones. I'm starting to get the feeling no one knows what's going on around here."

**4**

The dispatcher, Courtney Shaw, had finally reached a stage where emotion seeped into her radio voice. "Say again Echo 2. What is your ETA?"

"Thirty five minutes."

Courtney looked at her map and saw where Echo 2 was supposed to be—it was twenty minutes away with the siren hot. This meant Echo 2 had been *off route*, probably checking in with one of his mistresses. The man was notorious.

"You understand we have an officer down? One injured and one MIA?" Her anger rippled across hundreds of miles of airwaves and she didn't care in the least. This was one call that had turned into a nightmare. She was simultaneously trying to talk to the CDC, half a dozen frightened hospital workers, and Sergeant Heines who had no clue where his partner had gone to, or where the rest of the CDC team was, or really what was happening at all.

She checked the board for the third time that minute. She had rerouted three cruisers to the Walton facility—it didn't seem like enough, however she would need permission to send more. It was something she wasn't looking forward to.

Courtney rang Lieutenant Pemberton. He made a tired noise when he heard her voice. "Is this about the 'zombies' again?" It had been a mistake mentioning the word, she knew that now.

"Yes, sir. The current situation is a bit convoluted. There are twenty three personnel trapped on the fourth floor and thirty one, including Sergeant Heines trapped in a room on the first floor."

"And they're trapped by zombies?" The disbelief in his voice was obvious and annoying.

"That's the word some people are using," she answered.

He exhaled loudly into the phone. "I swear if this is some sort of prank, I will not be happy."

"Yes, sir," Courtney replied. "It's not. The CDC in Atlanta is thinking that environmental exposure to some toxin is causing the odd behavior."

She could hear him tapping his pen through the phone line. He asked, "And they're on scene?"

"We don't know. A team supposedly arrived about an hour ago. We confirmed one is dead, however the other two are MIA. The CDC is sending up another team, with an ETA of about midnight."

"Taking their sweet time, aren't they?" he growled as if it was her fault they were being so slow. "When do our own lab boys get there?"

She knew this was going to be sticky. "The Mid-Hudson team won't arrive until around eight." Before he could begin yelling, she added, "They were already on another run and their van broke down. I called Albany but they're making excuses. They're going to need someone with more authority than I have to send out a team."

"Did you use the term zombie? Because if you did…"

"I didn't, sir. I said we had a possible biological hazard with deaths involved. They're moving as fast as they can."

Pemberton was quiet for a moment before slamming his pen down in frustration. "Zombies…motherfucker! I don't want to see that word in anything official. Man, I hate this. We have at least three KIAs, who knows how many MIAs, and it feels like we're just sitting around. What about ambulance and emergency support?"

"The Kingston fire department has sent two trucks, Havilland and Millbrook have sent one each. Unfortunately, not only is the facility now under a Class 1 quarantine, we only have a Millbrook sheriff's deputy and a single trooper on site. I have three more troopers heading in, but I need permission for anything more."

"Yes, fine. Send what we have available, but keep everyone back until you hear from me," Pemberton said, hanging up abruptly. He made a call to his boss, Major Billups, who called his boss, Lieutenant Colonel Parks, who called the CDC in Atlanta, who called the New York CDC office, only to get a recording. Thus began a forty six minute pause in the chain of command.

Eventually, a half mile from the Weston facility gates, four fire trucks, five ambulances, three state police cruisers, and four local police cruisers sat parked with their lights blasting the rainy evening waiting for the word *go*. The minutes ticked by and, as each passed, the thirty one employees stuck in the first floor break room grew edgier and edgier. First they fidgeted or complained of headaches, then, when the migraines set in, they lay on the ground clutching their heads and groaning.

When the phone rang, Heines snarled at it through twisted lips and smashed it with the butt of his gun. The snarl felt good. Venting his anger and hate felt really good. Inside him was a nasty, evil feeling that hurting someone would feel even better. He was stuck on the idea that he could transfer his pain to someone else with his fists or with his teeth. It was an idea he fought for some time, but at 6:32 PM he'd had enough of being good, of waiting for the authorities to get their shit together, of living in pain. He was dying of *the disease* as everyone in the room had taken to calling it and he was fucking tired of it.

"I have to do something," Heines said. He tried to stand but his injured leg wouldn't hold his weight. "Fuck!" he raged. "What are we going to do? They're keeping us stuck in this room for no reason except to maybe watch us die. I bet they're laughing right now."

Everyone knew who *they* were and looked up at the ceiling. "They're laughing because they have the cure," Jodi Schmelling said.

Morgan no longer craved cigarettes; they were a pale vice in comparison to what she really wanted. "We should go get it." She wasn't really thinking about a cure, she was thinking how much she needed to wet her mouth with blood.

**Chapter 10**

**//6:39 PM//**

**1**

Von Braun's threat had effectively ended the crisis over torturing Anna Holloway. The group on the fourth floor was in too weak a position not to take his threat seriously and all thoughts of a fight between Chuck and Deckard evaporated in a blink.

"We're going to need more of your smarts," Deck said to Thuy after he'd toured the floor, looking for ways the infected people could get at them. There was a gaping hole in their defenses and it was a wonder it hadn't been exploited before.

"I'm using them at the moment," Thuy replied. She had just got off the phone after a lengthy conversation with Jaimee Burke. Thuy had quizzed her in the same manner as she had her father only to discover the young girl was of little help. Jaimee wasn't very bright to begin with and her mental faculties had deteriorated over the last two hours. She was still far better off than any of the other infected persons but there was a slight change that Thuy had discerned.

"You're smart, Deck," Thuy went on. "Whatever you need I'm sure you can figure it out. And there are other scientists running around here, some of them are smart, too."

"That's just it," Deck said. "They are running around *doing* things while you're holed up in your office. It almost seems like you're hiding."

Thuy sat back with arms folded and stared hard at Deckard. "It's called delegation. You job is security. I expect you to secure the place. I am a scientist. My job is to make hypotheses, test my hypotheses and, if possible, discover facts. What everyone else is doing is up to them. It's safe to say that I'm no longer in charge."

"If you're not in charge then nobody is and we're screwed."

"Then you be in charge," Thuy said. "You're all big and manly. They'll listen to you."

Deck went to the glass wall and leaned back against it. He found himself smiling at her. "Two compliments in one conversation. I feel like I'm getting a pat on the head and a push in the back. You must really want me to leave."

"I am busy…"

"Stop it," Deck growled. "The only reason you're not in charge is because you've given up. Milner said what he said and you just folded. I'd happily be in charge but I'm *just* security in your eyes and in theirs. If there's killing to do, everyone will turn to me, but in the meantime, I'm being treated like the help."

"And there's something you need?" Thuy wasn't about to address how Deck was being treated. There was definitely a pecking order in academia. Ph.Ds lauded their degrees and looked down their noses at those with only a master's degree, and rarely conversed with anyone who had only a bachelor's. It became ingrained in school and people forgot that although it was nice to get a degree, it was even better to actually do something with it.

"I need you in charge," Deck said. "Right now we have mayhem and bickering. If Von Braun can find a way through the doors we'll be dead."

"What about the police?"

Deck shook his head as he answered, "They're waiting for the CDC to give them clearance to come in and no one knows where the CDC is."

"Then it's just us for the moment." Thuy pushed back from her desk and stood. "Show me the problem." Deck opened the door for her and the sounds of the infected people out in the stairwell, struck her ears. Their groans and growls were muted by the doors but their ceaseless banging echoed throughout the floor. It was haunting and unnerving.

Thuy did her best to ignore it as she followed Deck. "It's the elevator," he said. "There's very little stopping Von Braun from just turning the control key. He could be up here in thirty seconds with a car full of zombies."

She raised an eyebrow at the word "zombie", but let it pass. "And we can't lock the doors ourselves." It was a statement. The outer elevator doors were flat, there was no obvious way to lock them or hold them in a closed position. She turned to Deck. "What about tools? There were workmen all over this place yesterday."

"They finished up here yesterday, too. Right now we don't even have a screw driver."

A number of scientists had followed them and Riggs was with them. "That's not exactly true," he said. "We can pry open the doors and I was thinking that maybe if we could run a line over from the gas supply, we could cut one of the cables."

"Show me," Thuy said, stepping back.

Riggs had armed himself with a sliver of metal he had pried from the inside of one of the centrifuges. It looked like a prison shiv. He stuck the edge in the crack of the doors and worked them just far enough apart so that he and Deck could get their fingers in. The two men hauled back on the doors until the elevator shaft sat like a black pit before them.

Thuy stepped forward and peered in at the cables. She then looked back at Riggs and saw a man whom she barely recognized. The stress had given him a ragged appearance. His sandy blond hair stuck up at odd angles and his eyes were very round as if he was walking around in a state of constant surprise.

"I'm afraid that won't work," she told him. "We have propane, yes, however we don't have pure oxygen, and even if we did we don't have any way to mix them properly. Riggs, don't you realize we're talking about a fifteen hundred degree temperature difference using only room air compared to pure oxygen. Propane alone won't be able to cut those cables."

Riggs was shaking his head with jerky little snaps of his neck. "But...but there's O2 on the second floor. If we can run a new line up..."

Thuy touched his arm and tried to smile away his fears. "No. We can't get to the second floor and even if we could there's no telling how the Com-cells are spreading. If it's in the air we risk getting contaminated."

"We need to do something," Anna said. "It wouldn't hurt to try using the propane." A few of the other scientists were nodding as were Dr. Wilson and Chuck. Deck was grim-faced and shook his head at Thuy.

She caught his meaning. If she didn't assume command they would try every bad idea under the sun until they ran out of time and Von Braun attacked. "No," Thuy said. "I will fix the elevator so it doesn't run. The rest of you need to split up into three teams. Each team will guard a staircase. Deckard, Mr. Singleton, and Dr. Riggs will be the captains. They will choose who's on their teams. It'll be like in school."

"So that means I'll be picked last," one of the smaller scientists said with a smile. She wasn't quite five feet in height and had the bones of a bird.

"I'd rather not be picked at all," Stephanie said. "But I also don't want to get turned into one of *them*."

"Go ahead, Mr. Singleton," Thuy said to Chuck. "You get first pick."

As they divided into groups, she turned away to stare into the elevator shaft. She squinted into the dark until a pale light streamed from behind her to light up the shadows. It was Anna holding up her cell phone.

"I'll be picked last, if I'm picked at all," she explained.

"Do you blame them?" Thuy asked.

"Yeah, a little. I'm in the same boat as the rest of you. If

Von Braun makes it up here it won't be like I'm immune or anything." The light dimmed and Anna touched the surface of her cell phone to brighten it again. She saw Thuy's wide eyes. "Don't worry, I'm allowed to have it. That idiot Deckard gave it back to me. He said: *It'd be stealing if I kept it*. He's like a pretend cop. I know he's hoping I use it to call my contact or whatever."

"Seems smart to me," Thuy replied.

"Yeah, except I don't have a 'contact' and if I did I wouldn't be stupid enough to use my own phone to call him. That's the problem with Deckard playing cop. Whatever evidence he comes up with will be illegally obtained and not admissible in court."

"Clearly you would have made a better a lawyer than a scientist," Thuy said, acidly.

"Well, one way or another we'll all be looking for a new career tomorrow...if we live to tomorrow. That's why I'm helping you. I admit I'm not a fighter and most of your people aren't nearly as brilliant as they'd like to believe.

"And you are?" Thuy asked. When Anna smiled, suggesting she was, Thuy said, "Show me. How do we stop the elevator from coming up here?"

The blonde swung her hair across her left shoulder and then eased closer to the shaft, shining her cell phone light up and down the walls. After a few moments she said, "We can cut the cable. We'd first have to fashion a saw from metal..."

Thuy spoke over her, "Von Braun is already late carrying out his attack. It could happen any minute now. Meaning we don't have time to be fashioning tools like a caveman."

Anna's smile disappeared and her lips drooped at the edges, making her look like a fish. "I don't know...maybe we could set a beam or something at an angle down in the shaft that would block the elevator from..."

"Do you see any spare beams lying around?"

Now Anna glared. "So, you're just trying to be vengeful?

Figure it out yourself."

She turned to leave but Thuy grabbed her arm. "I have already figured it out, I was just trying to see if you had a better idea. Dr. Riggs, may I borrow your knife, please?"

Slowly, Riggs brought it out and was even slower handing it over. "That's my only weapon." He was like a child being asked to give up a favorite toy.

"I need it to hold the elevator. You understand." It didn't look like he understood. It looked like he had been suddenly rendered impotent. To Anna she said, "Point your light across from us. See those concrete rings sitting one on top of each other? Those are the counter weights for the elevator car. When the elevator comes up, those go down. What I need you to do is wedge this knife right up against the rail underneath them."

"How? How am I going to reach that far?"

Thuy squinted into the shaft as if expecting to see something more than darkness. She then shrugged and answered, "You climb."

Anna looked down; the shaft was midnight black. It could've been ten feet deep or ten thousand, there was no way of telling. She backed into Thuy's hand. "No," Thuy said, holding her there just inches from the edge. "You've admitted you can't fight and you've proven you aren't up to snuff when it comes to problem solving. I hope you can contribute to our dire cause with the simple act of climbing, something any second grader could do. It won't be that difficult. There are a couple of handholds, and you can put your feet on that little pipe."

After a long moment, when Anna realized Thuy wasn't really giving her a choice, she said, "Alright. I'll do it, but just to show you that I'm on your side." She handed over the phone and accepted the knife, which she stuffed down the front of her blouse where her full breasts and her push-up bra held it in place.

She reached out for the first hold with the cell phone light full on her shaking hand. It almost seemed like Thuy was mocking her by showing each hold and then pointing out how frightened she was by letting the light linger on her quivering hands. She was dreadfully slow. Anna gripped every hold as though she was never planning on letting go. It made her palms slippery, which only added to her fright.

Finally, she made it to the counter-weight at the back of the shaft. "Just stick it up there?" she asked.

"Yes," Thuy replied. "Wedge it up as far as it will go and hurry. If the elevator starts now…"

Anna knew. She shoved the hunk of metal as far up as it would go and then hammered on it with the palm of her hand. When it wouldn't go any further she said, "I did it. That thing is stuck up there good."

"Problem solved," Thuy said. "The potential energy of the weights shouldn't be able to overcome the friction generated by the knife against the rail. We should be safe now. You can come on back." Thuy guided her with the light until Anna reached the first corner then unexpectedly she turned the cell phone off.

"Hey!" Anna froze in place.

"Before you come back, I need to know what you did," Thuy whispered. "What did you do to the Com-cells?"

"Th-This isn't f-funny," Anna stuttered.

Thuy was secretly pleased at the obvious fear. "What you did to the Com-cells wasn't funny either. Lives are at stake here, Anna, and more importantly to you, at least, is that your life is now at stake."

"I-I didn't do anything," Anna insisted. "Please, you have to believe me."

"I don't," Thuy said, through clenched teeth. Standing, she reached up and touched a small lever at the top of the elevator door. It held the doors open when maintenance needed to do repairs. "I'm going to shut the doors now and it's going to get very dark. You won't be able to see where the handholds are and eventually you'll grow tired and fall."

"Dr. Lee, please," Anna begged.

"I'll open the door only when you tell me what you did."

Anna shook her head. "I didn't do anything. But...if...if you want me to say I spied then ok I'll say it. I spied on your research and sent coded messages on to a professor at Cornell. Ok? That's all I did. I didn't do anything to the Com-cells. I swear."

Thuy had expected just this: admitting to a crime that she had already been fingered for. "I'll be waiting just outside when you're ready. I wouldn't be too long if I was you."

"Dr. Lee! Thuy, please don't." Anna's face was a pale oval and her eyes little glints of light. Thuy was moved to pity—she struck the feeling down. There were lives at stake, it hadn't been just a cliché. Besides, she knew Anna would talk.

"Sorry," Thuy said, and then hit the lever.


**2**


Four floors down, Von Braun was hooking up another bag of Diazepam with fingers that felt like they were made of wood. He had been sitting at the bottom of the stairs trying to figure out how to make his threat of killing everyone into a reality. Unfortunately the stairwell doors on the fourth floor had stubbornly resisted every attempt he and the other zombies had made to open them. So far they had tried pushing *and* pulling. When that didn't work they tried pushing and pulling really, really hard. He had a few tools at his disposal but not a crow bar or an acetylene torch.

Von Braun found himself out of his ideas, except the overarching idea that he had to get up there and find the cure. He hated the scientists who, he was sure, were laughing at him, but what he hated more was that his head was filled with such horrors that even he, one of the most loathsome humans on the planet, couldn't stand it.

It was like hell had hatched in his mind. He needed blood. He craved it. He wanted to bathe in it and he needed to drink it. The fresher, the hotter, the better.

As he was sitting there grinding his teeth and hating everything about humanity, a police officer came limping around the corner. The bag of Diazepam dropped to the floor, forgotten as he rushed at the officer intending to rip his throat open. Three steps away, Von Braun stopped in his tracks. It wasn't the gun pointing at him that halted his feet. It was the smell.

The man smelled like shit. There was nothing clean about him. His skin wasn't dusky with the spores yet and his eyes weren't black, but he still smelled nasty. Von Braun turned away in disgust and, remembering the Diazepam, he shuffled back to the stairs where he slammed himself down. He fumbled for the bag.

"Get out of the way," the officer demanded. Behind him were thirty others. They stank, as well.

"The doors are locked," Von Braun said. Finally, he got the Diazepam hooked to his IV. The relief was instantaneous. It doused the fires of his mind and he was able to regain more of his mental abilities. He looked up to see the cop staring at him.

"You can talk," Heines said, squinting. His vision was beginning to fade and yet he could see Von Braun's black eyes plain as day. "But you're one of them."

Von Braun grunted. "I think you mean you're one of us. All of you stink. Can't you smell yourselves?"

"Like shit," Morgan whispered.

"You're one of us," Von Braun said again. "But the doors are locked at the top where *they* are. That's where I need to go, where I have to go, but the doors are locked."

Although Heines' ability to think was quickly fading, he still had his training ingrained in him. "I can get us through a locked door," he said, picturing what he needed: *the hammer*. He remembered Brown used to say: 'It's hammer time' whenever they had to breach a door. There was a little dance that Brown would do as well only just then the memory of it was just out of reach.

It nagged at him, haunting him deep in the last clear area of his brain. "Something about how I couldn't touch it," he whispered. "And there were pants..." The memory worried at his mind until he was forced to give up on ever recalling it.

"Wait here," Heines ordered the others. He began lurching toward the way out and as he passed through the front doors he almost stepped on the body of his partner, Wendell Brown. He didn't notice and wouldn't have cared if he had noticed. Like the dance move, Brown was already fading from his memory.

But he still had his training.

When he reached the cruiser, he ducked in out of the rain and stared about its interior, again trying to recollect what he was doing—*the hammer* and *the cure*. Those were the two things that were important. The first thing he saw when he popped the trunk was his trusty twelve-gauge. Heines ignored it completely. The second thing he saw was *the hammer*. It was a twenty-pound breaching ram that had never met its match against any door.

He stuck it on his shoulder and slowly gimped his way back. The rain drenched him, but, surprisingly, he didn't feel the cold, nor did the gaping wound pain him. For the most part, he was numb both inside and out....unless his brain was taken into consideration. That mass of grey crap was still pounding as if the top of his head were just about to shoot off.

Von Braun watched Heines struggle with his wound and the weight of the ram, but he did nothing to help. Heines was a cop, a state trooper to be more precise. Von Braun could remember hating cops more than anything. "You a cop," he accused when Heines got back.

This was the last thing Heines had expected to hear and the only answer he could come up with was, "Huh?"

"That badge means you're a cop," Von Braun said, poking him in the chest. "It means you're one of them. One of the ones who did this to us."

"I'm not! I don't have the cure," Heines shot back.

"You're their guard dog." Von Braun stood in Heines' way. That the thirty people gathered all around the cop had far more to do with the clinical trial didn't enter into Von Braun's thinking at all. They looked like dull, middleclass, business types; it was as far as his mind could go in that direction. But the cop was different. He represented authority, a hated concept that was deeply ingrained in Von Braun.

And in this case authority meant he was one of them. One of the people in power. One of the people he hated. Heines might have the smell, yet his look wasn't right. He wore a badge and that was definitely wrong.

He reached out and snatched the badge off the trooper's chest. "This is what tells me…"

Heines smashed him in the chest with the ram and then proceeded up the stairs. Behind him came the admin workers. They ignored Von Braun who lay gasping for breath, and they ignored the other full on zombies, who smelled horrible: there was no salvation in their blood.

For the most part the zombies ignored them right back, though every once in a while, one would turn, see the clear skin, and attack. These attacks were always short lived and didn't amount to much. One taste of the diseased flesh was enough for a zombie to know it wasn't pure and quickly they would spit out the mouthful.

Heines slogged upward. The stairwell was littered top to bottom with lab equipment, shattered glass, tables, desks, chairs…it was like an entire office had been poured down the stairs. It made for slow going, yet he was determined.

At the top, a dozen zombies were pounding on the door

with their fists. The skin of their knuckles had long ago worn away and blood sprayed with every strike.

"Out of the way," Heines commanded. When they continued to pound, he reached up and began hauling them back from the door. Morgan and Jodi helped, throwing the zombies back down the stairs, heedless of who they landed on.

"Morons!" Heines yelled after them when he saw the door handle. "You're supposed to pull." He tugged the handle and when it didn't budge, he yanked harder, screaming, "Come on! Open you fuckers!"

The others tried to crowd him to get at the door, but he pushed them back. "No. *The hammer*. It's hammer time."

He hefted the ram and then sent it crashing against the metal door making a noise like thunder. It echoed throughout the building in a long wave that caused people to jump.

On the third floor, Dr. Hester heard it and made a little whimpering noise. A floor above, Deckard heard it and had his gun drawn in an instant. Thuy heard it and understood exactly what it meant: Von Braun was attacking! She made a split second decision and threw herself between the closing elevator doors. Anna heard it, panicked and lunged for a handhold, desperate to escape. In the dark she missed the metal bar.

3

"Anna!" Thuy screamed. Forgetting everything, she dropped to her belly and had just begun searching the dark with the cell phone when the doors closed on her waist. She groaned in pain and had to force her knee up at an odd angle to keep from being pinched in half by the heavy doors.

Another crash rippled through the building. *Von Braun is coming!* The frightening thought made Thuy want to up and run, however just then she heard a ragged, whiny breath from somewhere below her. Thuy turned the cell light toward the sound and saw Anna clinging to the side of the elevator shaft by one hand.

She was trying to reach for another handhold but she was too weak and couldn't pull herself up. "Dr. Lee…help…me." She was straining to hold her grip yet her fingers, even as Thuy watched, were slowly pulling back.

"Hold on," Thuy pleaded. It might have been the single dumbest thing she had ever said, but just then she wasn't using much of her brain. Her fear over Von Braun had been multiplied by the two thundering crashes and now, added to that, was her fear of Anna falling to her death. She was having trouble thinking straight.

The light in her hand shook and jitterbugged as it panned over Anna. The woman blinked and Thuy realized she was again being stupid, blinding her uselessly. She roved the light all around Anna as another boom shook the building. The vibration seemed to go right to Thuy's chest and shake her heart.

"Your right foot!" she cried. "There's an electrical conduit right above it. There…just lift…yes!" Anna used her foot to lift herself just enough for her left hand to find a hold. "Good job," Thuy said. "Now, move your left foot a few inches out…"

"Dr. Lee!" Stephanie Glowitz cried, running up to the elevator doors. She started to pull Thuy out from between them.

"Stop," Thuy yelled. "Anna's down here."

Stephanie dropped Thuy's ankle. "We need you. They're breaking through the central doors and no one knows what to do."

Thuy hesitated caught by indecision. Anna saw it, she hissed, "Don't leave me, please. Dr. Lee, damn it, you did this to me! You can't leave me!"

Guilt and fear tore at Thuy. Another of the crashes tipped her in favor of fear. "I'll be right back, Anna. Just hold on. It'll be ok." She squirmed backward and the doors began to close.

"No!" Anna screamed. "Don't leave…" The doors shut, cutting her off.

"You can't worry about her," Stephanie said, hauling Thuy along by her lab coat. "She brought this on herself and…and I'm sure she'll be fine." Stephanie had no idea if she would be or not, nor did she really care. She only knew that there were forty or fifty zombies trying to tear down the stairwell door. The scientists called them infected persons; everyone else knew better. Those things were zombies, pure and simple.

She also knew that fear was making everyone reactionary. Only Thuy seemed to have been able to keep any wits about her.

Stephanie dragged Thuy out into the hall where they found everyone standing in a semi-circle around the stairwell door. They wore blue surgical masks and latex gloves; all the protection that was available. The men were in front. In their hands was a mishmash of pathetic weaponry: two held brooms while three others had mops; Dr. Wilson had Thuy's desk chair raised and ready, Eng had a couch cushion held in front of him. Leading the group were Deckard, Singleton and Riggs. Behind them were the women, cringing at each of the loud crashes, and looking ready to bolt.

"Do something," Stephanie said, desperately. Thuy understood. The door wouldn't hold for long and their defenses were pathetic. At a minimum every one of them would be infected. At the worst they would literally be ripped to shreds.

"We can't just stand here and wait for them to get through," Thuy said.

Deckard shrugged, grimly, his brow hanging heavy over his dark eyes. "You want us to go on the offensive? Probably a good idea. I'll lead the first wave. We need to get that ram before the door comes apart." Thuy marveled at him. Even in the face of terrible odds he seemed so sure of himself. It was this absolute fearlessness that made him so striking.

She wanted to trust in him. He was correct, getting the ram was paramount, however she knew he would be infected in the process...and he would die. "No," she said again, letting her eyes fall away.

Suggestions flew around the open hall as everyone spat out different ideas about what to do, but she didn't hear them. Her mind was somewhere else. With her labs in ruins she had to find the solution by digging deeper. Thuy knew the building inside and out better than anyone, except maybe Hal Kingman, the architect. She pictured the floor plan on the first day she walked in when the place was half finished. It was the day Deckard had bitched out Kingman to get the labs completed on time. Half the drywall hadn't even been hung, the tile had been stacked in piles all over the place and she had been able to see down into the cafeteria.

She had seen something in the flooring...black lines of...

The ram crashed again like a great bell. The door was beginning to bow inwards.

"So much for my idea," Riggs complained.

"You never had time anyway," Deckard replied. Thuy was staring right through him, but he mistook the faraway look for one of confusion. Deck tried to explain, "Riggs wanted to weld the door shut."

Thuy blinked, remembering what the lines were. "Riggs! The propane!" She left everyone standing at the door and raced into the nearest BSL-3 lab with Riggs right behind her.

"What about it? What about the..."

"Shut up," she said, holding a hand out to him. She was trying to recall the exact layout of the gas lines. It started as a single line that came up from the basement in a heavy rubber tube running along a conduit in the elevator shaft. This line eventually went to the electrician's closet where it went into a meter before it branched five ways, heading out to the labs. She pointed at the nearest gas port. "Uncouple that line!"

Riggs said, "Huh?"

"From beneath, hurry!"

He rushed to the port and, with fear-driven adrenaline lending strength to his hands, he broke the panel with one big yank. Thuy turned and sped back to the elevators, yelling, "Wilson, Eng! I need you."

In the electrical room she found the gas valve and yanked it hard all the way to the right, turning it off. The valve sprang from a steel panel screwed to the wall; without tools they would have to find a different way to get at the gas lines.

"Kick that open," she said to Wilson. When he hesitated Eng shot a front kick that was shocking in its violence; a second one was all it took and the panel fell to the floor, clattering. Thuy could see the five lines heading out to the labs—thankfully, each was labeled.

"That one," she said as another crash rocked the air. "Grab it and pull!" The two men reached in and started pulling at the black hose. It jerked back about a foot giving Thuy room to grab, also. Together they jerked the hose clear of the wall, a foot at a time.

"Now what?" Eng demanded. In his heightened state of fear, his accent had practically disappeared, but in the heat of the moment, Thuy didn't notice.

"Turn the gas back on when I tell you," she said, pulling the end of the hose out of the room and to the stairwell door; already the metal door was bent outward at the middle and there were gaps along the edges.

Deck had his pistol in one hand and was trying to get a bead on the man wielding the ram. Thuy elbowed him aside. "Now, Eng!" She shoved the hose into one of the gaps. In seconds, the smell of gas blossomed up causing everyone but Thuy to step back. Afraid that too much was leaking into the hall, she pushed the hose further in.

Right next to her the door boomed with another strike. "Get everyone further back," she said to Deckard. "One spark and…" She didn't need to finish her sentence. As he herded the scientists back, Thuy tried to buy herself time in order to let the gas build up.

"Von Braun!" she yelled.

On the other side of the door there were a few seconds of silence and then a man snarled, "Von Braun? Who is that?"

"You aren't Von Braun?" Thuy asked. Another one who could talk? The idea rattled her. "Um…if you're not Von Braun, why are you banging on the door?"

"I want the fucking cure. Give it to me! Give it to me, now!" The man pressed his face right up to one of the gaps and held his mouth open as if she had the "cure" in tablet form and would just pop it in.

"Just…just hold on," she replied. The smell of gas was becoming overpowering, the air in the stairwell shimmered with it. She turned to Deck who was halfway down the hall. She mimed flicking a lighter.

He shook his head and whispered, "I'll do it. Get back."

"Hold on for what?" the man demanded. "I'm not holding on for anything, damn it!"

"I'm getting the cure," she said, easing down the hall. "I'll be right back." When she got to Deck, she whispered, "How do we do this without getting blown up?"

"You're asking me? You're the genius, I'm just the muscle."

She studied the door, the ceiling, and the walls around it. "We'll need to keep at least fifteen paces back...so, maybe I could fasten a pulley above it using double sided tape, and then I can use some wiring to..."

Deck interrupted her. "Why don't we just use this?" He produced a Zippo lighter and thumbed it alight.

"Ok," she said. Her eyes, round and large, were on the flame. Her breath quickened; there was no telling what was about to happen. Her hands reached out and touched Deck's black shirt; just then she needed some reassurance.

He pulled her in close, his eyes also on the flame. "Here

goes nothing." With a deft move he slid the lit Zippo along the floor and then ducked down, clutching Thuy to his chest where his heart beat steadily in her ear, sounding like a clock ticking down on a bomb.

They huddled together as the lighter skittered to the stairwell door. There was a pause and then there was a tremendous sound: *Whuump!* The air flashed brilliantly white for a fraction of a second before it changed over to a combination of orange and black that washed over the pair.

Deck felt the heat bake into his back and instinctively he pulled Thuy tighter until he was almost crushing her. At first she didn't fight it. She held him with all her strength, but after a few seconds when she realized they were still alive she pulled back.

The hallway was burning in places: the linoleum along the edge of the door, the ceiling, the metal door itself. It was charred around the edges and there were blue flames running up it, but it was still closed.

"How come the door is..." Her words faltered--her voice sounded strange to her, as though she had just come back from the pool and there was water still in her ears.

"It happens. Explosions can be tricky," Deckard said. He then yanked off his mask and yelled, "Eng! Turn off the gas before you burn the whole place down!"

She started to get up and before she knew it he slid his hands up her sides and lifted her to her feet. Compared to him, she felt small, weak, delicate; a flower next to a burly oak--she hated the feeling.

"I'm fine, thank you," she said, holding herself at her full, stiletto modified, height. She pulled the edge of her lab coat down to straighten out the wrinkles and lifted her chin.

His only reply was a smirk. He strode over to the stove-in door, stomped out the linoleum fire, waved away the smoke and then peered through one of the cracks. "Mother-fu...I mean, uh, you've made quite a mess, Dr. Lee." He took hold of the gas line and pulled it from the crack in the door. It was burning like a torch so he stomped on it with his once shined shoes.

Thuy went to peer in through one of the cracks, but Deckard pulled her back. "I have to get that ram," he explained. "Besides, it's not pretty in there." With a grunt he disconnected the steel cable, which had been holding the door in place. He dropped it and pulled his weapon in the same instant.

When he reached for the door, Thuy stopped him. "Wait." She fished in one of her pockets and pulled out a new surgical mask for him. "For the Com-cells. Here, duck down."

He could've put the mask on himself, however he liked the feel of her hands on him, even in such a small thing. "Thanks," he said, his eyes crinkling above the mask, making Thuy wonder if he was smirking at her again. She never found out. Very gently he moved her back and then opened the door.

The air wafting in from the stairwell was acrid with the stench of burnt hair and roasted flesh. It made her want to gag. The sight that struck her didn't help. There were at least a dozen of the infected people who had been torched by the explosion—most were still on fire. Their clothes and hair were burning merrily, filling the stairwell with grey smoke. They seemed not to notice.

For the most part, the blast had laid them back and they floundered amidst the wreckage. Heines was easily the worst off. His hands had been flash-welded to the ram, and as Thuy watched he pulled one hand off, leaving behind a sheaf of skin, like an old snakeskin.

Deck shook his head in wonderment and then said to Thuy, "I need your coat."

She clutched it to her chest. "Why?" The feeling of being small crept over her and although the coat was the flimsiest protection possible against the zombies, it was better than nothing.

"Because I need it," Deckard growled, holding out his hand.

"You can have mine," Riggs said. A number of people had come up to see what effect the explosion had on the zombies, Riggs among them. He slipped off the coat and handed it over without an issue.

Deckard took the coat, sunk his pistol into its holster and then strode into the stairwell. He was grim; no smirk was discernible as he walked right up to Heines who was struggling to his feet. Thuy let out a groan as Deck planted a foot on the trooper's chest and pinned him down. He then used the lab coat as an oven mitt, wrapping the head of the ram with it and pulling it out of Heines' grip. When he lifted it, long strings of flesh hung from the ram like hot cheese from a slice of pizza.

"Oh my," Thuy said. She pushed past Dr. Milner to find better air in the hall. She was very close to losing her lunch.

A warm hand came down on her shoulder. "It'll be alright," Chuck Singleton said to her. "That ain't pretty, not by a stretch, but it'll pass. Don't you worry on it."

"Make way!" Deckard barked. With the ram held out at arm's length, he walked it down to the north end of the building to the BSL-4 labs. Thuy watched him until he was halfway down the hall, until Milner let out a cry.

"Get it off of me!"

With his hands no longer welded to the ram, Heines was free to move, and for someone who's skin was either charred black or sagging like candle wax from the heat he was surprisingly spry. In a fury he leapt up and attacked the closest person: Milner.

Milner had taken his eyes from the smoke-filled stairwell for only a second to see what Deckard was going to do with the ram. He suspected that the Neanderthal in a suit would just toss it in the hallway, not realizing that it was now very likely a vector carrying the disease. Before Milner could spout his ridicule something slammed into his back.

Heines went after Milner's throat, but the scientist was just able to turn away so that the teeth sunk into the muscle on the side of his neck instead of the soft flesh where half a gallon of blood surged back and forth every minute. This also rendered him capable of screaming which he did with more gusto than he used in actually protecting himself.

Singleton was closest. He had stepped back to make sure the ram and its dangling tendrils of burnt flesh didn't touch him. Now, he sprang into action. He was armed with a broom handle which he whip-cracked across Heines' skull. The top of the wood pole snapped right off and Heines didn't even blink.

"Shit," Chuck drawled. Milner continued to scream. Heines tore out a chunk of flesh and swallowed it without chewing. When he went back for seconds Chuck jammed the jagged edge of his broken broom handle down his gullet. Heines gagged and Chuck asked Milner, "You just gonna lay there?"

Milner wriggled out of Heines' grasp and then tried to escape out of the stairwell door. Burke stopped him by shoving a mop into his chest. "He got the disease," Burke said. "He was bit!"

Some of the scientists had been edging around the door, hopeful that propane blast had killed all the infected people. Now, they began backing away. Thuy elbowed her way to the front. "We don't know that Mr. Burke. But even if that's true, we can't leave him out there to be mauled, or eaten."

With the other zombies getting to their feet, this was a very real fear. "Please!" Milner begged. "I'll stay in one of the BSL-4 labs. I won't come out, I promise."

"Listen to him," Stephanie demanded, grabbing Burke's shoulder with desperate hands. "We have to let him back in. We're not savages like them." She didn't particularly like Milner, her primary concern was for Chuck who was fighting to keep Heines pinned down. As long as Milner stood in the doorway, Chuck was basically trapped.

Burke hesitated while Thuy started pushing the scientists back. "Out of the way," she demanded. "Give Dr. Milner some room." When they had pressed themselves flat against the walls she said to Burke, "Let him in, John, quickly."

Chuck's situation had become desperate. He was forced to let Heines go and was now using the broken broom handle like a bloody spear, jabbing it at the zombies on the stairs to keep them back. When John finally relented and Milner passed through the doorway, Chuck backed out of the stairwell and Stephanie pulled the door closed.

"The cable!" she yelled as the first body slammed against the door. Riggs and Eng were quick to reattach the steel cables and for a few moments everyone watched breathlessly as the door shook under the renewed assault. Without the ram battering it, the door held.

"That was crose," Eng said.

Thuy rolled her eyes at the jarring accent and then began ordering people about: "Burke, walk Milner down to the labs at the end of the hall and stand guard over him. Sorry, Dale it's just a precaution until we know if you're really infected."

"Ya'll blind?" Burke asked. "Course he's done got infected. He got bit."

"I was scratched by one earlier and I'm fine," Thuy countered. "We don't know if the infected gentleman was in a stage that rendered his disease communicable. Time will tell. Now, Deck and Singleton, find some ethyl alcohol and wash any of your exposed skin with it. It also wouldn't hurt to wipe down your clothing. Riggs and Eng, I need you two to disconnect all the propane lines and run one to each of the other stairwell doors. Finally, Wilson, I need you with me."

She didn't wait to see if her orders were being carried out, Thuy headed straight for the elevators. "Are you strong enough to pry these doors open?" she asked Wilson.

"I'd like to think I don't look that old to you," Wilson replied, half-jokingly. He did look that old. The hours of near-panic had left him haggard. His warm brown skin hung from his cheeks like a Bassett hound's, while beneath his eyes bags had sprung up from out of nowhere.

"I'm sorry, but I, but…" Thuy yammered.

"Don't be sorry, yet. If I can open the doors then you can be sorry about judging my virility. If not then I'll be glad my ability to blush is less pronounced than some."

With a fair amount of grunting, Wilson was able to haul the doors open enough for Thuy to get her slim fingers in to help. Together they opened them completely and once Thuy locked them in place, she pulled out Anna's cell phone and shone the pale light down to where the woman hung precariously…except Anna wasn't hanging precariously.

She was gone.

## Chapter 11

**//7:14PM//**

**1**

Courtney Shaw stared at the grid map for her district: nine troopers on site, six local law enforcement, and a fleet of emergency vehicles...all just sitting there.

She punched the number for Lieutenant Pemberton. "Lieutenant, we now have fifteen officers on site."

Pemberton blew out sharply and said, "You don't have to tell me every time a trooper shows up, thank you." He was barely civil. She had called every few minutes; it was her way of trying to goad him into action. Of course she wasn't burdened by the knowledge contained in the three-inch thick volume of standard operating procedures concerning bioterrorism, which was the closest thing to what they were dealing with. It sat open in front of him, four hundred pages of crap.

He had alerted the area hospitals, local public health officials, and politicians. He had also set up a command post, opened communications with a dozen police, sheriffs, and fire departments. Slowly but surely, he was going down the checklist which was all well and good, however without authorization from the CDC or the New York State crime lab to enter the facility, he was stuck with little to do besides form a quarantine perimeter, something he lacked the manpower to do.

Courtney understood S.O.P. but knew that sometimes it had to go out the window. This was one of those times; there was nothing standard about this situation. She waited six minutes after Kilo-8 radioed in that he had arrived at the Walton facility before again punching the number for the station chief. He didn't pick up.

Pemberton was stewing. He had his orders: stay in

position until the lab boys arrived, but how long would that be? Another hour? Did those people trapped on the fourth floor have another hour? The hundredth sigh of the day was just escaping his lips when he jerked—Courtney was standing in his doorway.

"What?" he demanded.

"Kilo-8 is on site and is awaiting orders."

"He has his orders."

"Are those orders to rescue the people trapped on the top floor? Their last communication was that they were being attacked. Someone was trying to bash down the door with a *ram*."

"A ram?" Pemberton asked, feeling his stomach drop. The word "ram" suggested something he didn't want to consider, yet the idea strode his consciousness nonetheless and demanded to be addressed. "Any word from Brown or Heines?"

"Nothing."

"How long has it been?"

"I haven't heard from Brown since they entered the building over two hours ago. It's been forty eight minutes since Heines last checked in, and he was...strange." She tried on a smile but it was crooked as a dog's leg and only showed that she was embarrassed to repeat what had been said. "He called me a whore and then blamed us for leaving him there and for keeping the cure from him. Those scientists I've been talking to said there'd be personality changes."

Pemberton breathed out the word, "Right." He had known Heines for years; the man never complained about anything and certainly never cussed out a dispatcher. "You think he's got it? The disease?"

She tried to shrug noncommittally, but he read the "yes" written across her features clearly. "Ok. Get me Foster." Courtney put the call into the onsite commander and a minute later Pemberton was talking to Sergeant Foster, a man he'd once duct taped to a toilet to keep him from puking all over his carpet. A man he'd stood next to at the altar on his wedding day. A man he'd attended so many funerals with in the course of a twenty-year career. A man he trusted.

"I need to know exactly what's going on in that damn building. I need to know if they're really eating each other and who, if anyone is still sane."

"Are you suggesting a recon in force?" Foster asked. "I don't have much of a force. I have only ten troopers including myself and six local-yokel deputy dogs."

"Yeah, it's what I'm talking about. We're flying completely blind here, and...and I need to know what's going on with Heines and Brown. They're good men. Split your people. Leave half to man your perimeter and take the rest with you. Remember, try to keep contact at a minimum and also, everyone needs a mask. I'm talking a real mask."

The state police only had gloves and surgical masks, neither of which engendered much of a sense of protection. They would have to borrow gear from the emergency units. Foster snorted. "The EMTs and the fire-tards won't be happy."

Pemberton didn't care if they were happy or not. "If anyone won't give up their equipment, deputize them and make them come with you inside."

This had Foster chuckling. He knew that not a one of them would come along. He didn't question their courage, he only knew they had the courage of backcountry emergency workers who were accustomed to cleaning up after car crashes, wetting down a burning house every once in a while and dealing with assorted felines stuck up in trees. Then there were the parades and the school functions that had to be attended, and of course they had to make time to strut about for the local gals whose bodies were like soft bowling pins and who saw a man in uniform less as heroic figures but rather a man most likely to conform.

Foster had known many of these country emergency

workers. They wore their uniforms much the way a peacock wears his feathers—they would fold them in the second things got rough. He wasn't wrong. The locals huffed and puffed, staging hysterics strictly for each other's benefit, but when push came to shove and he threatened to deputize them they handed over their equipment just like that.

While the emergency personnel began hauling out the protective hazmat suits, Foster looked over the men he had to work with. He decided to go with size as his main criteria. From many years of experience he knew that even people who were high or tripping, or drunk, usually respected a man if he was big enough.

For this reason he chose four of his troopers and the three sheriff's deputies from Middleton who were huge both in height and girth.

He chose incorrectly.

Middleton had not yet made it into the twenty-first century: the three deputies had .38 caliber police specials on their hips, meaning that after six shots they'd be dry. Worse, not a one of them had ever reloaded their pissant little pistols under pressure, nor had they trained to do so. In their sleepy little burgs there had never really been a reason to.

"Let's get buttoned up," Foster barked. Under the watchful eye of the emergency workers, the eight men donned the protective gear. Foster was so concerned over the thought of germs and the integrity of the suit that he didn't realize that he had safely encased his weapon in plastic. It was germ free but useless, otherwise.

"Shit," Trooper Eddie Peels said when he realized the problem. "Our guns." Some of the EMTs started chuckling while the troopers all looked at Foster. Peels asked. "Is it too late? Do we leave them where they're at?"

Foster felt the ache of time getting by, however he wasn't about to go up against crazed infected cannibals without a gun at the ready. "Let's get them out." None of the men made a fuss. As the men struggled out of their suits, Foster went over what he expected to encounter, "We've all read about people on bath salts and some of us have had run-ins with people on PCP and meth, supposedly what's going on with the people in there is worse, so if we have to take any of them down, we do it hard and fast."

The men grunted or nodded, thinking they knew the score already. When they were ready, Foster formed them up, making sure to put the three Middleton men on his left where he could keep an eye on them. He led the way, sweeping through the abandoned gates and advancing on the brightly lit hospital. Rain pattered on their plastic hoods and coursed down their plastic suits in tiny rivers. It streaked across their face shields making them even more unrecognizable to each other. Foster knew the Middleton boys because their gun belts were different and because one of them had foolishly pinned his deputy badge to the outside of his biosuit. His own troopers were strange, alien looking blobs with guns at their sides.

"Hold," Foster barked as they came up on the CDC van. He glanced in, expecting to see only a corpse—it should've been a corpse. The man lying across the front seats looked as though a lion had gorged itself on his intestines. He was torn open across the middle, blood was everywhere, spattering the glass and the console and soaking into the seat cushions.

Still he wasn't dead.

Damon turned his head, ever so slowly, to stare at Foster. He started gnashing his teeth. "He's trying to say something," Foster said, waving his gloved hand to quiet the troopers who were gathered around. "Step back."

Foster opened the door. "It'll be alright, sir. Don't try to move. Just lay back." Damon had turned on his side and was trying to kill, but he was too weak and Foster ignored the hands scraping at his plastic biosuit. He also ignored the black goo dripping from Damon's eyes and nose, mistaking it for old blood. "Just settle down and try to tell me what happened."

Damon snapped his teeth and groaned in hunger and frustration.

"Can you hear me?" Foster asked, holding the man's hands down.

"He ain't hearing shit, sarge," one of the troopers said. That was true enough. Damon was solely focused on reaching Foster with his teeth and tearing out his throat. To the troopers, he seemed so far gone that he didn't appear to be much of a threat.

"Paul?" Foster asked. "Which one of you…"

"Right here," one of the alien blobs said. Jared Paul had been three years into a medical degree before he grew bored with school and traded in his books for a gun. Paul squinted from behind his face shield at Damon. "There's pretty much nothing I can do for him."

"Stay with him," Foster said, weakening his crew. "It's not right to leave someone alone to die like that."

Now it was only seven men who advanced on the looming hospital. At the front doors, Foster pulled his weapon; the others followed suit. Just through the glass he could see the body of a state trooper; the face was too torn up to be recognized. There were three other visible, living beings walking around the lobby; they didn't look right either. They looked like they should've been dead, too.

"Let's go," Foster said.

One of the troopers opened the doors for the others. The seven rushed in guns leveled and began to fan out. Foster stopped at the trooper's body—there was no need to check for a pulse.

"Who is it?" one of the troopers asked.

"Wendell Brown," Foster replied. The corpse's face had been eaten off but his nametag was shiny and looked new.

"Shit," the trooper said.

"Yeah," Foster agreed in a whisper that didn't make it through the respiratory filters on his suit.

There was little time to mourn. "We got incoming!" one

of the Middleton boys hissed. Two people were shambling at them—they were horrors. Blank faces, black eyes, wide, gaping mouths.

"That's the disease?" someone off to Foster's right asked. "What is it? Legionnaires?"

"It's not Legionnaires." Foster had arrested a junkie who'd somehow contracted Legionnaires; whatever this was, it was far worse. He held up his free hand. "Stop where you are! I said stop or we will be forced to detain...shit! Take them down."

The pair, Anita DeSota, one of the recently deceased cafeteria workers, and Mr. Mumford, charged straight at the law enforcement officers, ignoring the seven guns pointing their way. Neither of them was large but both were surprisingly strong and vicious, using their teeth as weapons. They weren't subtle about it; they led with their mouths open and snarling.

The troopers were not caught unaware, but still, it took two men to wrestle each down to the ground and a third to actually cuff them. "That was crazy," one of the troopers said. He was breathing heavily and a fog kept whisping across his mask with every other breath. The seven stood over Mumford and DeSota, watching as they bucked and grunted, trying to get at the living in spite of the cuffs pinning their arms behind their backs.

"Check your suits for any rips or tears," Foster ordered. Their suits, though streaked with the infectious black mold were whole and intact.

"What do we do with them?" asked the Middleton deputy who had pinned his star to his chest. He had been in the thick of it, struggling with Mr. Mumford, and now he was taking in spores through those twin holes every time he sucked in a breath.

"We leave them for now and get them on the way back," Foster answered. He too had been surprised at the ferocity of the two rather small and unassuming individuals, and he wasn't about to further weaken his crew by leaving someone to watch over them. "Let's take this floor room by room, nice and slow. The troopers will have point, the deputies will watch our six."

"Wait, where did the other one go?" one of the Middleton boys asked. "There was a third dude. Where'd he go?"

Everyone craned their heads around, trying to see out of the little clear windows in their masks. Other than the twitching body of Earl the security guard, there wasn't anyone around. "Forget about him," Foster said. "If he's anything like these two, he'll show himself sooner or later."

## 2

Von Braun wasn't like Anita or Mr. Mumford, at least not yet. He still had three bags of Diazepam left. "Three bags to find the cure," he whispered.

After Heines had cracked his sternum and he had been trampled by the admin workers rushing up the stairs, Von Braun had wandered into the lobby breathing like a broken accordion. His one thought was of revenge. He decided he would gather an army of his own and take the cure from that fuck-wad of a cop. The one problem was that the lobby was practically empty with only two morons wandering around.

He tried to gather them to his cause, but they kept wandering off and soon he became confused as well. His brain was a mush of hate—there were simply too many people he wanted to hurt: the cop, the gook, the nigger. And there were others. He remembered, barely, that his lawyer had been an asshole who had to die. And then there was Johnny Carew from the fifth grade...

"I gotta kill that fucker, too." There were more and Von Braun found himself staring at the distant flashing lights of two dozen emergency vehicles as he dwelled on all those he wanted to kill with his bare hands. The lights captivated him and, like a deer in headlights, he stood at the tall windows that made up the walls of the lower floor and simply stared.

Von Braun gazed blankly through the glass doors until he heard the explosion on the top floor that rattled the building. He then stared upwards for a full minute before a thought blinked into his brain, "My cure!" With the black goo draining from the ducts in his eyes, running was difficult. He stumbled like a drunk over to Mr. Mumford and Anita and began to shepherd them to the stairs.

They were annoyingly slow and easily distracted. They didn't understand that the cure was in danger, in fact, it seemed to Von Braun, they didn't understand anything. "Get up there you fat fuck!" he screamed at Mr. Mumford, pointing at the stairs where the smell of burnt flesh was overpowering. Had it been clean flesh Von Braun would have left the two and run to gorge himself, but the flesh had the underlying stink of shit which made his stomach turn.

Mumford hesitated in the doorway, growled and then scratched at his eyes, tearing off a piece of his eyebrow. Anita turned away. Von Braun was thinking of killing her when he caught movement through the glass doors—the police were coming.

There were many of them, too many for him to count, but not so many that they couldn't be overcome. "Go get them," he said, turning Mumford around. Mumford didn't need to be told twice. His brain was a black hole of misery, however he knew fresh meat when he saw it. He and Anita went after Foster's little force and Von Braun went for reinforcements.

In the little wedge of grey matter that was still operating he knew it would take lots of his kind to bring down so many cops. His stomach rumbled hungrily, thinking about it. As he climbed the stairs he encountered others and these he turned them around to point down stairs yelling into their ears, "The police are down there. Go get them!"

He sent a constant stream down. When he reached the

fourth floor he came on a dozen beings that no longer looked human. Their skin was black and ragged, their skulls burned down to the bone, but still they pressed onto the door and beat at it with hands that were little more than fused bone. Von Braun tried to get them to go after the police as well, but they could smell the fresh meat of the scientists and nothing was going to dissuade them from getting through the door.

Von Braun went back down to the third floor, rounded up another twenty or so and sent them downwards. They had been feeding on the newly killed. The six people trapped in the CAT Scan room, not understanding the breadth of the problem, had tried to make a break for it. They hadn't got far. Von Braun paused only long enough to take a bite from Dr. Hester's lukewarm corpse--the meat wasn't hot which meant it wasn't good.

Spitting it out, he went to the south stair and began pushing more of the zombies toward the first floor. It was then that the first gunshots began to rattle the air.

"Hurry, fuckers!" he screamed at the slow moving zombies. "There won't be anything left!" All told, eighty infected people were heading for the seven officers.

**3**

The troopers were surveying the bloodbath in the first floor break room when the first of the infected people broke out into the lobby and began wondering around. They could smell fresh meat but they couldn't pinpoint where the sweet odor was coming from. With their hoods stifling sound and cutting off their peripheral vision, the troopers were oblivious to them.

Foster was very glad for the concealing plastic. Yes, it kept the germs out but it also hid the fact from the others that he had gone a shade of green. He had never been to any crime scene that was comparable to what lay in front him. It was more than just the blood.

All over the floor were ugly hunks of flesh, long strands of hair still anchored to flaps of scalp, and a number of fingers. He counted eight, but no thumbs. There were also seven bodies, only one of which was actually dead. The rest were like the CDC man in the van, mostly dead. Most had been torn apart by something with vicious teeth and an eternal hunger, but a few sported gaping holes caused by a nine-millimeter handgun.

"Where's the rest of them?" one of the Middleton boys asked.

"Maybe Heines is trapped upstairs," Foster answered.

The deputy shook his head. "No, I meant, where are the rest of the dead?" He pointed at the ground. Amid the blood and the pieces of stray body parts were thirty-nine brass casings.

Foster stared all around, realizing that the deputy was right, the numbers weren't adding up. With so many shots taken, there should have been a couple of dozen bodies. Something caught his eye. There had been so much blood that he hadn't noticed it before. "Drag marks," he said indicating the floor where black streaks ran through the red. The color didn't make sense, but he had seen the telltale marks of a body having been dragged away enough times to know what they were.

They followed them out into the admin area to the nearest cubicle, fully expecting to see a pile of corpses, instead, there were just two, again grasping, half-dead creatures that made their stomachs churn.

"It looks like they just walked off," someone said. "How? How do you get shot up and then walk away like it was nothing?"

"And where did they walk off to?" another asked, quietly. The men were more like frightened boys. They clumped together, facing outward ready to shoot the nearest shadow if it looked menacing enough.

"We should've waited for the CDC," a deputy said. "We should've sat tight like the rules say. We..."

"Shut your fucking lip!" Foster snapped. "We still have a man in this building, not to mention there are civilians trapped upstairs. Now, let's do our fucking jobs."

There was an embarrassed silence broken when one of the deputies said, "Sir? There's more of them."

Attracted by Sergeant Foster's yelling, three zombies had come snooping around. One was Lacy Freeman, the pistol she had taken from Rory Vickers was long forgotten. Her meds had run out and now all she knew was hate and hunger.

The three saw the strange plastic covered figures and grew confused, not being able to juxtapose the sound of human voices with what their blurred vision showed. They advanced slowly until Foster said, "Take them, two per individual. Concentrate on pinning them first and cuffing them second. I don't want anyone bitten."

The officers knew what to expect this time and the take down went smoothly. The three were trussed up with only a little bit of fuss and then the seven officers stood around looking down at them. One of his troopers said, "My visor keeps getting fogged up. Is that normal?"

"Mine too," someone agreed.

"I think you should be worried if it wasn't," Foster told them. "It just means our suits are air tight. That's a good thing." He wanted to reassure them and himself. He had begun to sweat and, like the others, every breath sent a fog across his vision. "Maybe we should just take a moment to relax before we head up. Smoke 'em if you got 'em."

There was only one trooper with a nicotine addiction. "I would if I could," Trooper Bower said. "You think I can take a drag through these filters?"

"I think you could..." Foster stopped in midsentence. From the lobby, another dozen or so zombies walked into the cubicled admin area. Sudden fear gripped him and instinctively he dropped into a crouch. The others took one look and hunkered down as well.

"What do we do?" one of the Middleton men asked, his quivering voice at odds with his size.

"We, we...hold on, let me think," Foster said. His greatest fear was of the germs, of turning into one of *them*, however he was also extremely afraid of making a mistake. It was the age of blame and lawsuits, where every action was scrutinized later so that a sacrificial lamb could be produced whenever something really big happened. This is what had him nervous, not for a second did Foster consider the possibility of being eaten alive.

He peeked over the metaled edge of the cubicle and studied the people for a few seconds. "They're like the others. Whatever happened to them has messed up their minds, which means they'll come in stupid. I saw a printing room while we were coming in. I say we use it to funnel them in at us one at a time. We zip tie them and clear the floor that way."

Awkwardly in their plastic hoods, they all agreed to the plan. Foster led the way. It was all of forty yards to the printing room but they stopped after only making half that distance. There were a lot more zombies than they had realized. The first floor was teeming with them.

"Go back!" Foster said, urgently.

It was already too late. There were black-eyed creatures in front *and* behind. And worse, they'd been spotted. One of the zombies in a hospital gown let out a hiss and charged. This brought on a full stampede of the infected.

"Run!" someone yelled. Two of the officers took off in different directions. Another officer, with a zombie bearing down on him, fired his weapon twice in quick succession, dropping it at his feet.

"Stop," cried Foster to the fleeing troopers. One kept going, racing at top speed to who knew where. The other's mask fogged over at the wrong moment. He tripped over a chair that had been sticking out of a cubicle and went down hard. Three zombies attacked him, throwing themselves on him with their jaws gaping.

Coming to a split second decision, Foster yelled, "Quick! Follow me." He ran to the downed man and at first tried to do the humane thing: he kicked a horrible black-eyed woman full in the face with his boot. Teeth and blood flew; still she clawed and bit at the prone trooper. Next he used his gun and shot her in the spine. Her legs went jelly, but her hands continued to tear at the plastic and her mouth reached his abdomen where she began to rend threw the plastic and into his flesh.

Foster grabbed her by the collar of her shirt and hauled her back. One of the troopers fired into her chest twice at point blank range and she slumped.

Meanwhile gunshots were going off all over the place. The downed trooper was firing up at his other two attackers without regard to anything but saving his own ass. Bullets passed through them and around them, and a couple came within an inch of hitting Foster. He didn't notice. He had his own zombies to worry about. Six were charging in a line in front of him and he completely forgot his fear of getting in trouble. He began firing as quickly as his finger could pull the trigger.

The other officers were emptying their weapons into the advancing horde with very little effect. If one fell after absorbing the impact of five or six rounds, another took its place. For the span of a half a minute, the two groups fought to a draw and then the Middleton deputies were forced to reload as their guns ran dry. Reloading with gloved hands and fogged over masks, was impossible in the second or two they had to work with.

First, one was bowled over then the other two were gang rushed a moment later. They were swarmed under a pile of zombies. Foster and the other trooper tried to help. They shot into the mass until their guns emptied as well. Foster fumbled for a full magazine, dropping it. He didn't try to grab it from the ground. It was too late for the deputies and maybe even too late for him and the remaining troopers. There were just too many zombies, too close, coming from every angle.

"Run!" he yelled, grabbing the one standing trooper and pulling him along. Foster dodged between two zombies and ran along a corridor of cubicles until his path was caught off by three more of the walking horrors. He dodged to the right, jumped up onto a desk and then leapt a cubicle wall. He didn't quite make it and the wall came crashing down. He landed on the desk in the next cubicle and was up and running before he could draw a breath.

He ran low, keeping below the walls of the cubicles. At one of the little corridors, he paused to check behind him for the trooper whom he'd grabbed. The man was nowhere to be seen. There were gunshots from three directions and zombies everywhere--Foster's courage failed him and, for once in his career, he ran from the sounds of the guns. He ran for the lobby where he stopped in dread. There were dozens of the creatures between him and the exit.

His breath began to race clouding his mask completely. "Oh fuck," he whined, digging for a new magazine from the holder at his belt. One slid from his grip and clinked on the linoleum, the next felt turned around and wrong. It wouldn't seem to fit into his gun. With the fog obscuring his vision he was blind and afraid and all around him the growls of the creatures grew louder as they closed in.

Finally, he couldn't take the terror that was building in him, and he ripped off the hood and mask so he could see his death approaching. It was very close. The zombies were just feet away. The gun went ignored. Now that he could see, Foster sprinted away faster than he thought possible, leaving the beasts and the last of his troopers far behind.

He dodged in and among the zombies and when he came up to the lobby doors, he pulled them closed behind him and then backed away from the glass still trying to get the damned clip into his pistol. The zombies rushed up to the windows and stopped--the smell of sweet meat had suddenly diminished and the man they'd been chasing had, at least in their eyes, disappeared. All they could see was themselves reflected in the glass.

Gulping in the cool, wet air, Foster realized he was safe, he had lived! A twisted smile trembled his lips for all of a moment before he remembered his troopers. There was no sign of them save for a lone scream that barely reached his ears. It was an awful, painful sound that went right to his soul, twisting it into a gnarly, foul knot that made his chest ache. His hands shook as he tried to load the magazine into his pistol. Finally, it clicked into place and then he thought: *Now what?*

Loaded gun or nor, he knew there was no way he was going back in. But it hardly mattered, the scream ended in a high screech. "No," Foster said, stepping forward. He couldn't bring himself to go further. In fact, the accusing silence had him backing away again until his foot stumbled on the curb and he plopped onto his ass with a grunt.

The fall jarred him into a version of reality. He holstered the gun and then as quick as he could he pulled the plastic hood and mask back over his face. "I'm ok," he said, making sure everything was back in place. "I'm fine." He took a deep breath as if to prove the point.

Having convinced himself that he hadn't been near enough to any of the infected people to get their disease, he began to worry on his second greatest fear: he had royally screwed up. Six dead officers meant he'd screwed up worse than anything he could've imagined.

"But I was just following orders," he whispered. "This was Pemberton's fault." Excuses began to click through his mind: He'd been ordered into the building-not his fault; he'd been ambushed, again, not his fault; the masks were faulty and kept fogging up, that was the fire department's fault; the

Middleton boys were equipped with crappy little six-shooters that was Middleton's fault.

In the middle of this a voice spoke right in his ear: "What the hell happened in there?" Foster actually screamed. It was trooper Paul, the man he had left behind to watch over the CDC zombie. "It sounded like a frigging war in there," Paul went on.

"We...w-we were ambushed," Foster jabbered. "We...we...they were everywhere. They eat people!"

Paul stepped back trying to size up his sergeant through the little plastic window in his suit. Foster's eyes were huge and unblinking, he was pale as fish-belly and was dripping sweat down the inside of his suit. In a word, he looked crazy. Gently Paul asked, "Who wants to eat people?"

The sergeant's eyes went to slits at the question, realizing he wouldn't be believed, not yet at least. "The infected people. They're cannibals. They...they can't be stopped. You'll see. When they get out, you'll see." The idea of them getting out was deeply unsettling; there were just so many of them. Forgetting Paul, Foster started to head back to his cruiser, which doubled as his command post. He looked back over his shoulder every few steps, afraid the zombies had gotten out and were after him, again.

Paul stood for a moment, confused and worried. He then jogged to catch up. "But what about everyone else? Where are the others?" he asked.

Foster stopped short. He was the only one left alive...how was he possibly going to explain that? He'd been the leader. Leaders weren't supposed to be the first one out the door, they were supposed to be the last. Who would understand that he'd ran because he'd been without any other option? Who could possibly understand the truth about what had really happened?

They'd have to see it for themselves. "They're dead...sort of." The strange answer and the queer look on Foster's face had Paul thinking it was best not to ask any more questions.

Foster knew he sounded crazy--he felt crazy. "You'll see and then you won't look at me like you are with your judging eyes. You'll see."

**4**

"Anna!" Thuy whispered as loudly as she dared. As logical as she was, after the terrors she'd faced that day, the dark elevator shaft seemed as though it could hold endless evil. "Anna, if you can hear me say something or tap the wall. Anna?"

The dark was mute and deep. So deep that Thuy felt she could scream into it at the top of her lungs and her voice wouldn't carry to its furthest depths. She was on her stomach staring down, straining her ears to hear the slightest sound; there was nothing, not even an echo.

"She must've fallen," Deckard said. He was standing over Thuy, noting that her long, black hair so matched the darkness of the elevator shaft that she looked to be melding with the shadows. It was strangely enticing.

"She must've fallen?" Thuy snapped. "Is that right? You sure she didn't grow wings and fly away?"

So much for enticing. Deckard's eye went hard. "Ok, you trapped her, left her hanging in the dark, and then she must've fallen. Better?"

It wasn't, since it was true. She was guilty of killing Anna. That was the truth. "Sorry, I didn't mean to snap. I just...this is my fault. She's dead because of me."

"And we're alive because of you," Deckard said. "You made a choice, a good one if you ask me."

"It doesn't feel good." Thuy stood up, the toes of her shoes hanging off the edge. "I need to get a lantern or a torch. I can take some of the wiring from the..." she stopped at Deckard's sharp look. "We have to do something, Deck. We can't just leave her down there. What if she's hurt? She could be down there with a serious brain injury."

"And what if she is? I could climb down there, but what then? I'm not a brain surgeon. Dr. Wilson is the closest thing but I don't know if he could make the climb and even if he could, he doesn't have any supplies. If you ask me, if she's knocked out, we might consider her lucky. She's missing out on all of this."

Thuy didn't want to be so easily dissuaded, it made the guilt clogging her chest swell. "Ok, so we don't go down, at least not yet, but I can still fashion a light that we can lower..."

Below them Foster and his State Troopers had just discovered that they were surrounded. The sound of their gunfire rippled through the building and everyone stopped what they were doing to listen. This wasn't like when Heines and Brown had fired their weapons earlier. From the fourth floor it sounded like there was a platoon of soldiers blasting everything in sight. It lasted barely a minute and then there was silence.

"Was that the police or the army?" Thuy asked.

"The police," Deckard said, checking his watch. "It's about time, too. Wait here, I need to make sure Milner isn't getting happy feet over this and breaking quarantine."

Thuy didn't wait; if the police were here it meant the CDC had finally arrived and there were plenty of things to do before they showed up. She went to the first of the BSL-3 labs where everyone had gathered after the fight on the stairs. "I need someone to get in touch with the police again," she said as she strode through the glass door.

Dr. Riggs jumped up." Did you hear all the shooting? That means we're being rescued, right?" All of the other scientists looked at her expectantly, their excitement plain on their faces.

"It seems to be a safe assumption," Thuy answered. "But that doesn't mean we can rush out of here just yet. There are protocols that must be followed. Like I said, I need someone to call the police. I don't want them barging up here if they've come in contact with any of the infected people. Also we should ask for hazmat suits for each of us before we exit this floor. Riggs, put Milner up to it. It'll give him something to do. The rest of you need to gather up all the information we have on the Com-cells: any printouts, notes, blood samples, what have you. The CDC will want to see all of it."

The scientists rushed to the shambles that had been their workstations and began to make piles out of the mess, most of them were grinning at the prospect of rescue.

Before she left to arrange her own notes, she went to see Chuck, John and Stephanie. They were tired and pale, less excited than the others. Their being rescued only meant their deaths had been put off for another month or two.

Thuy dropped down onto her knees in front of where they sat. "I need some help with something. Anna fell while we were busy fending off the zom..." She caught herself just in time; unfortunately the word *zombie* seemed to fit so well. "I mean while we were fending off the infected persons. There are no sounds coming from the elevator shaft, but I want to make sure Anna isn't down there hurt and all alone."

"Y'all want us to climb down that bitch?" John asked.

"No. If you don't mind, could you sit by the shaft and listen for her? She's down there because of me."

Chuck snorted. "That's not the way I reckon the score. She's down there on account of what she did. She made her bed and I figure she's lyin' in it now."

"I'll stay with her," Stephanie said. "I made you leave her there. It's my fault, too."

Chuck went along with Stephanie because of the feelings he had for her and John went along with Chuck because he was uncomfortable around the egghead scientists. The three sat about, talking death.

"Mayhap gettin' bit by one a them zombies ain't the worst thing in the world," Burke said. "Y'all seen them burnt up ones same as me. They cain't die is all I'm saying. That's sumptin."

Stephanie couldn't get with the idea of becoming one of *them*, however Chuck agreed with John. "Supposably, they can be sedated, you know get put into a coma. That wouldn't be so bad. You just lie there until they find a cure and then..." he snapped his fingers, "you wake up good as new."

"And if they can't find a cure?" Stephanie asked.

"Then you'll never know," Chuck answered. "I'm not sayin' I'm going to let myself get bit. I'm just sayin' it's an option for when we're out of here. In the last couple of weeks, I've been enjoyin' life more than ever and I kinda want to keep it going if I can."

# 5

"Sir, you have to remain patient," Courtney said in her practiced bored-as-hell voice, she then put Dr. Milner on hold for the third time. She knew it wouldn't last; he'd wait five minutes, hang up and re-dial the emergency line just as he had the last two times.

She waited the five minutes, drumming her fingers on her desk and staring at the switchboard. Lieutenant Pemberton's line was still active. In eight years as a state police dispatcher she'd had her share of bad days, but this was the first time she'd been asked to get the Governor's home phone number. That was huge and scary.

Next to her, Renee was telling the owner of a trucking company that, yes, the state was commandeering his warehouses and no, there wasn't anything he could do about it. "Of course you can call your lawyer," Renee said. "Just make sure that neither of you are within two-hundred yards of the warehouse when you begin your protest. The State of New York thanks you."

She hung up and gave Courtney a look. "This is so

messed up," she said. "I can't believe Bill and Porter are dead."

"And Bower and Heines and Brown," Courtney added. She had taken the call from Foster when he had finally reported in after his disastrous recon. That had been scary as well. He'd spoken listlessly, in a dull monotone, reading off the names of the dead like he was reading off an order for Chinese takeout.

After that she'd been *officially* cut out of the loop. Foster had asked to talk to Pemberton. The second she'd transferred him, Courtney jumped out of her chair, raced down the hall to the station chief's office and stood outside the door, barely breathing. Pemberton's speakerphone was clear as day and she heard Foster repeat the same list of the dead in the same washed-out voice.

"How did you screw this up so badly?" Pemberton demanded. "I've got eight men dead! Eight! Bower and Porter and...Fuck! Fuck! Fuck!" The lieutenant's fury was so elemental that Courtney almost ran back to her place in the dispatch room. Her curiosity was too great and she stayed.

"They're not really dead," Foster said, quietly.

"What? You just told me they were torn to pieces. You said they had their throats ripped out."

"Yeah, but they're not truly dead. They'll come back as one of *them* and then it won't be so bad...officially speaking that is. You'll only have to list them as casualties, not as KIA."

Pemberton sat back, quiet for half a minute and the entire time Courtney thought he was going to go berserk, however he seemed calm when he said, very slowly, "Riiight, because they're zombies now."

"Yes," Foster agreed.

"Ok, Greg, Ok. I don't want you to take offence but I think we're going to need to authenticate this. You know, to make it official. Let me talk to Trooper Paul. We can send in another..."

"No," Foster said. His tone was low and dangerous. "No one else is going in. You wanted me to reconnoiter the building and I did. You wanted to find out what the fuck was going on in there and I told you. If you don't believe me then go in yourself but you're not sending anyone else in. Pemberton, listen to me! This is real."

"Greg, please. Listen to yourself. I can't go to Billups about zombies. You know what he'll say. I need proof. I need an objective observer to go in..."

"That's what I am!" Foster cried. "I'm your eyewitness and if you don't believe me, try believing those people trapped in the building. They are trapped by fucking zombies. I shot eight or nine of them and they just kept coming like they didn't feel a thing. They just kept coming and coming and..."

"Ok, Greg," Pemberton said in a softer tone. "I believe you. Just do me a favor and don't use the word zombie in anything official."

Courtney had heard enough. She went back to her desk feeling odd; her reality had been severely tested, and it had failed. She took Milner's calls and, in between them, told Renee everything.

"He said zombies?" Renee asked.

Before Courtney could answer, her call light began blinking. "It's that jack-ass again. He acts like I'm his secretary or something. You want to take it?"

"No, mine's going too."

Milner's call was tedious: he demanded to know what was happening and why everything was taking so long, and when they'd be rescued. Courtney didn't have much more to tell him besides, "We're doing the best we can. Sit tight and a rescue team will get to you soon." She had no idea when "soon" would occur. Every trooper within three hundred miles was racing to Walton, while local police forces were being stripped of their men. She could expect sixty law enforcement officers to be on site by nine that night.

Unfortunately, that didn't mean a rescue was going to happen immediately. After the last fiasco, Courtney didn't think there would be another attempt until the CDC team arrived, and she was sure they weren't going to spring into action either. They were notoriously pompous, officious, slow, and asinine. They did everything by the book and their book of Standard Operating Procedures was outrageously large.

There was a story circulating around about a CDC Intervention at an elementary school in Havertown, where three cases of small pox were discovered, only it hadn't been small pox, it had been chicken pox.

The school was in lockdown for twenty one hours until one of the cafeteria workers realized the mistake. Everyone was relieved and the teachers and students had thought they'd be able to walk right out after the mistake was discovered, but no. Regulations were regulations and it was five more hours before they were let go. Twenty six hours for chicken pox. Who knew how long it would be before the "rules" would allow for a rescue.

"Sorry, Dr. Milner," Courtney said. "They are working on setting up a rescue, however I don't know when it'll be. So, if you can please stop calling, I need all the lines as free as possible."

The call Renee took was far more interesting.

"This is Sergeant Thomas, from the Poughkeepsie P.D. We have a situation. We got a couple of guys in our drunk tank and they got some sort of black goo coming out of their eyes."

## Chapter 12

*//7:26 PM//*

**1**

"This is so not worth it," Bailey Cook griped, slamming her tray down. She'd been called in to the bar on her day off because some bug was making its way through the staff. Bailey wondered if it was true; she had a suspicion that the regular staff had taken one peek at the morons slopping it up in the corner and had taken off.

Next to her Danni Sparks rolled her eyes. "You haven't even been here twenty minutes and already you're whining. What the fuck?"

Bailey's eyes narrowed and she snapped back, "What's your problem, Danni? You should be happy I showed at all." Bailey wouldn't have bothered if it wasn't for the fact that her car was running on racing slicks. It had been four years since she'd bought new tires and now they were so bald that there were little zings of metal, looking like the bones of a snake, showing through the old rubber. Still, it wasn't worth it.

As she'd been coming in, the Poughkeepsie police were hauling out two guys; both bleeding and spitting curses.

This had been the third visit from the cops that night, a record for a Monday evening—Jack Cable, the front desk security guard at R&K, had been the first to be hauled off. He had driven his Mustang straight away from the Walton facility to the bar and plunked himself down, not realizing that he was practically coated in the mutated Com-cells. Soon his head was pounding, something he attributed to the cheap tequila he and the two gate guards, Randal and Wayne, had been downing shot after shot.

When the pain became too intense, he ordered his own

bottle and drank it like water. It helped for a little while. The alcohol dampened the worst effects of his disease, although nothing was going to stop the hate from building up. It made his head feel huge and bloated. He vented, in turns lashing out at the government, or the terrible service in the seedy bar, but mostly he complained bitterly about the scientists back at Walton, who he just knew were up to no good, experimenting on innocent people.

The other's at the table, Randal and Wayne, the two men who'd abandoned the gate and fled with Jack, and the other off-duty guards who'd decided to make themselves scarce after word of a quarantine filtered down to them, listened to his story with varying degrees of incredulity—at first, but as the Com-cells spread and invaded their bodies unchecked, they came to believe as Jack did.

Eventually, Jack's endless diatribes and the retelling of Mr. Mumford and the circumstances of Earl's death, reached the ears of a young tough at the end of the bar. His name was Ron Siltkis and he found joy in other people's misery.

"You were attacked by zombies?" he asked, elbowing the man on the stool next to him and giving him a wink. "Were you drunk then, too?"

"Who said anything about zombies?" In Jack's eyes, the bar was exceptionally dim and shady. There seemed to be more shadows than light; it was as if his eyes had aged forty years in the time since his alarm had woken him up that morning. He had to squint to see Ron. "I didn't mention any fucking zombies."

"Yeah, you did," Ron shot back. "You described them to a 'T' only you're too stupid to realize it. No wonder your friend got killed."

Tequila was a poor substitute for an intravenous infusion of Diazepam. Jack couldn't have stopped himself if he had wanted to. He stood, knocking the table and spilling drinks. Ron was almost gleeful as he came off his barstool. There was no stare-down or any more preliminary talk. Jack saw the young tough as a hulking blur. He seemed wrapped up in a cloak of shadows, and yet there was one thing Jack could see clear as day: the skin of Ron's cheek.

He had a bit of a baby face and his cheeks were high in color, like an apple turning in an orchard. The flesh was clean and fresh and for some ungodly reason it made Jack's stomach rumble.

It took five people to pull him off and when they did, Ron's apple cheeks were more like raw hamburger.

The police were back not forty-five minutes later to cuff the two gate guards and drag them out. They were just there to pick up Wayne who had inexplicably stormed into the kitchen and attacked the eight-person staff, bare-handed, however, Randal, who had been oblivious to the fight, assaulted the police on sight. He had no clue why they were there and really, he didn't care. It was the blue uniforms that sent him into a killing rage. His head was cracked by a dozen blows from the batons the policemen carried and he barely felt anything. He bit, he clawed, he spread the Com-cells to every one of them.

The rest of the Walton guards were asked to leave though it did little to make the bar a safer place. By that point, pretty much everyone in the place was infected to one degree or another. The patrons drank to cure the headache that gradually crept up on them. The employees didn't have that option. One by one they clocked out and the manager struggled to replace them.

Bailey was the last one to show and she was far from happy. The atmosphere in the room was edgy. The TVs were off and the music muted. People were moaning in the back along the wall where the booths were high, and it wasn't the good sort of moan that occurred sometimes among the friskier clientele. It was the sound of pain. Bailey kept to her station.

"The kitchen's closed, we should just shut down for the night," she suggested to Danni.

"I already fucking asked and that fucking Roger just screamed at me," Danni seethed. "He just told me to get back to fucking work. Man, I'm so pissed, and if one of those fuckers thinks about touching me tonight I am going to…"

"Spit in their drink?" Bailey suggested. She was also worried about the patrons touching her. Generally, it was annoying when it happened, but tonight the moody crowd skeeved her out. Most of them were pale or haggard, while some were downright nasty looking. Normally, she kept her uniform top zippered just above the sixty-percent line in order to maximize tips. Just then she had it at ninety percent, zippered almost to the soft cleft of her throat. She had also washed her hands four times since she'd walked in; touching anything made her skin crawl.

"No," Danni said, her lip sneering. "I'm not going to spit in anyone's drinks. I'm going to fucking kill 'em."

Danni seemed serious. Bailey took an apprehensive step away from her friend. "That's probably not the best thing to…"

"What do you know, you fucking goody-two-shoes?" Danni snapped. "Look at you all perfect, smelling like you're a fucking virgin or something."

Bailey pulled her drink tray to her chest using it as a shield against the unexpected words. She was usually an aggressive girl who didn't take much in the way of shit from anyone—she had to be, working in a dive like *Baker's,* however this wasn't a usual night. There was something very wrong going on.

"Y-you want me to talk to Roger for you?" she asked, trying to put a smile on to cover up the strange fear that was quickly building up. "I can see if he'll send us…"

A bottle sailed passed her head. A regular at one of Bailey's tables yelled, "What the fuck is taking so long? It's just one beer!" His name was Bob Jenkins. He always ordered the same: Newcastle Brown Ale and always had exactly three each night. He always tipped five dollars, and Bailey had never heard him curse unless his beloved *Knicks* were losing.

"I gotta take care of this," Bailey said. "But I'll talk to Roger, I swear." She was eager to get away from Danni, and yet the idea of going out into the main room was unnerving. There was a brittle edge in the air and an invisible line that couldn't be crossed without setting the twenty or so people gathered there off. She decided that speed was her best option. She would treat this as a Friday where she buzzed about without pause for six straight hours.

First she sped to the bar where she grabbed a Newcastle for the regular and a Corona for a pony-tailed dude who had just downed his last. "Here, go...here, go," she said to the two men. She then did a quick circuit feeling their hungry eyes on her ass as she passed. A shiver went down her spine as she made it back to the bar; those eyes were far hungrier than on any other day.

There were calls for more "shots"; Danni was simply pouring from the first bottle she grabbed and Bailey did as well. She poured a tray full of shots and then went back out. A hand grabbed her as she passed one of the tables; it wasn't gentle or sexy in any way. Her flesh was pinched and then twisted. "Shit," she said, through gritted teeth. She kept going, dropping off shot after shot, feeling that invisible line coming nearer and afraid what would happen when it was crossed. After the shots were dispensed she did another quick tour of the room and saw that everyone had a full drink in front of them. Her section was stable, at least for the moment.

Danni's was starting to get nuts. The waitress wasn't pouring drinks in the traditional manner, with the little silver jigger that Roger insisted everyone use. Instead, she was filling every drink to the top of the glass and if someone said anything or touched her, she would splash the drinks in their faces, sometimes following it up by throwing the glass as well.

Bailey watched for a few minutes and felt that her toes were just slipping over that invisible line. It was dangerous on the other side of the line, maybe even deadly. She went straight away to the office behind the bar.

The door was shut. She raised a hand to knock, but hesitated. Was there a line here as well? Danni had said he'd been grouchy, but Roger could always be counted on to be grouchy. The man hated his job as much as he feared losing it. But what if this grouchiness was different? What if he was like the others?

There was nothing she could do but try. Her knuckles rapped softly on the door and she said in a voice just above a whisper, "Roger? We need your help out front."

"Stop that hissing!" he screamed. "If you're a snake come in and try to bite me, mother fucker! Cause I'll bite the fuck out of you." There was the sound of glass breaking and then she heard him come stomping to the door. She fled before he could open it. Clearly, he was like the others and maybe worse. Bailey was seriously afraid, now. She ducked into the kitchen and dug out her cell phone to dial 9-1-1.

Unbelievably, the call went to voicemail. "What the fuck?" She dialed the number again. Someone picked up on the last ring.

"Emergency, please hold."

"Wait! I need…" A pre-recorded voice started telling her about how important her call was to them. "Son of a bitch," Bailey said. While the voice droned in her ear she cracked the door to the kitchen and stared out into the bar. Roger had Danni by the hair and was punching her in the face. Blood was splattering and her nose was bent to the side so that it looked like she was sniffing her own cheek but still she was cussing up a storm and vowing revenge. Bailey saw Roger had the face of a devil—his eyes were completely black.

Quickly, Bailey shut the door. She even reached over and clicked off the kitchen lights. "Come on!" she hissed into the phone. "Come, on. Please answer the damned phone!"

She was on hold twenty long minutes. "Thank you for holding," a woman said, speaking so fast that Bailey hadn't interpreted the first line when the woman spoke her second right over it: "What's the nature of your emergency?"

"Uh...uh, there's something weird going on over here. I'm at Baker's we're off of Underhill road, right by the..."

"I know where it is. What's going on?"

"There's a fight. The manager is beating up one of the employees, real bad." Bailey had to resist the urge to peek out into the main room again. Had the assault turned into murder yet? There was the feel of murder in the air; it was just a matter of time if it hadn't happened already.

"I'm afraid we won't be able to get someone out to you for some time," the dispatcher said in a rush. "What I need you to do is find a safe place. Don't put yourself in danger. Do try to remember any pertinent details of the assault. Write them down if you can."

It seemed like the dispatcher was just about to hang up. Before she could, Bailey asked, "How long 'til someone gets here?"

Six miles away, dispatcher Jenny McMann looked at her board and shook her head. The Poughkeepsie police department ran fourteen patrolmen on a Monday evening— nine officers and their cruisers had been lent to the State police and were on their way to Walton. Five off-duty officers had been called in to bring the number to ten, but six—the very six who had been to Baker's earlier—had already gone home sick with dreadful migraines. That left only four patrolmen, all of whom had left a few minutes earlier to deal with a spectacular brawl a half mile from *Baker's*. The Walton guards had not gone far when they'd been kicked out. They went to a college bar and it wasn't above a half hour before they were fighting eight against thirty...and winning.

"Maybe an hour," Jenny lied. The last she'd heard was

that two officers were being rushed to Saint Francis hospital, while the other two would be sorting the details of the fight for half the night. "Just find somewhere safe."

"An hour? Wait, just hold on, now. You don't seem to under…" The phone went dead in Bailey's hand. "Oh my God," she whispered, suddenly more frightened than she'd ever been in her life. No one was coming to her or Danni's rescue, not for an hour and she knew that an hour would be far too late. It was quiet in the other room, but she could feel the presence of people; she could feel their heated breath stirring the air. They seemed to be listening for her just as she was listening for them.

Her feet were moving before she even realized it, heading for the back door where the cooks would smoke and play craps in the alley when business was slow. She opened the door and came face to face with Bob Jenkins.

"I knew you'd come this way," he said. His breath was foul; it was akin to an open sewer. Bailey leaned back from it, trying to shut the door, only Bob stuck his foot inside.

He came closer, his face pressing into the crack of the door. She saw that there was a thin line of black fluid creeping from his tear ducts. "I always thought you were smart for a waitress. Smart and pretty and so tasty. Wait…why did I say that?"

His strength, for such an old guy, was prodigious and without even trying he opened the door halfway. But his own question so confused him that he straightened and looked about him. "I shouldn't have said…but you are so clean looking that I couldn't help…"

Bailey threw her full weight into the door, catching Bob by surprise, and knocking him back into the alley. She then pulled the door shut and rammed the bolt home. Half a second later, he tried to tear down the door with his bare hands, screeching in raw anger.

On the other side Bailey turned in slow circles hoping to see something that would trigger an idea or a plan to get out of there alive. She guessed that whatever was wrong with Bob Jenkins had also affected most everyone in the main room, which meant going out there was crazy, yet staying in the kitchen didn't seem much better. There was exactly one hiding place: the walk-in freezer, a six by ten metal box that was kept fifteen degrees below freezing. How long would it be before she ended up like the stacks of frozen hamburger patties? She guessed twenty minutes, give or take.

Without a hiding place she was a sitting duck. Any minute, Roger would come back to find out who was trying to break down his door; he would catch her and…she pictured the way he had mercilessly punched Danni in the face. It made her want to cry in fear. She held the tears back, barely, as a plan began to form. If Roger was going to come storming back, why not have him vent his rage on Bob Jenkins?

Before she could chicken out, she went to the swinging door between the kitchen and the bar, cracked it open and yelled, "Roger! Someone's trying to break in through the back door." The floor trembled as he came rushing down the short hall. Bailey ducked away from the door and knelt against the wall. The kitchen was in a semi-state of gloom and she hoped that in his blind fury he would miss her small form crouched out of the way.

The door banged open and he came rushing by, walking in an odd manner as if he wasn't certain where to put his feet. He went to the back door and screamed at it to shut up. When Bob kept up his attack, Roger grabbed his head in both hands and screamed again, before trying to open the door. His hands fumbled over the bolt, uselessly. He tried yanking it up and down. When that didn't work he yanked it left—unlocking it—and then right just as fast, locking it again.

"Fuck!" he cried and then began beating on the door with his fists.

Bailey watched this with her guts churning. Roger was

out of his mind and if he caught her just sitting there, she knew precisely what he would do: beat her to death like he had Danni. She left Roger fumbling at the door and went through the kitchen door in a crouch and stopped in surprise. Someone had turned off the lights. To her right the bar was dark with strange shadows roving over it. She could hear breathing and the sound of glass clinking glass. Suddenly the small fridge under the bar opened and in the glow she could see there were people behind the bar, grabbing bottles and drinking straight from the lip. Others were on the customer side or draped across the sticky surface stretching out long arms to get what they needed.

The rest of the room was a pure black surprise.

To get out she had to go one way or the other; she chose to risk the dark. Inside her was an urgent desire to run out of there at full speed, trusting to luck that she wouldn't trip over a chair, or run smack dab into one of *them—mouth breathers* as she had classified them. The sound of their breath was loud, the smell revolting. They were near in the dark, she could hear them all around. Cocking her head to the side, she tried to pinpoint where they were by listening. In this way she managed to dodge four of them, but one came up behind and grabbed her hair.

"Smell that. It's pure, so pure."

Hot breath on her neck told her he was inches away. In terror she spun away from him and heard rather than felt her hair tear from her head. It was like the sound of soft fabric ripping. Straight into the dark she pelted, knocking into something hard, a table, and then something soft, a person, one of the *mouth breathers*. She pushed him away and charged to the one light in the main room, a little orange glow that read: exit.

Between her and it stood Danni Sparks. The waitress wasn't a *mouth breather* yet and with her dark hair she wasn't easy to spot. They went down together and Bailey knew it was Danni by her small size and the smell of her perfume.

"Danni, it's me. Let's get out of here." Bailey jumped to her feet, pulling Danni up with her. She made to run out of there, but unexpectedly, Danni held her back. Her fingers were like claws digging into Bailey's arms.

"What makes you think you're so good? So fucking perfect?" Danni demanded.

"I'm not," Bailey said in a whisper, afraid to speak any louder in case she was overheard by a *mouth breather.* "But something's wrong. We have to get out of here before it's too late."

"It's already too late for you," Danni replied. "You and all your perfect friends are going to pay. Lording it over us, acting so superior, making us feel stupid because we never went to college or because we never had your money."

*What money?* Bailey wanted to ask. Everyone knew Bailey didn't have two nickels to rub together. "Danni, please," she pleaded. She was on the verge of blubbering which would be disastrous. The whispers were bad enough for it had already attracted some of the *mouth breathers.* "Please...I think they're going to eat me." It sounded incredible in her ears and yet very real.

"Afraid for your perfect skin?" Danni asked. "You should be, but I won't eat you. I am...hungry. It's odd to feel this want to eat a person, but I won't do it...I won't...not yet."

"Then you'll let me go?" Bailey asked.

"No. You're a fucking bitch and you're going to pay."

The pair grappled and with the dark, it was impossible to tell exactly what each took a hold of. Bailey felt hair and cloth and grabbed a handful of each. She was larger than Danni and figured she would be able to break the smaller woman's grip; she was mistaken. Danni threw her to the floor with ease, taking a position on top of her, straddling her chest, pinning her.

"Don't eat me, please. Danni, I'm begging you, please."

"I already told you I wouldn't. Do you feel that?"

Bailey felt it. Something sharp slid through her shirt and into the first layer of her skin. She guessed it was a knife and Bailey pictured one of the gigantic carving knives the cooks sometimes used. Whatever it was, it was sharp and the pain was immediate. The knife kept sliding in at her and she was unable to do anything but suck in her stomach; the metal seemed to follow her retreating flesh until she hardly dared to breathe.

"Please, don't," she hissed, high in her throat.

"Why not? You did this to me. You made me dirty. You and your kind did it."

Bailey tried to grab Danni's hands in the dark; it was too late. Danni slid the blade in very slowly and Bailey was paralyzed by the pain. She could do nothing as the knife entered an inch above her belly button at a shallow angle; it slid through the lower third of her stomach, spilling its contents into her peritoneum, sliced just the lower edge of her left ventricle before grinding to a halt against her fourth thoracic vertebrae.

The pain was excruciating. She could only fling her hands out and gasp. Danni bent lower, gloating. "I'm going to open you up like a lobster, pull out your heart and shit in your chest cavity." She wasn't lying.

## 2

On the fourth floor of the Walton facility, the scientists worked furiously, gathering everything for their coming rescue. As they worked they kept one ear cocked, hoping to hear more gunfire. They were sure that any minute they would hear the clatter of machine guns and assault rifles and, maybe, grenades. It would begin low and then creep closer and closer to the top floor as the infected people were "cleared" out. The scientists waited and waited and eventually the pace of their work slowed and then stopped altogether when they realized there wasn't going to be a rescue.

There was no more gunfire; there was only the steady banging as the infected people kept hammering on the doors. It felt endless. The sound vibrated the walls and rattled their nerves.

"Will the doors last?" Stephanie asked. Chuck glanced once to John Burke, who shrugged.

"I reckon they won't," Chuck said. "Especially that middle door, seeing as it's all bent and gnarly. It might last a few more hours, maybe a day, but it'll come down if them zombies keep at it."

"Yeah, but we gots fire, still," Burke put in. "Iffin' she'll use it."

"Y'all mean, Dr. Lee?" Chuck asked. "She'll use it. She's got some stones is what she has. Hell, she practically dropped that traitor bitch down an elevator shaft. She's not squeamish." They had stopped listening at the elevator shaft ten minutes before. It had remained deathly quiet the entire time and none of them really liked the idea of sitting over a corpse. They had shut the elevator doors and were now sitting across the hall from them with their legs stretched out.

Stephanie felt an odd and surprising twitch of jealousy at Chuck's words. She thought that with her death so close she'd be beyond such things. *It just means you're still human*, she thought. *Still alive*. That was good at least. She squinched over closer to Chuck so that the edges of their hips touched. "I'm hungry," she said, hoping to change the subject. "Do you think there's anything to eat around here? I could go for some Cheetos."

"I doubt it," Chuck said. Casually he put his wide hand on her slim leg. "Before the quarantine this place was sterile, you know, like perfect. I can't imagine Dr. Lee letting anyone get orange fingerprints all over the place."

"And don't forget them germs," Burke said. "This is where they be a makin' them. Who wants to eat in a germ place? Not me."

Stephanie was all set to be jealous again over Chuck's description of Dr. Lee, when a thought struck her. "Why not you?" she asked John. "The Com-cells germs didn't do anything to you. That's what I find so strange. You look normal when all the rest of them are so crazy."

Burke, who had zero practical knowledge of microbiology, said, "It's prolly gots sumptin' to do with my immune system, is all. Ain't no reason to go looking on me like that."

It was a second before Stephanie realized her lips had been twisted and her eyes heavy and suspicious, like a toad's. "I guess not," she said, making an attempt to hide the sudden nervousness she was feeling about being so near to Burke.

Chuck felt the way she'd gone stiff. "Hey, it's probably nothing. Maybe he got a bad batch. Or, hell, maybe he got the only good batch. Mayhap ole John here is what they were all supposed to look like." He slapped John on the shoulder and gave him a shake.

"Maybe, but…"Stephanie paused, not wanting to rain on the man's parade. " But how do we know? Maybe he's on a delay. Maybe the Com-cells just multiply slower with him. Maybe he's sick and we just don't know it yet."

Burke cast a nervous eye at Stephanie. He didn't know what was true when it came to all the science. For him, one theory was as possible as the next. Chuck caught the look and the chill between the two people on either side of him. He stood, unfolding himself to his full height and then reached a hand down to Stephanie to help her up. "We might as well go to the expert on this if we want some answers."

"We don't have to involve Dr. Lee." Steph said, feeling the jealousy like a splinter, needling its way closer and closer to her heart.

Chuck shook his head. "I got your piece of mind to consider and John's as well. He looks suddenly a might bit green. Sides, we all are just sitting around waiting on the next attack; might as well fill the time."

John was touching his face as if trying to feel the green. "Y'all really think I could still get it?"

"I'm sure it was all just speculation," Chuck said. "But to be on the safe side we should at least ask." He helped Stephanie to her feet and John, as well, as he hadn't made a move to stand up; he'd just sat there thinking about all the ramifications involved if Stephanie turned out to be right.

They went to Dr. Lee's office, finding her, at least in Stephanie's eyes, perfect as always. Her black slacks still had a sharp crease running up the front, her hair shone as if it had been very recently washed, her face was composed, her skin soft, her large doe eyes, calm. The only blemish on Thuy's appearance that Stephanie could see was a smudge of ash on her shoe from the fire she had set.

"I don't have any information concerning the rescue," Thuy said, preemptively. "The authorities are giving Dr. Milner the runaround, however I'm sure it won't be that much longer."

"That's not what we're here about, ma'am," Chuck said. "We wanted to know about John. Why he didn't get sick like the rest?"

"And iffin I'll get it in the future," John put in. "I don't wanna wake up some morn wantin' to be eatin' my baby girl."

Thuy grimaced slightly, and answered, "After what happened today, I can't say, unequivocally what will happen to you in regards to the Com-cells. I simply don't have enough information. What we know is that your body's immune system destroyed them so thoroughly that it is rather amazing." She paused for a deep breath and added, "I believe that there is a strong genetic component at play."

"Playin' how?" John demanded. He wasn't the smartest of men, but he was shrewd enough to see when someone was hedging. Amy Lynn's doctors used to act the same way whenever they had bad news to impart. They'd get all cagey with their words, hiding behind science when they didn't want to speak plain.

Thuy took another deep breath, confirming John's suspicion. "We should speak in private," she said.

The air seemed to up and leave John's body. It was just like when he'd heard Amy Lynn's terminal diagnosis—he felt like he'd been hit over the head with a two-by-four. "Naw, I'd ruther y'all jes tell me plain."

"It's about your daughter."

Suddenly, John lost all sensation in his extremities. It felt like his body was a loosely held cloud which was in the process of dissolving around him and that a stiff wind would finish the job. "What 'bout Jaimee? She get bit?"

"No, however she did come in contact with the Com-cells. She's stable at the moment, with her…"

John's legs gave out. Chuck said, "Whoa, big fella," and grabbed him on the way down. He helped John down to the soft carpet.

"Not my baby, not my baby," John said, over and over again. Tears leaked out of both eyes, dribbling into his thin hair.

Stephanie took his hand and squeezed, but she might as well have been holding her own hand for all the comfort it did for John. She looked up at Thuy. "Is his daughter like him, immune? You said there was a strong genetic component at play."

"Jaimee Burke is not completely immune to the effects of the Com-cells," Thuy replied. "It's been four hours and so far she is remarkably healthy in…"

John was well behind in the conversation. He heard the words as if they were coming through in Morse code. Each word seemed separate from the others; sentences had to be pieced together. "Four hours!" John raged. "It's been four hours and y'all didn't tell me?" he tried to get up; Chuck thought it prudent that he didn't and so held him down.

"If you don't recall," Thuy said, "you had run off, so you can hardly blame me for not telling you right off the bat. Then there were the attacks to deal with and Anna and...I'm sorry, I had a lot on my plate."

"Right, right, but how is she now?"

Thuy glanced at her notes on Jaimee Burke. "Stable. Temperature, blood pressure, pulse are all within normal parameters for a child of her age. Her eyesight has been dimming with the advancement of the spore production..."

"And her mind?" John asked, interrupting.

"Again, she's remarkably whole. She has suffered a slight impairment, mostly memory loss and certain higher functions. Math seems beyond her ability, all except simple counting, and reading comprehension is lower than her grade level. We don't know if this is going to be a permanent loss. These things she's lost might just come back on their own or she might be able to be re-taught. "

"And her appetite?" John asked, nervously. "She be gettin' a hankerin' for people? You know, like all them zombie whatchamacallem's."

"Not yet," Thuy said. "They say she likes proper human fare...I mean normal food." She added this last when John's eyes took on a vague look as he considered the word 'fare'. "Would you like to talk to her?"

John jumped at the chance.

**3**

In the big house, eighty yards away, Jaimee spoke to her father quietly, in a dull manner, not at all as she usually would. The phone was a tedious method of communication for her. She knew her daddy's voice and could remember his face and she remembered she loved him, but while she was on the phone, she couldn't put the three things together. So, one moment she would be basically talking to a stranger as she remembered how her father used to push her on the swings and the next moment she could hear her daddy, but didn't know what he was talking about.

She knew she wasn't coming across well because her daddy kept asking "You alright?"

Not being seen as smart or as one of them bothered her. She had hoped her daddy would be just like her. That would have made it better because he used to understand her meanings just fine. Now he was whining and his thinking wasn't right. His mind was clearly all catawampus and askew. That's what also made the call such a bother.

"Sorry, Daidy, I gotta do more tests for the doctors, so bye."

"Love you, pumpkin."

Half her mind was in an uproar about how awful and weak and puny he sounded, while the other half recalled what she was supposed to say back. "Love you too, Daidy."

Jaimee squinted at the phone, trying to see where the danged "off" button was hiding. It was there among all the other buttons but they was just so small. After a few seconds of searching, she decided to give up. She plunked the phone on her bed and promptly forgot all about it.

"Why did you tell your father you had more tests to do?" Dr. McGrady asked. His voice came through a speaker and Jaimee had long since forgotten the face that went along with it. She had begun to think of him as some sort of robot living in the house, or as part of the house. "You don't have any more tests scheduled for another hour."

"I jes didn't wanna talk, I reckon." She didn't like the robot voice of Dr. McGrady's none too much, neither. She moved away from her bed and began walking about the room she shared with the body. The body was still alive but just sleeping. At one time she'd known who it was, but now it was just a body to Jaimee, one that didn't smell none too good. It smelled like poopy.

She walked around the room because she knew there was a spot where the robot couldn't see her. She forgot where it was, but she knew it was marked in some fashion. On the wall next to the bed there was a stainless steel cabinet that, like all the rest of the furnishings in the room, looked to have been pilfered from a hospital.

The cabinet had a red line across its front—the mark! She remembered leaving it with a crayon; she glanced down to see if she was still carrying it. No. The crayon was gone. She'd eaten it and then looked in one of the windows at her reflection to see if her mouth had looked bloody. It hadn't, which was a might bit disappointing.

"Jaimee," the robot voice of Dr. McGrady said. "Can you get away from there? You know I can't see you when you go over there."

What was it he didn't want Jaimee to see? There had to be something. She began opening drawers and found all sorts of things that in her old life she would've found interesting: bandages, little bottles full of strange medicines, gauze, medical tape, needles, clamps, scalpels, and fine string with what looked like little fishhooks at the end.

"Jaimee, please get away from there."

"I'm jes lookin' and there ain't no crime in that," she mumbled to the robot voice. Most everything was in plastic. Some of the things she opened so as to get a better look at 'em. The scalpel was sharp enough to draw blood—hers was a very deep red. She glanced over at the body and wondered what color blood she'd have. Jaimee didn't want to find out. She was sure that if she cut open the body a whole mess of black poopy would come gushing up like a geyser and that was just gross.

She turned away from the body. It wasn't interesting. For all the time she'd been in there, the body had just lain there with its monitors making little mechanical noises every few minutes, either a beep or a boop or some such. Jaimee barely paid it no mind, not even to wonder who it was. She had once known. Sometime long ago she had known the name that went with the body. It felt like that had been in a dim past, years before.

"Jaimee, you are trying my patience," the voice said. "For the last time, move away from the cabinet."

"Why, whatchu got in it?" So far what she'd discovered hadn't been all that interesting.

"Boring stuff that doesn't concern you. Now go back to the center of the room where I can see you. Keep going; a little further, there. Is there anything I can get you? Something to drink or eat? A game or something?"

She had needs and wants but, like her memory, they were vague and impossible to form into words, and, at least for the time being, they weren't urgent. "Naw. I jes wanna git gone." That was something her daddy always used to say. Now that she wasn't trying to think on his words, her memory of him was perfectly intact. Gittin' gone was what she wanted. There was more to her life than the room. She went to the window and looked out, the dark was easier on her eyes.

A person appeared out of the rain and headed right for her. His skin was nearly dark as the night, his eyes darker. It was Earl Johnston. He came to stand right beneath the glass and stared up at her with his mouth hanging open; it looked huge like that of a gargoyles. There was blood on the tatters of his clothes and ugly open wounds across his throat and face. Jaimee wasn't afraid.

They stared at each other until Earl figured out she wasn't what he needed. He turned away at the sound of a car door opening. There was a man leaning into the driver's side of a Buick, digging around in the console. That's what Earl hungered for: someone clean.

Off he went to feed and Jaimee only watched without expression.

## Chapter 13

*//8:09PM//*

**1**

Even with his wife dying of cancer, Andy O'Brian couldn't quit. The cigs had a death grip on him. It's what drove him out into the rain to find a lighter, that and his mother–in–law's nagging ass, voice. He didn't need to hear it every time he went for a smoke.

"You have a four-year old daughter for goodness sakes," Alice Wepperman hissed, not wanting to wake her granddaughter. "If you get the cancer, too, who's going to take care of her? Not me."

Andy knew that was a frigging lie. First off, Alice loved Samantha more than she loved her own daughter, and second, if he died, Samantha would come with the proceeds from two life insurance policies. That alone would have cemented her position as permanent caregiver. Alice was a coupon clipper simply because she had a sharp aversion to work.

"It's one cigarette," he grouched, looking through his suitcase for his lighter. He'd had it earlier and he always kept it with his smokes, but it was plum gone. "Have you seen my lighter?"

"No," she lied, easily. She had his lighter stashed beneath the couch cushion. In a fit of anger, she'd taken it after his last cigarette. For the life of her she couldn't understand how a man could smoke around his children. It was easily the worst habit she could imagine. And her daughter! Barb had been just as bad right up until she got the news. "And good riddance I say," Alice finished with a flourish.

Andy felt the muscles in his jaw clench; they were hard,

like chestnuts in his cheeks. "You know what, Alice?" he growled. "Today is not the day and now is not the time." The quarantine was absolutely fucking him over. He had traded delivery routes just so he could stop by Walton to be with his wife for a few hours while she went through what was supposed to have been the miracle process of destroying her tumors. Instead the quarantine had descended on them like an iron curtain, trapping him on the wrong side. She was confined up in the hospital and he hadn't heard a peep from her all day. What was almost as bad, he and his truck were also stuck. Over a quarter million dollars' worth of whiskey was just sitting out in the parking lot.

It would be a friggin' Christmas miracle if he wasn't fired.

That's why he needed his cigs *and* his friggin' lighter. He popped up out of the suitcase and looked around the strange bungalow, hoping it had fallen beneath one of the poufy chairs. The O'Brian's were one of eight hardship cases among the forty-two patients who had been given free housing for the week. It was a smart little cottage with three bedrooms and two baths. Everything was perfect about it except for the damned missing lighter.

"It's never the day to quit in your book," Alice nagged, shaking her fat face. "While I think now is the best time. No lighter equals no cigarettes."

Andy snapped his fingers under her bulb of a nose. "Barb has one in her car, and if not, there's always the car lighter." She looked at him smugly and five minutes later he found out why: there wasn't a lighter in her car, not even the factory-installed push lighter.

"Son of a bitch!" he hissed. Not finding a lighter really got his goat, but seeing his mother-in-law gloating through the screen door nearly pushed him over the edge into rage. He held his temper in, letting the cool rain wash away his anger. As he was sitting there, half in and half out of his wife's car, a man came staggering up. He looked like he was walking a floor that wasn't just crooked but angled as well.

*Drunk by eight, sheesh*, Andy thought. "Hey, buddy, you got a light? I can't seem to…find…" Andy's voice trailed off as he got a better view of the man. He looked like his head had been near torn off, yet he was still walking. "Are you ok? Do you want me to call…hey!"

Earl Johnston attacked Andy, not as a man would with swinging arms and kicking feet, but as an animal, teeth first. In the first second, Andy actually thought Earl was falling and went to catch him and the next thing he knew teeth were tearing at his neck. He fought back but he did so against a foe imbued with great strength and an intolerance of pain. Andy was dead in minutes.

His dying screams alerted Alice, who ran to the door, thinking Andy had dropped a tire jack onto his toe or some such nonsense. She took one look at Earl chewing through Andy's throat and screamed herself raw. Foolishly, she reached for the screen door, jerked it closed, and locked it before shutting the main door. Losing those precious seconds doomed her. The main door was stout, solid wood and would have held Earl at bay for some time.

Earl was off of Andy's corpse in an instant. Unthinkingly, he went after Alice, rushing for her with a mad hunger driving him. He launched himself through the screen door just before the main door clicked shut. His weight and momentum sent it flying back on its hinges to bang square into Alice's round face, knocking her to the ground where she spent ten seconds just trying to focus her eyes.

Three feet away, Earl growled in rage and frustration. He was caught up in the screen door and a younger, spryer woman could've jumped up and run out of there. Alice was five years past fifty and had moved beyond chubby and into portly. Her head was spinning from the whack it had received from the door and in her heart she knew she'd never get up in time.

"Samantha hide! Hide!" she screamed. "Samanthaaaa..."

Earl bent the screen door in half with his bare hands and then he was on her. His right hand had her by hair, his left hand pinned her down. She was absolutely helpless as Earl stared down at her, trickling fresh blood from his glistening jaws. It wet her face and dripped into her open mouth. She screamed long and loud. Earl watched her spasms of fear through the black of his eyes trying to see the white flesh of her neck where the body's fluid was hottest. He was eager and his mouth kept opening wider and wider until he couldn't wait any longer and he ripped into her.

The blood gurgled and bubbled up like a hell-fed spring. It was scalding to his lips, it was liquid copper, it was like living fire, but it didn't last and his hunger was on him again just as soon as Alice's heart died in her chest.

He stood, breathing in great gulps. His mind was utterly blank. He was not capable of thought, he could only react. He reacted when he heard four-year-old Samantha say, "Ga-ma?" Her father's scream had woken her and she sat up bleary-eyed, confused and afraid. The room was strange to her and the crash and the growly noises had her stomach hurting and when her Ga-ma screamed for her to hide, she didn't hide, she just sat holding her blanket to her chest and staring at the door.

Instinct is the weakest of human drives. Learning is a thousand times stronger and she had learned to trust that her daddy and mommy would always make things right, would always be there when things were scary.

Earl only had instinct. He hungered to drink the freshest blood no matter what and the sound of the little girl's voice triggered his instinct as if his gullet were barren instead of sloshing with the blood of his previous victims. He charged the bedroom door and struck it square. The walls shook.

Samantha screamed, inadvertently egging Earl on to greater efforts. The door rattled in its frame and with each blow the striker gave way a millimeter at a time. In a minute the door blasted inwards and Earl rushed in. He was starving.

**2**

The CDC arrived for the second time that night. Leading the team of six agents was Gerald Brunson wearing his trademark *Braves* baseball cap. It never went with anything he ever wore, especially his tweed suits, but that didn't matter much to him. He loved his team more than he did fashion and was senior enough in rank that people rarely said anything.

In the hour and a half since Foster's reconnaissance had turned deadly, a large tent had been set up to act as command post. It was green and smelled like it had been sitting in someone's basement for thirty years, but it was large enough to hold a dozen desks and it kept the rain off.

Gerald swept in. "First, I need coffee," he barked. "Second, I need to know who *was* in charge and third, someone has to catch me up." He always made sure to let everyone know their place in his world the minute he walked onto any scene. For all intents and purposes, at least in his mind, he was the federal government.

The agents were pointed to the folding table where Sergeant Foster sat moodily staring at a map of the grounds. His head had begun aching thirty minutes before. "It's nothing," he'd told himself. "It's just stress." After all, who wouldn't be stressed after what he'd gone through? And who wouldn't be stressed considering what he was going to go through? Someone would have to pay. Eight officers had died that night, which meant someone was going to pay big time.

He saw the CDC people arrive, which only made his head hurt worse. In his pocket was a bottle of Tylenol. Six of the pills went into his mouth to go along with the six he'd already taken. His water bottle was empty so he dry swallowed them—a part of him wanted to the chew the pills, to grind them up in his teeth so he could taste in their bitterness that the medicine was working. It was a weird feeling

"Gerald Brunson, CDC," Gerald said, coming up. He didn't offer to shake Foster's hand. The CDC wasn't a place for shaking hands. "Give me a sit rep."

"Sit rep?" Foster replied, looking up at Gerald with dull eyes and wondering: who the hell talks like that? *Officious assholes, that's who*, he answered himself. "How 'bout I just give you a briefing?"

Gerald smiled through clenched teeth. "Go ahead then. Be thorough."

Foster pointed out through the tent flap. "That's the Walton facility. They were supposed to be finding a cure for cancer in there, but something went wrong and instead they've created…" he choked back the word 'zombie' and went with, "They created a disease."

"They created a disease?" Gerald asked with raised eyebrows. "I highly doubt that. We're probably looking at a reaction to a previously unknown mycotoxin. The study of fungal agents is…"

"Do mycotoxins turn you into a fucking cannibal? Because that's what's happening up there. They're fucking eating each other."

A put-upon sigh escaped Gerald and he said, "Side effects vary."

Foster laughed without humor. "Spoken like a true bureaucrat. Thank God the CDC is here!" Gerald glared from beneath the brim of his baseball cap; Foster ignored the look and went on in a strident voice, "What about coming back from the dead? Is that a side effect, too?"

A little, nervous smile cracked Gerald's lips; he was pretty sure that this guy was slipping over the edge. "Maybe you should start at the beginning," he said as reasonably as possible.

The trooper was slow to begin. The Com-cells he'd breathed in were collecting in his cerebellum making it difficult to remember the smaller details. "It started this morning. At…at…around ten, I think, but I'm not sure. You guys, the CDC issued a quarantine order. It was just a precautionary thing, but that was wrong. That was stupid. They should've known they couldn't control this. Not with so many."

"Many?" Gerald asked. "How many people are we talking about? Just the ones who are infected."

Numbers began clicking by the meter in his head. It started with the number eight, only that wasn't the right number. Foster shook his head and said, not quite under his breath "Not them."

Gerald glanced back at his fellow CDC officers and raised an eyebrow. Foster didn't notice, he was digging through his paperwork. "Ah, here it is. Forty…forty-two, I think, but there were more, later. Lots more."

"Let's just concentrate on the numbers when this started. How many people were on the grounds when this started?"

Again Foster looked at his notes. Everything on the pages seemed so miserably buggy that he wanted to swipe at the paper or crush it in his sweaty hands. Instead he turned the pages at an angle, squinted, and read, "Two hundred and fifty-seven give or take. That's how many people were at the facility as of nine this morning. That was the count of the desk guards."

"And who did that include?" one of the CDC agents behind Gerald asked.

That was a much harder question and Foster wanted to ask what difference did it make? Actually he wanted to scream the question in the man's face; Foster's head wasn't feeling better with all the stupid questions. "I don't know. Hold on," he said as he brought out the Tylenol again. This time it was a handful that he ate, chewing the bitter pills until nothing was left in his mouth but a nasty white slime.

"Here it is," he said, smacking his lips loudly. "Twenty four medical staff, sixty one family members, twelve security personnel...uh, there's also the patients...I said those. Uh, and the cleaning and cafeteria workers and, uh, like thirty construction workers. Then there were the admin workers but they're all dead...sort of. At least they're not really dead. They're like me. I-I mean..."

He stopped abruptly and looked up at Gerald with as guilty a look on his face as any criminal ever wore. "I mean...I mean..."

Gerald stepped back; he could feel his pulse in his ears. "Were you in the building?"

Guilt didn't sit well with Foster's frame of mind; it was like blood and water. No, that wasn't right. It was like blood and...more blood. "No," he said aloud. The CDC people were staring at him like he was some sort of freak; that wasn't right either. "No, I mean yes, but I was geared up. And it wasn't just me. Trooper Paul was there, too, and he's just fine. Just fine."

"But you were in the building," Gerald pressed.

"Don't you read the fucking reports?" Foster snapped. "I'm sure I forwarded them on to your office."

"I don't read them before I come on scene, they color my judgment. And I'm especially glad I didn't tonight, otherwise I would've probably missed the opportunity to see you in this state."

"What state?" growled Foster.

"There's clearly something affecting your mental faculties, Sergeant. I'm afraid we'll have to add this tent and everyone you've come in contact with to the quarantine list."

"You can't do that..." Foster stopped as he remembered that this CDC jack-hole could quarantine him. It was well within in his powers because he was one of *them*. Foster didn't know just yet who *they* were, still he had Gerald pegged.

"If I'm staying, you're staying," he said, getting to his feet.

Gerald wasn't about to be blustered by this police underling. "Wrong. We will keep a safe distance from the other…" In the middle of his sentence, Foster launched himself at Gerald, who squawked like a bird and tried to leap back. Too late. Foster had him by his tweed lapels and together they went sprawling.

The CDC agents tried to help but Foster was too strong and in seconds Gerald was flat on his back. Foster sat square on his chest and sneered, "You're staying with me, Mister High-and-mighty, Mister Perfect." Gerald wanted to cry out for help, but when he opened his mouth, Foster spat something foul right down his throat.

**3**

Thuy looked at the phone in disbelief. "Say that again. The CDC agents that just showed up are now part of the quarantine?"

"Yes," Courtney Shaw replied, tiredly. "We're still trying to sort things out, but we will be moving to rescue you as soon as possible."

Courtney had no clue when it would happen. Not only had the CDC agents quarantined themselves, they had also quarantined eighteen other officers. She was, in effect, losing men faster than she was getting them on scene.

"Look, ma'am," Thuy said. "The doors won't hold forever. You have got to make the attempt very soon. Do you understand? We don't have anything to fight them with.

"I would like to help. I really would, it's just we don't have the manpower."

Thuy's whole body slumped. Deckard, leaning against the wall, asked, "What'd they say?" When she told him he took the phone from her and barked at the dispatcher, "How can you say you don't have enough manpower? We can see the cruisers from our windows. There's got to be at least sixty of them out there. That's more than enough for a rescue. Just have the officers come in with guns hot. Don't play around."

"It would help if we knew numbers," Courtney said, biding time and thinking on the fly. "We can't seem to grip on just how many people we're dealing with. Do you know?"

"I don't," Deck replied. "Somewhere north of two hundred and fifty, but that's counting the family members in the cottages. They number about, I don't know, sixty. I think our worst-case scenario is there are about one hundred and seventy five of these zombie things to deal with here in the hospital. Just remember they may be strong but they aren't armed."

"And they really can't be killed?" Courtney asked, in a whisper. The official policy was not to give any credence to the idea of zombies, however these people so clearly believed it that it was unnerving to hear.

"Not that I can tell," Deck replied, his voice also set low.

Courtney checked her board again. Not counting the eighteen officers stuck in quarantine, she had fifty-six manning a perimeter a mile and a quarter in circumference. It seemed more than enough to her but the CDC agent on site wanted triple that number. This left nothing for an assault on the hospital.

And if those zombie things couldn't die, would fifty-six really be enough anyway?

"Can I call you back?" she asked. "I promise I will." Deckard grunted, his way of agreeing, involuntarily.

Courtney dropped her head set and stood, about to go see Pemberton when Renee grabbed her hand. "It's going to shit, Court," she said. "Poughkeepsie wants their officers back. Their dispatchers are going crazy over this massive brawl at a bar and from what I can tell they only have, like two or three officers left."

Courtney didn't need to look at her board to see they couldn't afford to lose nine men. "But we need those officers here, did you tell them that?"

"Of course, but they were like, we need them, too, and we need trooper support. And I was like, what troopers? I mean, look at the board." They had scoured the countryside for every available state trooper within two-hundred miles and now there was nothing left.

"Did you try Kingston?"

"Yes and Red Mills. We have all their extra men, which is like two."

Courtney forgot all about her promise to Deckard. She sat back down and shoved her headset back on. "I'll try Hyde Park and Milton. You try Highland and Myers Corner. Beg them if you have to. Have them bring in their off duty officers or their wives or whatever. We'll send half to Poughkeepsie and the rest need to come here."

In Walton, Deckard and Thuy sat in her office, waiting. Every once in a while their eyes would meet. They couldn't bring themselves to speak of trivialities anymore. The central stairwell door was failing. Deckard had inspected it: the hinges were loose, they could go at any time, which meant they couldn't risk using the propane again. Too large of an explosion would bring the door down, leaving them defenseless.

He made a single attempt using the gas line as a flamethrower and had managed to torch one of the zombies at the cost of melting off two feet of hose. That trick would only work once more before the hose would be too short to even reach the door.

"What do we do?" she asked. He shrugged.

They were still sitting there after ten minutes when the lights went out. Thuy leapt to her feet. "Von Braun," she whispered. In her gut she knew he was behind it.

**4**

Anna clung to the side of the shaft and knew two things: her strength wouldn't last another five minutes, and Thuy had it in for her. Even if she managed to hang there until Thuy got back, her fate wouldn't change all that much. At best, she could expect to be hauled up into the corridor and then later hauled to jail. At worst, Thuy would keep playing her sick games not realizing that Anna was innocent of what she was being charged with. Innocent or not, she'd still fall very soon.

With her choices being between dying and going to jail, Anna chose to try for a different option. Her left hand had the weakest grip, she let go and began feeling further down the wall for a better one. In the dark it came up against something smooth and cool. Whatever it was had a narrow lip, barely enough room for the tips of her fingers. It would have to be good enough. Next she scraped her left foot down the wall until it caught on some unknown piece of metal. It was small, like the jutting of a bolt. There wasn't much to it, still it held her weight.

Her right foot found something similar, then it was her left hand's turn, again. She began searching, blindly, however the wall had suddenly become smooth.

"Oh shit!" she whispered. Desperate, she began reaching further and further out as her right hand began to tire. It started as a little tremble in the fat muscle of her palm, but soon the weakness invaded her slim little fingers and then her wrist.

She redirected her hand upward hoping to find the old hold, but it seemed to have disappeared in the dark. A wild thought struck her: *Jump for the cable*! "Hell no," she said through gritted teeth. The darkness was so impenetrable that she had no clue where the cable was.

"Help!" she screamed at the top of her lungs. "Riggs! Dr. Lee, please!" Her voice echoed around the shaft but failed to penetrate the cement walls or the steel doors. Seconds passed without any answer. She was alone in the black, clinging to what felt like an endless sheer wall, disconnected from everything else in the universe. It began to feel as if there wasn't anything in the deep black but that lone wall and that she could stretch out her arm twenty feet and still not feel anything else.

A miserable whine broke from her throat as she began to stretch her arm to its limit. Her fingers found metal. Recklessly, she clung to her holds by the edge of her manicure nails and explored the metal as best she could. It was vertical and smooth. Her mind pictured either a fireman's pole, which made no sense, or some sort of guide rail for the elevator car.

Either way, she knew she was seconds from losing the precarious grip of her left hand. She gave her life up to chance or fate--but not to karma. Anna didn't want to think about the negative balance of karma on her soul. Trusting to luck she "jumped" from her perch; it was a jump of six inches; all she could manage in her position.

Her hand found the metal rail and discovered that at four inches in width, it was too big for her to grab one-handed. She scrambled at it but failed to find purchase and as she fell down the shaft a scream built in her throat. The darkness sucked her in and she didn't feel the metal zinging by against her left hand until it stopped her short.

It wasn't a miraculous save like one sees in the movies where the heroine finds herself clinging to a hold and looking up, desperate, but still beautiful. No, what stopped her fall was that the fingers of her left hand had hit a bracket holding the rail to the wall and became wedged in the metal.

The pain was exquisite. It hurt too much for screaming. She began to kick and flail at the wall until her feet found another bracket four feet down. Whimpering like a puppy, she lifted her weight off her mangled hand and pressed her cheek against the metal rail. It was then she cried. The tears were useless. She knew that and she had always given herself a lot of credit for being tough, but just then she was frail and weak. Her hand ached beyond the telling, especially when she tried to bend her fingers. Then the pain was like fire.

She had saved herself, but now she felt trapped, in too much pain to go up or down. She wept miserably in the dark, her small feet set on two slag bolts and her right hand gripping the rail on its thinner edge. She cried until there came an explosion from up above. Its violence moved the air in the shaft like an ocean wave and a second later she felt a thrum go through the metal pressed against her cheek.

"Shit," she hissed, gripping the metal as hard as she could. Either Thuy or Von Braun had done something. One of them had made a bomb out of who knew what. "It had to be Von Braun," she whispered. There simply wasn't anything left in the labs to cause that big of an explosion.

She didn't like the thought of Von Braun having the capability to blow things up. What if he took down the entire building next? It might be something he'd do if he couldn't find the cure.

This fear was the catalyst to get her moving again. Using the strength in her right hand and the three good fingers of her left, she was able to shimmy awkwardly down the rail, moving in four-foot increments, using the heavy metal brackets as hand and foot holds. It hurt like a bitch and she sweated fear out of every pore but, sooner than expected, she found herself standing on the top of the elevator. Her knees gave out and with a light thump, she dropped onto her bottom.

"I made it. Yes, I made it," she said to herself, grinning in the dark and shaking from head to toe. "I can't believe..."

A moan from below her stopped her tongue, making her realize that, yes, she had made it down the shaft, but that didn't mean she was in the free and clear. There were still an unknown number of zombies between her and the exit, and after that there were a bazillion police. And, even if she got past them, there'd be the prosecutors to deal with. They'd be out for blood. Someone would have to be blamed for everything and if the real saboteur wasn't caught, assuming there was one, they'd try to pin everything on her regardless of the fact that she had barely done anything wrong.

The most she could honestly be accused of was a little light spying and a single instance of theft. In her bra, under one of her heavy breasts was a vial of "the cure". The night before, back when she thought the damned stuff would work, she had switched out a single vial of the Com-cells that would have been used on John Burke. He had instead received normal saline. The real vial was for the nice people from France who, she assumed would pay her handsomely for it. She had carried it around ever since, at first because it was too valuable to set aside and now because...she didn't know why. In the back of her mind she thought: *Just in case.*

She hadn't known what *Just in case* meant until she was sitting right on that elevator. "Just in case I want revenge," she whispered. She promised herself that she wasn't going to jail even for corporate espionage. She was more terrified of being locked up than she was of a world full of zombies and they had her pretty much dead to rights. The hard drive Deckard had waved around had to have been stolen and thus wouldn't be admissible in court, however all the emails that she had sent from her own computer would be. Legally speaking, she was screwed...unless...

Anna's karma took a hit as a new thought struck. She stared upwards into the dark, not seeing the elevator shaft, but picturing the lab where Deckard had interrogated her. Even if she got rid of the vial, all the evidence needed to convict her was four stories up, and all the witnesses too.

Without the paper trail, or the hard drive, and without Deckard and the others pointing fingers her way, the prosecutors wouldn't have any reason to even suspect sweet, innocent Anna. She just had to think of a way to destroy all of it. "The zombies will eventually kill them," Anna mused, "only that would leave the evidence intact. But," and here her eyes narrowed, "a fire would do it. A big fire would take care of everything."

She sat back picturing it and for a time the throbbing in her hand went unnoticed. Fires weren't as easy to set as most people supposed, especially in this modern day of glass and steel buildings. Yet, Anna knew, these buildings were built around a skeleton of wood. There would be plenty to burn, it was simply a matter of getting a fire going and sustaining it.

"If only I had access to the labs," she said, pursing her lips. The dark hid the fact that she was subconsciously striking one of her "poses." As a teenager she had experimented with how she looked under different hues of light and in diverse poses. She practiced those which drew the most attention from the boys--even at a young age she was well aware of the effect she had on members of the opposite sex.

There, in the dark, even with a smudge of grease marring the perfection of one cheek, and her hand mangled and bloody, she was striking. This did her little good, alone in an elevator shaft, however she wasn't a one trick pony. Her beauty was a blunt tool; her mind was a fine instrument, which few could match.

She set her mind to the problems of starting a fire. First she created a mental catalog of the fourth floor labs--for the most part the paraphernalia was of a bio-chemical nature and, although she could've started a fire with some of it, it wouldn't be big enough to burn down a house let alone an entire hospital, and yet there had been an explosion.

"Think, damn it," she hissed to herself. "How do I start a fire without gas or...holy shit!" She began to grin. "I have gas. The release of propane in an enclosed space would account for..."

A sudden string of gunshots jarred her out of her thoughts and brought her back to the present. It was the sound of

Sergeant Foster and his men being ambushed. Like everyone else in the building she held her breath, listening, her full lips hanging open. Unlike everyone else, she was rooting for the zombies—if the police won through, she'd be screwed.

When the firing stopped, she sighed in relief. Out of those left alive in the building, she was the only one not blinded by hope. For her it was clear that the rescue had failed. She could hear the screams of the troopers as they were eaten alive. It was a sound that shivered her, but instead of causing her to give up the plan of burning down the building, the screams cemented it.

Anna rationalized that death by fire was far preferable to death by zombie--she'd be doing Thuy a favor by burning down the building.

As Foster escaped, alone, out into the wet night, Anna began the task of finding a way down into the elevator car, without the use of her sight and with only one hand. She was delayed a half hour when Thuy opened the door on the fourth floor and set Stephanie, Chuck and Burke to keep some sort of vigil over Anna's supposedly dead body.

It wasn't much of a wake, and the three of them didn't say much about her "passing" besides such sayings as *Good riddance* and *She was a bitch, anyway*. The words drifted down on Anna like hot, bitter ash, and when the three finally tired of their watch and shut the door, Anna went at the elevator hatch with even more eagerness than before.

There were two bolts holding the hatch in place. They were tight. Her fake nails snapped off one by one and then her real ones began to crack and peel back. Eventually, persistence paid off, the bolts gave way and the hatch swung down. A sharp, white light shot up, filling her with hope. The first thing she did was to inspect her aching hands: the right one was cut in a number of places and the nails were ugly, but otherwise unhurt in any lasting manner. The left wasn't as well off. Her pinky finger was cut to the bone near the base. Above the laceration the finger was dislocated or broken and went off at an obscene angle as did the ring finger next to it. The pain made her nauseous and the blood...

She wasn't one for blood. It was the reason she'd chosen the field of study she had. Because of the possibility of infection, the Com-cells being the most fearful in her mind, she had to glove the mangled hand. That meant she would have to straighten the fingers. Acting quickly before the fear of more pain could set in, she grabbed the two fingers, pulled them out and then up.

Bone grated on bone. It was like sawing glass with another piece of glass. A gasp, and then a small cry escaped her, as tears ran down her face. She balled her right hand into a fist and thumped it repeatedly against the metal rail that shot away upward.

The pain was a roar inside of her, muting the world beyond. She tried her best to cry in silence, but she'd been heard.

From below, a moan cut across her pain-filled mind. A zombie came up to the elevator doors and stood swaying slightly, looking in. Anna leaned back from the hatch for fear of being seen, however her morbid curiosity didn't allow her to lean too far. There was a question on her mind: *Did she know this person?* The hospital wasn't very large after all.

It had been a woman. The scrubs she wore narrowed it down to one of the medical staff. From her face it was impossible to tell who it had been since it was mostly eaten away; there was a lip hanging from her gaping mouth, but her nose was nothing but a ragged hole and the single eye she had left was black as the shadows in the elevator shaft. She still had most of her blond hair left on her head and since there were only three blondes on the med staff it narrowed it down somewhat.

Before Anna could figure it out, the zombie turned away. Another one took its place: from the blue work shirt and the belt at his hip, she knew it had been one of the construction workers. She was sure that he'd deserved his fate. For the past week she hadn't been able to walk ten feet without one of them making kissy noises at her ass, as if that would possibly turn her on in the least.

The construction worker zombie was shoved out of the way and another stuck his head into the elevator. "What the fuck?" it muttered. "What was that?"

At first Anna shrank even further back, terrified. It was Von Braun and his evil reputation preceded him; he was the boogieman being whispered about on the fourth floor. With his ability to think apparently somewhat intact, he was the most dangerous zombie of them all and if Anna hadn't been in such a dreadful position she would've remained completely silent, however it wasn't a secret how much he hated Dr. Lee.

*Maybe I can use that*, she mused. Injured as she was, she knew she needed help.

"Hey you," she said in a low voice.

Von Braun spun and glared up at the hatch his black eyes searching, his nose snuffling. Her perfume was pronounced in his nostrils, however he did not connect it with a human scent. The perfume was too sweet. What made him hungry was deeper, mustier.

Beneath the perfume he caught a whiff of her. "You're a girl," he said. "I like girls. I like them soft. I like them pure." His hunger came across unmistakably, almost sexual in its potency—this was something she understood.

"You can't have me," she said, in a sultry voice. "But you can have the others. I can get them for you."

His face squinched in puzzlement. "Who? Who can you get? The gook? The nigger? I'm so fucking hungry I could even eat a goddamned nigger!"

Anna didn't know the term "gook", she was too young to understand the racial slur, but she knew "nigger". She found it extremely distasteful, but that didn't stop her from using it as a tool. "You can have the nigger and all of them. I just need your help. It'll be like a trade. See that key?" She pointed at the elevator control panel where a silver key sat in a slot.

He turned and squinted. "This?" He slid the key out and held it up to the hatch.

"Yes! Just drop it on the floor and then press the button with the three on it. The number three, do you understand?"

"No," he said, truthfully. The gook and the nigger and all of *them* were on the fourth floor. Why did she want to go to three? He didn't understand and that made him nervous. His Diazepam was running down. He could see the little bag pinned to his hospital gown; there wasn't much left and he knew that when it was gone he'd turn dumb like the others. The thought scared him and nothing ever scared Von Braun.

"The three is right in front of you," Anna insisted. "Just reach out your hand and I'll direct you."

"I know what a fucking three looks like you fucking whore, bitch, shit! I want something out of this."

"What are you talking about? You're getting plenty. You're getting the nigger and the goot."

"It's *gook*, you dumb fuck!" Von Braun yelled in a rage. "Gook! Like slant or slope or fucking chink!"

Now Anna understood. "You mean Dr. Lee."

"Yes, I want her, badly, but there is something I need. I have to be able to think. I can't be like all of them." He pointed out into the hall.

She peered down through the hatch trying to decipher his meaning. There were two things which set him apart from the other zombies: the fact he could speak and the IV bag that hung from his shoulder. It was almost empty.

"You need some more medicine, don't you? What's the name of it?"

"How the hell-fuck should I know?" he cried, his diseased spittle flying. "I can't fucking remember. I just know it makes me normal." He tried to smile to show how normal he was. It was hideous. Not ten minutes before he had torn the throat out of one of the Middleton deputies and now his mouth was an ugly hole filled with black spores and congealed blood.

Anna coughed and turned her chin. "Just...just hold up the IV bag so I can read it. Oh, Diazepam. That's just Valium. Weird." Why would Valium make him lucid? It certainly didn't make him normal. He was far from normal. The scientist in her wanted to figure out the puzzle that Von Braun represented, however the criminal in her, who was on the verge of getting caught, wanted to please him long enough to escape.

"I can get you some more Diazepam," she told him. "Just hit the three button." He stretched out a hand and then paused. "Right in front of you," she said.

"No. It's on two. I know that much. Who do you think you're fucking with, whore-dick? Who do you think you're trying to trick?"

"No one," she said, thinking fast. "They have meds on both floors, but we can go to the second if that will make you happy."

"Getting the fucking gook who did this to me will make me happy," he replied.

"Ok sure. Hit the two and we'll get you fixed up." Now that the key was out of the control panel, Anna didn't think that she needed Von Braun and figured she would ditch him as soon as possible. He hit the button. Anna cringed as an awful screech struck her ears. "What the hell?" she asked. The sound was grating. It made the hair stand up on her arms. And it was a second before she realized what it was: it was the sound of metal on metal, it was the knife she had stuck up under the counter weights. "Thuy was wrong," she said with a smirk. "The knife didn't stop anything."

Thankfully, it was a short ride, only a single floor. "Go check to see if there are any zom...I mean anyone out there," she said, as the chime sounded and the door slid open.

He stared out into the hall for nearly a minute, ignoring

the doors that kept trying to close on him. He was having trouble counting the three zombies walking about; saying three and counting to three was not the same thing. "There's, uh, some of them. I'll get rid of those fucking retards." He left, snarling curses at the other zombies.

"About time," Anna said under her voice. Hurriedly, she slipped her feet through the hatch and dropped down into the elevator, making sure to clutch her injured hand to her chest while holding her good hand over the surgical mask to keep it from slipping.

"Move your ass!" Von Braun was screaming. "Come on, move it!"

Curious, Anna snuck a look down the hall and was surprised to see him herding three zombies before him. As docile as sheep they accepted his abuse. He slapped, punched, and kicked them to the north stair and then shoved them through the door.

"Wow," she said. A minute before, she had been all set to leave him there but, after what she had just seen, she changed her mind, realizing that if she could control Von Braun, then in effect she could control all the zombies. That was power.

She stepped into the corridor and he immediately charged, forgetting everything at the sight of her perfect skin. "Stop!" she ordered. "Remember your medicine. Von Braun, remember I'm the only one who can keep you thinking straight. I'm the only one who can get you back to normal."

This stopped him and for a few seconds he stood in confusion. "I am normal, damn it! I'm not like them."

"And you can stay that way as long as you do what I say. Now, point to where the meds are and I'll get them for you, but you have to stay put." He pointed at an odd collection of sheets, blankets, and shower curtains hanging off the side of the hall. Anna went to it, walking on her tiptoes, ready to race away if Von Braun even so much as twitched in her direction.

He looked like he wanted to do much more than just twitch. His hands were opening and closing and he had begun to drool. "Stay," she warned as if talking to a dog.

"Just give me my meds!" he screamed.

In order to get them, she would have to turn her back on him which meant she had to trust him. A shiver went down her spine as she turned to step through the curtains. There was no time to waste; she went straight for the med locker and began looking for Diazepam. The drawer was clearly marked and clearly empty.

There was plenty of Valium in pill form. She took one of the bottles and measured out triple the normal dose: six pills. They seemed so small and inadequate that she added four more to the med cup. The bottle went into the pocket of her lab coat for future use.

"This is for you," she said to Von Braun. "But if you want any more you have to do what I say." She set the pills on the linoleum and backed away. He ate them greedily, chewing them and then swallowing them dry.

"You'll give the gook to me?" he asked. She nodded and he smiled a mishmash of black spore, red blood, and white powder. "Then name it. What do you want?"

## Chapter 14

**//9:16 PM//**

**1**

In the fifty-six minutes before Gerald Brunson's migraine forced him out of his chair and onto the ground where he rolled around moaning, he did his level best to go through the CDC checklist, item by item. Yes, he was interrupted three different times as troopers went berserk and had to be restrained, and then there were the endless, tedious phone calls from his boss and his boss's boss, and this mayor and that dignitary and even someone from the governor's office, all wanting to know what was going on.

To each, he replied with a simple: "When I know, you'll be the first person I'll call."

Then he'd go back to his precious checklist because that was what he'd been taught. Follow protocol! Don't deviate from procedure. Stay the course, and all that. It had been drummed into his head, and now when there was simply no time to waste going page by page, he kept his team on task and focused on the manual. He even had them read each page aloud so that nothing would be missed, knowing that in the long run, it would pay off.

It cost them precious minutes; minutes they desperately needed and minutes none of them were ever going to get back. No one inside the white tent knew that their quarantine was on a countdown.

Even before Gerald and the second CDC team arrived, Sergeant Foster had accidentally infected half the troopers. After he spat in Brunson's mouth and went nuts, he got the other half good and germy as well. The CDC people, including Brunson, though it was obviously too late in his case, quickly suited up head to toe in their plastic bio-suits. They were safe against the Com-cells, but not against the infected troopers who gradually fell under the hateful spell of the disease and grew suspicious, angry and above all, jealous of the agents in the plastic suits.

When Gerald's migraine made it impossible for him to go on with his protocols, Rachel Jergen, the second in command, took over and she too "stayed the course", picking up where he had left off, attempting to catalog who was infected and where they may have gone and with whom they may have come in contact, but she, too, was interrupted.

Trooper Paul, his face twisted into a grimace from the pain in his head, came stumbling up to her. "How come we don't get a fancy suit?" The nasty look he wore, coupled with his size made him extremely intimidating. It didn't help that in order to see the face behind the plastic he had to stand very close to her. He was also armed with an extremely large gun on his hip, something Rachel glanced at every other second. "Where's my suit?" he demanded.

The CDC people looked back and forth at each other but they weren't trained to deal with such belligerence. They were used to throwing their weight around, not being cowed by the local "authorities" who they usually didn't feel were much of an authority on anything besides the locations of the local Dunkin Doughnuts.

"We...we have some coming," Rachel answered in a jittery voice. "It'll just be a few more hours before they arrive. We have additional agents on their way and they are bringing extra suits and extra, uh, uh extra of everything."

Paul had just begun to feel the paranoia. It wasn't yet the raging voice in his head that it would soon become and he allowed himself to be soothed by her words. He went back to sit with the other troopers, most of whom had been nodding along at his outburst. He sat and watched Rachel, gradually coming to the realization that there was something not right about her. The feeling built in his mind gradually, keeping pace with the growing numbers of replicating Com-cells.

Twenty-eight minutes later he got up, walked to her chair and without warning, punched her full in the face with all his strength—something that was extremely satisfying and good in his mind. Like a ragdoll, she flopped backwards out of her chair and lay on the ground unmoving. None of the troopers batted an eye, not even when he took out a utility knife and slashed open her mask.

"She's not human," he whispered. Behind the plastic shield her eyes were all wrong. She was either an alien monster that looked like a human or a fake, like a cyborg or a replicant, he couldn't tell which, but he was going to find out now.

"Get off her!" one of the CDC men screamed, pulling at Paul's broad shoulder.

"I have to see," Paul said. "She's not real. She's not one of us!" With little effort he threw the man off him. He bent again to the unconscious woman and without a qualm slit her face from forehead to chin. Blood gushed up, pooling in her eyes, and running to settle in her suit. Using both hands he peeled back her flesh. It didn't come off easily. Beneath were blood and bone and stuff he didn't recognize beyond the fact that he knew it was human stuff.

"Must be deeper," he said. The bone that made up Rachel's nasal ridge was harder than it looked and he had to punch the knife through it to get at the secret below. Someone screamed. "It's ok. She's not one of us," he said to reassure the screamer, he glanced back and saw the plastic people, and wondered if they were indeed real people. The CDC agents didn't look much like people to him.

"Keep an eye on them and someone untie Foster," he demanded of the other troopers. After his run in with Gerald Brunson, Foster had become increasingly irrational, but now Paul was seeing that his words had been more prophetic than crazy. "Foster was right all along about them. They can't be allowed to keep living like plastic fakes. We have to open them up, too."

At this, the remaining CDC agents broke for the exit with the troopers hot after them. In accordance with protocol, the door was zippered shut. The first agent got the zipper halfway down before the troopers were on them in a paranoia-fueled madness. The agents scattered like sheep, running around the tent uselessly screaming and begging for mercy.

"Don't listen to them," Paul ordered. "They ain't real. They're like her, underneath." He pointed to Rachel who, in truth, no longer looked human.

Since the troopers weren't full-on zombies yet, the CDC agents were spared the agony of being eaten alive. Instead they were stomped and beaten into a semi-unconscious state. Even then Paul wasn't sure about them. He mutilated their bodies with his knife, trying to find the hidden truth. "I'll find it," he whispered, growing hungry at the sight of all that red, red blood.

**2**

Outside the tent, time ticked uselessly away. The other troopers sat in their cruisers strung out in a wide circle around the hospital and shivered from more than the chill night.

The bloodcurdling screams of the dying CDC agents could be heard by everyone, even those on the other side of the hospital. They radioed back and forth to each other wondering what to do.

"No one does anything," Lieutenant Darrel Ford said. He'd been on scene for all of fifteen minutes, having driven down from Albany to take charge of the quarantine. "No one is to approach that tent. Maintain your intervals and keep your eyes open."

"But it sounds like people are getting skinned alive in there," someone said.

"I don't care!" Ford barked into the radio. "Our job is to enforce the quarantine. No one goes in and no one goes out for any reason." His orders were clear.

Eight minutes later things changed.

People in the little cottages had been waiting out the quarantine in relative comfort, watching TV or playing board games. It wasn't until the sun went down behind the clouds that things became unnerving. First it was the muffled gunshots, and then it was the ring of police cars with their flashing lights, and then it was the screams as Andy O'Brian and his mother-in-law were killed, and now there were people lurking around the grounds. Strange, scary looking people.

Instinctively, the people in the cottages turned off their lights and barricaded their doors. They also began calling the police over and over again until they got through. Their frantic pleas moved Courtney Shaw, who, on her own volition, ordered them to be evacuated.

"We have commandeered a warehouse for exactly this reason," she told Ford. "It's just up route 24 about fourteen miles."

"We don't have suits for everyone," Ford replied. "In fact I have only six available. That's not enough."

"It is," Courtney insisted. "Look, you don't have to transport anyone. They all have cars. Just escort them to the warehouse. The only ones you really have to worry about are those at the big house. Yes, they are infected, but one is comatose and the other is..."

"If they got the disease, they stay," Ford interrupted.

"But one is only a little girl and the other is..."

"I don't care. They stay here with the rest. Unless I hear from the superintendent himself I'm not moving them." Courtney, who had used the line: *You have new orders* as if they had come from somewhere higher up, relented.

Ford wasn't happy about the move; regardless he followed "orders" yet he did so with the very certain knowledge that he wasn't about to lose any troopers on his watch. He contacted each of the cottages personally and coordinated the withdrawal so that his men wouldn't be on the grounds for more than a minute.

The family members in the cottages were eager to get as far away from the hospital as possible.

In the big house, Dr. McGrady was checking the hall closet for his coat. "Someone has to stay," he said. "And I'm not volunteering. Sorry Ed, but you aren't paying me nearly enough to hang around here."

His cowardice bothered Edmund Rothchild who gave him a hard look from beneath his bushy brow. "I'll stay with Gabrielle and Jaimee myself, but you must show me what I need to do to take care of them."

"Of course," McGrady said. "It's not hard." Taking care of the little girl was nothing. So far, Jaimee's sickness hadn't progressed very far. She was moody and bored, but not cannibalistic. Gabrielle Rothchild was even easier. She hadn't so much as twitched since McGrady had put her under. All Edmund had to do was keep an eye on her IV drip.

"I'm going to stay, too," Maddy informed them, planting her balled fists on her hips. "Mommy needs me and Jaimee is my friend. I should be here for them."

"No," was all Edmund said on the subject. There wasn't time to argue. The sirens of the police cars had suddenly kicked on. It meant they'd be coming through the gates in precisely one minute.

As McGrady explained the simple procedure to replace an IV bag, Ms. Robins grabbed Maddy and rushed around the house stuffing their things in a suitcase. The little girl was like a whining anchor, needing to be dragged around by the hand. Ms. Robins barely noticed the weight. She had seen the creatures masquerading as people walking around the grounds and she had heard O'Brian's ghastly death as it happened. The screams had lanced her heart and she had bled courage ever since.

"Hurry, hurry, hurry," she repeated, over and over, desperately afraid to be left behind.

When the minute had passed, eight cruisers swept through the open gates. In each were two troopers, one literally riding shotgun. They screeched up to the cottages, nervously looking all around. In the glare of their lights they could see the strange people...the zombies in the rain.

Trooper Ian Andrews, in the lead cruiser disobeyed orders when he saw Ms. Robins. He rolled down his window long enough to yell at her. "Get in your damned car!" he screamed. "Forget all that crap!"

She had a suitcase in one hand, another under her arm and Maddy held by the collar to keep her from going anywhere. Mincing around the puddles in four-inch heels, she was the slowest by far of anyone fleeing the cottages. Before she even got Maddy tucked inside her Mercedes, Dr. McGrady's BMW was already pulling out, spewing mud in an arc. Right behind him was Mrs. Unger in her Cadillac.

"Don't leave us!" Ms. Robins wailed. A zombie almost caught her as she pushed Maddy into the car. It came splashing up out of the dark, its face half shorn away, one eye hanging by some grisly string of nastiness. Ms. Robins didn't have to be told to run. With a scream, she raced around the Mercedes, putting it between them.

As the zombie scurried around the car it walked right next to the police cruiser. "What the hell is that?" the trooper in the driver seat asked. His voice was girlishly high.

Ian didn't notice and when he answered, his own voice was two octaves higher than normal. "What do I do? Do I shoot it?"

"No!" the driver practically screeched. "Don't you fuckin' roll down the window again. Uh...Uh, use the spotlight."

"Right," Ian said. He had a death grip on his shotgun. It was as though the weapon had fused to his skin, and he had to will his right hand from the stock in order to work the spotlight.

The illumination, equivalent to 240,000 candles, blasted into the disfigured face of the zombie, transfixing it long enough for Ms. Robins to climb into her car. Just like McGrady, she didn't wait for the troopers. She pointed the Mercedes across the lawn and stomped the gas, tearing twin ruts in the new sod before bouncing over the curb and onto the street. She was so out of her head with fear that at the gate she swung left instead of right.

Lieutenant Ford, watching from the new command post swore into the mike: "Someone get that black car, damn it! And who's on the beamer?"

"Kilo-four is in pursuit of the BMW. That fucker is really moving."

"Watch your language, Kilo-four," Ford admonished. He relaxed a touch when he saw a second cruiser go off after the Mercedes. Ms. Robins wasn't going to get very far. "Let me have a vehicle count."

"This is Kilo-one," Ian answered, his voice slightly more under control. "Including the two that got away I have a vehicle count of seventeen. I say again, one, seven."

Ford had been thinking of just sending four cruisers to convoy the vehicles to the warehouse, however f seventeen vehicles was quite a number to handle. If the civilians decided to scramble and go in different directions the quarantine would be officially broken and he would be to blame.

"Kilos, one through eight, this is base. Once your stragglers are rounded up, reform and continue on to the warehouse. Do not let any stray. I repeat, no strays."

This was a terrible mistake. With the Poughkeepsie officers gone and eighteen of his finest going berserk in the quarantine tent, Ford only had forty-one troopers to work with and now sixteen of them were off trying to round up civilians, few of whom considered themselves part of the quarantine. Two drivers needed gas and broke off as soon as they saw a gas station. One car had kids who wanted pancakes; the driver thought nothing of searching for a late night diner. And one family just wanted to go home—the driver of that car tried to sneak out of line at three different opportunities.

The troopers were gone for nearly two hours.

Back at the Walton facility, Edmund Rothchild watched the police leave. When the lights and commotion was over, he could see seven or eight of the beasts he had helped to create, standing in the rain. They made him sick to his stomach. He wanted to go out and apologize to them and a part of him felt it would be fitting if they tore him into pieces—he deserved it.

If he'd been alone he might have done just that, but there was Gabrielle and Jaimee to take care.

"Hello?" Jaimee asked, when the house grew quiet. "Can I come out now? I been real good."

"Not yet, child," Edmund replied over the intercom. "But I'm working on it." He clicked off his mike and then dialed his partner Stephen Kipling. "Kip, it's me. I need a favor. I need an ambulance and a driver who isn't afraid of getting arrested. Money is no object."


## 3

In the hospital, Thuy was out of ideas. Offensively, they had few weapons: a single gun with a handful of bullets and a couple of broom sticks that had been converted into spears. Defensively they rested their hopes on a few bits of twisted metal.

Thuy suggested they keep away from the central door and not make any noise in the hope the infected people would just give up and go away. It was a vain hope. The zombies could smell the mass of humanity and it drew them on. They went at the door endlessly, pounding with bloody fists, completely unfazed by the broken bones and the pain.

Time and again, growing ever more desperate, Thuy wandered around in the dark, kicking at the debris in her labs, hoping to come across something that would save them. There was nothing but trash left.

"We could pick a door and make a break for it," Deckard suggested. "I have twelve rounds. Who knows how far that will get us?"

"Bullets don't seem to make much of a difference against them," Thuy said. "From a scientific view, it's fascinating. From a human point of view it's terrifying."

Deckard pictured Lacy Freeman, impossibly standing up with two fat holes in her chest. "It's disgusting is what it is."

"Yeah, disgusting," she said, absently. The image her mind conjured up was that of Heines burnt and blackened, but still moving, still trying to kill. He was out there in the stairwell, no longer sentient or aware beyond his endless hunger.

She let out a long sigh. Deckard dropped down beside her, their knees touching gently. She didn't pull away as she once would have. There was no reason to, not anymore, not with their time so close.

They sat in an easy silence until a little after nine when she asked Deckard for some privacy. "I need to do something," she said at his look. By the light of her fading cell phone, Thuy wrote out a quick last will and testament. In it she apologized for her role in what had happened. The last line read: *It seems fitting that I, who looked to end the death and suffering of others, but through my incompetence caused so much of both, will suffer at the hands of my victims. My death will not be long in coming.*

The others on the fourth floor waited bored but terrified. That Von Braun would attack before they were rescued was a foregone conclusion. It made every minute a dull torture.

Most of them prayed. Eng was among the few who did

not. He ground his teeth, thinking about what might have been. His right hand rarely left the front pocket of his slacks where the .38 snub nose sat. It was damp with the sweat of his palms. Despite all evidence suggesting that it would be of little value against the zombies, he was glad for it and he wouldn't stop touching it as if it held a spiritual significance.

The others would curl their lips at the way he kept rubbing himself. He didn't care. They would be dead soon and they would deserve what they'd get.

Alone in the BSL-4 lab, Milner paced. He'd been there long enough to know he wasn't infected; Heines had not yet been contagious when he had taken a bite out of him. Since no one was bothering to watch Milner anymore, he could've walked right out if he wished, however he chose to be by himself. The others were cretins. Miserable little bugs compared to him. Thuy was an abject failure, Riggs was falling apart under the stress, and Deckard, in spite of the bravery he'd shown was nothing more than a security guard. The rest were just morons. He figured if there was any justice in the world, they would all die a horrible death and he'd be allowed to walk out the front door.

John Burke fretted over his daughter. It ate him up inside knowing she was sick. "But she's a fighter, like her mama was," he whispered to himself. He'd been doing that a lot and the scientists had ceased cocking an eyebrow over it. John found it surprising that he liked the scientists and he had a real affinity for Chuck, whom he'd dubbed a *good ole boy*, despite that he hailed from that crap state Oklahoma. Then there was Stephanie, a fine woman in his eyes.

Good people. He was planning on leaving them when the fighting started. He would hold back, look for his chance and just split on out of there. Jaimee had to come first. He had to get to her.

Stephanie and Chuck sat with their long legs poking straight out in front of them. They were midway between the north stair and the central. They held hands like grade-schoolers and for the most part sat in silence. Chuck was built for silence; Stephanie liked to talk, but just then she didn't need to vent her frustrations, she needed to be reassured on one very important point.

"You won't let me get eaten alive, will you?"

He was quick to reply, "You know I won't let that happen to you."

His answer had come too fast for her, as though it had been an ingrained reflex as opposed to a thought out response. She shook her head. "No. I mean it. I can't be eaten alive, it's too horrible. I want you to do whatever you need to do to, you know, to keep that from happening to me."

At first Chuck was confused. She had to know he would fight his hardest for her, but that didn't mean he'd be able to guarantee her safety. Then the word *alive* kicked into his mind. *Ohhh*, now he understood. He wanted to bluster and "stand upon his honor" but that would've been just a load of bull. There was no honor in having the ropes of your intestines pulled out and fought over by undead beasts while you lay, half-alive, watching.

"I'll kill you if I have to."

"Just make it quick."

**4**

In Poughkeepsie, the darkened, windowless bar held the mindless zombies in; their olfactory senses weren't superhuman. They smelled the tacky, nearly dried blood of the dead waitress and they smelled the alcohol that had been spilt and they smelled each other, but they didn't smell the humans in the town just outside the bar's doors.

They drank the alcohol until it was gone, then they simply hung around, as aware as the sticky, beer-stinking furniture. Who knows how long they would've stayed there sealed up in the bar simply from lack of wit?

Just after nine a young couple walked in and paused in the doorway. They took one look at the black eyed, crazy people and took off running for their lives. The two got away, however the floodgates were open and the twenty-four infected patrons went out into the night. They scattered, each directed by the phantoms in their heads. Pedestrians were attacked, as were cars filled with people. Homes were broken into and gunshots began popping off all over town.

Three of the zombies attacked a movie theater. The girl selling tickets behind the heavy glass actually laughed at them, thinking it was some sort of performance art or a skit of some sort. Even when one of the zombies figured out how to work the doors and screams began in the theater, she only chuckled.

In all this, the police were of little help. The recalled officers from the Walton facility, not understanding the severity of the issue, took their sweet time, griping over their radios at being sent here, there, and everywhere. They tooled back to Poughkeepsie at a gentle fifty miles per hour, causing a backup on the highway, as no sane person thought it safe to buzz by one cop car, let alone nine.

Officer Shadrick, in the last car, was chortling in his seat as he kept a watch on the civilians growing aggravated over the slow pace. "Here comes one," he said into his radio. The car, a Ford Bronco that was mottled orange with rust, crept up, running at the posted speed limit exactly.

"Tell me when," Officer Megs said.

Shadrick's grin was so wide it pinned his lips back halfway to his ears. "Not yet...not yet...Now!" Just as the Bronco came up on Megs' bumper he flicked on his lights. They flashed red and blue in the wet night and the Bronco swerved and slammed on its breaks. Shadrick threw his head back and laughed.

"You guys are being juvenile," Sergeant Reynolds said from the lead car.

"What?" Megs asked, his faux innocence coming through clearly. "My hand slipped. Besides, you're the one doing ten miles an hour below the limit!"

"Are you saying you want to hurry?" Reynolds asked. It was a completely rhetorical question. A brawl in a college bar was nothing new. It meant a long tedious night of taking statements and going through the pain of booking a gazillion people on minor charges that would be plea-bargained down to practically nothing anyway.

There was no sense hurrying for that.

Twenty minutes later, the Poughkeepsie dispatcher, Erin Poole demanded, "Adam-six, where are you?"

"Be advised, Adam-six is engaged in a natural way," Shadrick answered. Reynolds had pulled over at a McDonalds and was currently stinking up their bathroom while the others were munching their way through piles of french-fries.

"Who is this?" Erin demanded, breaking protocol. "Is this Shadrick? Tell Reynolds to get his ass back here. Things are, I don't know, they're getting weird and scary. We have all these college kids here, and they're starting to get...I don't know, really aggressive."

Shadrick immediately ran to the bathroom and beat on the door until Reynolds came out, buckling his gun belt around him. "Something bad is happening at the station," Shadrick said. Within seconds the nine cars were racing out of the parking lot with their lights blazing.

At first, the dispatcher was relatively calm as she urged them along faster, however out of the blue their connection went to shit. "Say again, dispatch," Reynolds yelled into his radio. "You have to speak up. Who's right there? What do you mean?"

In answer, a scream lanced over the airways and then the radio went dead. All nine cruisers heard it. There was no need for Reynolds to say anything. He pushed the gas pedal to the floor and kept it pinned there until the lights of

Poughkeepsie came up. At the city limits they went loud, their sirens beating the air and drowning out the sounds of the gunfire coming from every direction.

It wasn't until they pulled up to the station that they heard the sporadic pop, pop, pop.

"What the hell?" Shadrick wondered aloud. It wasn't like a battle was raging in the town, but there was enough gunfire for them to know something was going dreadfully wrong. "What's happening?" Shadrick asked. No one could answer.

"First things first," Reynolds said and nodded to the police station which seemed unnaturally quiet.

They went in with guns drawn. The station was a cramped maze of offices, interrogation rooms and cells—a perfect place for an ambush. The guards from the Walton facility had managed to infect over thirty people during the brawl. When that was coupled with the police officers who had gone black-eyed after wrestling Jack Cable to the ground and then booking him, there were a total of forty people thirsting for blood in the police headquarters.

Reynolds went first and he was slow to fire on his friends, regardless of the black eyes or the putrid smell that came wafting off of them. "Bill, what's wrong with your eyes?" Bill Olson, a long time veteran, came stomping out of the 'bullpen' coming right for Reynolds. "Bill!" Reynolds yelled, backing up. He didn't equate the way his friend looked with the quarantine he'd just left, if he had things might have turned out differently.

"Stop right there, Bill!" Reynolds tried one last time. The other officers didn't know what to think. They could see Bill just fine and he looked horrible, but just like their sergeant they weren't going to shoot a friend out of hand.

With a grimace, Reynolds stuck his gun in his holster. Bill was on him a second later. It took five of the officers to pin him, but before they could cuff him the sounds of their fighting brought others who looked and acted just like him. First it was a pair of sorority girls, clawing and snarling. One latched herself onto Shadrick and though he was literally twice her size he found that she was impossible to shake off without resorting to overwhelming force.

He caught up one of the girl's arms, torqued it up behind her back, and then slammed her into a wall face first. At the very least she should've been stunned; the breath should've been knocked from her body and she should've crumpled to the floor. Instead of any of that, she spun in his grip and sank her teeth into his chest latching onto his bullet resistant vest.

Forgetting protocol, he grabbed a handful of hair and pried the sorority girl off of him. Holding her at arm's length, like a spitting cat, he cocked his arm back, prepared to cave her face in with one punch, however a gunshot stopped him.

The sound paused the fight just long enough for him to see that others had joined the bizarre brawl, many others. Cops and students, all dripping goo from their eyes were everywhere. Most weren't fighting the nine officers, there were so many of them that they were fighting to get at the nine officers. Reynolds, in front was buried beneath a pile of bodies. Right behind him, McCurry was pinned against a wall and there was what looked like a fountain of blood coming up out of him.

At the rear of their nine-person string Dave Morganstern was the man who'd fired his gun. He was wild eyed and shaking. There was a body at his feet. Unlike how the police are portrayed in the movies, no cop ever wants to fire his piece, especially at someone unarmed, it usually meant the death of his career; just then it was his life he feared for. The sound of the gun had drawn a dozen black eyes to him.

He was rushed and before he got two more shots off he was brought down, screaming curses. The officer next to Dave started blazing away with his 9mm. Astonishingly, the people jerked and blood flew but they kept coming.

All of the officers who saw this scrambled desperately for their weapons. Shadrick felt an overwhelming need to wiz in his pants--his gun was caught on something and didn't slide free until it was almost too late. He had the sorority girl clawing at his arm, pulling the skin back like she was peeling a banana and just in front of him was some college kid, no longer looking like a fresh-faced sophomore as he had when he'd woken that morning. He looked like death.

Shadrick's gun cleared his holster with the sophomore two steps away. He pulled the trigger directly into the things chest. The bullet tore through his right lung, sending pieces of bone and black lung spraying out behind him. The sophomore didn't blink, he just kept on coming, lunging like a drunken dancer and when he tore into Shadrick, the sophomore didn't bite into the vest.

His teeth crunched down on the side of Shadrick's jaw, cutting through the flesh easily and gouging the bone. The policemen did what came naturally, he screamed in terror and pain. He shot three times into the sophomore. The angle was an odd one so the bullets transfixed him from side to side leaving tunnels from one end of his body to the other.

Still the zombie bit and ripped with his bloody teeth. The pain was so intense that Shadrick couldn't think straight. Forgetting the gun he twisted his face away from those awful teeth, inadvertently exposing his neck to the zombie. The beast saw the beckoning flesh with its wonderfully strong pulse lying just beneath. It ignored the bullets slamming into his body, in fact they didn't even register as happening to him. All he cared about was his thirst.

He went for the throat.

Through the pain, Shadrick could feel his life gurgling up out of his flesh, strangely, it felt as though he was a boat with a leak. He was sinking. Sinking beneath warm red water.

**5**

Perhaps the busiest person in the state was Courtney Shaw. Sitting in the trooper station she was like the hub of a bicycle wheel that had sprouted a thousand spokes.

Before the CDC people had stopped transmitting, being mostly dead as they were, Courtney's night as a New York State police dispatcher had been hectic, but when the Poughkeepsie station went silent, her life became pure chaos, and each minute grew so hectic that she forgot to breathe at times.

Pemberton was stuck on the phone trying to explain a situation that was spiraling out of control. What was worse, he was forced to repeat himself over and over again, first to his boss, Major Billups, and then to Major Billups' boss, Lieutenant Colonel Parks. He then had to explain it all once again to the personal assistant to Gavin Ross, the superintendent of the New York State Police and not twenty minutes later to Ross himself.

After that he had to deal with the politicians. Every mayor, town manager and city council member from every little hamlet and village within a hundred miles demanded to know what was happening. Then there were the myriad of officials from the governor's office who had to be convinced that what was happening wasn't a hoax. Eventually, Pemberton was getting calls from congressional staffers.

With him tied up and with troopers heading in every direction, it fell to Courtney to direct operations; no one else had a handle on what was going on. Her first act was to call every trooper station in the state and beg for more men. She then put a call into the CDC in Atlanta to tell them the bad news that another team...another two teams had to be sent out--clearly the insanity occurring in Poughkeepsie had to be related to what was happening at the Walton Facility.

While on hold with the CDC, she took a look at her map and sighed. Using a red marker, she drew a circle that encompassed both Walton and Poughkeepsie. Within the circle were fourteen townships, with Poughkeepsie being the largest. She estimated there were 40,000 people living in that circle.

"Mother of God," she whispered.

Renee punched her in the leg. "Grab a freaking line. I'm getting killed here." The lights on the board were going nuts. There had to be a hundred people on hold.

"I can't. I have to call the governor." Pemberton's call earlier had been met with a not so polite: *Thanks. Keep me informed.* Who knew how many dead troopers there were and that was the Governor's response? Pemberton had thrown his coffee mug at the wall and had gone on a profanity-laced tirade that could be heard out in the parking lot.

"The governor?" Renee asked, incredulously. "Don't be stupid, that's Pemberton's job. Your job is to help me with all these freaking calls. Look at the board! Poughkeepsie is going crazy." It had been a half hour since anyone had heard thing one from the police in Poughkeepsie. "I'm getting like twenty calls a minute. Some of them say there are cannibals roaming the streets. Not zombies, Court, but cannibals." Her eyes were just as round as they could be.

Courtney glanced again at her map with the big red circle--the station was not a quarter-mile from the edge. "You're going to have to handle it, Renee." She reached for the phone and dialed the governor's home line and was proud to see that her hands were steady.

"Governor Stimpson, please" she said curtly when the phone was picked up. "This is Courtney Shaw with the New York State Police."

A man had answered; he sounded extremely starched and formal. "The governor is currently hosting a dinner party with..."

"I don't give a rat's ass," Courtney snapped. "Get him on the phone, now! Or I'll be calling the media next to tell them that sucking up to fat cat donors is more important to him than protecting the people who elected him."

"I see," the man said and then laid down the phone. Courtney could hear part of a muffled conversation on the other end of the line. She grew more and more nervous with every second, but when she heard: *Tell them I'm busy*, she grew frosty again.

The stiff man--she pictured a butler in coat and tails-- came on again, but before he could say anything, she said, "I forgot to mention this call is being recorded as was your entire conversation with the governor and it will be made part of the public record in five minutes."

"Oh...uh, one moment, please."

Stimpson came on the line a minute later. "Who the fuck is this?" he demanded at full volume.

"My name is Courtney Shaw," she answered, unfazed at his bluster. "I'm a dispatcher with the state police, section K. You need to call up the guard."

"What the fuck is this? You gonna tell me how to do my fucking job? A lowly dispatcher? A fucking nobody? What do you really want? I was told you got some sort of tape. Big fucking deal. Listen up bitch, I appointed the attorney general. He's not gonna listen..."

"Will you shut up!" she yelled into the phone. Next to her Renee was as still as a statue. She looked to be made of brittle porcelain that was on the verge of shattering.

The governor paused for half a second. "Sure, sure. Dig your own fucking grave."

"If you listen to me, you might be able to save you own ass, Governor. You need to call out the guard right this minute. The quarantine around Walton didn't hold. They're in Poughkeepsie now and if you don't act fast, who knows where they'll turn up next."

There was enough urgency in her voice to cause the governor to hold back his next curse-filled diatribe. "Look, I know about Poughkeepsie. I received an update from some sergeant named Pemberbrook, or something, forty minutes ago. He said they recalled their officers and that they were handling it."

"But..."

"But nothing. I also had one of my aides contact the local P. D. They said it was a brawl at a bar. So you see, Miss, I'm doing my job. The situation is under control."

"I'm sorry, but it's not under control," she insisted. "The Poughkeepsie police aren't picking up. Something terrible happened there. And something bad is happening at the local hospital, Saint Francis. The last call I had was there were eight confirmed deaths. We are sure it's..." Did she dare use the word zombie to the governor? No, she didn't dare. "We are sure, uh, that it's infected people from Walton doing this. Probably some janitor or family member slipped out of the quarantine before it was fully secure."

"Eight deaths?" he asked, quietly.

"Yes, sir."

"That's not a lot. It's sad don't get me wrong, but it's not enough to call out the National Guard over. We're talking millions of dollars just to mobilize a few battalions."

She didn't know how many men were in a battalion, however she knew it wouldn't be enough. "Would three hundred deaths be enough? That's my current estimate including everyone at Walton. It could be higher. We're getting calls from all over Poughkeepsie asking if there's a battle going on."

"Three hundred, Jesus...I'll need to confirm this."

Courtney didn't think there was time to play that game. "Who would you confirm it with? Superintendent Ross? All that will happen is he'll need to confirm it with, Lieutenant Colonel Parks, and he'll have to confirm it with Major Billups, who'll call Sergeant Pemberton, who'll ask me. You can't afford to waste any more time, Governor. You need to listen to *me*."

He blew out a sigh. "Look, I wish I could, only there are

channels to work through. I appreciate your, uh zest in this matter and I can assure you I will be calling Ross just as soon as we hang up."

"You're wasting time!" she pleaded.

"Yes, and now so are you." The governor didn't wait for a response. With another sigh he thumbed off the phone and then stared at it, thinking about the fucked up day he was having. "But the guard? Really?" Had it come to that point already? He didn't know and he didn't like being the man on the spot. Yes, he was governor, but he had a whole slew of aides just so he didn't have to make a decision. Not a real one. They'd present him with all the facts he would need to cover his ass one way or the other.

The governor straightened his tie before heading back to his party, pausing on the way to speak to his assistant. "I want the entire crew in house, in thirty minutes. No excuses. And get Ross on the line again. And that new guy, what's his name? Schemmel? From the Department of Health. Also, I'll want the Attorney General, and someone from the CDC who can explain what the hell is going on."

The calls were made and the meeting set and then delayed when the Attorney General couldn't be found. Eventually an assistant was located who could be expected to cover the governor's ass if things went to shit. The meeting moved ponderously along because the governor was clear on one thing: he wasn't going to be blamed for anything. The attitude was contagious. When Superintendent Ross was put on the spot concerning the current state of the calamity, he called his second in command, who called Pemberton directly, who ran down the hall to the dispatch room and asked Courtney Shaw.

One hour and thirty-seven minutes after Courtney had begged the governor to call out the guard, he made his informed decision. "We'll call out the guard," he said after taking a consensus and putting it on record.

Another twenty-three minutes slipped away before a

snoring Major General Horace Collins was poked awake by his wife. By that time the number of infected people had shot past the six-hundred mark.

**6**

Anna wanted to set her fire and go; the quicker the better, only there seemed to be an ungodly number of zombies wandering around the halls and stairs. They seemed to be in every nook and cranny. "Get them out of here," she ordered Von Braun.

"Why?" he growled.

"Because you don't want to have to share do you?"

"Share what?" He was easily confused.

She scoffed at his moronic answer, momentarily forgetting the delicate balance of power she held over him. His quick glare reminded her. "You know, Dr. Lee and the cure. There aren't a lot of the cures. Not enough for all of them."

He looked at the other zombies with a sneer. He hated them almost as much as he hated Anna. "What am I supposed to do with them?"

She thought on it for a moment. "Get them all down to the lobby. All except a few to guard the stairs." She could see his slow mind working and before he could ask why, she said, "To keep Dr. Lee from escaping. You don't want her to escape, do you?"

That was an especially tough question for Von Braun to answer because Anna's shit-fuck of a condescending voice had gone right to where his head was blackest and really he could barely remember Dr. Lee just then, not when this soft, pure, tasty treat was so close.

"Remember the cure!" she snapped, backing away. He followed after her, backing her almost into the elevator where there was no room to run. Again, the cure seemed like a distant thing to him, while she was so close, so haveable, so edible.

"What about your pills?" she asked as a last resort, holding up the bottle and rattling it to distract him. "If you hurt me, you'll end up like all of them. You'll be a freak just like them." She pointed with her chin at the hated zombies. He had his pressure points just like all men.

He sneered at them, too. "You want them in the lobby?"

"Yes, until the time is right. Then we'll turn them loose." It was her one way to get by the police. It would be dangerous as hell, but she didn't have many choices. Or any choice, really. She had begun to fervently believe that what was happening wasn't her fault. It was all fate. She was only playing her role.

Von Braun left to do her bidding. Anna didn't wait around to watch, she punched the "B" button. As before the elevator screeched and shook on its cable as it began to descend. She rode the car down to the basement. When the doors opened, she didn't rush out; she stood just inside the elevator, breathing as lightly as could, trying to hear anything that might sound like one of the zombies.

After a minute she crept out of the elevator, but only took a few steps before the door began to close behind her. Quickly, she jumped back and held the door open. "Son of a bitch," she whispered, taking off one of her shoes and jamming it in the crevice. "That was close." She didn't want to think about what would have happened if it had slid all the way to the top floor. Her plans would've been ruined for one and she'd be jailed for two.

"Don't think about that," she hissed. "Concentrate!"

Anna pictured the gas lines and the ovens on the third floor and realized that she was going to start a hell of a big gas fire and the one thing she couldn't have was it lighting prematurely. That meant no sparks and really the only way she'd get sparks on a deserted floor was through some sort of electrical short. She went to the breakers.

"Beautiful," she whispered at the sight. She had never in her life seen a set of breakers so well laid out and so perfectly marked in her life. The first thing she did was to kill the electricity to the fourth floor. "That'll fuck with any plans they might have," she said, gleefully. Next she snapped the breakers down on the third floor.

The cafeteria had six very large gas ovens—it would have been her next destination if a zombie hadn't come gimping toward her just then. It was between her and the elevator.

Without thinking, she began to race away, only she'd forgotten she had been going about with just one shoe on. It put her at an odd slant and made for a painfully slow get away. She ran in a hitching, hopping manner for the boilers where she hoped the maze of machinery, pipes, and shadows would conceal her.

Anna tried to hide herself within it all, but the zombie was too close. As she ran she could hear its breath wheezing in and out and she could imagine she felt the heat of it on the back of her neck. A scream was a second away from ripping up out of her throat when she saw a door along the wall that was partially open; she headed right for it and slammed it shut behind her. The zombie struck it a second later with such force that it jarred the breath out of her.

"Shit," she whined. She had her back to the door and through it she could feel the beast punching at the wood. It was a cheap door with a hollow core—but it held against the single zombie.

When she was satisfied that it wasn't going to be able to get at her anytime soon she tried to figure out where the hell she was. The room was just about as black as it could be. Splaying her fingers she swept the walls next to the door, looking for a light switch, but not finding one. The dark was impenetrable and the smell, nasty. She had no clue what sort of room she was in until her shin barked up against a solid object. "Ow!" She bent down and found something hard and smooth. Tracing its outline, she discovered it was a toilet. Even though she still wore latex gloves, she pulled her hands back in disgust.

Now that she had a point of reference she discovered the dimensions of the small lavatory: six by four. The light still eluded her until she felt something in her hair. Thinking it was a spider she did a gross-out dance until she heard the chain above her head clink sideways against the light bulb suspended from the ceiling.

"Well, shit," she said, feeling stupid. She reached out to paw the black air until she found the string. With a yank she had light, but no hope. The bathroom held an ugly little toilet and a sink, both of which were so filthy it was hard to believe they were as new as they were. Other than a mirror on the wall that showed Anna she was no longer the fairest of them all and a single roll of toilet paper, there wasn't anything in the little box of a room.

She was trapped.

In despair, she slid down the door, which thrummed against her back as the zombie beat on it, relentlessly. Ten minutes went by with nothing changing other than the conviction that she was screwed. The zombie wouldn't stop until either the door came down or the police would show up in large enough numbers to "rescue" her from it and put her in jail.

Since patience was her only option she clicked off the light and sat down again, and waited, and waited. In the world above, the families were being rescued from their cottages and General Collins, having just been debriefed was sitting in his pajamas studying a map of the Hudson Valley and realizing that the units of the $42^{nd}$ infantry division from New York weren't going to be enough to sustain a quarantine of the magnitude that was being asked of him.

Almost above her head, Von Braun was busy filling the wide lobby with every zombie within reach. Already there were over a hundred and fifty wandering around the lobby, knocking into each other. Further up on the fourth floor, one of the hinges gave out on the central door and Deckard found his hand being held in a tight, cool grip. It was Thuy displaying the full extent of her fear. It was there behind her breastbone, a point of pain that had been building with each passing minute.

"It'll be alright," Deckard breathed into her ear. "I won't let anything happen to you." She didn't believe him. Logic dictated that she would be killed in the same manner as the others: eaten alive.

Anna sat through all of this, waiting patiently, barely breathing as minute after minute ticked on by. No prayer crossed her lips. It seemed blasphemous to even consider a prayer when she was hoping to kill twenty-three people...*not that they didn't deserve it*, she thought to herself for the hundredth time. They were the ones judging without proof, sentencing her simply because they didn't know who the real...

A sudden touch of cool air at her wrist cut across her thoughts. She felt at the bottom edge of the door and found there to be a gap of at least an inch where cool air was slipping in. This little thing triggered an idea. Her greatest hope had been that the beast would stop its incessant hammering and go away. Only it never would on its own; it would need the promise of something else to lure it away.

She dug in her pocket and found two coins, both quarters, change from the vending machine on the third floor outside the cafeteria. Carefully she took one and set it rolling beneath the door. She heard the tiny clink as it hit the floor and for a second she heard the tread on its edges at it wheeled away. After that, nothing. The zombie, who hadn't heard anything, kept up its ceaseless banging.

Anna bit back a curse and produced the second coin. This time she got on her hands and knees, but instead of rolling the coin she slid it beneath the door as hard as she could. She could hear it skitter across the floor and then came a little sound: *tink*.

Immediately, the zombie stopped and turned. She could hear its heavy breathing retreat and then a slapping noise that she couldn't place came to her. It went on for some time and unfortunately it wasn't all that far away. Using her good hand, she undid the buckle on her one shoe and then stood, deciding right then she was going to make a break for it, no matter how close the zombie was to the door.

She would have to be fast and her escape would have to be all or nothing.

Pausing only to make sure her mask was square on her face, she threw open the bathroom door in a quick move and saw immediately that her escape was going to be very, very close. The beast was nine feet away, staring down at a pipe, with its hands raised. It had been faced away, but at the sound of the door it had begun to turn. Anna surged forward, seeing she'd have to pass within arm's reach of it. Speed was her only defense.

As she ran by, a diseased hand slapped down on her back, grabbing her lab coat, and checking her momentum. With a shrug of her shoulders she let the coat go and then she was speeding down the hall, racing on bare feet for the elevator, her soles slapping on the cement. The doors came up so fast that her momentum threatened to carry her beyond them. Skidding to a halt she bent, grabbed her shoe from the crevice and then leapt in. "Come on," she hissed in a panic as she repeatedly jabbed the button for the third floor. She tried to will the doors to close faster; they seemed to take forever.

With a thunk they closed in the zombies face. "Thank God! Oh, thank you, God!" she cried not caring that she was on her way to commit mass-murder. She bent over at the waist, panting, "Almost done. I'm almost out of here."

As slow as the doors were, the elevator seemed to speed to the third floor. Before she was really ready the doors opened. Nervously, she peeked her head out of the door just in case there were still zombies around. The only light came from the elevator, making it difficult to peer into the dark, but as far as she could tell there were none. She started for the cafeteria and was halfway between the elevator and the double doors of the cafeteria when the central stair door opened and a zombie stumbled out.

It was Von Braun. To him, she was nothing but a splash of white in the dark and the erotic, exotic aroma of a hot woman. He could smell the sweat of her fear as well as her pussy and he was after her before he could think.

"Von Braun! Stop!"

Hearing his own name made him blink, her face coming into focus. "You! You left me. You were supposed to cure me and look at me. Look at me, bitch!" He looked just the same to her—gross.

"I have your pills. Remember the pills make you better." She had the bottle out and was rattling it again. At the same time she was backing away because he looked on the verge of losing it. "Here they are, like I said. I also have the cure right upstairs with Dr. Lee. Remember her. Remember how you were going to kill her."

"I was going to kill you," he seethed.

"Then do it," she challenged. "Go ahead kill me and see what happens to you. There won't be any cure for you, and no more pills and…"

"And no gook," he said. It was all coming back to him. He ground his teeth, not even feeling it when one of his molars broke; he only chewed on the splinter and felt his hate grow. "Give me the fucking pills, bitch-whore-shit!"

"Here you go." She poured ten of the pills into the cap, which she held out to him. The pills clicked off each other as her gloved hand shook. It was clear to her he was on the cusp, seconds away from going full on zombie. His limited control was fading. "Here. Take them," she said.

A part of him wanted to just let go and eat her, but his head was killing him and he had a vague memory about the pills. They helped the pain. They helped everything. "Gimme," he said, taking the cap. Watching her, he ate the pills.

"There," she said. "You'll start to feel like your old self any time now."

He stared at her for a full minute, his eyes dripping black crap onto the floor; she didn't dare look down at the twin puddles, afraid he would attack her if she broke eye contact.

"It's not working," he growled, taking a step at her.

"I said it would take a *few* minutes, ok? Maybe we should finish up with our plan."

"I already did my part. Those fuckers are all down stairs. What the fuck have you been doing?" He took another step at her. When she took a corresponding step back, he grinned, showing his broken teeth. "What's wrong? You been going behind my back? What were you doing all this time?"

"I was busy hiding from one of the zombies you were supposed to have moved into the lobby," she snapped right back. She wasn't easily cornered but when it happened her claws came out.

Von Braun's grin widened. Once he got his cure, he would kill this girl and eat her. He was going enjoy ripping her open. Without realizing it he stepped into the elevator where she had her back to the wall. "Get out!" She held up the opened bottle. "I'll throw it, I swear."

"No you won't."

"And you won't attack me," she said, forcefully. "So back off. I need you to go down stairs to the lobby. It's time to release the zombies on the police. Do you understand?"

His black eyes gleamed. "Yeah, it's time for a pig roast." The idea excited him and wearing an evil grin, he left her, and headed for the stairs.

"Thank God," she said again and hurried through the cafeteria to the kitchen where she stood in front of the six ovens. In the dark, without their usual gleam, they seemed old and dead. But they weren't, not yet at least.

Anna went to each, checking for the little blue flame that would indicate a burning pilot light. They were all dark. She tried to start one of the burners, without success, but she could hear the hiss of gas; it was surprisingly loud. "Alright, alright," she said as she dialed all thirty-six burners to high. The smell of the gas was immediate and overpowering.

Now, she was stuck with the dilemma of how to start the fire without blowing herself up in the process. A number of labor intensive and farfetched ideas came to her: a fuse made out of *Wesson* oil soaked sheets that she could run all the way from the first floor, a flaming zombie, enticed to wander up the stairs using strategically placed cell phones to draw him on. She discarded these ridiculous ideas and decided to use a primitive drone: the elevator.

She took the elevator down to the second floor where, after a quick search of the nurse's station, she found a bottle of rubbing alcohol, a lighter that was stashed in one of the desk drawers and a heavy sweater—everything needed to start a fire.

"Now all I need is that dumb fuck, Von Braun to come through." She went to a window that faced the front and saw that the entire lawn of the facility was covered in people…zombies, actually. They were everywhere. There must have been two-hundred of them. They milled around for about ten minutes and then suddenly the *pop, pop, pop* of gunfire reached her ears. Coming through the glass it was a soft sound. Outside it was loud enough to attract every single zombie. As one, they began marching through the gates.

The gunfire picked up and Anna felt a stab of queasiness. People were going to die, hell, they could already be dying and it was all her fault. She could blame Thuy, but deep down she knew better. She was trading the very likely chance of her going to prison for all the lives that were going to end that night.

"They made me do it," she said, trying to convince herself. "They set this all in…" The smell of gas caused her to stop her blame shifting. It was just a whiff, still it was shocking how quickly the air in the building was being infused.

"I better hurry," she whispered, heading for the elevator with her little bundle under one arm. She took the elevator down one floor and again paused to see if there were any stray zombies. There were two of them. Fortunately for Anna they had their faces pressed against the glass and were staring out at what was beginning to sound like a major battle going on beyond the gates.

With little choice, she turned her back on them. She piled the heavy sweater into an ugly pyramid and then doused it with the alcohol. Then she reached up and pressed the button for the third floor and as the doors were closing she lit the sweater. It blazed merrily and then the door closed and she was running to get out of the building before it was too late.

## Chapter 15

**//11:40 PM//**

**1**

Two minutes earlier, Stephanie was sitting in the hall with Chuck, lazing her head upon his broad shoulder, trying not to think about the drumbeat from hell that the zombies had kept up all this time or that the central stair door was a millimeter from losing another hinge. She had kicked all this out of her mind and was simply breathing in this man with whom she had found such a connection to, when she smelled the gas.

After being confronted with her looming death for so long, alarm over the smell was not her initial reaction. Curiosity was. "Do you smell that?" she asked Chuck. "It smells like gas."

"It wasn't me, I swear," he drawled out, grinning at her.

She shoved him, unable to help her own smile. "No, I mean it. I smell gas. Should we be worried?"

He took a big sniff. "Well, hell, I smell it, too. Maybe it's nothin' but to be on the safe side, I should mention it to Dr. Lee."

"No, I'll do it," Stephanie said, getting up. "I'm feeling much better." She'd been sitting for the last few hours and had regained much of her strength. With barely a cough, she walked down to the central door where most of the scientists were sitting. They had given up hope and for the most part they were doing little besides waiting for the zombies to break through.

"Excuse me, Dr. Lee," Steph said, coming to squat close to where Thuy and Deckard were sitting. She felt bad for interrupting them. They'd been holding hands, but now Thuy quickly pulled her soft ones from his callused paws.

"Yes?"

"There's a gas smell down the hall. You know, like natural gas. That sort of thing. I thought you should know."

Thuy's brows came down as she gave a tentative sniff to the air. "You can smell it from down there? That doesn't make any sense." She jumped up and hurried down the hall toward Chuck. Over her shoulder, she asked, "Deck, can you check the control room? If there's a leak, it would be coming from there, not down…"

She stopped, struck by an urgent feeling of déjà vu. A memory was shifting in her mind, trying to come to the surface: it was the first time she'd come to the Walton facility. She'd been standing pretty much right where she was now, staring about at her half completed lab and wondering how all the work was going to get done on time. Then Deckard had come in. He had stood right where he was standing now…but he hadn't remained there. He had walked past her and right around the hole in the floor where he could see right down into the cafeteria.

"The kitchens are down there," she said to herself. Gas could only be coming from two sources: the huge industrial sized kitchen ovens below her, or from the lines Thuy had pulled out from the walls—except the lines were shut off. "Von Braun," she hissed. It had to be him behind the gas leak, which meant… "Chuck! Get over here. Everyone move to the south end of the building. I think Von Braun is up to something with the gas."

Stephanie watched Chuck slowly get to his feet. Nonchalantly he put his fists into the small of his back and stretched. "Damn it, Chuck!" she screamed. "Stop playing it cool!"

A heavy hand grabbed her arm. It was Dr. Wilson, sweat lining his brown face. "Come on, Ms. Glowitz. We can't wait on him." The smell of gas was heavy in the air. The scientists started to run and Wilson ran with them, pulling Stephanie along with him.

Thuy counted them as they ran past. "Twenty-one...who are we missing?"

"Riggs and Milner," Deck said. "They're down in the last lab." Thuy started running. In her mind, she saw herself running down there, getting them and running back, no problem. She made it three feet before she was pulled up short by Deckard. "Don't be stupid," he growled in her ear.

He had her by the arm with one hand and in the other he had his cell. It took two second to find Riggs' number. "This is Deckard. You and Milner have to get out of there."

"Did the zombies get through?" Riggs asked. He was already hurrying for the door.

"No. There's a gas leak," Deck yelled into the phone. "We think it's been intentionally set. Grab Milner and get down to this end of the building, quick." After a second as he felt a strange fear ripple the air, he added, "You better run."

Deckard thumbed the *off* button and looked up. Chuck was just passing the elevator and glanced at it—he thought he'd heard the machinery going. Riggs and Milner came fast walking around the corner at the far end of the hall. On the floor below, the elevator, with the sweater burning and puffing out black smoke, let out a pleasant *ding!* The doors opened about a foot and a half, just far enough to allow the methane to come swirling in.

A fraction of a second later the gas exploded with an indescribably, deafening roar and a shock of light. In a blink it turned night into day for miles around. Every window on the third floor blew out, sending shards zipping through the air for hundreds of yards.

The explosion rocked the building, shaking the floors and cracking the support structure in a hundred places. Water pipes burst sending thousands of gallons water cascading through the interior walls to flood the basement. As a crescendo the glass walls of the labs came crashing down in a noise like raining thunder.

One second, Thuy was looking at Riggs and screaming for him to run and in the next she was knocked off her feet. She slapped up hard against the linoleum. With her cheek pressed to the floor she was in a perfect position to see the hall undulate like a low wave, like water. Then her vision was filled with clear crystals and sharp glass so that it seemed like she was looking at the world through a kaleidoscope.

Then something heavy covered her and a large hand hid her face from the flying glass. It was Deckard. He had thrown himself across her. Glass cut him in so many places he could barely feel all the wounds. They didn't matter to him. They were nicks only. What mattered to him, he realized, was not himself but Thuy.

"Are you ok?" he asked Thuy. "Are you hurt?"

He was shouting, but he came across in a mumble as her ears rang from the explosion. "I'm ok, I think." In truth she was numb and couldn't feel anything, good or bad. "How's Riggs?" she asked. "Is he ok?"

Deckard wasn't nearly so numb; there was a slashing pain running up and down his back, but what stung worse was that she would ask about Riggs first. He squinted through the grey pall that was gradually overcoming the clean air. Halfway down the hall, Chuck was on his hands and knees, spitting blood onto the rubble and glass strewn floor.

Further down, Riggs was just getting to his feet, while next to him Milner was screaming and holding his hands to his face. Deckard turned to look down the other end of the hall, Burke was climbing out from beneath a clump of skinny scientists—if asked he'd say they fell over on top of him. A few feet away from John, Wilson was helping Stephanie to her feet.

"Riggs looks ok," Deck answered, and then worked his jaw around on its hinges. His head felt plugged with sawdust.

"You're bleeding," Thuy noted, seeing all the blood on his face.

"Probably," he said with a shrug. He winced at the move, something Thuy also noticed. She began to inspect him closely, and he felt like a chimp being groomed, right up until she pulled something that seemed to be made of fire out of his shoulder.

"Son of a..." he seethed through gritted teeth. She shrugged and held up a bloody shard of glass the size of her hand that had been stuck in his back. She tried to hand it to him as though he might want to keep it as a souvenir. "No thanks," he said. "I've got one just like it at home."

Chuck came up then. "You know y'alls bleedin'?"

"You, too," Deck answered. They both were running red from a hundred tiny cuts and a few larger ones as well.

Thuy looked past Chuck. "Oh no, Milner!" Milner was being helped along by Riggs. Milner had one hand thrown out questing blindly for a wall that had basically disintegrated, while the other sat across his eyes and, from beneath his palm, blood ran wet. Thuy turned to the others. "Wilson? Dr. Wilson, we need you." She heard the fear in her own voice. "Quickly!"

Grimacing, Deck got to his feet, just as Milner's flailing hand finally struck something solid: the central stairwell door. It swung back on its broken hinges with a groan. "Riggs!" Milner cried in a panic. Even blind he knew the touch of the door and it didn't take a genius to guess that the danger from the zombies hadn't ended with the explosion.

Riggs had been moving in a daze but as he glanced at the open door he cried, "Oh God!" Before he could react, zombies rushed up from the stairs. Milner was closest and there were three of the black-eyed creatures on him before he knew it. Riggs tried to kick them off his friend, however two more came through the stairwell door and latched onto him, sinking their teeth into him, one at the shoulder, another on his arm.

Chuck and Deckard pulled their surgical masks over their noses and ran to help, while everyone else hung back. Chuck had a spear made from a broom handle with which he stabbed down into one of the zombies chewing on Riggs. The point went four inches deep, slipping between ribs to puncture a lung—the zombie continued ripping into Riggs' shoulder as if nothing had happened.

Deckard had his pistol with its twelve bullets. He brought it up to shoot one of Milner's attackers, but a movement to his left attracted his attention—there were more zombies coming up out of the stairwell. Some were whole and strong, like Rory Vickers, who was the color of old oatmeal and had black goo in his eyes and mouth and up under his hair, but otherwise looked like his old self. It took three shots to the chest to drop him.

Some of the zombies were downright horrifying.

Sergeant Heines had most of his skin burned away and what was left was charred black and hanging in strips. He was gruesome and smelled so bad it turned Deckard's stomach. A strange pity awoke in Deckard, which ended up saving him…for the moment. He shot Heines in the head, hoping to kill any thinking part of him that was left and was happily surprised to see the zombie fall straight over from the single bullet.

"Go for the brain!" he shouted to Chuck. The Okie had been stabbing over and over again into the back of the zombie, slowing it down but not killing it. Now, he aimed for the back of the head. The spear broke but not before sending a killing shard into the thing's brain.

While Deckard made head shot after head shot at the zombies coming up out of the stairwell, Chuck used half a spear to kill the second zombie that was on Riggs. He stepped on the thing's head with one shit-kicking boot to hold it still and then drove the shaft right into its eye socket.

Riggs rolled out from beneath the corpse and then kicked away from the zombies eating Milner who was still very much alive.

Chuck raised his hand to the others showing his broken spear. Only Thuy seemed to understand. Chuck would continue to fight but he needed a new weapon. Thuy yelled, "Eng! Wilson, come on, don't just stand there. Burke, you're immune, damn it. Go help."

None of the three were eager to go into battle. Eng went first, carrying Thuy's desk chair as a combination weapon and shield. He used it to pin one of the zombies down. Burk and Wilson came next with makeshift spears; they went for the eyes.

In short order the zombies attacking Milner were dead. The scientist just laid there and cried blood; he wasn't going to make it. Even without the Com-cells busy replicating in his system, he wasn't going to last so grievous were his injuries; the floor was slick with his blood.

Deckard shot down the last of the zombies coming from the stairs. He went to check his ammo, but the slide was back; the gun was empty. "Huh," he said and then showed Chuck.

"Close," Chuck said. He then began coughing and backing away from the stairs. They all did. A heavy black smoke broiled up out of the stairwell and the air was shimmering with heat.

"What do we do about Dr. Milner?" one of the scientists asked. Milner was trying to move away from the stairwell door, but one of his arms was dislocated and the other ended at a mangled and bleeding stump.

"We don't do anything!" Riggs spat. "We let him die. The smoke is a blessing for him…and for me." He started for the stairwell door, but after a quick look from Thuy, Deckard grabbed him and shoved him back.

"Not yet, Riggs," Deckard said, wondering why Thuy wouldn't let him end himself before he became a danger. "You have lots of time left."

Riggs cackled, madly. "I have all the time in the world.

It's you who's out of time. Can't you feel it?" He knelt down and put his hands on the floor. Blood trickled down from the bite on his shoulder to pool around his hand. "You can feel the heat through the floor. You can feel the building dying."

Everyone but Thuy knelt and touched the floor. Riggs wasn't lying. Burke was the first to stand. He went as close to the stairwell as he could, his face twisted from the heat. With a curse, he turned away. "It's clear of them zombies. I says we kin wet down all our clothes and make a run for it."

Deckard rolled his eyes at the stupidity of the idea. Thuy was more circumspect. "The heat will shrivel your lungs in seconds. You will die. But...but maybe it doesn't matter. We're trapped. I think we're all going to die here very quickly."

As if to prove her wrong, the elevator took that moment to *ding!* Freed from the key that had kept it penned on the first floor, its tiny electronic brain had gone through its floor sequence and ended up on the fourth floor.

Everyone jumped back, all save Deckard who took Wilson's spear and advanced like any primitive stone-age warrior would. The door had been warped by the explosion and it took a full thirty seconds to grind back.

"What the hell?" Deck poked at the remains of the sweater with his spear. A thin grey smoke lifted up from it.

"Was that a shirt?" Wilson asked. "Did someone spontaneously combust?"

"Wilson, please," Thuy answered. "Let's not be ridiculous. This is how Anna set off the gas." Before anyone asked how she knew who had caused the explosion, she showed the obvious clues. "Look at the open hatch. Anna must have climbed down the elevator shaft and entered there. She started the gas going in the kitchens and then used the elevator with a burning shirt in it as a trigger."

"What about Von Braun?" Deckard asked. "Couldn't he have done this? You were pretty sure before."

"I let my imagination get the best of me," she answered.

"His Diazepam must have run out hours ago. He's just as brainless as the rest of them." Her eyes inadvertently slipped over to Riggs.

He scowled at her. "Maybe it was just a shirt that caught on fire when the elevator went by the third floor."

He was in such a pitiful state that she almost didn't want to correct him and, if hadn't been for the renewed fear in some of the eyes of the scientists, she would have let it go. "That sort of heat would have ignited the carpet as well. No, it'll be hot in there but it will be survivable, at least for a little while longer. If we hurry."

"Then what are we waiting for," Burke demanded. Without looking for permission he walked onto the elevator and kicked the remains of the sweater out.

"I guess some men should ride in the first car," Thuy said. "Wilson, Riggs, and…" Her eyes went to Milner who was no longer moving. "And…and uh, Rajesh, take the first group down. Deckard, Eng, and Mr. Singleton will escort the second."

"No, I go wit firs group," Eng said. He started forward, just as Burke had done, but Deckard grabbed his arm.

"Don't be a chicken, Eng. You're going down with me." There was a real reason to fear waiting on the second trip. The heat and the smoke were fast becoming unbearable, and the sound of the fire eating away at the building came to them in tremendous crashes that rumbled the floor every few seconds.

Eng was no chicken, however he had reached a breaking point watching Milner mewling around on the ground with everyone pretending he didn't exist. It seemed a particularly horrible and lonely death. "I'm going on this elevator right now," Eng said, suddenly reverting to perfect English. Before Deckard could reply, Eng pulled the .38 with his right hand and grabbed Thuy around the neck with his left forearm.

"Why do you have a gun, Eng?" Deckard asked, feeling

like he had missed something big. It made no sense that this geeky scientist would have a gun and that he hadn't used it before this moment to fight the zombies.

"That's my business."

"And why are you talking like that?" Thuy asked. She was in the exact same confused boat as Deckard.

"Because I chose to," Eng answered. "Now back off Deckard or I will kill you. And you too, Mr. Cowboy." He meant Chuck who had angled to his right as stealthily as he could. "In fact, everyone get away from the elevator."

"Ah ain't going nowheres," Burke said from inside the car.

"I will kill you," Eng said, leveling the gun at John. "You have until the count of three. One…"

"Burke, get out of the elevator!" Deckard snapped. The way Eng held the gun close, how he had snatched up Thuy so easily, so fluidly, and the fact of the gun itself had Deck thinking Eng wasn't what he seemed. It was suddenly very clear that Eng was something beyond the nerdy caricature of an Asian scientist he had appeared to be.

"Two…" Eng said and then thumbed back the hammer.

"This won't get y'alls little girl back, John," Chuck said. "Bein' dead won't help her at all."

John dropped his head. "Ah-rat. Y'all win," he said and then eased out of the elevator with his hands up.

Eng didn't waste a second. He thrust Thuy at Deckard, stepped into the elevator and hit the one button. As the door ground closed he kept the gun pointed out at the scientists who all kept well back. The elevator, making a high-pitched squeaking sound, dropped slowly through the fire engulfed third floor. The heat, baking through the concrete walls, staggered Eng. It was like stepping into a man-sized oven. His skin stretched tight across his cheekbones and he was forced to hide his face beneath his lab coat to keep it from blistering.

When he got past the flames eating away at the innards of

the building, the relief was immediate. He dropped to his knees and, when he finally got to the first floor and the door came open, he jumped out and sucked down huge gulps of air, forgetting for a moment the threat of zombies. What brought him around was the sound of the elevator door shutting behind him.

"Oh, no you don't," he said, sticking his arm out to stop the door. A few feet away a potted plant sat overturned. Eng used it to hold the door open, in effect trapping everyone on the fourth floor once again. "So solly, Dr. Rhee," he whispered as he headed out the front door.

## 2

The quarantine had always been an illusion. There were forty one troopers stationed around the hospital and not a one of them knew exactly what would happen if someone tried to break the ring. Their orders were to "maintain" the quarantine without coming into contact with any potentially infected person.

"Can we shoot them?" one of the troopers asked.

"Only to protect you or another civilian from attack," Lieutenant Ford answered.

"And if someone just wants to leave?"

There was no good answer to that. Ford cleared his throat before replying, "Just use your authority and order them back into the quarantined area."

This didn't work out so well when Von Braun's army came marching out of the front door. The now ex-prisoner pushed and punched and yelled the zombies out through the gates and at first they only meandered about, not realizing precisely what all the flashing lights meant. Then the trooper directly in front of the gate used his loud speaker to "command" the zombies back inside.

The human voice drew them on and in seconds they

swarmed the trooper's car and before he knew it they were all around him, hammering on the windows with their greasy fists. It took twenty eight seconds for the windows to break. The trooper got off three shots before the zombies crawled in and ate him alive.

A hundred yards back at the command post, Ford was screaming into the radio, first for a sitrep from the now dead trooper and then, belatedly to order all available units to "get their asses" to the front of the facility. Again, the first cruisers on scene were swarmed by the undead with the same bloody result.

Ford listened to the frantic cries for help over the radio with his stomach in knots. The situation was deteriorating, quickly. He could've gone in with guns blazing but in his mind he was still thinking in terms of maintaining the quarantine, when he should've been thinking about saving his men. "Use CS," he yelled as more troopers came flying up. He jumped out of his cruiser and ran to the trunk. "We'll disperse them with tear gas."

He had a very commanding voice, a very loud voice. It carried into the quarantined tent that sat fifty yards away. For the last hour, eighteen former troopers and three badly mauled former CDC agents had walked in circles in the canvas tent leaving trails of black drool behind them. There was no reason for them to do anything else but to mindlessly walk along the inner wall of the tent. The night had been quiet; the troopers guarding the perimeter stayed in their cruisers where their voices and odors were masked, and so the zombies, who couldn't think beyond the walls of the tent, just walked.

Now, there were gunshots and voices and the smell of clean humans. It awakened the hunger in them and, so powerful was that force, that they attacked the zippered door. The zipper itself was beyond their ability to comprehend, but they understood ripping and tearing. Just after the first tear gas canisters thumped down-range to land amid the horde of zombies, a wall of the tent ripped wide open.

The former troopers saw their former friends and charged. They came out of the dark and, with all the noise and mayhem, no one noticed them until they were only a few feet away.

Ford saw the uniforms only. "I need you to dump all available..." His words caught in his throat as he recognized Sergeant Foster—it was a grotesque, demonic version of Foster. Ford went for his gun, however Foster was on him too quickly, his teeth searching for the neck, his hands pulling the head back. The two went down, Ford on his back, Foster full on him.

So greedily did Foster go for his flesh that Ford gave up the gun which was still half-holstered. He needed every ounce of strength just to keep his throat from being torn out. Ford was a strong man and gradually he pushed Foster back until he was practically at arm's length—that was when a second zombie suddenly appeared.

She dropped to her knees and lunged right at Ford's face. Her teeth tore into his cheek, and then ripped off part of his ear, and then finally got into his neck. He fought back, wildly, trying to buck off his two attackers, but to no avail. They had their claws hooked into his hair and were holding onto his shirt at the collar and sleeve. When he fought off one, the other was always there, taking huge bites of him and chewing in his ear.

Ford was so strong that his death took twenty, very, long minutes. By then half of his troopers were dead and the others, many of them infected, were racing away at top speed.

The quarantine had failed its only test.

3

The briefing General Collins received while sitting on the

side of his bed in his pajamas had him grim faced. An infection that was worse than Ebola was spreading along the Hudson River Valley and it was going to be his job to contain it.

"There are, uh, strange side effects to the disease," a man named Ross told him. "The victims show, uh, an increased aggression and, uh, there are reports of cannibalism." At the time Collins had shrugged off such talk. There wasn't much in this world that a spinning, fiery-hot chunk of lead couldn't take care of.

His second briefing, which came five minutes later, had him thinking all of this was some big prank. "Zombies?" he laughed. "Ok, that is funny. Who's behind this? Is it Colonel Becker? That old dog is going to pay for getting me up in the middle of the night for a joke."

"It's no joke, General. Like I said, you will be dealing with zombies."

"Listen lady, I don't know who you are or who you think…"

"General, I swear this is on the up and up. I've diverted a helicopter to your home. It will be there in four minutes. I suggest you get dressed."

"Who is this?" he asked.

"Courtney Shaw." She had already overstepped her bounds to such an extent that it didn't seem right to start going half-assed now. She had commandeered an air-ambulance unit from a hospital in Newburgh by invoking the governor's name—she figured he'd thank her later.

"I've also taken the liberty of starting your call-chain for the 27th, the 50th, and the 86th infantry brigades. When can we expect full muster, do you think?"

Collins sputtered at this: "You did…you did what? I'm only authorized to call up the 27th. Who is this?"

"Courtney Shaw. I'm sorta with the governor's office. Listen, General. I've been on the ground from the beginning with this. Until you see for yourself, you're going to have to trust me." The sound of the helicopter overhead had him thinking he didn't really have any choice.

Half-dressed, Collins kissed his wife goodbye and then ducked under the spinning blades of the copter that sat smack down in the middle of his street. Eight minutes later he was circling over the Walton facility. The little craft bounced and rocked as the heat of the fire roiled the air.

Down below people were walking around. There weren't nearly as many of them as he'd been led to believe. "I only count sixty or so, Courtney. What happened to the hundreds you mentioned?" Sixty didn't seem like a lot when he was safe in his helicopter.

Courtney had a fair count going that matched up with the breathless tales of horror the fleeing state troopers had given her. "They must have dispersed, sir. I've taken the liberty of calling up the 3$^{rd}$ battalion of your aviation unit. They're the ones with the Blackhawks, right?"

"I...I...yeah, but..." Collins was about to ask who she was again and how she knew so much about his own unit when she answered the unspoken question.

"It's all on Wikipedia. I figured you'd need to start ferrying your troops as soon as possible, though we should begin with Poughkeepsie. The outbreak there is far worse and the containment logistics are a nightmare."

"What can we expect from local law enforcement?" Collins asked into the mike.

Courtney looked at her board. It was a chaos of flashing lights. Next to her, Renee was busy trying to find out where all the state troopers were, who was dead, who was driving off to who knew where and who was coming to their rescue. "Until morning you won't have more than a handful," Courtney answered. "Which reminds me, what are your orders concerning the zombies? I hope to God they are to shoot on sight."

"I don't have that authority," the general replied.

"Then I better call up the Pennsylvania guard because

your men don't stand a chance."

"You're out of line," Collins snapped. "My men are some of the most highly trained warriors in the world…"

"But you just said they won't be fighting. By the time the zombies are on you, it's too late. Hold on, General. I'm going to put you through to some of my troopers. If they don't convince you, then God help your men."

"Stop with the melodramatics!" Collins growled. "The rules of engagement are not up to me. They're up to the governor and maybe even the president. You need to convince them that killing their own citizens is the best course of action."

Courtney sat back in her chair listening to the steady hum of the other operators. Two more had been called in. They were under strict orders to ignore all calls from within Poughkeepsie—the general consensus was that the little city was doomed. They were to concentrate on anything suspicious outside the city limits; they had to know how far this thing was spreading.

The callboard in front of her was blinking like mad, almost all the lights were representing people in dire trouble. Ninety-nine percent were coming from within the city. The board made Courtney sick. "There's only one way to convince the governor and that's to convince you, General. I'm going to send you to Poughkeepsie so you can see for yourself."

Collins resented the idea that this nobody was going to "send" him anywhere, but she was right. He had to see for himself.

The helicopter touched down in a field outside the city where the remnants of the state troopers and the emergency personnel who had fled Walton had congregated. He began barking orders the second he stepped away from the rotors and such was his presence that very quickly he was outfitted with a bio-suit and a handgun. Volunteers were asked for to escort him into the city. They were a dispirited and beaten lot and only one man held up a hand.

Trooper Gavin Jones had killed four zombies that night, two at point blank range and he was starting to get a thumping bad headache and being surrounded by pussies annoyed him.

He donned a bio-suit as well, and then they were off. Jones tore down the two-lane road without his emergency lights flashing. He noted the general holding onto the *oh shit* bar with both hands and smirked. "You'll be fine, General, there are very few drunks out on a Monday night. 'Sides, it might be a blessing if we roll this bitch."

They didn't crash. The trooper drove right into the heart of Poughkeepsie and killed the engine. From all around them came sporadic gunshots and every once in a while a scream or two.

One was particularly close. The trooper slid out of the cruiser, dropped his hood over his face, and drew his weapon. Collins hesitated until the trooper ducked back in. "You wanted to see what's going on, now's your fucking chance."

Collins started to make an angry reply, but Jones was already walking off down a side street. General Collins hurried to catch up and again was about to snap at the trooper, but just then they passed two bodies: one completely inert, the other crawling. "That's going to be one of *them*," the trooper said in a low voice. "See its neck? See all the bite marks? That used to be some guy but now it's a zombie."

The zombie started crawling toward them and Collins took a few mincing steps back, completely disgusted by the thing. "How's it even alive?"

"I thought you were with the government," the trooper said. "You should be telling me not the other way around. Oh, wait...here we go." An actual walking zombie had just come out of someone's garage and was crossing the street, coming toward the two men. Its face dripped red with fresh blood. "That's a real walking zombie. It can't be killed, I don't think. I saw one with four bullet holes right through it, walking around like it was nothing. I'd love to know why you government boys started all this shit."

"The government didn't start this," Collins shot back. "And you had better start speaking to me with a little respect if you want to keep your job."

"Ha!" the trooper laughed derisively. "That's a joke. After tonight I'm pretty sure you can take this job and shove it up your ass."

He was being extremely loud and the general grew even more nervous. "If that's your attitude, why did you volunteer to come out here with me?"

"Because...because I'm in the mood to kill." The trooper raised his gun, turned his head so that he could see better through the mask and then squeezed off a round.

"Did you miss?" Collins asked. The zombie hadn't even twitched.

"Of course I didn't fucking miss, look at his fucking shirt." There was a hole in the thing almost dead center. The trooper shot twice more, hitting dead center both times. The last shot definitely slowed the beast. It staggered and began to walk off at a little diagonal as if he were a sailboat fighting an unfavorable breeze.

"See? You can't kill them." Forgetting the zombie, the trooper began to walk back to his cruiser.

Collins took aim with his own weapon. It wasn't easy with the hood threatening to drop down over his eyes and his hands encased in rubber. He waited until the zombie was practically right on top of him before he shot it through the forehead.

It flopped right over. "Not impossible to kill, but very, very difficult," he whispered to himself.

When he got back into the cruiser he dialed Courtney Shaw. "You were right. These things have to be destroyed, especially if they're as contagious as you say."

"It may be worse," Courtney replied. "Do you want me to

schedule you to see the governor?"

He agreed that it had to be done and a meeting was set up. After giving a few instructions to the state police and the fire fighters gathered at the edge of town he left to convince the governor of the necessity of mass scale murder of his own constituents.

While he was gone a command post was supposed to have been set up by the troopers, but it was left half done because, after about an hour, some of them took it upon themselves to kill the rest.

Just like that, the disease had spread outside the city limits.

**4**

Anna ran for the front door, afraid that the explosion would drop the whole building on her head, however once she hit the rainy night air, a new fear struck her as far more urgent: a zombie battle was going on just outside the gates, and there were others of the undead going here and there, crisscrossing the lawn right in front of her.

She knew she couldn't stand right there in the open so she scurried beneath one of the cherry trees. Under its new blossoms she paused to put her shoes on and that was when Von Braun materialized like a ghost out of the dark. He looked like a cross between a zombie and a psycho-killer. Clearly, he was out of control. His splintered teeth were like fangs in his dank mouth and his hunger was obvious.

In a fury, he came right at her. "Where the fuck have you been, you little whore-bitch-cun..."

The explosion on the third floor saved her. It started with a pulse of air that first went in toward the building and then blew out a millisecond later striking them like a wall of solid wind. Anna was thrown to the ground where she hid from the violence tearing up the sky behind her up-thrust arms.

Von Braun went from being on the verge of murdering Anna to lying flat on his back, staring up as the night went from a dull black to a painful, brilliant white. "Holy fuck!" he cried as the light seared his eyes and then he too was squinting and cringing as a rain of glass and steel came down from the angry heavens. Anna had the tree to protect her, but he was exposed and bled from a thousand holes.

Half a minute later she had recovered from the explosion and tried to make a run for it, thinking that pain or injury would have slowed Von Braun down, but he was on his feet even faster than she. "Where the fuck are you going?" he raged.

In her fear of him she backed away, tripping on a root and plopping down. "To…to find you. I came out here to find you. The way's clear. Look." She pointed up where the building was blazing away, casting the night in an aura of yellow. In all its destruction, the building was such a captivating sight that she stared opened mouth until he cursed at her.

"What did you do?" he cried, pointing up at the building. "You fuck-bitch. Shit! Shit! Fuck! You destroyed it. You killed the cure, didn't you?"

"No, I swear. It's…it's still there. They…the cure is in paper cups right upstairs. On the fourth floor remember? Remember the stairs?"

His mouth came open as his mind struggled to understand. "Upstairs?" He looked up and the fire was reflected in the wet blackness of his eyes—it looked as though his brain was alight and burning him up from the inside out.

"Yes, right up there is the cure," she said in a whisper. "You can be normal again. How do you like the sound of that?" She was so close to escaping, so close to being done with this whole hated night that her desire must have been heard in her voice.

Von Braun looked at her with contempt. "What about the

doors? They're still locked aren't they? And what about the fire? It'll burn me, I fucking know it."

"Not if you use the elevator," she said, quickly. "It'll shoot you right past the fire."

"Yeah...it could. Ok, let's go." He reached for her hand and she pulled back. "You're coming with me," he growled, advancing on her. She couldn't run, not barefoot and not with the ground covered in glass.

"Yes, but let me get my shoes..."

"You'll just run away, won't you? That's right, isn't it whore-bitch-shit."

"No, I won't, I promise. See? I'm with you." Stuck, she began to pick her way back to the hospital. With every other step she winced as something stabbed or sliced at her feet.

Von Braun smirked, enjoying her pain and the smell of her blood. It put him in a good mood. He even kicked glass at her bare legs just to watch her squirm. It was intoxicating to him and a boner started to form in his pants. *Will I fuck her corpse*? he wondered. It was a given that he would kill her, but what would he do after he ate his fill? The thought was enticing. He followed her to the building, drooling out a line of black phlegm from his grinning mouth.

The sudden appearance of a stranger with a gun in his hand killed his mood.

"Eng," Anna said, amazed. She saw the gun. It didn't make sense. Eng was the epitome of a nerd and nerds didn't carry guns. Though just then she didn't need it to make sense. "You have to help me. Kill it, please. Use the gun on him."

Von Braun was slow to realize she was meaning himself. "What the fuck?" he demanded. "You can't do that, we're a fucking team." He knew what a gun was for. He couldn't tell you what a tea cozy was or who the Vice President was, or even the names of any of his nieces or nephews, but guns were deeply entrenched in his memory.

"Don't listen to him, Eng," Anna pleaded. "He's a

zombie. You can't trust him."

A snort escaped Eng. "I can't trust him? You were the one who set the fire. I'm pretty sure I can't trust you either."

Anna's brows shot up. "Your accent! Where did your accent...it was you! You sabotaged the experiment." Eng's gun shifted from Von Braun to point square into her face. The black hole in the front of the barrel was so small yet so deadly. It was captivating; she couldn't stop staring at it. "Don't...don't waste the bullet on me," she whispered. "Think about it, Eng, there's too many of them. If you shoot me, they'll hear and you'll never get away. I'm not worth that, ok? I'm not worth a bullet."

His eyes flicked to the battle between the state troopers and the zombie horde. It was winding down with more screams than gunshots. He still had time. "But you're the only one left alive who knows my secret. I can't leave loose ends." He smirked suddenly. "I know I've been in America for too long when I start to sound like one of your movies."

"Please don't," Anna begged. "I'll do anything." The gun wavered as his eyes swept up and down her. She began to nod. "Anything. Anything you want."

Despite her disheveled appearance, Anna was still strikingly beautiful and many of Eng's fantasies concerning her popped into his mind. The gun wavered. He smiled and Anna tried not to blanch at it. "Ok. I like that. But it will be anything or else."

"Yeah, sure...anything you want," she said, feeling relieved and sickened at the same time. "Just one thing, kill him." She jerked her thumb at Von Braun.

With the blackness eating away at his mind, Von Braun couldn't understand any motivation beyond his own. He had watched the two scientists talking and couldn't follow a word of it until Anna said, *kill him*. That he understood all too well.

"No! Shit-fuck, no!" he yelled. "You promised me the cure and I want it." He pushed Anna aside and advanced on

Eng who leveled the gun but didn't pull the trigger.

"Shoot him!" Anna demanded.

"Why?" Eng wondered. "If he wants to go inside that's fine with me."

"I do," Von Braun said. He hated the gun and he hated the chink, but damn it, he needed the fucking cure. "Get out of my way, you uppity chink. The cure is in there."

Eng stepped aside and Von Braun rushed inside. He ignored the potted plant that Eng had stuck in the elevator doorway and began jabbing the number *four*. When the door repeatedly bashed up against the plant he flew into a rage, kicking the plant over and over again even after it had rolled out into the lobby. Behind him the door finally closed.

"Fuck!" he screamed, before attacking the door with his fists. He was still hammering on it two minutes later when it opened and an amazing number of people spilled out. The first thing Von Braun saw was a mop smacking him in the face. It was wet and stank of the worst aspects of a men's room.

Before he could grab it and pull it away, something sharp bit into his right shoulder; then something else jabbed him in the abdomen. He was thrust backwards until his feet tripped over each other, where upon he was practically trampled as the elevator emptied.

All he could do was curse until the mop was removed. He leapt up spitting mad, intent upon revenge only he was now confronted with a real choice. He could either attack the shit-fuck with the mop and make him pay in blood, or he could stop the elevator door from closing. The zombie in him wanted to kill and rip and gorge himself. The man wanted to live and think and reason once again. It didn't matter that his reasoning before getting the disease wasn't all that much different from the way it was now: filled with hate and rage, he wanted his mind back.

He went for the elevator.

Eng saw none of this. He had grabbed hold of Anna's

arm and had marched off into the parking lot, glad for another reason about keeping her. He was fully prepared to throw her at the first zombie to come his way. The .38 in his hand seemed pathetic against the ferocity of the beasts.

Fortune was with them. The night's darkness and the pelting rain hid the two of them, making them look like little more than passing shadows. They made it to Eng's Nissan Sentra; he thrust her into the passenger seat and walked around to his side with the gun pointed at her through the windows. He needn't have bothered; she wasn't going to risk running away when there were a couple of hundred zombies somewhere out in the dark, not barefoot and with her feet bleeding all over the place.

When he climbed in he gave her a long greedy look. "Anything I want," he said as a statement, not a question.

She had no choice except to agree. Eng was clearly cold-blooded. He had committed mass murderer on a tremendous scale and all he could think about was getting laid. She was sure he would kill her if she was anything but his perfect fantasy. "Of course, anything."

## Chapter 16

**//11:59 PM//**

**1**

A mile behind the quarantine line at the Walton facility, strung out along route 24, were sixty emergency vehicles. They ranged from boxy, ambulances to seventy-foot hook and ladders. There was even a pumper truck and two water tenders, though no one had expected there was going to be a fire. As it turned out, no one knew what to do when the fire started. They couldn't break quarantine even if they wanted to and really, with the radio alight with the sounds of the state police fighting for their lives, no one in that whole mess, other than Bobby Dern wanted to.

Bobby and his partner Karl had spent the greater part of that very long day taking turns napping in the back of their ambulance. They had been bored to tears right up until they got the call from Edmund.

"My name is Edmund Rothchild. Do you know who I am?"

"Yeah," Bobby answered. He knew who Edmund was. Everyone knew, especially after he had announced he had a cure for cancer.

"I'm willing to pay you one million dollars for one ambulance ride. You will have to come into the quarantine zone and it will be dangerous, possibly deadly."

Bobby was all in, Karl was not.

"No. Absolutely no way. A million dollars is great but only if we live to spend the fucking money! We can't spend it if we're dead."

"And how do we live on fifteen an hour?" Bobby shot right back. "We don't. All we can do is exist on so little. Come on, man! This is like a one in a million chance."

Karl shook his head. "No, it's a fifty-fifty chance we get fucking eaten. I can't deal with those odds."

"Then get out," Bobby said. "Go on." The hard truth was he didn't want to split the money, anyway. The dollar signs were lighting up his eyes and he didn't care that even then the other emergency vehicles were jerking around in awkward U-turns, trying to get the hell out of there as the last of the state troopers screamed down the road in a full retreat.

Karl watched them zip past with his mouth hanging open and a panic growing in his eyes as he searched into the dark. "Shit, no. Bobby, come on man. You know what's out there. Zombies, man. I can't do..."

Bobby punched him. The blow struck him on the side of the head. It wasn't a knockout punch. Bobby was a good person, generally and he had pulled the punch, making Karl cry out in shock and anger. Bobby had to hit him again. This time Karl was dazed and Bobby was able to force him out of the ambulance.

Rain and the ache in his temple had Karl blinking up at him stupidly. "You...you shit!" he screamed. "You're choosing money over..."

"Shut up," Bobby hissed. "You don't want to be so loud. The zombies, remember?" He started to shut the door on his friend but then paused, and added a lame sounding, "Sorry."

Again the truth was that there was no sorry in Bobby. The thought of the money had too strong a grip on his mind. He neither knew nor cared that he sprayed mud all over Karl as he gunned the ambulance toward Walton. He was all about the money and not even the zombies could dislodge the million dollars from his mind. Nevertheless they could scare the hell out of him.

"Shit!" he cried as he drove past the first one. It was missing an arm and there were easily half a dozen bullet holes running through it, yet it still stumbled on. It looked into the ambulance with slow, stupid eyes. Bobby stared right back, keeping his body rigid, hoping not to be seen. The zombie turned and began following after the red ambulance.

"Oh, no," he whispered, as a second one turned to watch him pass. He stomped the gas and barreled down the road as fast as he dared. More zombies came at him, a lot more, and soon he was dodging the ambulance all over the road to keep from hitting them, only his speed was too great, and their numbers too many. He caught one with the edge of his grill, sending black blood spraying across his windshield and causing the ambulance to bounce as though he had run over a log and not a person.

He drove on, his face stretched into a grimace, but he found that after hitting that first one, the next four that he crushed weren't all that bad. The last came just as he drove through the gates. There was no room to dodge and he simply plowed right over the dude, whispering another lukewarm: "Sorry."

The big house came up quickly and there was the rich old dude, Rothchild, crouching next to a bush by the driveway. He had on a bio suit. Bobby didn't have a bio suit. All he had were gloves and a mask. Before putting them on, he reminded himself about the money once more, and then he climbed out into the rain.

Rothchild waved him over and said, quite unnecessarily, "Hurry."

*No shit*, Bobby thought to himself as he followed at a fast walk. Out loud he asked, "How am I going to get paid? A check?"

"A check is fine, but you have to do the job first. She's right through here." Rothchild led him through a rich man's house and to a first floor bedroom where he pushed through plastic curtains that hung from the ceiling. Bobby paused just on the outside of the bedroom. Looking through the plastic gave the room a ghostly vibe, the people, Rothchild, a little girl, and a woman sleeping on a gurney, looked more like specters than actual real humans.

"Just do it," he whispered to himself. "It's a million dollars, Bobby. Just do it."

With a sharp intake of breath, he pushed through the curtain and stopped at the sight of the little girl--she was a freaking zombie. "Hey! You never said anything about transporting zombies."

"She's harmless," Rothchild snapped. "And she is still a person. You agreed to transport three people, now help me with Gabrielle, damn it."

The little girl didn't seem harmless, not with her black eyes looking like they belonged on some sort of freaky, giant bug. It was unnatural. Everything about her was unnatural. The way she stood like a manikin, the way her fingernails were cracked and how that same black pus oozed out of them. It coated the inside of her nostrils and ears as well. Bobby gave her a wide berth as he went to the foot of Gabrielle Rothchild's bed.

"Who's this?" Jaimee asked. When she spoke it looked as though she had been drinking ink. Her teeth in all that wet black looked very sharp.

"He's the ambulance driver," Rothchild answered. "Now, step back, dear."

She did, cocking her head this way and that like a puzzled dog. Jaimee was curious over the man, the way he kept glancing at her as he wheeled the gurney along; the way his eyes looked so big above his mouth. Something dawned on her. "He's all ascared of me, ain't he? He be lookin' at me like I's a haint." Strangely, she liked the idea that he was afraid of her. His fear made her happy.

Bobby was just about scared shitless. He knew the house was full of germs. He could almost feel them eating at his eyes or drifting into his ears or burrowing down into his very pores. And he knew that if the germs didn't get him the zombies would. He had a horrible feeling that, at any moment, Gabrielle's eyes were going to pop open and she would attack him like something out of a monster movie. *Hell,* he thought, *I'm even afraid of the little girl zombie, just like she said.*

She kept staring at him, hungrily, and breathing through her mouth in something like an urgent pant. It was eerie and distracting. Twice, he rammed the hospital bed into a wall.

"Ignore her," Rothchild ordered. "As I said, she is harmless." It was like trying to ignore an alligator walking next to you.

When they went out into the rain her demeanor changed. She stopped eyeing him and took to staring at the burning building. "Daidy?" she asked, in a little voice. "Is my Daidy up in there?"

Edmund had heard the explosion and had seen the fire. Fearing the worse he had tried calling Dr. Lee, only to have the phone ring and ring in his ear. More deaths on his conscience. "I'm afraid so, my dear."

Her face twisted, not with sorrow, but with anger. She was suddenly spitting mad. "Who did it? Who made that fire? Was it him?" She pointed a small hand at Bobby who actually took a step back, shaking his head.

"No," Edmund said, kindly. "This man is here to save us. He didn't do anything wrong. Now, I have to insist that you get into the ambulance so we can escape. Your daddy would want you to escape."

That was something at least that made sense to the little girl. Her mind was all sorts of mixed up and jumbled, but she was sure her daddy would want her to escape, at any cost. She climbed into the ambulance and sat on a little bench with her knobby knees pressed up against Gabrielle's gurney and at first everything was alright. Then Bobby closed the back door and she suddenly felt like a coon in a trap.

"It'll be ok, my dear," Edmund said. "You can come and stay with me on Martha's Vineyard. I have a compound there where you will be safe until we figure out what's going on."

*A compound?* She wondered what that was. An image of a cell was the first thing that came into her mind. That wasn't escaping.

## 2

As the fire spread and grew, the situation on the fourth floor became desperate. The air was choked with a reeking black smoke and the only way to get relief from it was to crawl on the linoleum. No one did. With the inferno just below them, the floor was radiating heat like an oven. Bare skin touching that floor blistered in seconds. Only at the far, southern end of the building was it bearable. Twenty people huddle at the end of hall where the temperature was a balmy hundred and twenty three degrees and rising by the minute.

Most had given up. Some had fainted and were being held up by those who had the tiniest bit of strength left. Thuy was among those who were done fighting. She was conscious, however she no longer had enough spit in her mouth to form words and every breath seared her dried out lungs. She leaned on Deckard who swayed on his feet. He hadn't given up, but he was altogether clueless on how to save them--or really how to save *her*. His world had shrunk. He was only mindful of the dreadful heat and of the woman holding onto his arm.

With determination he fought to stay lucid, in case luck would favor them. He was under no delusion that it would. Their one hope had been for the elevator to come back up. It hadn't. Instead, the building shook and trembled beneath them as the fire gorged itself. The air roiled from the heat and shriveled their lungs with each breath. They were going to die; it was a certainty, or so Deckard thought.

Then fortune announced itself with a soft *ding!*

It was a second before he understood the meaning of that

little noise: it meant the elevator had miraculously come back for them. In a flash he had pushed Thuy toward Dr. Wilson and was running for the elevator at a flat sprint, filled with the fear that the doors would close again and that the elevator would make its slow journey all the way back to the first floor. How long would it take to come back for them? Two minutes? Three?

Three would be too long. Three would mean the death of some of the people around him. The unconscious ones couldn't be held up for long and, if they fell to the floor, they'd be cooked like pieces of chicken.

These unpleasant thoughts spurred Deck who got to the doors just as they began their journey back on the track. They jerked to a stop when his arm interfered. "Come on," he wheezed to the others, waving to them. They were shadows in the smoke, but they were moving shadows, moving with a purpose. Thuy came first; without thinking he thrust her into the elevator, however she resisted.

"No...the others first," she said, through a coughing fit. "My fault...all of this...I'll be last."

He wanted to argue but his mouth was too dry to talk. She leaned into him, laying her face against his chest. Gently he placed one of his large hands across her cheek, hoping to block some of the heat.

The others straggled up, none so much as pausing as they stepped into the elevator where the temperature was twenty degrees cooler. They groaned in relief. Deckard reached out and grabbed Wilson, Chuck and John Burke, holding them back. They were the only ones with "weapons."

"Last on, first off," Deckard said. "Just in case of zombies."

There were twenty of them on the fourth floor and seventeen of them forced themselves into the one working elevator like sardines--no one wanted to be left behind. Amazingly, there was room for one more and the only ones left in the hall were Riggs, Deckard and Thuy.

Deck tried to push Thuy in once more, but she wouldn't go and since he refused to leave her side, that left Riggs, however the other passengers refused to let him on. "He's got the disease," someone said. Since he had been attacked by the zombies, no one had gotten within ten feet of him, not even to look at his wounds. He had smears of black all over his clothes.

"We all got it, probably," he said in a whimper. To Deckard he looked like he was trying to cry, only he didn't have the moisture left in his body to form tears. "Please let me on, I can fit."

"The elevator will come back for us," Deckard said, letting the door go. Three minutes, he thought, was a hell of a long time to wait in those conditions. Still they had hope now and he knew they would be able to hold on for a little longer. The creaking doors closed in their faces.

The elevator was slow, painfully slow. It dropped down to the level of the fire and the heat skyrocketed. Everyone hid their faces from the intensity of it, but it was for seconds only and then the temperature of the air sank and with every foot further down the shaft they went, life became more bearable until at last the doors opened and cool air rushed in.

The zombie Von Braun greeted them and was immediately smacked in the face with Burke's mop and, when Wilson and Chuck stabbed him with their makeshift spears, he went right over. The other passengers were so eager to escape that they poured out of the elevator and like water, swept all around the struggling zombie, some trampling him in the process. They didn't care. They figured their nightmare would be over as soon as they got out of the building.

In fifteen seconds they were out in the cool, wet night. Only Stephanie remained with the men and it was not by choice. She had been one of those who had fainted on the fourth floor, her tumored lungs unable to handle the smoke. On the elevator ride down she regained consciousness and now she could only stand by leaning against a wall.

"Run," Chuck yelled to her. She took one step before dropping to the ground.

"Go, get her out of here," Wilson said to Chuck. "We got this."

Burke, who was struggling to keep Von Braun pinned with the mop didn't think they *had* anything. As far as he could tell they were only pissing the zombie off. He kept wondering what would happen when it got to its feet? What would he and Wilson do then? A mop and a sharp stick simply weren't real weapons and they weren't much in the way of warriors. Besides this wasn't a part of his plan. Burke still had Jaimee to consider. She was the only thing that really mattered to him.

Chuck went to Steph and hoisted her in his arms and then swayed, nearly fainting as well. Blinking like a drunk, he waited until his head cleared before heading for the lobby doors.

"They made it out," Wilson said of Chuck and Stephanie. "We should go, too."

The two men stepped back from the zombie who struggled to his feet, swearing in a weird staccato of mismatched curse words. John was sure it was going to attack them and he honestly felt bad for Wilson, because he planned on running if it did and he was fairly certain he could out run the middle-aged doctor. He was amazed when Von Braun did not attack the two and headed for the elevator instead.

Wilson and Burke looked at each other, both thinking the same thing: Deckard and Thuy were going to die. Deckard was weaponless and Thuy was barely surviving the heat. Neither of them gave Riggs a thought. In their minds he was already dead; he was just waiting for his body to turn into one of *them* to make it official.

"Ain't nothin' we cun do," Burke said, with a shrug, before he headed for the front doors. For a few seconds

Wilson spluttered angrily at Burke's callousness; then an almighty crash occurred somewhere high up in the building causing the very foundation to tremble. Part of the structure had given way. The doctor, realizing that Burke's assessment was spot on, hurried after him, afraid that if he waited any longer he'd be buried alive.

He found that being outside was only a little bit safer. Everywhere there were screams.

The scientists had rushed out into the rain, rejoicing over their liberation and smiling up into the falling rain. With the light of the building behind them, they were all too human appearing and the remaining zombies in the area, about sixty in number, came swarming to feast.

The defenseless scientists ran in every direction. Some made a dash for the cars in the employee parking lot, others ran for the supposed safety of the little cottages, and some just ran off into the night. With Stephanie so weak, Chuck hoisted her as far up as he could into one of the low cherry trees and then climbed up himself. Like a pack of dogs treeing a cat, five zombies sat below, staring up hungrily.

John Burke paused in the middle of the mayhem to get his bearings and to catch his breath. His cancer wasn't as far along as Stephanie's, still, the smoke had done a number on him and he was unable to take a full breath. Wilson came up behind him and took his arm. "I have a car in the lot. We can..."

"Get off," Burke snapped. "I gotta find my girl." An ambulance was pulling away from the largest of the cottages. John hurried as fast as he could to intercept it before it drove through the gates. With his lungs clogged with ashy mucous he was too slow to get in front of it. The best he could do was hammer on the side as it drove by.

He tried to scream, "Jaimee? You in there?" only his lung capacity was that of an infant's and the words came out soft and wet. He hacked up something black and for a moment he thought he'd been infected, but then he remembered he was immune. "Jes the smoke," he said to himself.

A second later Wilson was at his side. He was wide-eyed and frightfully scared. There was a woman in a white lab coat being eaten twenty feet away. With so many zombies on her, Wilson didn't know who she was. "We should get out of here," he whispered to Burke.

"Not yet," Burke replied. He started heading for the rich man's house where he had eaten dinner the night before. On the way a zombie tried to eat him. It wasn't much of a zombie. It had been one of the CDC agents and had been partially devoured with great chunks of flesh missing from its neck and face. One of its arms hung by a strap of tendon and it was missing a foot. Burke used his mop to topple it.

Wilson walked around it, staring as if it were a circus freak, his medically trained eye trying to make sense of it. How had it not bled out? How could it stand to walk on the root of its tibia? The pain of that must be excruciating, worse than almost any torture.

It was a horrible puzzle that he hoped he would never have to contemplate a second time, however, not a minute later, as they were approaching the big house, they encountered another poor creature that defied logic and sound medical reasoning.

It was a little girl.

"Is that your daughter?" Wilson asked, hoping to God it wasn't. There wasn't a lot left to the girl's face. One eye missing and nothing but a hole in its head where it had been; both ears, most of the nose and its bottom lip had been chewed off.

"Elp eee. Oooh elp eee," she said.

"That ain't her," Burke said, his face twisted in disgust. "Jaimee got legs on her like a ger-aff. That one's too small."

"It sounds like she's trying to talk," Wilson said, bending low to look at the girl. He saw she was missing her tongue on top of everything else. The sight made him shudder. "I wonder why some of them can talk and others can't."

"Cain't say as I give much of a shit 'bout that," John replied. He held the girl back with the business end of the mop and glanced up at the house. It was altogether quiet. "Ah'm goin' in. Y'all can stay here iffin you wanna."

Wilson didn't want to be alone; even though he thought John wasn't much more than a hillbilly, he was a better companion than the grotesque little girl zombie. They went in and knew right away that the house was empty. The air didn't feel right. It was stagnant and dead.

"Jaimee?" John called out softly. "Jaimee?"

He went room to room searching, fearing he would come across more bodies, afraid that he would find his little girl's among them. On the third floor he found Jaimee's little traveling case. "Oh, no, that ain't right," he said, fighting back tears that wanted to jump on out of his eyes.

A girl traveling needs her traveling case, he figured. For some reason he flipped it open; sitting on top was a pair of her worn underwear, looking as though a family of mice had got at them. John began to cry.

Without Jaimee, he had absolutely nothing in this world and no reason to live.

"Mr. Burke?" Wilson asked from the doorway. He hesitated stepping in; it seemed wrong to step over the threshold and into the man's misery. "We can't stay here. We really should go."

"To where?" John didn't know where he fit in or where he could go that would matter.

"Anywhere away from here," Wilson said. At that particular second he didn't have a destination in mind. The idea of going home appealed to him, but he couldn't chance it. How the Com-cells were transmitted was still a mystery and he wasn't going to risk infecting his family.

*Anywhere* wasn't much of a draw for Burke. Nowhere might have been a better answer. He glanced out the window, wondering if she was out there walking around with all the rest, trying to eat people. Or had she been in that ambulance?

"Would they have tooken her in that am-ba-lance?" he asked Wilson. "She don't got no money for no am-ba-lance."

"Of course they'd take her," Wilson replied. "She's probably on her way to the nearest hospital even as we speak."

Burke's initial reaction to this was one of suspicion. After the last day, a hospital was the last place he wanted her to go. "Could we go find her?"

Wilson jumped at the chance to get the man moving. "Yes, of course."

Imbued with a new purpose, Burke led the way, running down the stairs and out the front door, only to freeze just outside. The grounds were thick with roving bands of zombies.

"Shee-it," John swore. There was no getting through all of them and there was no staying in the house neither. Already many of the closer ones were turning to stare at the two men. They'd be charging next and the house, with its large windows wasn't going to be much of a refuge.

Fortunately for them, General Collins' helicopter came swooping in from the north. All the zombies stopped what they were doing, even the ones eating the screaming scientists, and canted their heads up at it. Burke was staring up as well, but not Wilson. He saw that the helicopter represented a moment frozen in time. It was a chance to get away. A hundred and twenty yards to the parking lot where his Lexus sat beading rain on its newly waxed metal hide and if the copter would hang around for just a minute he could get to it.

"Come on," he said, taking John's arm and pulling him down the porch stairs and running. They ran among the mindless and mesmerized zombies, over the pretty lawns in front of the cottages, and across the front of the hospital which burned with a white noise that was like radio static turned up to an ungodly volume. Lastly, they ran past the cherry tree where Chuck and Stephanie were stranded in its thin branches.

Chuck yelled, "Burke! Hey, Burke!"

It was then that Collins' copter swung overhead on its way to scout out Poughkeepsie and neither Burke nor Wilson heard the cries. And even if they had there wasn't much they could've done, they were now the focus of every zombie in sight.

When Wilson saw this he let out a breathy, "Oh…man!" Both men were already winded and they still had forty yards to go. The zombies gave chase and for some reason Wilson began laughing. It made no sense whatsoever, still the giggles came bubbling up out of him and there was no stopping them. Next to him, Burke was coughing himself into a fit and looking at him as if he were crazy.

With the laughing and the coughing, both men were barely at a jog now and only just made it to the car ahead of the first zombies. They climbed in and the pounding on the glass followed immediately. It wasn't like someone thumping with the soft part of their hand below the pinky, these were full on punches; the back window cracked after three blows.

"Go, go, go!" Burke cried, slapping the dash with the flat of his hand.

A little touch of Burke's *good ole boy Dixie* rubbed off on the normally staid Wilson. He gunned the Lexus, letting the wheels scream, not caring that he clipped a stray zombie or two or that he bounced the car over a couple of curbs. He was even going to let out a rebel yell as the gates came up, but then he happened to glance back and caught the full extent of the death all around the hospital.

Bodies were everywhere. Most were very dead, but some of the scientists were still alive and screaming as zombies ate their fill. There was nothing Wilson could do. He pointed the car through the gates and left the grounds, turning south at the first intersection.

"Is this the way to the hospital?" Burke asked.

It was the way home for Wilson. The image of his wife: tall, stunning, and statuesque, drew him on. He knew he couldn't go home but he wanted to be close. He needed to be close because he knew this wasn't over, not by a long shot. "Yes," he lied to Burke. "I'm sure it is."

3

Deckard had long before shed his jacket, now he draped it across his and Thuy's faces. The heat had become torturous and anything that could come between their exposed flesh and the inferno was a blessing.

Thuy rested her forehead on his chest, her normally large doe-eyes were heavily lidded; she was fighting to stay conscious but losing.

"Another minute," Deckard whispered. "Hold on, the elevator will be right back." The elevator had slowly dropped away, leaving the three of them alone and in pain. It felt like ages ago. She nodded, her eyes drooping further closed.

"You'll let me get on, too?" Riggs asked. He was a miserable creature. The Com-cells were barely into his system, nevertheless he looked more than half zombie already. He seemed to be shedding his humanity at an alarmingly quick rate.

Regardless, Deckard answered, "Of course. We won't leave you behind."

Thuy pulled the coat away. "I'm sorry," she said to Riggs. "I'm so sorry."

"Not your fault," Riggs said. "Someone messed it up. I don't blame you at…"

He stopped as the sound of the elevator could be heard grinding it's way upward. Their excitement peaked with the light *ding!* And then vanished altogether as Von Braun emerged, resembling a fiend from the lowest plain of hell. The unbelievable heat was making him into a mad thing. He was in such a rage that he completely forgot his desire to have his revenge on Thuy and flew directly at the first person in his way.

It happened to be Riggs who had been so terrified of being left behind a second time that he had taken up a position right in front of the elevator doors. Von Braun struck him with an overhand punch breaking Riggs' nose and squashing it sideways on his face—he dropped to the linoleum, his eyes going in two different directions.

Von Braun resisted the urge in his black heart to leap down on Riggs and tear open his throat. As much as he wanted to, there were two other humans close by and they smelled much purer than Riggs did.

Deckard pulled Thuy back, shielding her with his body as Von Braun charged. With a quick move, Deck threw his coat over Von Braun's face and followed it up with a swooping haymaker. His fist connected with such force he felt the jolt run straight up into his shoulder; there was an ugly *crunch* sound and he felt something give beneath his fist.

Von Braun yanked away the coat. His face was misshapen, one of his cheekbones had been crushed by the blow and yet he was completely unfazed. Again, he charged and now Deck was down to one very poor option: he kicked the zombie in the chest, striking with the flat of his shoe. It was about the only method of attack left to him that didn't involve direct touching.

It was basically worthless. Despite the fact that it had been vicious and that Deckard had put his all into the kick, Von Braun ignored it completely and came on.

Now Deck was seemingly done offensively, while defensively he had shot his wad by throwing the coat. This left retreat as his only option—a retreat down a dead end hallway where the heat brewed the air to over a hundred and forty degrees.

Deckard shoved Thuy aside and waved his hands at the foul beast. "Come on, Von Braun! You want to fight? I'll fight you, man to man." As he spoke he began walking backwards, in the hope of drawing Von Braun away from the elevator. It seemed to be working.

They were thirty feet away from it when Thuy jumped at the elevator door, which had been slowly closing. She caught it with an inch to spare. Maybe because the explosion had warped its inner workings, the door took that moment to *ding* once again. Von Braun began to turn; Deckard waved his arms wildly at him.

"Over here, jackass! I'm right..." He was still walking backwards when his foot came down on the face of one of the zombies they had killed earlier. His ankle rolled, sending a bolt of pain up his leg. He fell backward and could only watch as Von Braun turned his back on him. "No! Over here!"

The zombie ignored the yelling. He had spotted Thuy and his hunger flared to new heights. He bore down on her and she was stuck with the terrible choices of run or die.

She turned on her heel and raced into the smoke, under no delusion that she could actually get away. The heat and the ash made it so she could barely sip at the air and yet it didn't seem to be doing anything to Von Braun. He came on fast. One moment he was just a dim figure in the haze and smoke and the next, he was running past the open elevator twenty steps behind her. He would catch her for certain.

And he would eat her.

If she'd had the lung capacity she would've screamed. All she could do was make a whining noise in her throat as her inevitable death came for her, but then, amazingly, Von Braun fell.

Riggs had grabbed his ankle as he passed and now the two were rolling around on the raging hot floor, each looking for a death grip on the other.

It was a foregone conclusion that Riggs would lose the

fight. Everyone knew it, including Riggs himself. Von Braun had been an accomplished killer before, now he added zombie strength and an invulnerability to pain to his abilities.

Riggs only had guts and no reason left to live—it wasn't enough.

With a grimace and a grunt, Deck got to his feet; he would help Riggs even though he knew he would die trying. Von Braun was covered in the black residue of the Com-cells which meant Deckard would get infected the second he touched him and that meant death, a real death. Deck wouldn't leave the building if he was infected. He'd let the fire and smoke kill him before he turned into one of *them*.

With grim determination he began hobbling towards the two men wrestling around on the ground. He had only taken six gimpy steps when his phone started ringing in his pocket. He was sure it was going to be Stephen Kipling demanding to know what the hell was going on in his hospital. Deckard was sort of looking forward to this last minute chance to scream at his former boss.

"What?" he barked as he kept going. His ankle was a storm of pain and was already swollen to the size of a baseball, making his progress slow.

"You can't fight him bare-handed." It was Thuy speaking to him from the cooler end of the hall where the interfering clouds of smoke hid her.

"I don't have a choice," he said. Although he seemed to be inching along, he was getting closer and now he could see Von Braun and Riggs more clearly. The killer was atop the scientist with one hand crushing down on his throat and the other trying to tear Riggs' eyes out.

"You do," Thuy said. "The ram, where did you put it?"

Deckard stopped eight feet away from Von Braun. He had a weapon after all. "Son of a bitch!" he cried, feeling stupid for having forgotten it. He spun on his good foot and began to run/hop towards where the heat and smoke were the greatest. "I'll get it, but you have to promise me to get on that damned elevator the first chance you get."

Thuy did not promise anything; she hung up on him instead. He didn't have time to argue or call her back. The environment around him was no longer able to support human life. The air seared his lungs and the smoke closed his throat. Even keeping his eyes open was next to impossible. He hobbled on dropping the phone and then ripping off his shirt and holding it to his face. It was the only way he could breathe.

The ram was somewhere up ahead, he had left it sitting against the wall at the far end of the corridor. Without the ability to see, he had to shuffle painfully along waiting to trip over it while his skin went cherry red from the heat. Two seconds later his shin barked into the metal. It would have hurt if he wasn't already in so much pain; as it was he barely felt it.

His hand certainly felt the heated metal. There was a sizzling sound and he had to let go. Again, he didn't have time even to cry out. With both hands he ripped his shirt in two. One half went across his face and the other he wrapped around his hand to act as an oven mitt.

Then he was hurrying back the way he had come, the pain in his ankle diminishing with each step as his fear for Thuy overcame everything else.

Ahead was Riggs' lifeless body. It was laid out in front of the elevators. It was alone. A scream ripped the dark air, "Deck!"

Deck's ankle was totally forgotten now. He raced through the smoke and saw them, struggling together in a standing embrace—he was touching her! The vision sent a spike of fear right to his heart. She was diseased now. All his efforts to save her had been for nothing.

The fear in him abruptly switched to hate as Von Braun threw her down and jumped on top of her. Deckard, at a full sprint now, was on Von Braun before he knew it.

"Hey!" Deck yelled. He paused just long enough for Von Braun to turn and look in his direction before he swung the heavy ram.

It struck Von Braun just under the jaw sending splinters of teeth flying and snapping the bone square in two. The zombie's head flew back, while his hands shot outward. He toppled off of Thuy; Deckard stood over him just long enough to take a deep breath. He raised the ram and then brought it down with all the strength he could muster, striking Von Braun on the temple where the bone was thinnest. The metal head lodged there four inches deep. Von Braun took one last rattling breath and then his hands dropped to floor and his eyes slipped into the back of his mangled head.

Deckard stood, swaying and feeling dizzy from lack of oxygen. He was on the verge of fainting when Thuy grabbed him and started pulling him to the elevator. The door was opening and closing on Riggs' ankle; she pushed it all the way open and shoved Deckard inside.

"What are you doing?" he rasped.

"Saving us," she answered. She pushed Riggs' foot out of the way and as the door began to close she shed her lab coat, which was streaked black with the Com-cells, and threw it out into the hall. She surprised Deckard by hitting the button for the second floor.

Slowly the elevator sunk into the shaft and as it did, Deckard gulped in air. Thuy shook. There were scratches on her face and a thin smear of the black stuff on her forehead.

"There's still a chance," she said at his look. "The Com-cells might not be able to hold their form in this much heat and there...oh...God!" They were passing through the third floor where the heat was simply unbearable. She started to faint and he grabbed her. "No...you can't," she whispered from the edge of consciousness. "You can't touch me."

He could. There was a feeling inside him and where it had come from, he didn't know, but it had been building in him all day…really since the first time he had laid eyes on her. She was precious to him. The feeling inside him was indescribable other than to say she was precious in his eyes.

He held her and shielded her body from the intense heat and the Com-cells covered his chest.

They were blasted by the heat for what felt like an eternity, but in truth was less than a minute and when they managed to survive the third floor, the temperature dropped so fast that Deckard, who was half-naked, actually got the shivers.

Thuy stood swaying and blinking until the elevator doors opened to the second floor; she then put her hand on the wall and used it to guide her to the nurse's station. "There's a chance. I just need the right stuff." She started throwing open drawers and cabinet doors searching for what, Deckard didn't know.

"Here it is!" she cried when she found a shelf stacked with brown bottles.

"Hydrogen-peroxide?" Deckard commented, surprised.

"Among its many uses is that it actually kills molds of all types," she answered before dumping a full bottle all over her face. "Ahhh," she hissed; whether she was in pain or not he couldn't tell. What was obvious was how quickly she was reviving.

Even if it didn't kill the Com-cells, Deckard thought it looked wonderfully cool. He poured a bottle over himself as well and then took a second and began washing every inch of his exposed skin. When he was done he watched her for a few seconds as she worked the fizzing liquid into her shallow wounds.

Even after what had to be the worst day of her life, she was delicate, beautiful, and softly feminine. Underneath she was brilliant, determined and hard.

"I, uh, I should do your hair," he said.

"And I should do your back," she replied. She reached out for him touching his side, feeling the heat radiate off of him. The touch was soft and meaningful and…suddenly her world shook. Not in any romantic way. Something in the building fell in with a thunderous crash. "We should hurry," she said.

He grabbed two of the brown bottles and dumped them unceremoniously over her long black hair. The peroxide began to froth as he worked it through her scalp. As he went at her hair, she splashed some on her hands and then reached around to clean his back.

"You're burned," she said, feeling the hundreds of small blisters that had formed across his shoulders.

"Yeah, and I don't want it to get worse so let's get out of here."

With the building shuddering around them, they decided to take the stairs and were happily surprised to find them free of zombies. Then it was a matter of crossing through the lobby and in seconds they were outside. Thuy stopped just beyond the door, struck speechless as she surveyed the death all around her.

The Walton facility was supposed to have been her pride and joy. She was supposed to have made history here. In a sense she had. How many dead? How many infected? How far did the quarantine zone stretch now? Judging by the dozens of cold police cruisers, looking like the corpses of a herd of metallic beasts, she had to guess the edge of the quarantine zone was far away now.

Deckard urged her to move. "We're attracting attention. We should get out of here." There weren't many zombies in evidence. Most had given chase to Wilson's Lexus, leaving only the feeders and the very gimpy behind. There were also the five who had treed Chuck and Stephanie.

Stephanie saw Thuy and Deck. She wasn't shy about screaming across the fifty yards of open ground for help. With the cold and the rain, Stephanie figured that she and Chuck would have to add pneumonia to their list of worries if they weren't rescued soon.

"Please, do something," Thuy said. She felt personally responsible for every death that had occurred that day and she wasn't going to add to the count if there was anything she could do.

"No problem," Deckard answered. "Come on." They jogged to the black Shelby Mustang that sat like a sinister shadow in the lot. In the glove compartment was a Sig Sauer P229. With a feeling of relief, he checked the load: fourteen fat .45 ACP rounds in the mag and one in the chamber.

"Is that a good gun?" Thuy asked. She was relatively clueless about guns.

"It's not the gun, it's the shooter," he answered. When she frowned a bit at this non-answer he added, "Yeah, it's a good gun. Lots of stopping power." He keyed the ignition, revved the throaty engine for a second and then took them to the edge of the parking lot closest to the cherry tree. "Cover your ears," he suggested, before firing five times, notching five headshots and five dead zombies.

Chuck and Stephanie climbed down and hurried to the Shelby. When they were squished into the back, Deckard shocked Chuck by handing him the warm pistol. "We might be infected," he explained. "And I don't want to be one of them."

"We might all be infected," Stephanie said, lightly. Despite the zombies and the corpses and the horror of the night, she felt almost giddy. She had lived. Not only that, she had Chuck holding her hand. "So where are we going?"

Thuy answered when no one else would. "As far as we can. To the edge of the quarantine zone. I don't want to be anywhere near Walton."

This was agreed upon by everyone and Deckard drove south, fully expecting to come across a police checkpoint at every turn. An hour passed and there was nothing but open road before them.

"This doesn't make any sense," Thuy said. "They have to have a quarantine perimeter."

"Not if they're incompetent," Deckard said.

Chuck gave a little laugh. "We got a saying back home: dumb-shits do dumb shit, ma'am. Maybe they're thinking about reasoning with the zombies. I wouldn't put it past the government."

"Then I'm going home," Thuy said, tiredly. She'd been renting a room ten miles outside Walton, but where she called home was a townhouse just north of New York City. "You two are welcome to stay, I have a guest bedroom," she said to Chuck and Stephanie.

"You have a couch for me?" Deckard asked. "I don't need much more than that."

She cast her dark eyes toward him and then shrugged as if embarrassed. "No, you can't stay on the couch. You, uh need to be observed for signs of the disease. You should stay with me to be on the safe side."

It had been over an hour since their escape and he felt fine, while she looked stunning as always with the only difference being a touch of shyness in the way she was now having trouble looking him in the eye. "So what you're saying is that I should stay with you for the sake of all mankind?"

Thuy grinned at this and touched his arm. "Sure, let's say that's the reason.

**Epilogue—After Midnight**

As it streaked east, the boxy ambulance swayed, causing Jaimee's feet to kick off the underside of the metal bench, making a small thump-thump sound every other second.

"Could you stop that, dear?" Edmund asked.

She shot him a look. Through the filters of her black eyes he looked even older than usual and that was something. Behind his bio-suit mask, his bushy brows drooped and his wrinkled face sagged. He was grey with sorrow and looked close to death, as though he was right on the edge and that a little push would send him over....where he belonged.

He belonged with the dead.

*What a strange thought*, she said to herself. Why would she think he belonged with the dead and why was she even thinking about the old coot's death in the first place? It was a minute before she came up with the answer: "Because he deserves to die," she whispered. The old man was supposed to have saved her father, but he killed him instead. He had been part of all of it: the strange looking people walking around in the night, the screams, the fire, the fact that Jaimee no longer felt like herself. The fact that now she had strange urges. That was all his fault. He had started this whole business.

A mind reader might have noticed that she had put the cart before the horse. A dark part of her wanted Edmund to die and so she looked for a reason. And she didn't just want him to die, she wanted to be the one to kill him. It was such a natural feeling that she didn't question it.

"Did you say something, dear?" Edmund asked, turning towards her. "I can't hear well in this suit. It crinkles every time I move."

Jaimee hadn't realized she'd spoken aloud and didn't know which part of her sordid thinking had escaped her mouth. She only knew for certain it had to do with death. Her mind was crawling with thoughts of death. "I...I was just wonnerin' iffin y'all be goin' ta heaven when y'all die?"

Edmund's wrinkled face went sour. "Before today I would have said yes. Now, I feel like I deserve hell."

His words and her perception of them did not correspond. In the underworld of her mind where evil covered itself with rationality she heard a vindication of her thoughts. Her father was dead and here was the only authority figure in her life, practically giving her permission to kill him.

In her pocket was his cure. She had found it where they didn't want her to look. She took it out into the light where it gleamed brightly. It was a scalpel and it was wickedly sharp. It was one of the few things that she could see clearly, that and the aura of death surrounding Edmund.

The blade sat in her hand but he didn't see it. The plastic suit blocked his vision and his age clouded his judgment. For some reason he was completely at his ease around her, which made no sense. She may have been small, but she was still infected and that meant she was dangerous. And the fact that her mind still operated meant she was doubly dangerous.

The scalpel could attest to that. Without warning she stabbed Edmund. The blade slid through the plastic suit and into his chest, gliding easily between two of his brittle ribs and puncturing his right lung.

Shocked, he turned to see her grinning face leering into his mask. All up her arm flowed a malignant electricity. It was as if she was feeding on his soul as he slowly died. And his death was indeed slow. The punctured lung deflated like a balloon and he had to fight to suck in the smallest amount of air. Gradually, his arms and legs went numb, feeling as though they were no longer attached to his torso and then slowly, ever so slowly he slid to the floor of the rocking ambulance and died a temporary death.

He would later come back just as the driver, Bobby Dern would, though it would take Bobby a few more hours because his injuries were much more severe.

Jaimee opened the little door between the cab and the

crew space. Before Bobby even knew who it was she had poked the scalpel in his side. She had no way of knowing that she had stuck him in the liver; she didn't even know what a liver was.

The pain was immediate and galvanizing. He slammed on the brakes so that his scream mingled with the screech of the tires as they drew two long black lines down the roadway. Jaimee was thrown forward and if she was hurt she didn't know. Nothing could really hurt her now.

She picked herself up and, while Bobby was still trying to comprehend what was going on, she laid into him again with the blade. The first stab went into his neck and blood sprayed out. The second sunk into his cringing face just below the eye. The third went into his open mouth sliding through his tongue and coming out beneath his chin.

After that she didn't know where she stabbed or how many times. Bobby's blood, pure clean blood shot into her mouth and from that moment on she didn't know anything beyond a ravaging hunger. Only when his blood had pooled and wasn't so wonderfully warm did she finally climb out of the ambulance. In front of her was a sign that read *Hartford 14 Miles*.

She began walking and within minutes she was hungry again.

So it was that as General Collins was sitting with the Governor of New York explaining the need to shoot the zombies on sight and why he needed such a huge quarantine zone, Jaimee was already fifty miles east of its furthest edge and heading towards a brightly lit city where over a million people lived and worked and would eventually die over the next few weeks.

Jaimee smiled at all the lights and her tummy rumbled.

The End of the First Day

Author's note:

Thank you for reading The Apocalypse Crusade, War of the Undead Day One. I sincerely hope that you enjoyed it. If so, I'd like to ask a favor: the review is the most practical and inexpensive form of advertisement an independent author has available in order to get his work known. If you could put a kind review on Amazon and your Facebook page, I would greatly appreciate it.

Peter Meredith

If you are in the mood for more zombies, a ton more bullets and a whole lot more blood(and just a bit of sex thrown in), please check out my other ghoulish series: *The Undead World*.

Greed, terrorism, and simple bad luck conspire to bring mankind to its knees as a viral infection spreads out of control, reducing those infected to undead horrors that feed upon the rest.

It's a time of misery and death for most, however there are some who are lucky, some who are ruthless, and some who are just too damned tough to go down without a fight. This is their story.